A CURSE OF MALICE & MERCY

A Curse of Malice & Mercy

Courts of Malice Book 1

Miranda Joy

Spellbound Souls

Paperback ISBN: 979-8-9859148-2-5

Developmental edits by RaeAnne from LavenderProse - www.lavenderprose.com - Instagram: @lavenderprose.editing

Line edits by Brittany Corley from ThisBitchReads - www.thisbitchreads.com - Instagram: @thisbitchreads_

Cover designed by Maria Spada - www.mariaspada.com - Instagram: @mspremades

Map by Cartographybird Maps - www.cartographybird.com - Instagram: @cartographybird

Spellbound Souls
www.authormirandajoy.com

Content Warnings

This book contains fictional depictions of physical abuse, emotional abuse, brief attempted sexual assault, references to slavery/servitude, murder with blood and slight gore descriptions, nightmares, grief, post-trauma PTSD, manipulation, slight bullying, descriptive/detailed sexual content, foul language, and more. This book is intended for mature readers. As always, read at your own discretion and comfort. Your mental health comes first. If you would like further information, please email me at authormiran dajoy@gmail.com.

For those who make friends with the monsters instead of fearing them.

Contents

ONE

THE LORD'S LITTLE DOLLY

ALESSIA

I can't resist gossip about the fae.

So, when I overheard Sir Dougrey telling his tablemates about the faerie trees eating men alive, I was drawn to him like a moth to a flame. I should've remained silent. I should've kept my eyes downcast and carried on serving the cranberry-almond apple pie. It took me all afternoon to make, after all, and seeing their eyes light up as the sweet, tart, and toasty flavors exploded on their tongues would've brought me a spark of elusive joy. Plus, I could've lingered in the wings under the guise of service and eavesdropped longer.

But I messed up.

A dozen questions ran through my mind, and instead of setting down the dessert and retreating, I gaped at the back of Sir Dougrey's bald head and asked, "humans went to Avylon?"

The lord's refined friends grew silent, and Sir Dougrey slowly turned to scowl at me. A dozen gazes had penetrated me with open disdain.

I hadn't meant to speak—to be seen—but it slipped out and now I'm paying for it.

Char—who served the other end of the table at the time—met my eyes with a flash of disappointment, the frown lines on her pallor skin more prominent than ever.

Normally I pester Char about faerie tales and she obliges, albeit with an ominous warning, telling me stories filled with magic and wonder, but in that moment, I had taken my interest too far.

"How dare you make a fool of me," Lord Edvin says after dragging me from the dining room.

His beady eyes prick me with unease as he leers over me.

I glance away.

The kitchen's hearth sits off to my side, tucked into a brick mantle. It crackles with the room's heating, the flames dancing like the fae in the stories Char told me about. A few feet beside it sits the door to the wine cellar, and next to the cellar is a small servant's stairwell that leads up to my and Char's shared room.

I'm half-tempted to bolt up there and hide away. Better yet, I'm tempted to escape the door on the opposite side of the room—the one leading out into the pastures and stables beyond.

Perhaps I could flee through the field and into the forest. Escape from the lord for good. But there isn't anywhere to go.

Or maybe, like in my dreams, I could be stolen away by a faerie. They have *magic*.

Plus, Sir Dougrey said the *trees* were eating the humans—not the faeries themselves. Surely they can't be *that* dangerous.

"Look at me girl!" Lord Edvin grunts as he grips my shoulders, spinning me away from him and shoving me down on the cool oak table in the center of the kitchen. "I said how dare you make a fool of me!"

He grips my hair, keeping me in place on the table and I wince. At least he has the decency to dole out my punishment in private, away from prying eyes, with only his wife present, watching on with amusement. Then again, it's probably so my cries don't disturb his fancy friends as they dine on their pie.

A sharp clank fills the room as he unfastens his leather belt and frees it from his belt loops.

It's a warning sound—one I've heard many times before—and my body automatically tenses at what's to come.

In the background, soft classical music plays. Silverware tinkles against expensive porcelain plates, and the lord's guests speak in *polite* tones. Never too loud, nor too quiet. Never with a show of open emotion, and never directed at *me*—a mere Tradeling.

"Why are you misbehaving tonight, Dolly?" he whispers, his hot breath scorching my cheek. He smells of malt liquor and cigars. My stomach churns. "What has gotten into you?"

I stay stock still, my upper half resting on the table with my toes on the ground. I forgo a response, fearful that if I acknowledge the lord it will only fan his fury. Or worse, my voice will crack and my words will come out weak. Instead, I use Char's counting technique and work to keep my breaths steady.

Inhale.

Two.

Three.

Four.

Exhale.

My right cheek flattens against the table. My lungs fight to expand against the wood beneath my chest. The kitchen's ugly, painted, paneled walls fill my sideways vision as I focus on counting my breaths. Walls that the lady insisted Char and I paint navy of all colors. It's horrid, making the kitchen seem dimmer, smaller, and more suffocating than usual. Especially with its poor lighting and stone and oak furnishings.

"You are to apologize to Sir Dougrey." Lord Edvin inhales sharply. "You are also forbidden from speaking another word for the rest of the evening, even if spoken to first." When I don't reply, the lord runs the end of his belt across my forehead, over my cheek, and down my neck in a quiet threat. I shudder involuntarily. "Do you hear me, Dolly?"

Acid burns in my throat at his nickname for me. I'm tempted to sass back, to ask him how I'm supposed to apologize if I'm not allowed to talk, but I keep my lips clamped shut. I've learned the hard way the lord likes it when I fight back.

"Yes sir," I whisper, my face heating.

"Good."

As he moves back to deliver my punishment, Lady Nilda steps into sight with her arms crossed over her willowy frame. Her face is overly powdered, drying out her pale complexion and making her appear older than her forty-odd years. She holds my gaze over the table as her husband whips me raw, not a sliver of guilt present on her face. I stare back into her vacant, feline eyes.

Tears of rage fill my vision, blurring the lady, but I refuse to look away.

"The girl deserves it," she says smugly. "Release your aggression, Edvin. Take it out on her."

I chew on my lip to keep from crying out as the belt strikes me, biting into my skin. When it lands, my breath hitches and a swarm of black dots swim through my vision. Knotted, ashy curls fall into my face, like a theater curtain closing, hiding me away.

Only, the show goes on.

With his next strike, I can't help but flinch. My body tenses after the initial shock of pain subsides.

"Don't move, Dolly," Lord Edvin hisses. "Make a noise, move a muscle, and you'll get more."

Lady Nilda tilts her head to the side and laughs.

I imagine her chest is hollow, missing the rhythm of a beating heart. Perhaps that's why she takes so many lovers behind her husband's back—she's desperate to borrow the warmth she's lacking. Maybe if he was sober long enough, he'd catch on and *she* would be the one receiving his wrath for once...except I refuse to wish this on anyone.

Even Lady Nilda.

I tense my muscles, squeezing my arse tight and bracing myself for the next strike—

Clang.

Clang.

Clang.

The music of the estate's gold-plated knocker rings out. The chatter in the dining room ceases, and the lord pauses with his arm raised and ready to strike. He sighs with impatience as he pulls away, looping his belt back through his trousers with a *swish* and a grunt.

"The door, Nilda," he says, annoyed.

"The other Tradeling will get it," she spits back.

"The other one is tending the guests. Get to the damn door before whoever it is freezes their cock off."

"Yes, husband." She narrows her eyes at me before squaring her shoulders and trodding off.

I exhale in relief, thanking the gods for their timing.

Leaning forward, Lord Edvin pets my hair and lets his sour breath wash over me. "Clean up and get back to work, like a good little Dolly." He pats my head aggressively, and I school my expression. "And no speaking, or I will find another use for that pretty mouth of yours."

His pudgy thumb caresses my lip, and I swallow down the burning bile that rises. It takes everything in me not to flinch from his touch or knee him in the groin. One thing I've learned over the years is that it's better not to react. I might not be able to control many things in my life, but I can control my reactions.

He spins, striding out of the kitchen with the confidence of a man who doesn't believe in the word *no*. If his ego was a living, breathing thing, it would be larger than his entire estate—and that's saying something.

Once he's out of sight, I wobble to a stand, letting my serving smock fall to my knees. The skirt conceals the red textured stripes that surely now line my backside. I'll be in pain for a few days as they turn to raised purple welts before healing, but this is not the worst the lord has done to me.

At least my bones are intact.

The chatter in the dining room picks back up, carrying down the hallway as I make my way from the kitchen into the corridor. Instead of returning to the guests in the main dining room, as I should, I skim across the glossy hardwoods on the balls of my feet. I pass a few closed doors and scurry past the open dining room doors. Making it to the entryway, I duck down beside the foyer's grand staircase. The oak railing curls outward in a dramatic flourish, offering me cover as I eavesdrop.

"—this combined with unrest about the taxes," an unfamiliar voice says in low tones. "Queen Wyetta requests your presence in Ryalle immediately."

The queen's caller.

Whenever the queen's caller knocks, the lord leaves immediately. The palace is in the bustling port city of Ryalle, which controls most of Dovenak's imports and exports. It's an entire day's ride south of our village of Lyson, which means he'll be gone for a few days at least.

The lord curses. "Again?"

"Again."

"I am hosting a dinner party," Lord Edvin hisses. "We will leave in the morning."

"We will leave now."

"I refuse to entertain—"

"Due to *your* inability to properly monitor the Gleam, this cannot wait." The caller's tone is bored, but I'm anything but. My ears perk up at the mention of the mysterious border that lies deep in the woods behind the lord's house. "The situation has escalated. There is no room for debate."

I hadn't realized the lord was in charge of *monitoring* the Gleam—the portal between our realm of Dovenak and the fae realm of Avylon. Before tonight, I hadn't thought anybody went near the Gleam. Other than Char's make-believe stories, I don't hear much about the fae. It's almost like they don't exist, more myth than reality.

But the Queen's caller mentioning the Gleam, combined with Sir Dougrey's gossip about the faerie forest *eating* people...it could mean the faeries are stirring up trouble.

I should be frightened. At the very least, I should be apprehensive. But I can't help the way my stomach tightens and excitement prickles at the base of my neck.

"There's a treaty in place," Lady Nilda drawls, as if the caller is ignorant. "There is no threat from a few feeble sodding faeries. The queen can wait."

"With all due respect, my lady," the caller continues, "these matters do not concern you. But if you must know, the faeries are no feeble things. You might be thinking of pixies, which are notoriously tiny and adorable, but the bloody *faeries*, the shifters, the sirens—well, they'd eat a bitter-hearted shite like you alive, and use your scrawny femurs to pick their teeth clean."

Lady Nilda squawks, and I slap a hand over my mouth to mute my own gasp. I squirm, discomfited by the caller's words, but they have done nothing to quell my interest.

"Do something, Edvin! This Tradeling scum can't talk to me like that."

"First," the caller says quickly before Lord Edvin can speak up, "I am *not* a Tradeling. Second, as an official employee of the crown, I outrank your status as small-town noble."

There's a silence and I carefully peek my head around the carved banister to witness the lady's mouth gaping open. She shuts it and opens it a few times, like a fish. My lips curve up in a smirk, and it almost makes the sting on my arse worth it.

Her eyes swing in my direction and I duck down behind the banister, heart pounding against my rib cage. Quiet as a mouse—one of the perks of being out of sight and sound for so long—I scurry back to the dining room, as if I'd been there all along.

No one spares me any mind as I join Char's side clearing dessert plates. She gives me a sidelong glance but says nothing. My cheeks heat, more embarrassed at letting *her* down than I would ever be for disobeying the lord.

Char and I work in a silent tandem, removing dishes from the dining room and bringing them to the kitchen. She hobbles around the room, and a pang of guilt hits my chest. While I was gone, she must've done double the work, even if it was only for a half-hour. It was enough time for pie to be served and finished by the greedy Lyson nobles.

As we're heading back to the dining room, the front door slams shut and Lady Nilda rounds into the hallway.

"Woman!" the lady snaps at Char. I grit my teeth. "Go arrange digestifs in the parlor for our guests. Now."

"Yes ma'am." Char bows her head slightly, limping down the hallway.

"You!" Lady Nilda sets her sights on me. She grabs my arm with her needle-like fingers, nails biting into my skin. Once she drags me into the kitchen, she flings me to the floor. My knees crack into the slick hardwood. "Clean the floors."

"I just cleaned them before the guests—"

Her hand whips out and strikes me. My head jerks to the side, and I catch myself before tipping over.

"Are you talking back or are you cleaning?"

"Cleaning," I mumble.

My cheek barely stings. It registers more as shock than pain, but I keep that to myself.

Reaching for a bowl of stew, unfinished from a guest, the lady tosses the chunky mess out onto the floors.

It lands in a symphony of sloppy, squishy thwacks onto the ground.

"Now you have something to clean. You're welcome."

Halfway out of the kitchen she pauses and reaches into her dress pocket for a compact mirror. When I'm sure she's paying me no attention, I grimace, rise, and dust off my knees. I stride to the far wall and fetch my pail and scrub brush from the cupboard beneath the sink. The pipes have a tendency to freeze in the winter, but at least today water flows. It's cold though, and my fingers scream at the contact. As the bucket fills, I add lemon-scented soap and watch out of my peripheral as the lady continues to fluff up her hair and line her lips with a ruddy color before finally leaving.

I catch a glimpse of my sorrowful reflection in the darkened window. The girl reflected back at me appears sad, lost. The plain dress she wears hangs off her thin frame. She has a forehead marred with worry-lines, and the ragged tattoo from jaw to chin acts as a sharp reminder of her place in life.

I quickly glance away, not wanting the confirmation of how exhausted and bedraggled I am. How knotted my ash-blonde curls are. How bloodshot and lined with dark half-circles my grey eyes are. I remove the bucket and plop it onto the ground with a splosh.

Glancing around, I inspect where the stew landed. The counters stretch along the wall across from the main entrance, with a variety of cooking apparatuses laid out from dinner. Bits of brown goo drip from the underside of the counter in one section, tainting the cupboards there. So I address that area first, wiping it clean with a rag.

I work the base of the counters, where stone meets wood, and keep a repetitive pattern that causes my shoulders to ache instantly. Most of the stew is contained to one area, so I scrub the liquid from the cracks between floorboards, doing my best to return them to their shining glory.

I've barely gotten anything done when the lord enters, scratching his potbelly. My stomach sinks into my bowels as his dark eyes narrow on the mess I'm cleaning.

"What are you doing, Dolly? You vomit on my floors?"

"Lady Nilda, sir," I croak out. "She—"

"Just finish and get back out there with the guests!" He strides over to me, lifting a riding boot and hovering it over my left hand. My fingers are splayed out on the floor, and if he lowers another centimeter, he'll crush my hand. I swallow the lump in my throat.

"Mind yourself while I'm away."

My gaze locks onto his shiny black-leather boot. "Yes, sir," I whisper.

"What was that?"

"Yes, sir," I say, louder this time to appease him.

He grunts before turning away, his heavy steps pounding out of the kitchen.

Gritting my teeth, I exhale a long breath. My eyes flick up to the textured ceiling above, and I mentally repeat the words that always inflate my hope:

I am not weak.

I am strong.

With as much energy as I can muster, I continue to clean, upholding my duties like a good little Tradeling—the lord's little Dolly.

Two

In the Trade We Will Die

Alessia

B y the time I finish scrubbing the kitchen, my fingers are wet and wrinkled, and my knees are red and raw. My bones threaten to collapse, on the verge of disintegration. Curls fall into my face, and I tuck the strands behind my ears, letting my tired arms hang loose at my side after.

"The lord is gone for the evening, my Alessia." Char limps to my side.

My gaze snaps to the older woman, and a genuine smile overtakes my face.

"Charlotta. There you are." I want nothing more than to jump up and give her a much needed hug, but I'm sopping wet and covered in grime.

I toss my cleaning rag aside, wincing as I struggle to a stand. My face contorts with pain, but when sorrow fills Char's eyes, I force another smile at her.

"Oh, what has that wretched man done to you now?"

"Nothing I can't handle."

"Let me have a look." She lifts my skirt, peeking at the raw skin on my back and legs. "Stay here. Give me a moment. I know of something that might help."

"The lady will notice when you don't return," I warn, beckoning toward the hallway behind her, where the lingering voices have grown louder, more confident, more belligerent.

Char chuckles, it's a comforting sound. "She is quite—preoccupied at the moment. I was on my way to the wine cellar for another bottle of the tawny port. If you would do this old lady a favor and fetch it, I will tend to your wounds."

She gives me no room to decline as she hobbles out of the room and back down the hallway, past the parlor where the guests enjoy their evening drinks. I chew on my lip, guilty she's stuck taking care of me on top of her regular house duties

Char might be spared from the worst of the lord's temper, but she went through much worse than I ever have prior to being purchased by him eighteen years ago—right around the time he purchased me. I was sold into the Trade at age five, simply because I was unfortunate enough to lose my parents in a house fire. Being an orphan is reason enough to get sold like cattle in the Wessex Peninsula. It's as simple as being in the wrong place at the wrong time.

As much as I despise the lord, there are much less favorable positions I could find myself in. I could've been purchased by a brothel in Ryalle, forced to offer my body to nobles for coppers I'd never see. Or worse, sold to the sweltering iron mines of Illynor down south.

That's where Char came from. The mines.

She suffered severe burns to her leg, rendering her incapable of the labor required in the mines. The lord bought her for a hefty discount—out of greed rather than compassion—but if he hadn't, she would've been killed instead.

A life in the Trade is a short life for many.

Worse, it's an inescapable life. We bear the mark of Tradelings—a thin, black zigzag tattoo down the left side of our faces, from temple to jaw. Like a dark lightning bolt. It ensures that Tradelings will never be free, even if they escape. And even *if* we somehow bypassed the village scouts without being seen, we're stuck in the Wessex Peninsula. We face the Valor Sea to the north, south, and west, and the Barrens to the east—a stretch of inhospitable land with no shelter, no water, and wide open, dusty space, separating the peninsula from the rest of Dovenak. Queen Wyetta's troops, plus others from various countries in Dovenak, are stationed throughout the Barrens. From what I've heard and read, it would be impossible to pass through without being spotted.

Once, when I was younger, I tried to run. I made it to the outskirts of town, having no idea where I was headed, only to discover that the lord has eyes everywhere.

It ended with a broken leg and crushed hope.

The memory of my attempted escape makes me shudder.

Later, Char held me while I cried. "Bide your time, my Alessia," she said as she stroked my hair, "All broken things heal, and broken girls heal into indestructible women."

I've held onto her words all these years. But I've never tried to run again, because things could be worse. They could always be worse.

I oblige Char's request to grab the port, locating an extra oil lamp from beside the hearth. I wince as I sidestep down the rickety old steps to where the surplus of wine and spirits are stored.

I hold up the lamp, illuminating the. cellar. It's a dim, cool room made of mismatched stone with a dirt floor. Two walls are lined with racks of bottles—some so old they've acquired a layer of thick dust. A couple of whiskey barrels sit around the space, with potent liquor aging and soaking within the wood.

"You know why they're called spirits, don'tcha?" A low voice says. I gasp, but before I can whirl around, a warm, muscular body presses against me from behind. Soft lips find my neck, and I squirm—out of embarrassment more than desire. His breath caresses my ear as he whispers, "because they bring out a man's true spirit."

He releases me so I can face him.

I hold up the lamp and he recoils from the light, giving me a charming grin. His pupils are blown out and the top of shirt is unbuttoned near the collar. His fingers grip my skirts, tugging the fabric up. I swat him away.

"Felix," I scold, taking in his state of disarray. "How much have you had to drink, you scoundrel?" Clearly enough that my poor state of dress and the sickly smell of beef stew does nothing to dissuade his wily ways. "Sneaking up on me like that!"

"Forgive me, my lady, for the lack of greeting." He drops to a single knee in a flourish, reaches for my hand, and plants a kiss on the back of it. I eye him warily as he rises. He acts like a gentleman, though the gleam in his eye says he is anything but. "The party above has grown rather stale, and I was in search of something prettier to occupy my time."

My cheeks flush, and I tuck my hair behind an ear. It's too easy to fall for Felix's charms and give in to the temporary distraction.

I met Felix a few years back when the lord hired him as a groundskeeper and stablehand. His father is a close companion of the lord's, so he often joins them for dinner events and hunting parties. He even has his own living quarters in the stables across the pasture. And unlike me and Char, he is an actual employee. He bears no mark, and he's listed on the ledgers. He's afforded true freedoms.

Like eating with the guests tonight.

"I have to get back up there." I sigh. "The lady is waiting for me."

His grin grows. "Nilda left with Father, and trust me, they won't be back tonight." He steps forward, tracing my jaw.

Lady Nilda might act like a doting wife in the day, but she wastes no time seeking out one of her many illicit lovers to whisk her away when her husband is gone.

"What would your mother think, Felix?" I scold.

She's a beautiful, kindhearted woman who has treated me like an actual human the few times I met her.

"She's on a gals' trip." He winks, and I frown at him. "So long as she doesn't find out, she can't be affected."

Felix's nonchalance to the adultery is appalling, but I shake my head, not wanting to fight a battle that isn't mine.

"I should really—"

"I'll be quick."

He leans forward, planting his lips on my collarbone and trailing to my earlobe. I sigh, my body easily giving into the comforts he offers. I favor him for the touch of his rough, callused hands—a delicious contrast to the rest of his silky skin.

Felix spins me around, hiking my skirt up and parting my legs. I shiver.

"Cold, darling?" he whispers in my ear. "Aren't you a lucky girl. I can warm you up tonight. Just say the word."

After a beat passes, I nod and set the lamp on an empty shelf, giving in to his request. I'm sure I'm not the only one Felix explores—he's handsome, young, and charming—but I don't care. I'm hungry for these small moments that make me feel alive. And luckily, Char makes the lady quarterly protection tonics for her escapades, and she always sneaks an extra one for me. The last thing I'd want in my current situation is pregnancy or a disease. The tonic also keeps me from menstruating, which is a blessing on its own.

After a few minutes of prodding and poking between my legs, Felix presses his bare erection against my slit. I'm barely wet yet, and the rushed foreplay certainly doesn't help matters much.

"Ouch," I cry out, wincing as he jams himself deeper.

I bite the inside of my cheek to keep from crying out. My arse smarts, still raw and tender.

"I'm sorry. Am I hurting you?" It doesn't stop him from holding me still and pushing deeper into me.

I sigh, shutting my eyes. "I'm fine. It's just—I wasn't ready."

"I'm sorry," he repeats.

When he kisses my temple, I relax into his touch. I'm able to access my clit, rubbing it to summon my natural lubrication. It helps, and he's able to pick up his pace, sliding in and out with more ease. I grip the wine rack in front of me with one hand, holding on for stability, while my other continues to work myself closer to climax.

It's nearly impossible to lose myself to the pleasure with how bad my wounds ache from the lord's whipping. Felix won't be able to see the marks in the dim lighting, which is fine because I don't care to discuss them.

Less than a minute later, and before I have time to achieve my own pleasure, Felix groans as he pulls out, spilling on the floor.

He chuckles in my ear. "I told you I'd be quick, darling."

"Yeah," I mumble, fixing my dress. "Char is waiting for me, so..."

"That was delightful." Felix watches me like a contented cat. "I really needed that tonight. Thank you."

"Sure." Despite the chill in the cellar, my hands grow clammy as I snatch the lamp from the shelf.

"Was it good for you, too?" he asks.

"Yes," I lie, refusing to look at him.

Well, it's a half-lie. The distraction was good, and the sex wasn't bad. I love his warm skin against my own. But something tells me if it were truly satisfying, I wouldn't care about returning to my tasks upstairs.

"Wait for me tonight. We can go again." He kisses my temple before darting up the stairs, tucking himself back in at the same time.

My shoulders slump as the loneliness settles back in. I'd rather Felix's company than none at all.

Raising the lamp, I scan the legible wine labels. It takes me more than a few minutes of wiping the filth off labels to locate the dessert wine. Coughing at the small plume of dust I've summoned, I snag the bottle. With the oil lamp in my other hand, I trudge back up the stairs.

Char stands with her hip popped, arms crossed, and lips tight with displeasure.

"Took a long time."

My neck and cheeks heat. "Yeah I... couldn't find it." I hold up the bottle.

"Do not lie to *me*, Alessia." She takes the bottle from me with a sigh, walking unsteadily to the table and setting it down before facing me again. "That boy is no good."

That *boy* is the only man who pays me consented attention. For all his faults, if I'd told him no in the cellar, he wouldn't have forced me. That's better than most men that step foot into this house. However, I choose not to argue with Char.

"I know."

Her eyes narrow sharply. "You are in luck today." She holds a familiar jar. "I have a bit of salve left."

"Char," I hiss. I grab her hands, covering the small jar. "What are you thinking?"

"If I cannot protect you, the least I can do is alleviate your suffering."

I shake my head. "No. I'm not using it."

They'll notice that I've healed so quickly, and the punishment will be so much worse—for both of us, not just me.

"The lady will not take notice and the lord is gone for the week. I guarantee he will be too drunk to keep his eyes open when he returns."

I bite my lip as I hesitate, weighing my options. The salve is enchanted with magic from the fae. It will heal my wounds immediately, but magic is banned here. Not only here in Lyson, but in the entire realm. Anyone caught using magic or enchantments is deemed a fae sympathizer and hanged without trial.

Simply having the salve around is a risk for us both. I've only agreed to using it a few times, when I was in too much pain to rest. But the paranoia almost isn't worth the relief it brings.

I scan the room nervously, afraid someone will overhear. My worries are unwarranted, however, because drunken chatter spills down the hallway, but no one is in sight.

"Are you ever going to tell me how you get it?"

"Mind your business." She says it with kindness, but it's the same answer she gives me anytime I ask.

"It is my business since you're using it on me."

She sighs. "From someone in the village."

"Someone or something?" I ask. Fae?

"That is all you are getting from me, my Alessia."

I narrow my eyes at her. We both know none of the regular shops would risk selling enchanted products or magical salves. Either there are fae in Lyson, or there's a sympathizer who imports their products. Both prospects intrigue me.

That Char refuses to confide in me only piques my interest.

"I thought you said the fae can't be trusted," I accuse. "They can't be so bad if they give humans healing—"

"Alessia," she warns.

"I'm simply saying, they can't be that cruel compared to the horrors we've faced here. Perhaps we could leave and cross the Gleam—"

"And succumb to certain death?" It's not the first time she's said these words, and it won't be the last. She squeezes her eyes shut, her crows feet and frown wrinkles more prominent than ever, making her look even older than her sixty-something years. "At least you are alive here. Stop romanticizing things you know nothing about."

Her harsh tone puts an end to my questioning, and I change tactics.

"Okay," I tell Char. "Keep your secrets, but this is the last time I'm using this cream." I level a stern look at her. She's heard these same words from me before, too. "I mean it this time. Stop putting yourself at risk. *Please*."

Char doesn't respond as she lifts my skirts, soothing my backside with a generous helping of the cream. I flinch as she slathers the cool cream around. The pain is alleviated almost immediately, and I know without looking that the balm leaves unblemished skin behind.

"Are you finally going to use the salve on *your* wounds?" I prod, turning to face Char when she finishes.

She sighs. "I already told you—"

"The lord is an idiot. He won't notice."

"He is a drunkard, yes. Quite oblivious, but not dense." She reaches out and squeezes my hand. "Even if he did not notice my decades old wounds have healed, I would notice. My scars are reminders of my survival, my Alessia."

I eye her skeptically. It's incomprehensible why she refuses to let go of her pains. She could move about better without the ache in her leg. But I let it go. Anytime I bring it up, she shuts me down. The horrors are too awful for her to rehash, so it's best I don't press her.

She wipes her hands on her apron, before embracing me. Even though I don't want to dirty her, I'm glad she doesn't mind. Her familiar scent of lemon soap and peppermint cream softens my shoulders.

After a tender moment, I break the embrace. Without the lingering pain on my backside, I move more swiftly. Heading to the hearth, I stoke the fire, allowing its warmth to fill the air. It's a nice reprieve from the otherwise bitter bite of winter.

"You said the lord will be gone all week?"

"Yes, dear."

Thank gods. "He's been called away a lot lately. Not that I'm complaining. I'll take any blessings we can get."

Rowdy laughter echoes down the hall, followed by a shattering.

Char shuffles toward the door with a groan. "We best get out there. We have dallied long enough."

Her sharp eyes pierce me as she reaches out to fuss with my hair. I avert my gaze, wishing she didn't know what Felix and I were up to in the cellar.

But it's Char. Of course she knows.

Hours later, the party is still going—even in lieu of the the lord and lady's presence. Liquor sloshes around, chatter and cigar smoke pollute the air, and there's a hum of randy energy found in aggressive touches and non-discreet kisses. It's an entirely different energy from the stuffy dinner earlier.

Char stands at the long, cherry bar stationed at the parlor's far wall, refilling glasses, while I fetch ice from the icebox out back and get more wine from the cellar. Even with Char's cream, my legs and arms scream at me every time I run an errand. On the last trip to the icebox, I was tempted to ask Felix for assistance.

Unfortunately, he's preoccupied.

Sitting on one of the four couches perched around the room, a beautiful older woman at his side, he leans back leisurely, one arm thrown over the back of the couch behind her perfectly coiffed head. She grips his thigh with one hand while she tosses back her liquor with the other. He gives her a charming grin—one I recognize all too well—and she leans forward, purposely giving him a view of her abundant cleavage.

Sure enough, his eyes fall to her breasts before slowly dragging up to her face.

I fight an eye roll, leaning against the wall and fisting my hands at my side.

My stomach flips over, but I can't stop watching them. It's not jealousy—not in the way Char must think as she shoots me motherly glances every few seconds. No, it's jealousy of their freedoms.

I wish I could be the one sitting on the plush couches, being fed alcohol and pastries for once.

It could be worse, I remind myself. *At least the lord is gone.*

Felix throws his head back with laughter at something the woman says. His eyes catch mine, and the joy dies out on his lips. He shifts uncomfortably, but does nothing to stop the woman as she leans in and plants her lips on his neck. His hand shoots to the crotch of his pants, and he adjusts himself, giving me an apologetic look.

My cheeks flush and I turn away, heading to the other side of the room, away from him and away from Char's judgment.

I don't need their pity.

A group of five of men are playing cards, smoking cigars, and speaking in hushed whispers at a round table at the back of the room. Sir Dougrey's shiny head peeks through the haze of smoke like a beacon, and I slink over there under the guise of checking for empty beverages. Really, I'm hoping his lips are even looser now that he's intoxicated and the lord isn't here to punish me for eavesdropping.

No one notices as I meander past their table.

"I went to take a piss and accidentally ended up in Edvin's office," one of the men says.

"Just like last time, when you accidentally ended up in his bed with his wife's lips on your cock."

A few hearty chuckles litter the air. I frown at the crude conversation, tempted to turn around. But it's the promise of gossip keeping me rooted in place.

"Couldn't help but spy a letter on his desk," the man continues, "and it would seem the queen is not happy with our dear friend."

My brows raise imperceptibly; it's a challenge to keep my expression neutral. I keep my eyes locked on the floor, to downplay my presence as I lurk by the nearest wall.

"He is woefully incompetent at his job."

"Stop the riddles, Timothee. Get to the point."

"The point is—"

"Concern about the Gleam, it seems," Sir Dougrey says with a scoff. "I told you imbeciles at dinner. The trees have a penchant for feasting on human flesh. They sent Jeremiah's body back over with flesh wounds that would make a grown man lose his lunch. His eyeballs were missing, his blood drained—"

Someone scoffs. "That is a mere rumor, Doug."

"No. No way. He's right. The village is slowly perishing because of the feckin' fae," another man says, slamming a fist on the table and rattling the glasses. "We pay the same damn taxes as the south, for a lesser quality of life here. It's time we do something about the damn Gleam. About those damn faeries."

Timothee clears his throat, leaning forward conspiratorially. "The letter said little about the Gleam or the fae." He narrows his eyes at Sir Dougrey. "For all we know, there are no damned fae. The stories are made up to keep us in line. Have you ever seen one yourself? Have you ever crossed the Gleam? Hell, did anyone truly see Jeremiah's—"

"They are not myth," Sir Dougrey growls. "Just ask the boy. He's the lord's—hell, the queen's—communication line with them, from what I hear." He lifts a glass up, tilting it toward someone in the room. All eyes follow, including mine.

And I spot Felix, who's now alone, and watching me with a concerned expression.

"Looks a bit gangly to be dealing with the fae. Can't be that tough after all."

"Looks can fool ya, Tim."

Communication line? Felix? He's a stablehand. A groundskeeper. He tends the horses and maintains the yards. There's no way he's seen the fae. He would've told me. He knows how intrigued I am by them and their stories. Anytime I repeat what Char's told me, he brushes me off like I'm an annoying child.

And the lord works as the queen's liaison here in Lyson, rounding up the villager's taxes and corresponding with locals on behalf of the royal palace. He runs the village. The amount of time the lord has spent away lately is an indicator things are not going well, but I thought it was due to high taxes and civil unrest. Boring political factors that affect me little. I never realized he has so much involvement in the Gleam.

"Do they really feast on human blood and kidnap babies?" one of the men asks. "Are they covered in scales with fangs and—"

I jump when Felix appears at my side. "Char could use your assistance, Alessia."

His hand gently presses into my low back as he steers me away from the men and toward the other side of the room. I turn to him, intending to ask about what the men said, but his lips tighten and he shakes his head, walking away without sparing me another glance.

Once everyone filters out of the house around the crack of dawn—including Felix and his new woman—Char and I clean the parlor.

Exhaustion clings to my eyelids, weighing them down. I yawn, stretching my arms overhead. Despite the tiredness, my mind flits to Sir Dougrey's conversation.

Curiosity has always brewed where the fae are involved. Most people tend to refer to the creatures in Avylon as 'the fae' when speaking of them—as if they're one single entity of being—but as Char has told me time again, there are many different beings that live across the Gleam.

I repeat the question I overheard tonight. "Char, are the fae truly as cruel as everyone thinks?"

"Some are as hideous and cruel as you have heard, but some are also more beautiful and kinder than you could possibly imagine.

Just like humans, fae are diverse. You should know this by now, my Alessia."

A flicker of hope lights in my heart. "Maybe we could—"

"We are *not* crossing the Gleam." I flinch at Char's scolding tone. She's often stern, but her voice takes on an unusually sharp edge. "How many times must we have this conversation?"

"But—"

"I do not need you to go on romanticizing them now, do you hear?" My eyes widen as I nod my agreement.

"I simply said that not all fae are as cruel as the stories say, but it does not mean there is no truth to the darker tales either. You do not belong with the fae. They are not fond of our kind."

"To be fair, *I'm* not fond of most humans either," I mumble, lightening the mood.

This brings the smile back to her face. "I know."

"One of these days, I'll get you to give me more details about them, you know," I tease. Once again, it snuffs out my budding idea of being saved by the fae. It's a sobering reminder that there is no other life for us outside the lord's estate. "Less stories and more truth."

"All stories stem from some truths."

I twist my hands in my skirts, dropping my gaze to the floor. Perhaps Char has told me all she knows. Or perhaps she tells me tales to placate me.

Char places a coarse hand on my shoulder and gives me a knowing look. Her sleeve rises to reveal a secondary marking on her wrist, a large black 'X' that signifies her discharge from the mines due to injury, along with textured skin—scars older than I am. The wounds from her time in Illynor.

"Maybe it's a blessing in disguise that the lord bought us," I say.

She was a broken woman, and I was young; we were both discounted for being unworkable. But much to the lord's pleasure, Char healed and I grew, and we were no longer unworkable. Char's aching joints, stiff walk, and scarred hands are a constant reminder of what she's survived. It could always be worse.

"Make no mistake, it is no blessing to be sold into the trade, my girl."

"No. Not the sale itself. I'm grateful to have you as my family, Char."

"Yes, I understand, but *this*"—she points at herself then at me—"is not what family is."

I shake my head. "You're wrong. We are family, Char."

"If I was family, I could protect you better," Char mutters, her voice cracking along with my heart. "One day you will be freed of this circumstance to build your own life. You will experience what a true family is. This here is not a life anyone should live. Do not be blinded."

After cleaning up and changing into our nightgowns, we get comfortable in our cots, both of us lying down and drawing the threadbare blankets over our bodies. I close my eyes and inhale her comforting scent.

"Char?" I ask. "Why do humans and fae hate each other so much if they're so alike?"

"The story changes depending on which side of the Gleam you stand," she says. "Here in Dovenak, human lore says the fae were created to destroy humans, but on the other side, in Avylon, lore says fae were created by the gods. They were gifted magic to protect the earth—caretakers, if you will."

I hang on to her every word, desperate for more. "Well, which lore is true?"

She chuckles. "Truth is nothing more than a perception. Some stories say the humans and fae lived together peacefully, until one day the humans grew jealous and fearful of their magic, causing the two groups to clash. Those sentiments intensified, turning to hatred and bigotry. The humans began slaughtering any magical beings unprovoked. In turn, those with magic did not sit idle. They protected themselves, as one would expect.

"The feud grew remarkably bad, resulting in the War of Chaos. Neither side won nor lost, and the devastation was catastrophic for all. The fae feared for the earth, and in an attempt to keep the peace, they requested a truce with the human rulers at the time. The treaty came at a high price—a price of which I do not know."

"The Treaty of Wessex-Iorworth," I say. Named after the two families who established it. Queen Wyetta Wessex's ancestors, and whoever the Iorworths were in Avylon. It's one of the few things about the fae mentioned in the history books in the lord's office—the ones I snuck peeks at after Char taught me to read. It also says the Iorworths are the most treacherous family of all, so it was a surprise to many when they initiated the treaty. At first, the Wessexes were afraid it was a trap. But it's been hundreds of years, and nothing bad has happened… yet.

Char nods. "Yes. Put simply, fae are forbidden from entering Dovenak, and humans are not to enter Avylon."

"What happens if we disobey those terms?"

"Then we are are on our own—at the mercy of their magic."

My mind flits to what Sir Dougrey and his companions spoke of at the party. Trees eating people, men mutilated, Felix being a communication line.

Tomorrow, if the lady is still out, I will pay Felix a visit and ask him directly.

"If the fae are so powerful, why didn't they win the war by simply wiping the humans out?" I ask.

"If the Dovenak lore is true, they would have. If the Avylon lore is true, they would want to protect the lands from devastation out of respect for the god who created them. Power is not always about exerting force, sometimes it is about knowing when to quit for the greater good. Standing down does not make one weak. In fact, it may make one the strongest of all."

Her words are heavy, as if they are an additional burden to carry.

"But, my words are nothing more than fairytales," Char says as she rustles around on her cot, getting comfortable.

I yawn, my mind foggy.

"All stories stem from some truths," I mumble, repeating her words from earlier.

My fingers mindlessly trail up to the ink on the side of my face—the mark that mirrors Char's. The one damning us. Even if there was a way out of this life, there's nowhere for us to go.

In the Trade we were raised.

In the Trade we will die.

Three

Survive My Forest

Rainer

R ich, moist soil offers a cushion for my knees as I work, hunched over, tending to the roses. Moving carefully, I clip any dead growth, pruning away the old so new can flourish. Unlike the flora of the forest and the experiments in my mother's greenhouse, these flowers require a green thumb, hard work, and…fine, perhaps, a touch of magic to survive.

Ideally, roses prefer at least six hours of strong sun per day to flourish. The soil here is impeccable for gardening, but the climate often leaves much to be desired. Though I am not partial to admitting it, a touch of magic—not my own—allows the roses to blossom.

As if responding to my weather-related disdain, a rumble cracks through the sky. I turn my eyes toward the grey abyss above, and a raindrop splatters onto my forehead. One by one, bulbous droplets splash the petals around me. Standing, I swipe my soiled hands on my dark trousers and take a large inhale.

The scent of fresh rain is delectable. Earthy, musky. Dirty, yet clean.

The stone castle to my left stretches into the clouds, the rain darkening its stone.

"Rainer," a jovial voice calls. My spine goes rigid, and I spin toward the garden entrance, trudging toward my dearest friend as he speaks. "We found another body." I quirk a brow." In the woods."

"Imbeciles," I mutter.

Kenisius grins from just inside the doorway, out of reach from the pattering rain.

I wipe my brow with the back of my arm.

"You could always keep it for—"

"Send it back."

His forehead wrinkles. "They'll think you're sending a message."

"Precisely." I brush past Kenisius, entering into the dim hallway and stomping my boots on the stone floor. He uses an oversized boot to nudge the glass-door shut behind us, and I wince when it rattles with the impact. "What condition is the human's body in?"

"Worse than last week."

I glance up to catch him grimacing, pale light from the sconces illuminating his profile. Kenisius is not easily rattled, so the sight sends a flicker of concern through my bones.

"Worse than the male who clawed his own eyes out?" I cock my head with a frown. "How so, exactly?"

"This one chewed off his own foot to escape the vines. Clawed off his own skin in chunks." He scratches his beard. "It was almost impressive."

"Hmph." I inspect my nails, wondering if I have time to scrub them clean before the court meets.

It's only a matter of time before Terra Court shows up at my door, demanding answers, per usual.

Despite the treaty with the human queen being broken, I still abide the terms. I'm sure I'm the only one who's even noticed the expiration. Besides, it was always implied that any humans who cross the Gleam do so at their own risk.

I don't offer protections to the humans, nor do I owe them any. Returning the mutilated bodies is a courtesy at best, an inconvenience at worst. *They* might see it as an act of aggression, reading into it from the wrong angle, but that has much to do with their inclination of assuming the worst, and their limited perspective.

"Send the body back, Kenisius," I repeat. "Drain its blood for the trees and send it back over the Gleam."

Kenisius gives me a mock salute and saunters down the passageway, ready to uphold my orders.

For a moment, I stand in the grand hallway, shadows flickering on the walls from the growing storm. Thunder ricochets through the space, followed by a blinding flash. The rain pounds on the windows, as if its demanding to be let in.

I inhale deeply, letting my eyes flutter shut. Despite the storm's aggression, it's a moment of pure peace. Where blood is the lifeline of flesh and bone, rain is the lifeline of roots and roses.

"Sir," a squeaky voice calls, shattering my illusion of peace.

My eyes fly open and I locate the pixie speaking. He flutters in the air just a few yards away, no bigger than the size of my fist. His wings move so quickly they're a mere blur of sapphire.

The pixie clears his throat. "The prince from Terra Court is in the parlor."

"Perfect," I say sarcastically.

Ignoring the dirt caked under my nails, I run my hand through my hair, allowing myself one moment to wear my disdain. Then, I harden my bones, stand tall, and stomp in the direction he waits.

The beloved golden-prince of Terra Court is once again here to save the day. Protect the fae *and* the humans. It's vomit-inducing.

Unlike his false, convoluted sense of reality, I'm *truly* working to protect the fae here. He is *not* taking my land.

Let him try. He could never survive my forest.

FOUR

LEAVING THE NIGHTMARES BEHIND

ALESSIA

Time passes much too quickly, stealing away our illusions of freedom. With the lord gone and the lady busy with her suitors, it's as close to freedom as we will ever get.

At the very least, I'd expected to see Felix, but he was nowhere to be found. In this blustery weather, I can't imagine what groundskeeping duties he could be completing, and the words from the dinner party earlier in the week ring through my head: "*He's the lord's communication line with the fae.*"

There's no way that's true. He would've told me.

But it begs the question: where is he?

I shake away the thoughts, clearing the fog, so I can tend to my duties before the lord's return this evening.

Even in the bright light of day, the estate is still dim with its dark wood paneling, dim oil lamps, and drawn curtains. I'd like to rip the curtains open, let the natural light in, but the lord likes them closed. It's easier on his often-hungover eyes.

Despite my hurriedness, I double check everything I clean, ensuring I don't miss a spot as I dust and scrub alongside Char.

Most often, Lord Edvin is too drunk to lift a hand, but on occasion he'll swipe a finger across various surfaces in search of a single speck of dust. As if it excites him to catch my error and punish me.

So, I am unwilling to take any chances.

In the evening, the lady returns as I'm scrubbing the hardwoods in the foyer. She scowls at me, then kicks over my bucket. Murky water stretches across the floor.

My eyes squeeze shut as I curse her mentally.

"Clean that up," she says. "Then draw me a bath."

"Yes, Lady Nilda." I keep my eyes on the puddle of water spreading out beneath my knees.

"Snap to it." She inclines her head, staring down her nose at me before gliding out of the room.

I toss the rag down with a sigh.

Once I'm finished in the foyer, I brace myself for the lady's foul mood. Heading to her chambers, I draw her a bath complete with chamomile flakes and lavender soaking salts—the overwhelmingly floral scent makes me gag. I don't know how she can stand to marinate in it.

She enters the room, sinking her nude body into the water and tipping her head back with a soft sigh.

"Stop gawking at my breasts," she says coldly. "Have the cripple serve my meal here and get back to work."

She waves a hand in my direction, dripping water onto the wood.

Turning away from her, I clench my fists at my sides. She deserves to fall asleep and drown in her own filth for speaking about Char in such a manner.

I deliver the message to my friend, sparing her the horrid name calling. As Char prepares the lady's plate of boiled cod and potato stew, I go through the motions of tidying the kitchen, nothing more than a shadow slinking around. There's some leftover stew in the hearth, and I dip my fingers in, sneaking the few remaining scraps.

When Char finally limps back into the kitchen, my heart tugs at her gait. She's moving slower than usual, a hint at her level of exhaustion. It's clear the estate demands are growing more grueling for her.

"I can finish here. Please rest, Char." I nod toward a wooden stool.

"Nonsense. These responsibilities belong to me as much as they do you."

"You're already worn out."

"Such a kind heart. You will be free of these invisible chains one day, my Alessia. I promise you."

I avoid eye contact. "Don't make promises you can't keep."

Char obeys me for once, lowering herself onto the stool with a heavy sigh. "I fully intend to keep my promises to you, dear."

I don't reply as I stare at the grimy stack of cooking pans on the counter. As I begin lathering the washrag with soap, the foyer door creaks open, shutting with a slam that reverberates down the corridor. I tense at the sound, counting three heavy footsteps before the entrant belches and grumbles a string of foul words.

Good gods.

The lord is back—drunk. Of course.

Part of me is relieved he'll be too incoherent to inspect my cleaning. The other part of me is downright dreading the vomit I'll likely be scrubbing out of his sheets later.

Neither situation is ideal.

Char exhales with resignation, rising from the stool and shuffling to my side at the sink. Her dark eyes narrow at me, full of fire.

"The vermin drank too much again. You stay as far away from that son-of-a-wretch as you can tonight, you hear?" She blows a salt-and-pepper colored tendril off her forehead, tapping her temple with two fingers. "He can only get in here if you let him."

Grabbing a plate from beside me, she drips water onto the stone.

I sigh, staring down at the darkened spots. "Maybe he's so drunk he's forgotten about us entirely."

The stale stench of cigar smoke wafts through the estate.

"Wassit en here, Dolly," Lord Edvin slurs as he stumbles into the kitchen, his face blotchy and wind-burnt. Dark purple bruises form beneath his eyes, as if he hasn't slept the entire week. His coat is worn crookedly, buttons misaligned with the holes, and his short silver hair sticks up in wispy angles. He's more depleted than normal.

At the sound of his nickname for me, Char's eyes narrow with disgust.

"Hello Lord Edvin, it appears you require assistance to your chambers, if I may," she says, gesturing toward the corridor.

"Nah. Dolly ah eye have bish ness." With a hiccup, he lurches toward me.

Char pulls me behind her back as the stocky man fumbles with his belt. Fear swirls in my gut.

"Ten lasheeths," he slurs.

"For what!? I did nothing wrong!" I should keep my mouth shut and take his punishment, but I can't help the exclamation from slipping free.

He yanks Char's elbow, pulling her out of the way. It sends her tumbling to the ground.

"Char!" I move to help her, but the lord swings his belt at me. It whistles through the air and I jump backward, the leather barely missing my thigh.

"Now for talkun back."

Cruelty without reason. That's what this is. To someone as powerful and conceited as the lord, this is merely a game. I'm nothing more than a little mouse—a dolly—for him to play with. He had a bad day—a bad week—and he's ready to release his aggression on me, as the lady would say.

Without thinking about the potential consequences, I turn to run.

The lord is quicker, even in his deep state of intoxication. He grabs a fistful of my hair, yanking my head back, and I cry out, legs flailing as he hauls me backward. He shoves me face down onto the stone island in the center of the kitchen.

The cool stone bites into my flesh. He rests one meaty paw on the back of my head, pressing my face into the cool stone, while his other hand begins lifting my skirt. My muscles tense and I squirm, desperate to wiggle free. Tears stream down my face, puddling beneath my cheek.

Please, gods!

I want to beg, but I refuse to give him the satisfaction. It will only encourage him. He loves the power, the control, and my pleads would be a gift to his wretched soul.

The belt whistles through the air, biting into my bare skin and catching me off guard.

I gasp, clenching my teeth as tight as I can to keep from yelling out.

Before the sting can settle, he lands a second lash.

Then a third.

Each lash comes in quick succession, building on the pain from the previous strike.

My body jolts involuntarily each time the leather finds its mark, and my vision begins to fade. A metallic taste fills my mouth from biting down so hard on my cheek.

Only three out of ten strikes down, and a dark fog fills my vision. My limbs go limp beside me.

Char's face fills my thoughts. She'll help me heal. I only need to survive this first.

"Poor leetle Dolly." The lord leans over me, hovering so close I can almost taste the whiskey on his breath.

His palm travels up the back of my thigh, and he strokes my bare flesh.

Bile rises in my throat and I gag as his hand rises higher, and higher, until it meets the curve of my arse. Skin that is once again ribboned red and raw.

His aggression tonight is different. These touches are different.

They're urgent.

Desperate.

I'm horrified Char will have to watch this, and I'm ashamed I'm so defenseless.

The lord releases me for a moment, grunting as he fumbles with the buttons on his trousers. Taking a deep breath, I summon my inner strength and scramble away from him. His thick fingers grab my ankle, dragging me back toward him.

"No," Char whispers. "This has gone on for far too long."

Time slows as she hobbles into view, gripping a butcher's knife with deadly calm.

"Char—no! Don't—"

She juts the blade into the lord's side before he can register what's happening. The slobbering, red-faced man makes the noise of a dying animal. He rolls off me, thumping to the ground.

I stumble to my feet as he struggles with shaky hands to rip the blade from his gut. It clatters to the ground beside him as his hands rush to find the gushing wound.

"You—You!" He coughs and blood trickles from his lips.

Heavy numbness roots me in place as his eyes flutter shut and his body stills.

"What did you do?" I whisper to Char, my voice cracking.

"He needed to be stopped. I—"

"No. I don't care about *him*." I shake my head. "Char, we need to go." I grab her hand, my eyes flitting rapidly between her and the lord. "*Now!*"

She yanks her hand free of mine with more force than expected, and gray tendrils fall loose from her messy updo. "No, my dear, I cannot."

"Yes you can!" I grab her sleeve, tugging her toward the back door. Lady Nilda surely woke from the lord's screams. It's only a matter of moments before we're found. We'll be taken to the village center and hanged for murdering one of the queen's lords.

There will be no trial.

We're Tradelings.

We've committed treason.

My lungs burn, collapsing and suffocating me.

Once again, Char pulls free of me, standing firm. Tears and snot stream down my face; my body is light, airy, yet weighted at the same time. However, Char's hands are still. Her expression is serene. Her voice is calm.

"There are things you have yet to understand. Reasons why I cannot go with you, my Alessia."

"Please, Char. I'm not leaving without you." My eyes widen at the thought of leaving her here in this place. It pains me to know both options she faces right now are death sentences. "Whatever it is, we can figure it out together. We need to go before the lady finds him."

"Listen to me." Her voice takes on a stern tone as she steps forward and grips my cheeks in her hands. "*You* need to go. Cross the Gleam." Her eyes glimmer with unshed tears. "You need to take the risk and go."

"But the fae—"

"Are dangerous, yes. But at least in Avylon you stand a chance at survival. Here is inevitable death. You must go, and do not *ever* return."

I wince, knowing she's right even though my heart disagrees.

"But you're my only family, Char." My voice cracks. "I *can't* leave you. You'll—"

"I am not your family. You will find a family one day, but it will not be me. Run to the north side of the forest where the mushrooms grow. Do not stop until you cross into Avylon. Do not linger in the forest, on either side, especially if it calls to you."

My heart pounds erratically in my chest, adrenaline and fear merging into one uncomfortable emotion. Despite her always swaying me away from the Gleam—the fae—I know she's only directing me there now because I have no other choice at survival.

I want to ask how she knows where the Gleam is, ask why she thinks she can't join me, but footfalls in the corridor alert me to the lady nearing.

"What is all the ruckus in—" Lady Nilda's face turns ashen, her mouth dropping open as she spots her husband's bleeding body on the floor.

The lord is alive, but his breaths are ragged and shallow.

"Edvin!" Lady Nilda screams.

She charges toward Char, and a glint of maroon-stained silver clutched in her hand catches my eye. I open my mouth to warn Char, to scream, anything, but she cocks her head and offers me a soft smile.

"No!" I cry.

"I am sorry, my Alessia. Forgive me for ly—" Char's words are replaced by a squelching gurgle as Lady Nilda runs the blade across her throat. I squeeze my eyes shut, whipping around to keep from losing it.

Vomit rises in my throat, threatening to spill. I swallow it down, willing my feet to move.

I refuse to look back at Char. Refuse to be haunted further by something I can never unsee.

Selfishly, I don't want to remember her like that.

My hands tremble uncontrollably as I reach for the doorknob. I had daydreamed about running so many times before. But I never imagined I'd be leaving without Char.

I throw the heavy wooden door open and a snowy gust of wind snaps me to reality. My legs remember how to work again, propelling me forward.

Dashing barefoot across the snow-dusted field, I keep my focus on the dark tree-line ahead. My breath comes out in white puffs, and the cold air stings my skin. As I bolt past the stables, Felix's voice reaches my ears. He's calling my name, but I don't spare him a glance. I can't.

The only thing on my mind is survival.

Tears blind me as I bolt, and I can only hope I'm leaving the nightmares behind.

FIVE
FIND STRENGTH IN FEAR
ALESSIA

B are branches reach for me like bony claws as slivers of moonlight glitter off the forest frost. The unforgiving weather eats me alive as I struggle barefoot, with only my threadbare dress on, against the elements.

As the adrenaline wears off, the pain sinks in, slowing me down.

I need to find shelter soon, or else Char's death will be for nothing.

Do not linger in the forest on either side—especially if it calls to you. I wonder if this is what she meant. The call to quit. The ease of giving up. The forest is certainly calling to me in that sense, but it's Char's voice that keeps me going.

A sob escapes my throat and I stumble. My hands catch a thin, gnarled tree trunk and I steady myself, pushing the suffocating images aside.

Somewhere behind me, shouts carry on the wind.

I need to move forward.

Must get to the Gleam.

It can't be that far or else Char wouldn't have encouraged me to run for it. And it's only a matter of time before someone catches up to me. I might have the advantage of a head start, but Lady Nilda will have the advantage of horses, warmth, and stamina.

I try to keep up my pace, knowing my trail through the snow can be tracked. Strands of hair whip across my face, knotting together as my teeth chatter uncontrollably. There's nowhere to hide where I won't be found. I half-run, half-wobble until my legs grow stiff and my chest burns.

Until I can no longer smell the fresh pine of the forest, and each breath turns razor-sharp in my throat.

I've never felt so alive yet so close to death at the same time.

My head pounds with Char's words on repeat: *I am not your family.*

She *was* my family. She died for me, that's how much she loved me—believed in me. She had her secrets, but she loved me fiercely.

We both knew it. She even apologized for it with her last breaths.

She died so I would keep going.

I need to.

Keep going.

But it's so hard.

I'm so tired.

Right when I'm about to collapse from fatigue, a glimmer of light snags my attention. At first glance, it's a faint iridescent mix of blues and greens. The closer I get, the brighter the colors glow, like a translucent, shimmering wall. A thick swell of mushrooms stands near the colors. Vibrant, standing calf-high, the fungi contrasts with the low saturation of the woods.

They're unlike any mushrooms I've seen before.

I made it.

My breath hitches and my joints creak in refusal as I try to pick up my pace one last time. There's no portal. No door. Nothing magical about the border other than the vibrant hues the Gleam clearly gets its name from.

On the other side, through the shimmering wall, there's nothing out of the ordinary. It's the same expanse of Lyson forest, stretching as far as the eye can see.

"Alessia!" Felix calls from somewhere behind me.

My heart jumps into my throat and my body jerks. Half delirious and trembling with cold and fear, I turn to see Felix approaching me. I hadn't heard him or the steed beside him, the one he presumably rode in on.

He shrugs off his cloak, stepping toward me with it outstretched in his hand.

"Gods, Alessia. You're freezing." The concern in his voice sounds genuine. "Let me take you home."

Home.

That place was never my home. Especially not without Char.

"I—I can't go back there, Felix."

"Let me protect you," he says, his voice cracking. "Whatever happened, let me protect you."

"Like you've protected me so many times before?"

"What are you talking about?"

I scoff, my vision spotty and weak. "I really thought you cared about me," I whisper.

"I *do*!" He steps forward and I jolt backwards—closer to the Gleam. His eyes widen, and he looks over my shoulder then back to me. His voice softens when he says, "I *do* care about you, darling."

But I think of all the times I tried to ask Felix for help, subtly bringing up Lord Edvin's violence, only to be shut down. Whether

Felix was truly ignorant to the lord's cruelty, or he purposely tuned it out, it doesn't matter.

So many times the lord hurt me when Felix was just one room over, letting other women plant their lips on his skin, their hands on his muscles. While the lord violated me, he received pleasure.

I'm not disillusioned enough to think Felix loved me back. But I thought he was my friend. I thought he cared.

I thought he could protect me, but in the end, it was Char who freed me.

And now, it's up to me to save myself.

"You're only here because the lady sent you," I mutter dejectedly. "Aren't you?"

He presses his lips together, his shoulders slumping. "It's not like that. She told me to come after you, yes, but—"

"And you're not just a stablehand."

His eyes widen in fear. "I don't know what you heard, Alessia, but you have no idea what—"

"It's much too late for that, Felix."

I turn my back to him, stepping closer to the Gleam.

"Don't, Alessia, please," Felix begs. "You have no idea what lies beyond that border. The monsters I fight to protect you from!"

"I loved you, Felix, and it was all a lie," I mumble as I close my eyes and step forward.

Felix's desperate cry is cut off as a rush of energy overtakes me. My skin prickles. The hairs on my arms stand up. I've never felt anything like it.

A sizzle of heat scurries up my legs and a flash of neon color assaults my eyes, forcing them shut.

My whole body thrums with energy, and I grow warm as I thaw out, thinking of all the stories I've heard over the years: how the fae are terrible, magic-wielding creatures who partake in shenanigans purely for entertainment, at the expense of human lives.

They're cruel.

Unforgiving.

Dangerous.

At least that's what the whispers say. But how is that any different from what I face with the lord and lady? It's a risk I've been pushed to take.

Char had also said the fae can be beautiful and kind, and I only hope to find the ones who are. Only one irrevocable step through the Gleam stands between me and what I hope is freedom.

It feels like an eternity passes before my foot hits the ground on the other side. The tingling subsides. When the colors fade to a soft orange glow, I cautiously open my eyes.

I gasp, squinting at the unrecognizable landscape before me.

The sun beats down on a meadow of cheery blossoms, a sea of lush magenta and periwinkle wildflowers that reach up to my waist. They sway lazily in the soft breeze, as if they don't have a care in the world.

A delirious laugh bubbles up from my throat.

The meadow is no more than a small circle opening in the middle of a forest. Dense trees, endlessly tall, stand guard at the edges of the clearing. The woods are lush, thick with vegetation.

Birds flitter and tweet around me, their sweet lullaby soothing. With each exhale, my adrenaline subsides, but the grief grows. Exhaustion soaks me to my bones. Char had said not to linger in the forest, but I need a moment.

I can't—

I don't know how—

Curling myself into a ball, I whimper and tremble, trying to hold myself together. I'd rather endure a thousand lashings than lose Char. My hair soaks to my wet face, and I keep my eyes pinched shut to slow the flow of tears.

It's unfair that my blood continues to pump through my veins while Char's stains the lord's floors. I was right when I told myself things could always be worse. And now, things *are* worse.

I wake with a violent thrash.

The thin material of my dress clings to me like a second skin, soaked with sweat. I grasp at the grass around me, as if I'm desperate to physically hold onto the earth. As if I might fall off if I let go.

Even in sleep, I cannot escape the harsh reality: Char is really gone. I'm alone.

My head throbs and my mouth is dry and sticky with thirst. I need to press on.

Standing to stretch, my legs ache from running, and my arse screams from the lord's last whipping. Not to mention my feet are caked with grime—dirty, angry, and sliced up from the stones and sticks littering the forest floor.

In a bout of good luck, they are still intact. Somehow I managed to avoid frostbite.

I weave my way through wildflowers, trudging to the treeline. My stiff legs loosen up as I hobble deeper into the forest.

The sun hides behind a knot of silver-blue clouds, and combined with the thick canopy of leaves above, it's quite dark in the forest. It's a maze of shadows and looming shapes. Twisted branches and towering trunks stand in silent isolation, stretching intimidatingly into the skies. Other than my quick breaths and crunching steps as I traipse over rotting leaves, it's utterly silent. Like a world of its own.

I shiver, wrapping my arms around myself.

I move past the hickories with their craggy bark, the oaks with their gnarled branches, and the beeches with their pale trunks. Unsure of where I'm going or where I started, it's as if I'm traveling through an endless loop. I've trudged on for what feels like hours, but I'm failing to track the true time spent out here

After a while, the thousands of trees blend together.

I try to pay attention to which side the moss is growing, but it's everywhere—crawling over the forest floor, roots, and rocks in every direction.

Right as I'm about to take a break, something shatters the beautiful monotony of the forest. A glimmer of joy sparks. Between the trees sits a small clearing, no bigger than the estate's kitchen, filled with an abundance of forget-me-nots.

Flowers I recognize from the lady's gardens.

In late spring, when her roses and tulips would bloom, Char and I were tasked with pruning the wild forget-me-nots that popped up relentlessly. Lady Nilda called them unwelcome weeds. She said they were parasites, sucking the beauty from her garden.

I always liked them. For their resilience, and for the fact they bothered the lady. Most of all, they gave me and Char a reason to get fresh air.

My heart swells at the memory of working side-by-side with Char, knuckle deep in dirt, and I try to hold onto that image of her instead of her final moments.

I head closer to the forget-me-nots, placing my hands on rough bark as I peek around a hickory tree. Movement catches my eye and I gasp, jerking backwards.

A figure stands with their back to me, between two thick elms on the other side of the clearing.

Ever so slowly, the person turns.

My pulse rages in my temples, and my eyes widen.

"Char?" My mouth drops in shock, and my battered, blistered feet move toward her as fast as they can. "Oh gods, Char!"

"My Alessia," she whispers. "Come with me, dear."

A smile grows on her face as she swiftly walks toward me, her gait agile. The trees bend and sway almost imperceptibly as she passes them. I squint, wondering if I'm seeing things. There's no breeze—everything is otherwise still.

My gut swirls with warning as she reaches for me.

But I find myself moving toward her anyway, closing the gap. She grabs my hand, tugging me with her. I trip and stumble trying to keep up with her quick pace. Glancing over my shoulder, I notice the clearing is gone. There's nothing but dim forest behind me.

"Char?" I ask in a whisper, frowning. "Where are we going?"

"Keep up," she hisses.

I try and fail to pull free of her. A few paces later, two other figures step into sight. There's a large stone behind them. I blink, and at second glance, it looks an awfully lot like a table. Like the one from... Lord Edvin and Lady Nilda's kitchen.

"Come 'ere, Dolly," the lord says, beckoning me closer with a stubby finger.

His gut hangs over his pants, and he grunts as he undoes his belt.

I try to rip my hand from Char's, to turn and run, but her grip is steel.

"No, Char, please," I gasp. "Let me go."

The lord appears to float toward me. Before I can fight him, his hands wrap around me, pulling me away from Char.

"I am not your family," Char says, her voice monotone. "I am not your family. I am not your—"

She continues chanting as the lord drags me to the stone table, shoving me face down. I squirm, tears streaming down my face, but he holds me in place.

I'm stuck helpless, rooted in place, as I watch the lady approach Char. When she slices the blade across her throat once again, a guttural scream rips from my lungs.

Through it all Char keeps chanting, even as her blood spills from the wound in her neck and from her mouth.

I scream and scream, until no sound comes out and blackness consumes my vision. I waver in and out of consciousness before it consumes me entirely.

Fear and exhaustion are a lethal concoction.

***

Something nudges my side, and slowly, I peel my eyes open. My breath quickens as I take in the stone beneath me, remembering where I am. Only, it's not the lord's table I'm facedown on after all. It's only a rock. A regular boulder.

I swear I saw the lord and lady.

And Char.

Is my mind playing tricks on me?

Blinking a few times in confusion, I try to push myself up, but something presses on my back, holding me in place.

I think I hear the word, "*stay.*"

"No." My voice is weak, hoarse. "Get off me."

I thrash around in slow motion, unable to fight back.

"Stop moving," a velvety smooth voice hisses in my ear. "You're tangled in the vines. If you keep moving the thorns *will* pierce your skin. Trust me when I say you would like to avoid that at all costs."

My body quakes and a strangled cry escapes me. My hands search for purchase, and I fumble to press myself up.

"I said *stop* moving."

The heat of his breath warms the back of my neck, but I can't turn my head to see who's there. Based on his voice, it's definitely not the lord, nor is it Felix, but that doesn't make him any less dangerous.

"Please," I croak out. "Please." In my hazy vision and the abundance of shadows cast around me from the towering trees, I see a figure staring at me. "Char!"

"Quiet."

The figure gives me a sad look, one I know too well. Blood starts pouring from her eyes and I scream. Then she turns her back, leaving me here.

"Char! Come back." My voice cracks as I scream and cry for her. "Please don't leave me here. Please!"

There's a rustling behind me, and a few tugs as someone works to free me. I close my eyes and rest my face on the cool stone, trying to quell my body's trembles.

"Char," I murmur, my throat raspy and aching.

"She's still hallucinating," another male voice says from somewhere off to the side of us, this one more boisterous than the first. "I don't sense anyone else. Already scanned the area."

The person holding me down grunts. There's a ripping sound and air hits the back of my thighs. *My dress.*

"Get... off of... me!" I try and jerk away, only for his grip to tighten. "Stop—don't do this!"

My heartbeat pounds in my ears.

"I said don't move," he hisses at me. His voice warbles between the lord's and something smoother. I wiggle—kicking and growling with mayhem. "The thorns have a toxin that will—" Something sharp pricks my skin. "Fecking ignorant human! Kenisius, I need you to—"

"Get away—" My words slur as the voices fade out. My body sags against the stone. I can't move, not even to blink or breathe voluntarily. My body simply functions without my control. I'm a prisoner caged in my flesh.

The voices grow distant.

"...it won't survive the woods...throw it back over with the other..."

"...so young..."

The voices cut in and out as I'm consumed by an unsettling darkness. It's disorienting. Ice encases my bones. The darkness sucks air from my lungs.

A presence approaches me. I can't see her, but I feel her.

"Find strength in fear, my Alessia," Char's voice whispers to me through the blackness. All the sounds grow quiet as I fade away again. "Find strength in fear."

Six

I Miss Char

Alessia

A wave of dizziness grips me for a brief moment, as I press myself up with a groan. When it passes, I take a quick inventory of my body. My hands tremble as they run the length of my dress, inspecting every inch. My fingers meet skin at the back of my lower thigh area, where my dress was ripped, and the rest is tattered and covered in muck. Other than that, I'm still covered and everything is intact. Nothing throbs or aches with violation.

I shudder with relief.

Only the injuries from the lord's recent whipping and my escape remain.

"The little human lives."

I flinch, recoiling into myself and wrapping my arms around my stomach as a large male steps into my line of sight. I recognize his boisterous voice from before I fainted.

He's a burly fellow, thick with muscles, and a mess of brown hair curled into a bun at the nape of his neck, with a beard to match. He tosses a small, purple berry up into the air, catching it in his mouth with a dramatic flourish.

My head snaps to the side, wary, as I scan the rows and rows of moss-covered trees. Wisps of fog roll across the ground, caressing the trees' roots and trunks.

I search for the lord. The lady.

Char...

No.

I must've hallucinated.

That was—

"Want one?" he offers, stepping closer with an outstretched hand.

"Stay away from me," I command hoarsely.

Climbing off the boulder, I duck down on the opposite side, keeping the large rock between us. Thankfully, it isn't the lord's table after all.

"Whoa." He shakes his head. "You were dead there a moment ago. I figured you might be hungry. That's all."

"Dead?" I blink a few times, wondering if I heard him correctly.

He plops another berry into his mouth, eyeing me curiously. "What'd it feel like?"

"What do you mean I was *dead?*"

"The toxin." He points at a pile of severed, snake-like vines with long, needle-like thorns adorning them. "Slowed your heart rate allllll the way down. Couldn't hear a rhythm at all for a minute or two. Thought for sure you weren't going to make it."

I exhale a long breath, not knowing what to make of that.

"Fate must be on your side because slowly your pulse picked back up and *bam*"—I flinch when he yells the word—"here you are! Right as roses." He snickers to himself then mutters something that sounds like, "he's gonna love that irony."

My eyes scan the woods around us as I squat behind the boulder, desperate to make out an escape. My body is much too weak to outrun this muscular brute, but I'll be damned if I don't try.

I open my mouth to speak, but he cuts me off.

"I don't know what to do with ya now. He said to throw ya back over the Gleam when you died. But technically, you're back alive. Or still alive. Or...whatever. Humans are weird."

"Please," I whisper. His eyes widen as he goes still. "Don't hurt me."

This causes him to chuckle, his shoulders shaking vigorously.

"I've no such intentions, little human." He glances toward the sky, and shifts his weight. "I *knew* you were gonna make it." He punches the air with a wide smile. "But we gotta get going. You've been out a while and I need to get back. We've spent far too long in the woods. Guess you're coming with."

I glance around the trees, looking for signs of the other male who was here. The one who tried to rip my dress off. Or worse—for the lord or lady.

"There's no one here," the male says, presumably reading my body language.

"Where'd they go?"

"There's no one else here. It's the trees. They play tricks."

He gives the lanky elm tree next to him a knock, and the sound echoes around me. Something slithers through the grassy area beside me, and I shudder.

The male steps forward, crouching down in front of me as if I'm a frightened child. I suck in a sharp breath. He sniffs the air and his frown deepens.

I keep my palms on the rock, studying him cautiously, ready to push off and run if I need to. Perhaps it's the exhaustion that gives me pause, but I find myself listening to him.

"We were surprised to find you alive." I can only stare at him, his molten-brown eyes filled with concern. "Twice now, you've defied death."

Three times, actually, if I count avoiding certain death in Dovenak.

I clear my throat, trying to instill some strength into my voice.

"Where's the other one that was with you?" *Was* there another one? Or did I imagine that too?

"Oh, Rai?" He jerks a thumb over his shoulder. "He's gone back to court."

"*Court,*" I whisper. "Are you fae?"

At this, he laughs, flashing a set of white teeth that contrast with his dark copper skin. It's a loud, rumbling laugh that causes a small animal to skitter through the bushes.

He's terrifyingly large, yet he looks human.

"I am." He cranes his head and sniffs again. "I can smell the terror on ya, but I promise, it's not me you should fear. It's the forest. We need to leave before night falls." It's the second time he's mentioned the woods, and my confusion must show on my face because he continues, "The trees are pretty, but they are cruel things. They play tricks, and when night comes… you shouldn't be here. Figured you had enough by now, anyways."

Char's words hit me again: Do not linger in the forest, on either side, especially if it calls to you.

I might not trust this… fae, but his words match up with Char's. I can't stay here any longer. Squinting at him, I take him in from head to toe. His pants and tunic are cut from brown leather, adorned with black accents and various weapon holders. I'm not sure what they're called, but I've seen a similar outfit once or twice back at the estate. They were escorts—guards—for the lord.

Though the outfit gives me pause, the joy and kindness radiating from his broad smile and relaxed posture put me at ease. As much at ease as I can possibly be in this situation, that is. I can only hope he is genuine, because I am far too exhausted to fight for my safety.

"Please be one of the good ones," I mutter under my breath.

"I'd like to think I am," he says with a grin. When he catches my horrified expression, he chuckles. "Shifter hearing. I'm Kenisius, by the way." He steps closer, carefully, as if I'm a frightened animal. "It's a mouthful, I know, but Ken is fine."

My pulse picks up and blood rushes to my cheeks.

"Your heart is pumping furiously." Ken slowly steps around the boulder, and reaches out to pat me on the head with a meaty hand. I flinch away from his touch, stepping around the rock to keep it between us. "Relax, little human."

I'm not sure what exactly being a *shifter* entails, but his senses certainly are animalistic. I gape until a movement catches my attention. Past him, a dozen or so yards away, a large chestnut steed steps into sight and begins chomping on a berry bush.

He follows my gaze over his shoulder. "That's Merry. She's just a horse. Nothing to fear with her either."

My mouth clamps shut. If he was going to hurt me, he could have already done it when I was unconscious. He seems...nicer than I expected. If I have any chance for survival, I need to understand my surroundings and adapt as quickly as possible. I don't have to trust him to accept his help.

Taking a few steady inhales, I heed Ken's advice to attempt to relax, focusing on the breathing techniques Char taught me to stay calm, to quell my mind. Right now, I'm stuck between fight or flight mode—biding my time until I determine my next move—and that doesn't help things.

"You're… what kind of thing do you shift into?"

"Thing," Ken mimics, cocking his head at me. "Rude."

"S-sorry," I stutter. "Little human is equally as rude though."

He simply laughs. "You *are* a little human. Look at you—you're a third of my size. You need a decent meal or seventeen."

I grimace. He isn't wrong, I could use a good meal.

The fog hovering near the ground thickens. It tickles my ankles with a cool caress. The sense of being watched consumes me, and I swear the wind whispers my name from between the trees. I glance around nervously, but see nothing other than endless forest.

"Look, ones like you don't normally cross the Gleam." His humor subsides and he grows serious. "Nor do they survive the woods… especially not after nightfall." He gives me a stern look and strides toward the horse. "You survived this far, so clearly you have a decent will to live. Don't be stubborn now. Merry is waiting, and we need to move."

Ones like me? Do others cross often?

"Is there a… sanctuary village around here?" I ask, remembering a rumor Char had briefly mentioned.

"A *what* now?" He gets to the horse and turns toward me, beckoning me forward.

"I—nevermind." Of course it doesn't exist. Char already told me that.

Reluctantly, I follow him, ditching the safety of my boulder. Once I reach him, he offers me a broad smile. He grips me by the waist with two massive hands.

I scream, thrashing against his hold. But he simply lifts me up with ease and plants me on the horse. My heart pounds in my chest.

He ignores my outburst and says, "You're running from something—or someone."

Taking a few deep, calming breaths, I nod. "Something like that."

"I recognize that marking." He gestures toward his own face, referring to my Tradeling tattoo. "Must be a scary something you're running from, if you thought you'd be safer here."

"Others have come?" I ask breathlessly. "With this mark?"

"Yup."

"Where are they now?"

"Dead," he says, matter-of-factly.

My heart drops at that, but I try not to let his words affect me. I grip my skirt, glancing down at the tattered thing.

"Your friend ripped my dress," I mumble lamely.

He scratches his neck. "It wasn't—we weren't—" he pauses and taps his foot, as if he's contemplating an explanation. "The trees had a hold of you and we were trying to cut you loose. Some of the thorny vines were stuck in your dress, and we had to rip it free. We weren't trying to tear it off."

"Then why did he run away?"

Ken's mouth turns up. "The thorn pricked you good. He figured you were going to die and left me to take care of you." My brows rise at how brash the truth is. "Plus you were bleeding and he didn't want to…get soiled. Blood has a tendency to stain, you know. He is not partial to it."

"Trust me, I know," I mutter. "Good thing he doesn't menstruate."

The shifter throws his head back and laughs. "You're a funny little thing."

I frown. There's not anything funny about menstruation, but I'm also not about to dissect that with a male shifter.

"You ever ridden a horse before?" he asks.

"No."

My fling with Felix has offered me basic knowledge about horses and riding, despite never having actually been on a horse before.

"Come on."

He waves a hand around, instructing me where to place my hands and feet. I don't know if it's fear or excitement, but my stomach flutters at being atop such a majestic being.

"Wow," I say in awe.

"She's a beaut, eh?"

He holds onto the reins, showing me where to place my hands on the pommel, and giving me basic instructions.

I squeeze my thighs tight against the horse, and immediately realize it's a mistake.

"Whoa!" I yell, as Merry lurches.

Ken chuckles. "I got her. Just hold on."

The horse prances in circles around Ken, and after a couple of tiny laps, a hysterical laugh bubbles out of me.

"This is amazing!"

I can't believe I've never asked Felix to let me ride a horse before when the lord was out. I was always too afraid.

"It's going to be a bumpy ride, but we really need to get out of here, so hold on tight."

Movement in my peripheral catches my attention, but when I whip my head toward it, there's nothing there. The breeze stills and the chirping in the trees grows awfully quiet again. Goosebumps rise on my arms.

"Aw, here we go," Ken says. I'm expecting him to jump on behind me, so I'm caught off guard when he slaps the horse on the rear and yells, "Take her back to court, Merry!"

"Wait—ahhh!" The scream rips from my lips as Merry bolts through the forest, zigzagging through the trees and soaring over the bushes and brambles that line our path. I squeeze my eyes shut and throw myself forward, gripping the poor horses' neck for dear life.

Everything Ken instructed me to do goes out the window, as I grab ahold as tight as I can, battling to stay centered.

Felix once said I'd love horseback riding.

He was wrong.

It's awful.

All my thoughts of Char, the lord and lady, the woods, and Ken's mysterious friend fall to the wayside. If there was anything in my stomach, I would've spewed it all over Merry.

With each gallop, my still-raw arse aches, reminding me of my unhealed wounds. My thighs scream and bugs pelt me in the face. It's a new form of abuse.

Maybe it's the circumstance to blame, but I hate horseback riding.

By the time the horse slows, the skin between my mid-upper thighs is chafed as raw as my backside. I ache in new places. Ken is nowhere to be found, so I decide to dismount. It's a battle to swing my leg over the horse, and when I finally succeed, I plop down and my legs buckle beneath me. I crumple to the ground.

My eyes fill with tears.

"Oh gods," I cry out. "Sorry, Merry," I tell the horse as she stomps away to chomp on nearby vegetation.

I shake out my hands, reminding myself that I'm alive. That's what matters.

With a few deep breaths, I push myself back to a stand, biting my tongue to keep my groans at bay. I need to be okay—for Char.

Though the sun has tucked itself away behind silver clouds, the air is still comfortable—warm even. I sniffle away the tears, finally taking a moment to observe what lies before me.

Roses wind around the bars of a tall, pointy, black-iron gate built into a towering stone wall. From between the bars I can make out a stepping stone path that leads through a vibrant green yard, right up to the most magnificent structure I've ever seen.

The pale, weathered stone of the castle matches the wall and pathway, with moss stretching up four or five stories high. Spires and steeples stab the overcast sky, as if attempting to poke holes in the clouds. Some of the windows are colorful, the glass stained with art.

It's breathtaking.

Merry whinnies from somewhere behind me. An eerie feeling crawls up the back of my neck, and I twist around, squinting at the trees.

When the overgrown bushes at the edge of the woods rustle, my forehead crinkles. I hope to the gods it's Ken and not something else.

The bushes shake again, and Merry whinnies, taking off alongside the stone wall. My jaw slackens, my mouth falling open as an animal clamors out.

It's a large, terrifying creature. With an abundance of brown fur, dark beady eyes, and claws larger than my head. It prowls toward me on all fours.

My chest tightens as I scurry backward until my back hits the iron bars. "Gods, no. Please no!"

The bear moves at an unhurried pace, eyeing me with curiosity. It doesn't snarl or snap. It shows no signs of aggression, but that does little to reassure me. Maybe it's another hallucination.

When the bear reaches me, I slam my eyes shut.

"Please—" Tears stream down my face, and I'm sure I'm seconds away from a heart attack.

Hot, moist breath blasts my face, but instead of taking a bite out of me like I expect it to, it nudges my cheek with its furry face.

"Okay," I whimper, sliding down to the grass and curling up into the fetal position. "This is fine. Everything is fine. Good bear."

Even as it pulls away I stay in place, curled up against the gate for what seems like forever.

When a crunching sound fills the air, I finally open my eyes. The bear begins to contort. I watch in stunned silence as the form takes on two legs, shrinking slightly in size. The fur melts away, revealing rippled muscles. When the transformation is complete, a very humored, and very naked Ken stands before me.

I squeeze my eyes shut again and grip my chest. Leaning back, I suck in air desperately.

"Oh my gods. Oh my gods."

"That's what they all say when they see what I'm slinging." His voice is teasing, but it does nothing to soothe the terror still coursing through me.

A sound between a groan and cry escapes my lips. My stomach roils with nausea, and I lean forward, retching all over the ground.

"That's a new one." Ken scratches his head. "You're the first one to puke after seeing me naked."

"I can't do this." I lean my head against the bars, sobbing with my eyes shut.

"Oh, oh. Hey now." Concern laces his booming voice. "I was only kidding. I have clothes in one of these bushes…" There's the sound of rustling leaves. "Somewhere over here. Oh—here." There's more rustling, and the clank of a belt buckle. "I forgot humans find nudity offensive," he mumbles. "Okay, the ol' tallywacker is tucked away. It's safe to peek again."

I hesitantly open my eyes to see Ken emerge from the nearby brush. He's dressed in brown leather pants, a snug long sleeve, and worn boots. Some sort of weapon is tucked into a holster on his belt.

"Come on now," he says. "Let's go see about getting you a room and some food. I'm sure the prince will let you stay."

Prince.

Now I'm to meet a fae prince.

All I can do is nod and numbly follow him, my footsteps shuffling heavily, as he opens the iron gates.

The last of the daylight dips behind the castle, casting night's shade on us. As we head toward the grand structure, an ominous tingle creeps up my spine.

Slowing just enough to glance over my shoulder, I squint at the forest. At the edge of the tree line, I swear I make out a human-shaped shadow—faceless and terrifying—as it watches us without eyes.

I shudder and try to keep pace as best I can with my battered body, desperate to put distance between me and the creepy forest. It's hard enough to keep track of reality right now as is. More hallucinations are the last thing I need.

We enter the castle, and my brows fly to my hairline at the grandiosity of the space.

The inside of the castle is as jaw-droppingly gorgeous as the outside. The foyer is striking with painted floors and opulent patterns. Two identical sets of dark staircases with ornately carved banisters mirror each other as they curve up, joining as a mezzanine on the second floor.

My head tips back, taking it all in, and I almost stumble.

An obnoxious off-white chandelier dangles precariously above us. I stare for a few long seconds, wondering if it's made of bone.

If it's made of *human* bone.

Fear courses through my veins at the haunting sight.

A feminine giggle carries down one of the many hallways, echoing around us.

Ken sighs and scrubs at his face with both hands, clearly unimpressed by whoever the laughter belongs to.

Goosebumps decorate the back of my neck. For such an imposing space, especially one so well kept, I had expected there to be a plethora of servants milling about. The emptiness is eerie.

"Where is everyone?" I whisper.

"Out of sight, out of mind," Ken replies. Gone is his lighthearted demeanor. He stands taller, his frown stretches further, and new lines appear on his forehead.

"Rainer," Ken bellows. His voice echoes back. "We're baaaack."

A few seconds later two figures emerge from the hallway beneath the staircases. One is a beautiful female with flowing burgundy-colored hair and dark, hooded eyes. She wears a low-cut dress that hugs her slim frame. Smoky lids and a bright red lip are painted dramatically on her face. Her high-heels teeter slightly as she tries to walk and sip from a goblet at the same time. The excess of golden jewelry bracelets on her wrist clank together in a sharp melody as she leans on the male beside her.

"Fern," the male says sternly. "Get off me."

She whines. "Don't you want more?"

"No."

The male sports unusually sharp ears. The tips peek through his shaggy charcoal-colored hair. Thin, gold, decorative chains wrap around his lobes, climbing up each point. He's very clearly fae. No doubt about it. And though I should perhaps be frightened or hesitant, my eyes widen with intrigue.

Dressed in muted shades of grey, his disheveled hair and rumpled clothes seem at odds with the elaborate room. Like he, too, is an outsider. Whorls of ink peek out from beneath a half-buttoned up top. I squint to make out the design, until I realize he's grimly observing my unabashed staring.

When his eyes lock onto mine, a flash of surprise crosses his face. He stops in his track and the female at his side nearly topples over.

My cheeks heat, embarrassed, but thankfully he doesn't say anything as he shoves his hands deep into his pockets. He steps closer until he's only a few feet away. Then I can see just how blue his eyes are.

A pale, frosty blue. Cold as ice.

There's a beat of silence as he peruses my body, and my stomach quivers. He's handsome in an unconventional, unkempt sort-of way with strong cheekbones, thick brows, and a pale complexion.

"It lived," he mutters before turning his scowl to Ken. "What were you thinking, bringing it here?"

That voice… I recognize it from the woods. *He* was the one trying to free me from the vines.

"I'm not an it," I whisper, fidgeting with my dress.

The fae—Rainer, as Ken called him—glowers at me. Ken's shoulders shake with silent laughter. The girl ignores us completely, in favor of pouting at Rainer.

"Rainer, this is—" Ken leans toward me. "What was your name, little human?"

"Alessia," I whisper.

"Alessia," Ken repeats to Rainer. "And *she* is not an *it*." He winks at me.

Rainer evaluates me with a set jaw. "I don't know how you possibly survived. You're a pathetic thing."

My cheeks burn at his assessment. Meanwhile, Fern giggles, and I wonder how much she's had to drink. I recognize that flushed, bloodshot look from the lord and lady's parties

Rainer's scrutinization grows so intense that I quickly avert my gaze to the ground.

Ken grunts.

I swallow the uneasy lump in my throat. My stomach chooses that moment to rumble.

Fern gives me a pitying look. "Poor thing is hungry, Rai." She tugs on his arm. "You should feed her. You of all people know what hunger does—"

"Stop talking." Rainer grabs Fern's goblet with one hand, and pinches the bridge of his nose with the other. "What it needs is to get cleaned up."

My hands ball into fists at my side. Considering I expected to die a million ways since yesterday, a bath and food would be more than I could've ever hoped for after today.

But the one thing I'm unable to let go of is the derogatory way he calls me an *it*.

"I am not an it," I mutter, louder this time.

Rainer narrows his eyes.

"I thought we were to meet the prince?" I whisper to Kenisius. There's no way this is the prince. Not with his unhinged aura, attitude, and not to mention, he was in the woods with Ken. Princes don't wander the woods.

Do they?

Rainer smirks. "The prince is busy." He turns to Fern. "Take her up to a guest suite. I'll send Das Celyn with food."

Ken gives me a thumbs up before he and Rainer head down one of the hallways that spill from the foyer, leaving me and Fern alone in the enormous entranceway. I wonder where the prince is. Ken and Rainer must be his guards of some sort. Surely both are built like warriors—Ken especially in his leathers and boots.

As soon as they're out of earshot, Fern whines. "That cad took my wine!"

After the day I've had, it's absurd she's throwing a fit over wine. She appears to pick up on my disinterest, because she scoffs at me.

"Faerie wine is phenomenal." She teeters on her heels, then shakes it off with a giggle.

"Are you—?"

"Human? Yes."

I was going to ask if she was drunk, but relief shoots through me at her admission. "Is this…a refuge for humans?" I choose my words carefully. "Is it safe here?"

She snorts. "Nowhere's safe. Though it's better than whatever's…out there." She waves a hand and a hiccup bubbles out of her. "The fae are arseholes. Oh! And you better thank the gods Ken found you before dusk. The fae barely survive the woods at night, and you definitely wouldn't have made it." She shrugs, eyeing me up and down.

She's beautifully done up, and awfully composed despite her drunkenness. Meanwhile, I'm covered in muck and grime, bogged down by grief. Rainer was right. I need a bath.

As if Fern can read the expression on my face, she says, "Well, come on, then."

She turns away from me, leading me toward one of the grand staircases.

Reaching down, she unsnaps the clasps on her heels before tossing them aside with a dramatic sigh of relief. They clatter to the floor in the foyer. She leaves them there as she trounces up the stairs.

"Don't those hurt your feet?" I ask.

She turns to look at me, gripping the banister so she doesn't lose her balance. "Obviously. That's why I took them off."

My cheeks heat as we resume our ascent. I've never seen those kind of shoes before. Not even the lady wears them.

"What kind of... creature is Rainer?" I call from behind her.

We hit the second floor, and Fern spins around to face me again, but this time she cracks a grin.

"He would be appalled if he heard you refer to him as a creature. He's a—" she hesitates and glances around the dimly lit, paneled hallway. "A faerie."

"A faerie," I repeat.

"Yep. You can always tell a faerie by their sharp ears and ethereal beauty," she rushes out. "Look, I don't know why you're here, but you can't stay."

I can only balk at her, unable to determine if she's threatening me or trying to help me.

"Ken is nice enough, but Rainer—" her eyes widen as she glances nervously over her shoulder. "He's a scary fecker."

"And what about the prince? Is he—should I fear him?"

"Funny you should ask." She hiccups again, wiping her mouth with the back of her hand. "They call him Prince of Fear for a reason."

Prince of Fear?

My skin pebbles at the ominous title.

Fern gives me a look like she wants to say more, but someone else enters the hallway, grumbling to themselves. They're shorter than me—and that's saying something—with a black bob and bangs. Sharp ears poke through their hair.

Another faerie.

They hold a tray of food in their hands.

Fern giggles, clapping her hands. "Das Celyn! It's a party now!"

"Oh hush, girl," Das Celyn scolds. "Get yourself together."

Fern rolls her eyes. "Get yourself together," she mocks.

"You have a problem."

"And you have an attitude."

"I cannot wait for the day the prince drains your body of blood and feeds you to the forest."

Fern frowns. "That's rude, even for you."

"One human is bad enough, I don't need two pestering me. Scram."

I avert my eyes, glancing to the floor as Fern mocks Das Celyn and strides away.

"Remember what I said, Alessia," she calls over her shoulder. "I don't know what monsters you ran from, but you better hope they weren't as bad as the ones you just ran to."

Das Celyn narrows their eyes, giving me a disgusted look.

Shrinking back from them, I say, "Hi. I'm Alessia?" I hadn't intended for it to come out like a question, but it does.

They click their tongue and thrust the tray of food toward me.

I accept it, eying the plate of breads, cheeses, and fruits cautiously. There's even a small kettle of what I presume is tea, and an empty mug. I sniff it.

Chamomile.

When they turn to leave I call out, "Wait! Celyn?"

They whip around. "Don't you Celyn me. I earned my title."

"What?"

"It is *Das* Celyn to you." Their voice is much sharper than it was with Fern, and I recoil.

"I'm… sorry," I mumble.

"Don't you ever apologize to the fae!" They shake their head and their bangs swish across their forehead. "What is wrong with you, girl?"

"I'm—" I pause, unsure of what to say.

I'm so out of place here. Glancing around the wide hallway, with its ruby-red runner and plethora of doors, I realize how easy it would be to get utterly lost here.

"Fern was supposed to show me to a room," I say lamely.

"That girl is no good. An addict. Can't rely on her for anything."

I don't care what or who she is, other than human, and I hope she'll be an ally.

"Come on then."

I carry the tray of food as I trail behind Das Celyn. They lead me another floor up the winding staircase. I wince with each step, struggling to keep up.

We trail down a gloomy hallway lined with weird, obscure art. Nonsensical paintings that appear to be dark splatters of color without any rhyme or reason. Oversized windows stained with glass line the hallway—more decoration than actual use.

Flickering sconces cast shadows in every corner of the walk. Everything—the paintings, the runner, the stained glass windows—consist of hues of brown, black, and blood-red.

Das Celyn, having purposefully ignored me for the last few minutes, opens the door to reveal an extravagant room with a four-poster bed, brick fireplace, and beautiful window seat perched beneath a wall of oversized casement windows. It appears perfectly comfortable, but I drag my feet, reluctant to enter.

"Get in here, girl."

I oblige, exhaustion winning. That bed is much too inviting to ignore, and I have nowhere else to go.

They point to a door beside the fireplace. "Bath and toilet are through there." They wave a hand toward the opposite wall. "The armoire is fully stocked in a variety of sizes. *Enjoy*."

Without another word, they turn and leave. The door slams behind them, and I flinch at the harsh sound slicing through the otherwise quiet room.

Between Fern's warning and Rainer's wintry gaze, I'm on high alert.

My stomach growls again. I place the tray of food on a small table in the corner, and continue to stand, afraid sitting will irritate my wounds further.

My chest tightens with the ache of missing Char as I force myself to choke down some food. It all tastes bleak and bitter—like ash on my tongue.

Afterward, I clean up and tuck myself into the grand bed, barely registering the soft sheets. My hand trembles as I cover my mouth, trying to muffle my sobs. Tears pours down my face until my vision goes blurry.

Gods above and below, I miss Char.

Seven

Welcome to the Umbra Court

Alessia

Subtle hints of clove and rose linger in the air, blending into a unique, soothing scent, rousing me from my slumber. The bed beneath me is unfamiliar. Too soft. The sheets lining my body are too smooth. The air is perfectly comfortable—no bitter bite of winter nibbling on my flesh.

My head is clear and intense pain no longer wraps around my legs. Only the whisper of a dull ache lingers, a fraction of the agony from before.

"It can't stay here."

I recognize Rainer's voice. It comes from somewhere nearby. I crack open an eye, relieved to see I'm alone. The door is cracked, however, and the voices spill in from the hallway.

"Calling her an 'it' doesn't make her any less of a being. You can't lie to yourself and say you don't care."

"It's not a lie, Kenisius. I *don't* care."

"Then why did I catch you checking on her just now?" Ken's voice holds a hint of humor. There's a scoff, but no response from Rainer. "Exactly."

I keep my eyes shut, feigning unconsciousness to eavesdrop. I'm vulnerable lying here, and I fight the urge to wrap my arms around my midsection and curl into myself. But I stay stock-still to gather as much information as I can before facing them.

"She could be a spy, sent by the queen," Rainer says flatly.

"You saw her face. She's marked. She *ran*."

"That's exactly what the queen would want us to think."

Ken chuckles. "The human queen knows you wouldn't take pity. It'd be like sending a lamb to slaughter."

My muscles tighten. I was under the impression no one ever neared the Gleam, but after Felix's revelation about guarding the border, it's clear the two realms have more interaction than I assumed.

"My life is riddled with troubles," Rainer says.

"Then what's one more?"

"One too many."

"Oh come on, Rai. Sending her back is an early death. If they don't already want to kill her for escaping their trade, they will most certainly kill her for breaching the border."

"As if it's any safer here," he snarls. "You of all people know better."

"We can protect her."

"I *can't*."

"But you *want* to?" Ken asks eagerly. My heart squeezes.

"No."

"She survived the woods."

"Only because your demanding arse got to it in time," Rainer deadpans. "I was keen on leaving it."

There's a soft knock on the door, then a shuffling across the room, pacing. Floorboards creak and groan under their steps. After a few moments, they draw closer and the bed dips next to me as someone perches on the edge.

Someone heavy.

"Might as well tell her yourself then. Go on, tell her you're signing her death warrant, Rainer. She can hear how much of a right bastard you're being."

The room grows silent, so after a few seconds I muster up bravery and crack open an eye. I'm greeted by the view of Ken's blindingly warm smile.

He scoots off the bed to stand, hovering over me. His thick hair falls loose of its bun and he straightens to retie it at the nape of his neck.

"You're a poor eavesdropper. At least fake it next time." He chuckles.

"I *was* faking it." The lump in my throat makes it hard to speak.

"Well, not good enough. I heard the change in your breathing."

"Why are you here?"

"Checking on you, of course, little human."

Sitting up against the headboard, I glance around. The only source of light comes from the oil lamp beside the four-poster bed I'm resting in. To my left, beyond the shifter, it's dim. I can barely make out a few pieces of furniture encased in shadows. To my right, there's a wall of heavy drapes with slivers of light peeking out from the edges, concealing the casement windows I saw when I arrived.

Rainer is nowhere in sight, so it's safe to assume he's lurking in the hallway still.

My pulse speeds up.

Ken cocks his head at me. "Calm down, little human."

I inhale through my nose, holding it for a few seconds before exhaling through my mouth. I do this a few times until my heart rate evens out.

"What time is it?" I ask cautiously.

Ken strokes the fuzz on his chin. "Just after dawn. You slept through the night."

"I don't even remember falling asleep."

I ate and drank the tea, took an extended bath, and changed into a clean nightgown from the armoire. But I barely remember lying down for bed. It's all a blur.

"Valerian root," Rainer mutters, entering the room. His boots clack ominously as he strides toward me. He leans against the armoire, crossing his arms. "In your tea. Helps induce a deep sleep."

A flash of panic flows through me. I've been unconscious here, with two brute fae who could've done gods knows what to me. I lift the blankets, glancing at the clean dress I changed into last night. My breath hitches when I notice all of my wounds are missing. Jagged slices, from racing across a wild forest, no longer mark my feet. Bruises and swelling are nowhere to be found.

I blink a few times, unable to tear my gaze away, even though I should be perfectly used to this. Char healed me with her magical salve many times before.

A sweat breaks out on the back of my neck.

"Das Celyn used a healing salve on you." Rainer's voice is hard and his expression is something akin to disgust as he picks a piece of lint off his shoulder. "And valerian root is a very rare herb around here. Hard to come by. Yet we spared some for you."

I'm unable to form a coherent response, because the healing salve reminds me of Char.

I wish I had Char.

I wish she was the one to help me heal.

My chest caves in and I clutch it, as if I can reduce the pressure there.

Rainer's eyes latch onto mine, and even in the flicker of the lamp, I can make out the light blue coloring. His gaze drops to where I grip my chest, and his features soften a fraction.

"Does it still hurt?" he asks.

It will always hurt, I want to say. Instead, I lie. "No."

His lips tighten, and he gives a sharp nod.

I shiver despite the room's warmth. I bring my knees to my chest and wrap the sheet around my shoulders. Ink peeks out from beneath his half-buttoned top, catching my attention. I squint, trying to make out the design, but he catches me staring and raises an eyebrow. The sharpness of his features and his unfriendly demeanor intimidates me.

Flustered, I look away again.

Ken clears his throat. "I hate to break whatever weird tension you two have going on—"

"For fae's sake, Kenisius," Rainer snaps, rubbing his forehead.

"—but I do think a spy would be far more competent than the little human has proved to be."

"I'm plenty competent." My hands tremble as I throw the sheet off me, swinging my legs over the side of the bed. My bare feet make contact with the wood, and I flinch at the coolness.

I'm sick of males—human or not—telling me what I am, what to do, how to act.

I wince as my backside screams with the movement. Das Celyn might've rubbed cream on my wounds, but only the wounds they saw.

My fingers flex at my side, tempted to reach back and touch the welts and cuts on my arse. The wounds tore open on the horseback ride, and now it'll take them longer to heal. I'm tempted to ask if there's any healing salve left, but I'm unwilling to ask for another ounce of help from them. Especially with how uncomfortable I am with the aid they've already given.

Instead, I straighten up, trying not to flinch as I take another step.

Both males watch me with dark expressions.

"Leave us, Kenisius," Rainer says in a deadly tone. The two exchange a glance and Ken nods before thudding across the room.

"See ya soon, little human," Ken says, slamming the door shut behind him.

I eye the exit, but Rainer steps into my line of sight. A wrinkle forms on his forehead as he scrutinizes me. His lips purse together into a thin line. His eyes roam me from head to toe, like he's assessing for damage, rather than in the predatory way Lord Edvin's eyes had always felt roaming my body.

Regardless of the reasoning, the attention rattles me. I wrap my arms around myself again, trying to quell the ill-timed fluttering in my stomach.

"You're still hurt," he says through clenched teeth. "Where?"

"No, I'm not," I lie.

His face contorts into something deadly, his eyes darkening. "You're bleeding. I can smell it from here."

My nose scrunches at the invasion of his senses. I could be menstruating for all he knows.

But I'm not.

My hand reaches up my skirt, brushing gently over my backside where the sting of pain is most persistent. Sure enough, my fingers come away tainted with the rusty smear of blood. I must've reopened my blisters by moving too quickly.

They'll never heal at this rate.

Rainer snarls. "I hadn't realized you had… been wounded prior to arriving in Avylon."

My mouth dries out. "I'm used to it."

"Who is responsible for this?"

"It doesn't matter who it was." I shrug nonchalantly, hoping it hides my unease.

His jaw clenches, and violence fills his eyes. "You are not to leave these grounds," he commands. "And for the time being, you're not to leave this room."

A brittle laugh escapes me. "I'm leaving. Now, actually."

"You're not." He shakes his head, turning away. "Clean yourself up. Ensure there's no blood on those sheets."

His shoulders are tense. He's uptight about cleanliness, which is odd, considering his borderline unkempt appearance. But I remember what Ken implied about him being uncomfortable around blood. And suddenly, though I tell myself I shouldn't care, I'm hoping I didn't stain his sheets.

I smooth my hands down the front of my dress, standing a little taller and feigning confidence, though I'm highly unsettled. Glancing toward the doors, I try to gauge how quickly I can bolt out of here—assessing whether or not I can outrun this… fae.

Taking my chance, I move swiftly toward the exit. His arm flashes out, stopping me in my tracks.

He leans in, his lips hovering beside my neck. When he speaks, his warm breath caresses my skin and I shudder.

"I said *clean yourself up.*"

My hands tremble at his tone. He refuses to meet my eyes, continuing to stare at the wall.

"And I said I'm leaving."

I ball my shaking hands into fists, wanting to get out of here sooner than later.

"All right." He steps back, piercing me with his gaze. "Feel free to thank me for all I've provided you, and you can be on your way."

The lord would whip me for my lack of gratitude. The thought alone is enough to instill fear in me. I compose myself.

"Thank you for the meal and bed. And for having Das Celyn heal me. Truly."

As soon as the words are out of my mouth, a sizzle of warmth spills into my veins. Everything tingles for a moment before the heat subsides. The sensation was vaguely reminiscent of when I crossed the Gleam.

"What was that?" My voice trembles.

Rainer strides to the door. Finally, he turns to me with a smirk. His eyes sparkle mischievously. "What was what?"

"What did you do to me? I felt it…*magic.*"

I charge forward, eager to get out of here, but when I get to the threshold, I smack face first into an invisible wall and stumble.

Grimacing, I step forward, trying to exit the room once again, to no avail. Something solid stands in my way, despite the doorway appearing normal and open. Some sort of magical force field blocks me from leaving.

I bang my fists against it, but it makes no noise. There's nothing there but air, yet I can't physically pass.

"Why are you—" Desperation laces my voice, but I trail off as I recall the conversation he had with Ken. The reasoning for why he's trapping me here. "I swear to the gods, I am not a spy. I'm not! I've never even met Queen Wyetta." It's true. Even though the lord worked for her, I never came near her. "I'm only a Tradeling! I'm a nobody." My voice cracks.

Rainer stops in his tracks. When he turns, my breath hitches at his cruel indifference.

"Oh, I know."

"No!" I scream after him, irritating my newly healed throat once again. "Get the prince! Please just get the prince, let me explain! *Please.*"

A flash of amusement creeps onto his face. "I hear the prince is a cruel bastard. Something tells me you won't care much for him. But since I'm not entirely heartless, I'll send Das Celyn to tend you in the meantime." With that, he strides away, leaving me sobbing in the enchanted doorway. "Welcome to the Umbra Court."

Eight

I Am Conflicted

Rainer

I storm into my office, planting my hands on my desk and letting out a roar. It echoes off the tall ceilings. With a quick swipe of my arm, I clear my oversized desk of its piles of parchment. After I compose myself, I slowly roll up my sleeves and turn to Kenisius.

"You shouldn't have brought her here."

"Well," he says with a sheepish grin and half-shrug, "too late?"

He plops sideways into one of the ornate couches with red and gold velvet, kicking his feet up and placing his arms behind his head.

"Too damn late."

I eye the papers scattered across my office floor with distaste—correspondences with Terra Court, and, worse, with the human queen, Wyetta. Another thorn in my side. "We're lucky the girl isn't a spy."

The human girl with grey eyes and pouty lips. A beautifully sad girl that stunned me silent—not because of her appearance, but because of the charged energy between us.

The pull I felt to her.

"I would've sent her back like the rest if she was."

"That's not my point. My point is that you had no way of knowing she wasn't, Kenisius."

Stooping, I angrily snatch up some of the papers, placing them in a neat pile. I can't stand messes.

"It's clear as day, Rai. Don't be like that."

He isn't wrong. It's obvious she isn't a spy. She's timid. Scrawny. Clearly unskilled. She might've survived the woods, but barely. If Kenisius and I hadn't found her, she'd likely be dead right now.

It'd be another tally to my body count.

"It's almost worse that she isn't a spy." I slam my fist on the desk, and my rings bite into my fingers. The wine decanter rattles, threatening to shatter. "She's a Tradeling. She has an owner. And if anyone saw her cross, there could be trouble."

This isn't the first time a Tradeling escaped from Dovenak into our realm. We always send them back. Granted, the forest normally gets to them before I do, so they often return in corpse form, but Queen Wyetta never once specified they had to be returned *alive*.

If only they stayed away from the Gleam—from Avylon.

If anyone saw the girl cross, and we don't produce a body soon—dead or alive—it's likely the girl's owner will send someone more skilled after her.

A spy.

An assassin.

Those are the ones who *do* occasionally make it through the trees, at the behest of Queen Wyetta, only to meet death at my hands. I always blame it on the woods, of course, but the queen isn't dimwitted. We both know the unspoken truth.

The woods and I really aren't that different, after all.

"So you're not sending her back?"

Without hesitation, I say, "No."

Fingering the stack of papers, I carefully push them together so their edges are flush with the desk.

"Interesting." Kenisius strokes his beard. "So, are you pissed at me for bringing her here? Or are you pissed at yourself that you can't tell her to leave either."

"I'm not conflicted."

"Seems like it. Which begs the question: why?"

His smile grows in size, and I turn to face my bookshelves instead of my friend. I scan the old leather spines and bindings. I squint, noticing a thin layer of silver dust accumulating. I'll need Das Celyn to send someone up to clean and rotate the books immediately. I should have them send the girl some books too, in case she—no.

No.

I *should* send her back. Or neutralize her—put her out of her misery and send her lifeless body back. At least that will spare her the pain of returning to the life she ran from. But the thought of doing so sickens me. The thought of *her* lying dead in the woods like so many before her is painful enough to steal my breath.

Kenisius is right. *Why* am I so reluctant to part with her? *Why* did I almost lose control entirely at the realization someone had hurt her? My immediate reaction was to hunt the bastard down and rip off the fingers that touched her, one by one.

She's a human. A mere *human*.

But she's throwing my entire world off-center, and she's only been here for less than a day.

She might hate me for using an ancient fae trick to bind her to me—to keep her here—but I couldn't risk her going back to whomever hurt her.

Kenisius and I both know what I refuse to say: she survived the woods.

She survived her *fear*.

And part of me can't help but wonder if she could survive me, too.

Hope. The girl gives me hope. It's a strange feeling I haven't felt a tickle of since I was a child.

Frowning at the bookshelf, I notice a title juts out further than the others: *The History and Banishment of Avylon's Demons*.

I push it back so its spine is in proper alignment with the rest.

"You smelled it, too," Kenisius says.

"Smelled what?" My frown deepens as I turn to look at him. "Her human blood? Her terror? Her desperation?"

"No—something different." He gives me a coy look, pressing himself into a sitting position. "She smells human, but *different*."

"I have no idea what you're referring to."

He hums, raising a brow at me. "Doesn't matter. You're saving her life, you know."

"That's if I don't take it first," I mutter, silently holding onto my hope.

"Your self-control is impeccable, Rai. You've mastered it. Have faith in yourself."

I lean against my desk, toying with a quill pen. "Find out who she ran from. I want to know everything about the girl." Glancing over my shoulder, I see Kenisius's eyes twinkling. His mouth opens, as if he's ready to crack a joke. "*Don't* Kenisius."

He nods, his attention snagging on a letter I missed from the floor. He stoops to pick it up. It has the green seal of Terra Court.

Kenisius is the only one who knows all of my secrets.

All of them.

I couldn't care less if he peeks at my correspondence with the other courts, and we both know I'd confide in him sooner than later about it anyway.

"Eoin wants your court?" He asks, barely concealing the shock in his voice as he reads the letter. I grunt in response and the shifter shakes with laughter. "We wouldn't accept him, does the kid not understand that?"

I shrug, tapping out a rhythm on my thigh as my mind works overtime to balance my many current problems.

"*You* might not—you're loyal to a fault. But the rest of the court might."

"They would never accept him over you. He doesn't have Umbra blood in his veins. You do everything for the court, Rai. From protecting our side of the Gleam, to employing the local families and offering a fair wage, to—"

"It doesn't matter what I do to protect them or our realm," I roar. "What matters is their perception of the situation. And if they deem my bloodline impure, they'll rip the court from me. Eoin's blood might not be Umbra, but it is Royal Fae down to the very last drop—"

"So you think," Kenisius says. He tosses the letter down on my desk, and I quickly snatch it up and add it to my stack. "I've bent his mother over a few times. And I'm sure I'm not the only one. For all we know, he could be my kid."

I rub my temples. "Never subject me to that imagery again."

"At least it wasn't adulterous. Her husband was well aware—"

He takes in my lethal expression and cuts off, gripping the back of his neck. "I'm just saying." He gives me a toothy grin. "It's very easy to taint a bloodline."

"Keep Eoin out of my business. Ensure this doesn't become a larger problem. And speaking of Terra Court, send for Sennah's best warrior. We could use assistance in the woods."

"Even their best will need training. Do you have time for that, Rai?"

"No." But we need to make time. It's better than the alternative.

"Perhaps it's time to assemble your own—"

"*No.*"

We've been through this so many times. Kenisius knows why I don't want an entire army—why I rely on him only. The two of us—and the forest—are plenty enough protection most days.

I run a hand through my hair, trying to hold it together. Damn this human girl for showing up and throwing another problem into the mix. I turn to the window, gazing out at the forest beyond.

"Is now a bad time to mention Ostara is coming up in under two months? And that Sennah will be here to help plan it in just a few weeks?" Kenisius pauses. I turn to catch him giving me an apologetic look. "With Eoin?"

I grit my teeth at the reminder of the spring equinox celebration. That is the least of my priorities. I hate festivities, and even worse, I hate planning them.

I slam my palm into the wall beside the window. "It's always a bad time for that."

"How can I help in the meantime?"

"Get information on the girl…and keep her far away from me."

"Got it." He chuckles before leaving the room.

Let's see how long the new human survives here. Hopefully, for her sake, I wasn't wrong about seeing a glimmer of fight in her. Because, by the gods, Kenisius is correct.

Something inexplicable draws me to her. I hate it, but I don't know how long I can fight it.

I *am* conflicted.

NINE

PAY OFF MY DEBTS

ALESSIA

I'm suffocating.

Though the room is spacious—even with the carved wooden bed big enough to fit four, the massive armoire, and a seating area complete with an unused fire mantel and other various furniture—it's as if the walls are closing in on me.

I've escaped one prison in favor of another, and this time I don't have Char by my side to comfort me. It's not entirely surprising the broody, blue-eyed faerie trapped me here—not after the tales of the bloodthirsty trees and vicious fae I've heard—but it's infuriating nonetheless.

Worse, almost, is when the fae are *nice*.

Ken lured me in with his niceties. And though I don't believe it to be fake, it still managed to fool me into a false sense of safety.

Perhaps I can request an audience with the prince and appeal to him. Surely his rule will outrank that of the shifter and faerie. Except, Fern called him the Prince of Fear, and Rainer called him a cruel bastard. It seems unpromising.

I'm trapped.

For what must be the hundredth time this hour, I crash my fists against the invisible forcefield locking me in. My fists meet an invisible, solid wall each time. Once again, my hands roam the entire doorway, searching for a weak point or opening to push through, but there isn't any.

"Let me out of here you pointy-eared arsehole!" I scream.

Oh gods, the lord would skin me alive for that attitude. My neck heats up and I instantly regret saying it. But when no one stalks toward me with a belt, ready to whip me, I grow emboldened.

Testing a theory I have, I scurry to the armoire and pull out a shoe, throwing it out the door. It lands with a thump in the hallway.

An incredulous laugh leaves me.

I throw a pillow next. It lands beside the shoe, confirming that it is only *me* who cannot cross the threshold.

It's mind-altering, trying to understand magic and how it works, and the ridiculousness of the situation fuels me, giving me the confidence to act out. I have absolutely *nothing* left to lose. Everything has been taken from me—my body, Char, my freedom, hell, even my sanity.

With an ear-splitting shriek, I begin throwing anything I can get my hands on. One-by-one things fly out the door into the hallway.

Shoes.

Pillows.

Skirts.

Tunics.

When I run out of things to throw angrily, and my arms shake, lacking the strength to continue, I slump in a heap on the floor.

Throwing a fit has done nothing to help me. All it's done is deplete my energy. I need to be smart, find a way out, or bide my time and strike back efficiently.

I gather myself together and snoop around the bathroom space. Various hygienic creams and fragrances sit scattered about by the vanity, but other than a clawfoot tub in the center of the space and a toilet, there isn't anything useful in here.

Passing by a mirror, I catch a glimpse of myself. My eyes are wild, my hair even unrulier, like an untamed animal. I slowly trace the zigzag marking on my face and squeeze my eyes shut to prevent the welling tears from spilling over.

If only I could rip the tattoo from my skin, I could stand a chance at freedom in Dovenak.

Crossing back into the bedroom, I approach the windows and tug the tassel to part the heavy velvet drapes. Daylight bathes the room in a pale hue, the sun still tucked away in the colorless sky.

My eyes focus on the landscape beyond the window. I'm three floors up. Too high to think about escaping this way. Even worse, there's a stone wall outlining the entire property, containing the expansive lawn and overflowing gardens within. The wall is massive, and I can't help but wonder if its job is to keep things in or keep others out.

Red roses climb the wall, snaking around the strategically placed iron gates. With the gloomy, overcast sky, and drab colored stone everywhere, the roses are what give the property life.

Someone moves below my window, in the gardens, fussing with the flowers. I squint, making out Rainer. He's a smudge of black, like a shadow tainting the garden. He holds a tool in his hands as he carefully snips at the buds.

Interesting.

I didn't take him for a gardener. I thought perhaps a warrior or advisor.

When his eyes flit up to my window, I step back out of sight before he can spot me staring. Instead, I glance into the distance.

The castle is perched on a hill, with dense forest surrounding the wall in every direction I can see—a deadly forest, based on everyone's reaction to it. The thick blanket of green slopes down toward a pale grey sea in the distance. Nestled by the water's edge, a congregation of sprawling wooden rooftops merge together in bland streaks of brown. I wonder if the water glitters when the sun shines, or if it always appears so glum.

From up here, the buildings look like toys. They're just large enough to be seen, but small enough to appear fake, unreachable.

If I can escape, perhaps I can run to the village. It doesn't appear to be *that* far away on foot.

Peering down at Rainer again, at the way he takes his time with each stem, as if he's an artist creating a masterpiece, an idea forms.

I unlatch the window, slowly pushing it open just enough that I can reach out. Then, I scan the room.

"Shoot," I say, when I realize I threw most of the stuff out the door already.

I bolt to the bathroom, grabbing as much of the beauty products as I can in my arms, and make my way back to the window.

If Rainer wants to keep me locked up here, I'll make his life difficult. Ruining the flowers brings a pang to my chest—Char would be so disappointed. But this is a matter of survival, and the roses are simply a casualty of war.

I uncork the caps on the products and grab a bottle in each hand. I lean out the window, tilting the bottles and dumping the bright-colored, scented goop all over the bushes.

It lands in thick streams, painting the roses and landing on Rainer in the process.

His head jerks to the window, and even from this distance, I can see the fury on his face.

A thrill ignites my blood. Once the bottles are empty, I chuck them at his head. He jumps backward, barely missing the glass bottle as it shatters on the grass.

"Human!" Rainer roars, his voice practically rattling the windows. "What on earth is wrong with you?!"

Mustering up the last dredges of confidence, I chuck the bottles at him one by one. I find no humor as he dodges my sloppy throws, but I refuse to let him think I'm weak. That I won't fight back.

With the lord, I rebelled in quiet ways: eavesdropping, sneaking around with Felix, indulging in Char's stories, stealing books from the library. Look where that got me.

Perhaps it's time I rebel loudly.

My cheeks heat with fear and fury as I yell, "Let me out of here you monster!"

"Just for that, I'm never letting you go!" he roars back.

"Then I'll ruin your pretty little flowers."

He laughs darkly. "Not if I seal your windows shut!"

I throw a small tin at him, and it hits him square in the forehead. My hands fly up to my mouth as I gasp.

"I'm—" I stop myself before I apologize.

No.

He deserved that entirely.

Rainer's body goes rigid, and he cocks his head at me, leveling me with an intense stare. I swear his lips quirk with humor, but it's too far away to be certain. Either way, butterflies take flight in my ribs. I'm oddly proud of my defiance.

Whatever moment passes between us is gone, and Rainer turns and strides out of sight.

Once the pride fades, my gut knots with guilt. I expected Rainer to come up and unleash his rage on me. I sat trembling in the corner for a few hours before I realized he wasn't coming.

He spared me a punishment.

One I certainly deserved for acting like a heathen. If only I had fought back like this sooner, with the lord. Perhaps I could've spared myself and Char. Except I'm certain the lord would've murdered me for such actions. Considering he broke my leg without a second thought when I tried to escape, among the various other punishments he doled over the years, it's a realistic assumption.

But for some reason, the faerie spared me...at least for now.

My door creaks open and someone clears their throat.

Peeling my eyes from the floor, I blink away my tears and give the newcomer a cautious once-over.

Das Celyn stands in the doorway in a stained eggshell apron, their shaggy, banged bob framing their face. They keep their distance, which eases my discomfort slightly.

They toss a matching apron down beside me, then rub their temples with a sigh.

"You've redecorated." They jerk a thumb toward the hallway, where the stuff I threw is scattered.

"Perhaps if you let me out, I'll put it all back," I mutter.

They grunt, ignoring me in favor of striding to the window.

"You've been here a day, and already, you've managed to piss off the prince."

"I don't see how that's possible, considering I haven't even left the room!"

"Well, a few bottles of perfume thrown at one's head surely ought to do it. Not sure what you were trying to accomplish, but—"

"Rainer?" I cringe as the question leaves my mouth.

I'll be damned. He *is* the prince.

"Oh gods have pity. The prince was right. You truly are a dense thing."

My cheeks flush and my face falls. "He called me dense?"

"He summoned me to heal the welt on his forehead." They stifle a laugh. "*Everyone* is calling you dense for assaulting the crown prince of Umbra."

"I didn't have proper schooling," I whisper, as if it makes a difference.

Char taught me plenty enough, but nothing could've prepared me for entering a new realm.

Standing up, I spin toward the window, resting my forehead against the glass with a groan.

"For fae-sake, get your oily face off the glass!"

A hand wraps around my shoulder, prying me from the window.

I jerk away from their touch, mumbling my apologies.

Das Celyn shakes their head, their bob shimmying with the movement. Pulling a cloth from their apron pocket, they vigorously wipe away the smudge I left on the glass.

"I'm sorry. Really. I didn't—" My brows pinch in confusion. "I hadn't realized you cleaned by hand."

"Stop apologizing." They scowl. "Of course we do." Then their face softens, as they tuck their hair behind a pointed ear. "What—did you think we used magic to clean?"

I nod.

They bark a short laugh. "Magic isn't limitless, especially not for Low Fae." They tuck the cloth back into their apron with an eye roll. "Full of assumptions, you are."

I want to ask what Low Fae are, how magic works, but the returning scowl tells me I'm pressing my luck. If I stand a chance at earning their favor to escape from here, I need to win them over instead of alienating them.

"Thanks for answering my questions," I say.

"What is wrong with you? Haven't you learned anything?" They swat at me, and it's not violent, but it's also not playful. "Don't *ever* thank the fae. You should stop apologizing while you're at it, too, unless you want to get eaten alive." I blanch at the imagery and Das Celyn chuckles. "Not literally, ya dolt."

"What do you mean don't thank them?"

Lord Edvin whipped manners into me as a young girl, going the extra mile to withhold my food when I was too slow to offer pleasantries. The prospect of being impolite discomforts me. I can't help it. Even in my borderline catatonic and grief-stricken state, my manners are firmly in place. A natural reflex.

Das Celyn's voice lowers an octave. They gesture toward the closed door.

"Thanking the fae implies a debt is owed. It's a powerful magic that binds you to whoever you give thanks to until the debt is cleared. Think of it like a bargain of sorts. You thanked the prince, so you admitted you owed him a debt."

"I did no such thing!"

Except, oh gods, I totally did.

My heart sinks into my stomach. What a conniving cad! The magic I felt—it was some sort of binding oath I invoked without meaning to.

I step closer to Das Celyn, pleading with wide eyes. "I need your help to break it."

They purse their lips. "Can't."

"Please. I'll do—"

"I *cannot*." They shrug. "However, *you* can repay your debt and earn your freedom." They point to the apron they tossed at me when they entered. "Put your room back together then put this on and meet me in the kitchen. Prince Rainer says you have pent up energy that can be put to good use, and we could use the extra pair of hands."

"But I can't leave." I gesture toward the door.

They smirk, but it doesn't reach their eyes. "Magic is a fickle thing. You can exit and enter the rooms Rainer allows you to, at the times he allows. Meet me downstairs in an hour."

My pulse doubles as I realize what this means. If the barrier is gone, if I can exit the room, I can escape.

"The barrier—?"

They laugh darkly. "Won't be fully broken until you pay your debts. You won't be able to run, if that's what you're thinking."

The hope I felt comes crashing down. "But—"

"You need to sharpen up if you're to survive here," Das Celyn says. "Come downstairs. Earn your keep. Then earn your freedom. You'll be better for it. Stronger."

How incredibly unfair that I've fought to survive the lord, only to be forced to fight for freedom once again stolen from me.

How can my freedom belong to everyone but me?

Tears fill my eyes. They finger the velvet drapes, eyeing me with obvious discomfort.

"Are you crying? I don't do tears." They glance toward the door then back at me.

I sniffle, and they reach into their pocket and toss something onto my bed. It's an identical jar of the magical healing salve Char used to sneak me, and it only causes the tears to fall faster.

"This is for your other wounds. I'd rather not touch your backside anyway."

Das Celyn scurries past me, mumbling something about humans under their breath. The door clicks shut behind them, confirming I'm alone, and sure enough, the tears I was trying to hold back overflow, cascading down my cheeks.

After a few minutes pass, and I'm sure Das Celyn is gone, I bolt to the door and throw it open. I hold my breath as I reach forward, and when my hand passes the threshold, I squeal with excitement.

Without looking back, I run as fast as I can down the hallway toward the staircase, only to hit an invisible threshold at full speed.

"Ow!" I yell as I'm knocked flat on my ass.

No.

No!

I bang on the barrier with my fists until someone behind me clears their throat.

Spinning around, I blink through the tears to see the lovely Fern, adorned in gold bangles and gem earrings. With a slinky red number on, her willowy frame looks exquisite. And risqué—in a stunning way that works well for her.

A new sense of hope bubbles up inside of me.

"Help me," I whisper to her. "Get me out of here."

She watches me warily as she steps closer, and a cloud of vanilla perfume chokes me.

"I can't."

I pause, cocking my head at those words. "Okay," I say carefully. "I understand—"

"No. You don't understand anything." She squints at me, then alarm passes over her face.

She grabs my hand, yanking me back into my room. Then she uses a heeled sandal to kick the door shut, almost losing her balance in the process.

"You're bleeding." She kicks off her heels and darts to my bathroom, coming back with a cloth. "You need to clean this up." She presses the cloth to my nose, and I wince. "It doesn't look broken, but damn. You ran right into the barrier."

"How do I get past it?" I ask. "It was at the doorway first, and now it's further down the hallway."

Fern smiles sadly. "You don't. It's magic. It reads your intention. If you intend to leave, it will hold you here until Rainer considers you even."

"You know about the oath?"

She chuckles, her eyes crinkling adorably at the corners. It's such a change in demeanor from last night. She appears so grounded, so normal. Her eyes are clear, her words crisp.

"Everyone at court knows about it," she says, swiping my upper lip and cheek gently.

"So, what, I trick the magic into thinking I'm *not* planning to leave and then sneak out?"

"You can't trick it." She sighs, reaching into her pocket and pulling out a small white pill. She plops it into her mouth with a resigned look then returns to dabbing my nose. "Trust me. I've tried."

"Wait." I grab her wrist, pulling it away from my face. "You have your own magic oath keeping you here, too?"

"Something like that." She squirms uncomfortably, then she purses her lips.

The ache in my nose reminds me of the healing cream Das Celyn gave me. I pardon myself from Fern for a moment, using the bathroom to apply the cream on my backside and my face. Quickly, the ache in both places subsides.

When I return to the bedroom, Fern frowns at me.

"Do you have any wine in here?" she slurs, pulling open the drawers on my nightstand with shaky hands.

My stomach knots as I take her in, wondering what happened in the few minutes I was gone. "I don't think so." Upon a closer look, I see her eyes are bloodshot, pupils dilated. Likely from whatever drug she took. It must've kicked in while I was cleaning up. I'm not one to judge, but something about the shift in energy feels wrong. "I don't think you need any wine right now, either, Fern," I whisper carefully.

"You don't know shite about what I need," she snaps, and I recoil. "Look, just do whatever Rainer asks of you and be on your way. You shouldn't be here."

My body grows hot and clammy at her unexpected tone, giving me whiplash. It's like talking to an entirely different person now than it was five minutes ago.

"I'm sorry for overstepping or making you uncomfortable, but—"

"And stay the hell away from the prince," she says.

A nervous laugh bubbles out of me. "I've no intention of getting near him."

"I mean it. If I lose my spot in the Umbra Court because of you…" she sniffles, tears forming in her eyes.

Part of me yearns to reach out and comfort her, but I wrap my arms around myself instead.

"If you need help or something, we can help each other," I say. "We can figure out a way to—"

She wipes away the rogue tears that trek down her cheek and chuckles. It's a snotty, bubbly laugh. Bordering on hysterical.

"I don't need your *help*. I need you gone."

As she moves toward the door, she stoops to snag her shoes, wobbling in the process. Even though I don't know her, and she's being rude, my heart aches for her. It's clear she's troubled.

"Are you okay?" I whisper.

Her eyes narrow at me. "I'll be better than okay once you leave."

My concern mingles with irritation. "I swear, I want nothing to do with your… evil faerie boyfriend. Truly."

She snorts in disbelief. "You're an idiot if you think that's why—just stay away."

"Easy enough considering I'm stuck here." I give an exasperated sigh and wave my arms around the room. It's pointless arguing with Fern in this state. "I'm not your enemy."

"You're threatening what I've earned here. You *are* my enemy, even if you don't want to be."

Her eyes bounce around the room wildly. I know Das Celyn is waiting for me in the kitchens, and I'm supposed to be cleaning up the mess I made in the hallway, but right now my concern is solely for Fern.

I'm afraid to let her leave in this state.

Is she safe?

What if something happens to her?

"You said something about having a spot in the Umbra Court?" I ask, imploring her to stay and continue the conversation. She eyes me cautiously before nodding. "How many courts are there?" When she doesn't respond, I continue, hoping to ease her mind that I don't plan to stay here. "I'd love to visit the others—find a place to settle down."

"Oh," she says. She sniffles again, then smiles at me before plopping on the bed. "There are six courts in Avylon—used to be seven, but not anymore. Only Umbra, Terra, Ignis, Aqua, Aer, and Lux remain."

"What happened to the seventh?"

"I dunno." She shrugs. "Umbra and Terra are the only two on this side of the Illustris Sea." She waves a hand toward the window, and I wonder if that's the body of water in the distance. "Ignis and Lux are on the other side of the sea. Aer Court is atop the peak of Mount Altum. And Aqua Court is beneath the Illustris Sea."

Under the sea?

I can't imagine what that entails.

My mind spins, trying to comprehend the various courts and creatures living in each court. It's beyond anything I've heard before. The fae were always lumped into one large group for me. It's news to me that there are not only various subspecies of fae, but multiple courts and royals as well.

The Umbra Prince might not be as powerful as I first assumed, if Avylon has six royal courts, but he still must be important to hold such a title.

"And the Umbra Prince... what exactly does he rule over?"

"The Prince of Fear oversees all of the Umbra Court and its surrounding villages." Fern takes a big inhale and lies back on the bed with her eyes closed. "Everything you see around here is part of his court—the forest, the village by the water."

She mutters something else but I have no idea what she says.

"And what's your role in the Umbra Court?" I ask softly, not wanting to rile her up again.

I want to know more about what she's doing here, why she's afraid of leaving. Fern doesn't have the Tradeling mark, so I'd imagine she could return to Dovenak. Surely, if she's not a Tradeling, she has family who misses her.

But the only response I get is a snore.

She's curled up on her side, with an arm under her head and her mouth half-open.

Careful not to wake her, since it's clear she needs to sleep off whatever substance she's on, I fold the silky sheets over her. When I'm certain she's not waking, I tiptoe out of the room.

"I'm going to the kitchen," I whisper in the hallway, as if the magical barrier will hear me and allow me to pass.

Perhaps it's because I mean it this time, but it works. Nothing stops me as I trek two flights down in search of the kitchen. It seems safe enough here. For now.

I certainly need to leave this castle, but I suppose I need to pay off my damn faerie debt in order to do so. And in the meantime, I'll figure out how we can pay off Fern's and get her out of here, too. I'll be damned if I leave behind anyone else in a life of captivity.

Char gave her life so I could find freedom, the least I can do is pay that forward and help someone else. Hopefully it won't result in my life ending to do so.

I can only pray it's not too big of a hassle to pay off my debts.

TEN

DID THE FAERIE PRINCE JUST FLIRT WITH ME?

ALESSIA

I spend the entire day with Das Celyn, helping them cook, clean, and care for the castle. I wanted to hate it. Wanted to hate them. But there was peace in the routine. And luckily, the prince still hasn't sought me out for punishment.

If *this* is his form of punishment, I will take it over the lord's nicest days, a thousand times over.

When I return to my room, I notice all the stuff is picked up from the hallway. Everything is placed back in its spot, and Fern is long gone.

There's a piece of paper on my bed with nothing but a bright red kiss on it—as if someone pressed the paper to their mouth. Fern's lipstick. Something tells me she cleaned up as a way of saying thanks.

Gods know we can't actually say the word around here.

The next morning, after a fitful bout of sleep, Das Celyn wordlessly brings me a tray of fruits and oats. I dress and follow them around the castle again, mopping, sweeping, washing, and keeping the space impeccably clean.

It's almost soothing, going through the motions embedded into my being.

Anytime I test out the magical barrier, it stops me. Like Fern said, it acts like it truly knows my intentions. When I'm upholding my tasks, it allows me to move freely throughout the property. But when I intend to divert or escape, it traps me.

As the days continue to pass, I do as I'm told like the good little Dolly I've been taught to be, minus the leery looks, whippings, and grabby fingers. I notice that with the healing cream, proper nutrition, and rest, I'm feeling better than I have in a very long time.

It almost feels safe, but perhaps that's because the prince hasn't been around.

Sadly, I haven't seen Ken or Fern either. When I walk the hallways with Das Celyn, assisting them with tasks, I find myself scanning for the shifter and human, only to come up short.

The few other faeries I cross paths with either ignore me, or they're obnoxiously rude toward me. They make Das Celyn and Fern seem like saints. The only solace I have is that their cruelty is doled out in narrowed glances, sharp tongues, and silent treatments. At least I'm spared the physical violence I've grown accustomed to.

"They blame you for the prince's foul mood," Das Celyn tells me as we knead dough for fresh baked bread.

I punch the dough, taking out some of my annoyance on the rising yeast. Das Celyn snickers beside me. They throw a hand-towel over my shoulder so I can wipe my hands when I'm finished. There's flour everywhere, but there's also no pressure to clean it up as I go. We're able to focus solely on baking right now—one thing at a time—which brings great relief.

"Maybe they should blame the arse responsible instead," I mutter.

It's been a week since I pelted him with that tin in the garden. Clearly he's harboring a grudge.

"Aren't you growing sassy?" Das Celyn's lips twitch, and my chest flutters with pride at cracking the stoic faerie's shell.

A few days later, Das Celyn surprisingly tells me I have the day off. I've never been given a day off before, and I almost expect it to be a trick. The only reason I believe them is because they're dressed in white slacks and a maroon top—no eggshell apron in sight.

Unsure of what to do with myself, I dress in a pale pink sundress and try to exit the room, only to hit the invisible barrier.

With a sigh, I decide not to press my luck. I'm biding my time. I'm safe. And I'll be out of here soon enough. And honestly? It hasn't been all bad. I'm growing fond of my time around Das Celyn.

Standing by the window in my room, I watch birds and squirrels flit around the garden. A moment later, Ken enters the grassy area in the middle of the yard down below.

He's in brown trousers with a leather vest and scabbard attached to his back. I wonder if he's been out in the woods, protecting the castle.

But if the woods are as terrifying as everyone says, then how come he can navigate it unharmed?

A flashback to the hallucinations I experienced my first day in Avylon causes me to shudder. I wonder if the woods affects humans more deeply—some sort of protections should they enter the Gleam uninvited.

Before I can ponder that question any further, the prince steps
into sight down below.

My stomach flips over. I press my hand against the window,
leaning closer to the glass for a better look.

His outfit matches Ken's in style, but his layers are
black—leather vest and boots included. Once again, he's an otherwise bleak contrast to the vibrant green yards and colorful flower
beds.

Rainer unsheathes a sword from his scabbard, and my eyes
widen when I see that even his blade is matte-black. But it would
be a lie to say it wasn't utterly intriguing.

Ken follows suit, drawing a gleaming silver blade. They exchange words, and Ken's deep laugh floats up to the third story
where I watch.

I try to push open the window to eavesdrop, but sure enough,
it's sealed shut. A flurry of frustration blows through me and I scoff.

The two cease their conversation anyways and begin circling
one another. Their faces grow serious as they angle their weapons.
Then, without warning, they begin clashing their swords in a flurry
of attacks and blocks.

Rainer moves like a shadow, a dark blur of lethal grace. Though
Ken is broader and taller, he's almost equally as quick on his feet.
He reminds me of an animal, a beast, even in his humanoid form.

Engrossed in their skillful battle, I stay glued to the window. I'm
not sure how much time passes, but both males are drenched in
sweat by the time they shake hands and sheath their swords. They
toss their scabbards and vests to the ground, likely for a break.

I'm in awe, my mouth agape.

They chat, their voices still too low to make out. As Ken tilts his head back to laugh, he glances up at my window, and it's too late to duck. He gives me an animated wave before nudging Rainer with his elbow.

Ever so slowly, Rainer's head tilts to the side. Whatever joy was on his face a moment ago melts away, replaced by a cruel scowl. He lifts his shirt, using the hem to wipe the sweat off his brow. A preview of his chiseled abs and tattooed chest comes into sight and my breath catches in my throat.

Heat overcomes my cheeks, but I can't look away. The blaze spreads, encompassing my entire body. I'm glued to the spot as I stare. When he's finished wiping his face, he cocks his head at me.

Breaking free from whatever weird spell I was under, I jump up and yank the curtains shut, bathing the room in darkness.

"Great," I mutter to myself.

The last thing I need is the rude faerie prince to think I was ogling him.

I pace back and forth in my room, the hardwoods creaking beneath my feet every few steps.

Raised—if that's what one could even call it—by Lyson's lord and lady, I learned how to be patient. When Lord Edvin would strike me during my punishments, or *lessons* as he so fondly referred to them, I couldn't fight back. When I was younger, I tried. It never ended well for me. Crying, fighting, squirming, or any sort of protesting made it worse. My lashings would multiply, the strikes would grow harder and faster. My meals would get smaller.

Instead, I learned to bide my time, focus my mind, and patiently wait for the moment to pass without making it worse for myself. I bit back my words and learned to control my temper, because Char taught me neither would do me good.

Then, the remainder of my time was spent patiently waiting to finish chores. Patiently waiting for the nights Lord Edvin and Lady Nilda left the estate. Patiently waiting for Felix to sneak in and distract me.

Patience. Patience. Patience.

I've been patient for my entire life, and look where it has gotten me: a fresh start in a familiar situation.

Another day. Another owner. Another dolly—someone's plaything.

And though I tell myself I must be patient a little longer, bide my time and come up with a viable plan, I'm bursting out of my skin.

Perhaps my self-restraint is finally running out. My fingers tap incessantly against my leg, and I do the only thing I've been able to do the past couple weeks: distract myself and try not to dwell on the hollow ache left behind from Char's death.

In the early afternoon, a short series of raps on my door startles me.

"Fern?" I ask as the door slowly creaks open. "Is that you?"

When Rainer steps inside my room, a sharp look in his eyes, I perk up.

"Enjoying your stay, human?"

My pulse pounds in my head as the prince crosses the room, slinking into the chaise by the fire mantle, with an unbothered arrogance. Hints of clove and rose drift into the room with him. He leans back, resting an ankle on his opposite knee, branding me with his gaze.

The first few buttons of his shirt are undone and his slightly wrinkled slacks could use ironing. His onyx hair is tussled. I'd expect the owner of this castle to be primped and proper, not as disheveled as this.

But his laid-back demeanor and dark aura send a thrill through me, and I can't look away.

"Enjoying the views, too, I noticed," he says. He cocks a brow and I flush, thinking of him sweaty after sword fighting with Ken this morning. "You're trying to make friends with Fern? Why?"

"What do you mean *why*?"

"From what I heard, she was rather nasty toward you."

So were you and Das Celyn, I want to say. But none of that compares to the lord and lady's treatment. I can handle attitude and privilege with ease after years of reckless abuse and sadistic punishment.

"She told you about that?" I ask, surprised, standing awkwardly before him.

He chuckles. "No." He licks his lips, contemplating, before his eyes lock onto mine. "The pixies did."

"Pixies?"

"Tiny, nosy, winged creatures with an incredible hearing ability and proclivity for gossip."

I glance around, searching for such creatures and coming up short. To my shock, Rainer chuckles. The sound sends a burst of warmth through me.

"That's an invasion of privacy," I say, squinting at him.

"Then you'll be pleased to know there are none in here. They've been banned from your room."

"They—what? Why?"

Rainer turns away, no longer meeting my gaze. He clears his throat, ignoring my question, then turns back to me. "You're under the impression Fern will be leaving with you?"

My cheeks flush. Stupid blabber-mouth pixies. I square my shoulders and step over to the chaise, standing directly in front of Rainer with my back to the unused fireplace and my arms crossed.

"Yes," I say. "I'm not leaving her behind."

He chuckles again, this time it's much crueler than before. "And what makes you think she *wants* to leave?"

I think of her popping that pill, slurring her words. Her overindulgence with alcohol. "You're keeping her here. All drugged up and—"

He leans forward, resting his arms on his thighs and piercing me with his crystalline eyes. The eye contact is almost too much.

"You assume to know exactly what the situation entails?" he asks. "After being here only a couple of weeks?"

"She's hurting without you making it worse for her."

"You gathered that from a few encounters with her?" He taps his fingers casually on his thigh, glancing around the room.

"It only takes a second to see that someone is in pain. All you have to do is look. See them."

His fingers pause their rhythm, and his eyes snap to mine. A line mars his forehead as his brows scrunch together. Languidly, he peruses my face, as if he's searching for something. I squirm, my core turning molten with his attention on me.

After a few seconds of intense eye contact, Rainer licks his lips and nods slowly.

"See them," he repeats. A flash of sorrow crosses his face. "You're being awfully compliant. Why?"

"What do you mean?"

He blinks, giving me a hard stare. "Based on the attitude I saw when you first arrived, I know you have quite a fight in you."

"What's the point?"

"The point?" He laughs incredulously. "Of fighting for yourself?"

"I won't win any battles here. You have magic. A whole court. I have nothing. I won't win against you."

I'd rather uphold the bargain and be on my way. It's easier. Safer.

"What makes you think I'm your enemy?" He cocks a brow.

I scoff, my features scrunching. "Uh, the fact that you trapped me here."

"Did I trap you? Or did I give you exactly what you sought?"

I pause, his words catching me off guard.

"What did you seek when you crossed the Gleam?" he asks, his voice softening.

"Safety," I mutter. "Freedom."

He points to the bed, then to the empty tray of food on the table beside it. Then gestures toward my outfit.

"You are clean. Fed. Healed. *Safe.*" He stands, striding to me. I'm forced to look up to hold his gaze. "So, I will ask you again, human, what makes you think *I'm* your enemy?"

The heat radiates off his body, and his delicious scent makes my head swim. Quickly, I back away, putting space between us.

His features tighten. "And to answer your question from earlier: the point is to take back your power. No one will do it for you."

"Fighting a battle I know I'll lose sounds exhausting." There's a squeezing sensation in my ribs, and I can't breathe. I mask it by focusing on my inhales and fiddling with the hem of my tunic.

"So you'd rather submit and let others take advantage of you? Dictate your life?"

"It's not like that," I whisper.

"Isn't it though?"

I shake my head, whispering, "No."

"Fighting is hard, but yielding is harder. One is about dying to survive, and the other? Surviving only to slowly die. Choose your hard."

His words shred a layer inside of me, revealing a new truth I'd never considered. My eyes slowly meet his. My stomach flutters.

"You never answered my question when you arrived." He strides toward me again, and with each of his steps, my heart rate increases. "Who made you bleed?"

"They were old wounds that had scabbed over. And the—the," I stutter, unsettled with the faerie prince's attention on me. "The scab must've come off during the ride here."

He places a single, strong finger under my chin, gently tipping my head up and forcing me to look at him. His jaw tightens. He leans in, so close that his warm breath fans across my face, causing every nerve in my body to perk up.

"I didn't ask how it happened. I asked *who* did it to you."

The deadly tone and attentiveness evokes a newfound dread in me.

Though I've always been submissive and compliant with the lord—acting up put me in a worse situation—I never had an issue with my confidence. But in front of the faerie prince? Well, I can't seem to shake the way he watches me. It makes me self-conscious.

"The Lord of Lyson," I whisper. "I've served him and his lady at their estate in a small village near the Gleam since I was five." Rainer's lips tighten. "The lord likes hurting others." I tuck my chin, knotting my tunic in my hands. "The only friend I had stabbed him to protect me and got herself killed because of it."

He stays still, watching me. Waiting for me to continue, I think.

"I ran because if they caught me, I'd be executed. The lord's property is near the Gleam, so I crossed it in hopes to find safety. Like I said earlier, freedom."

Rainer runs a hand through his dark waves. His expression is grim, as if he's conflicted.

I try to ignore how ethereally handsome he is, but it's impossible. Heat floods my cheeks and I nibble nervously on my lip. Despite my ability to remain calm under pressure, I'm terrible at hiding my emotions. The last thing I need is for him to think I'm attracted to him, so I stand and face the window, putting my back to him.

"And what of your parents?" he asks.

"They died." I shrug, wrapping my arms around my midsection. I don't remember them, nor do I remember the fire that consumed our house. And it's for the best. It would only serve as yet another heavy trauma to carry, and my bones are already tired enough.

Rainer's ice-blue stare stays locked on me. It's invasive, as if he can see right through me, my flesh, and the many layers beneath.

"Inconvenient." His scowl deepens as he drums his fingers on his chin.

"What's inconvenient?" I stand a little taller, glaring at him. "The fact that my parents died? That my earliest memories are of the lord's disciplinary hand and his wife's taunting?"

He frowns. "That's not—"

"You keeping me here like an—another one of your little human pets is inconvenient," I snap, starting on a tirade. "Your ridiculous magicked barrier is inconvenient. You being attractive is inconvenient."

The last part slips out, but I'm too angry to care.

His lips twitch, and if I'm not mistaken, he almost appears humored.

"Ah. There's that fight."

I squeeze my trembling hands into fists. "This isn't funny."

"Nobody is laughing."

"You seem amused."

"On the contrary. I am quite displeased by many… revelations." He runs a hand through his messy hair.

"So you'll let me out of this prison?" I spit, despite my earlier acknowledgement that this is far from a jail cell.

He waves an arm toward the grand room. "You think this is where I keep my prisoners?" He chuckles, and it's barely audible but it makes my stomach weak. "You think I send Das Celyn to feed my prisoners? That I line their beds with silken sheets and offer an array of bath salts and oils?" He mindlessly rubs the spot on his head where the tin hit him, and I bite my cheek, ashamed I threw it at him. "You think I give my *prisoners* a familiar job to occupy their time and quell their mind?"

My brows shoot up at that tidbit.

He reaches forward, pushing a lock of hair behind my ear. His fingers linger by my jaw, and I hate that I enjoy his touch. "Trust me, if you were my prisoner, the only thing you'd wish for is death."

With that, I jerk away from him.

"Do not overlook my kindness, human. You'd be wise to appreciate the hospitality you've received."

"I *am* appreciative. So appreciative that it got me trapped here!" I yell. "Please just let me go." At this point, I'm begging, but I don't care.

"No."

"Then it doesn't matter what spoils you provide me. This might not be a prison, but I am your prisoner."

"Would you prefer we return you to your realm?"

Return me to Dovenak? Absolutely not. I would have to cut through the forest behind the lord's estate and trek through the village to get to any of the other cities, and the risk of being caught certainly isn't worth it.

I sigh, squeezing my eyes shut. "No," I admit.

As arrogant and rude as the prince is, he doesn't seem interested in harming me. At least not yet. He might not be as bad as the lord, but alas, I didn't come here to be enslaved by another.

When I reopen them, his head is cocked and he watches me with something akin to amusement dancing in his eyes.

He's so hot and cold. One second he's terrifying, the next, he's stirring something dormant in me. It's an inexplicable pull.

"What do you want with me?" I ask.

He studies me, a strange, distant look taking over his face.

"I'm not sure yet," he whispers.

A few moments stretch between us as his eyes flicker around my face—searching. For what? I don't know.

I wonder if he finds it, because a moment later he shakes his head and quickly strides toward the door. He hesitates at the doorway, glancing at me over his shoulder. Then he exits, shutting the door behind him.

Though he's dangerous, untrustworthy, and makes my blood boil, some small part of me grows a little lonelier with his departure. I can't help but wonder what it means.

What *he* means.

My heart beats rapidly, as if I've run for miles. My head grows light, woozy with Rainer's visit. I can't help but want more.

The feeling he gives me—it could easily become an addiction.

Or perhaps I'm simply falling for those dangerous faerie tricks I've heard about.

One day, I leave the room on my own to get food. Luckily, no barrier stops me as I carefully stride out the door.

Just as I make it to the staircase, I'm alerted to a presence behind me.

"If you're thinking about making a run for it, don't bother," Rainer calls out.

I jolt, turning to see him striding toward me. His lips tip up into a smirk. "I haven't declared us even, yet, human. You still owe me. You're still bound to me."

"How does the bind even work?" I ask dejectedly. He opens his mouth to speak, but I cut him off. "And *magic* isn't a good enough answer."

"What, you expect me to explain the laws of nature to you?"

My shoulders slump. "No. I only want to know how—or why—I'm bound to you for trying to be polite, of all things."

"Because I helped you, and now, you owe me. Simple. The magical signature of our souls bind us until the debt is resolved."

It still isn't clear what he's getting out of the deal. Surely he doesn't need my help in the kitchens and around the castle. I barely do anything at all most days.

And he's much too cunning to *not* be getting something out of it.

"Magical signature," I repeat. "I'm not even fae."

He glances at me with his brows pinched. "Of course you aren't. I can smell your humanity from a mile away."

"Then how does the magic bind my soul if I don't have magic?"

"Your soul *is* magic, human." I scoff and he leans forward, lowering his voice. "Every breath that expands your lungs, every surge of blood rushing through your veins, every healed wound—magic. Every night your mind takes you on a subconscious journey through your dreams, every morning your eyes open and you rise—magic. Every story you experience from reading words on a page, every flower that blooms despite the odds—magic."

Figuring that's as good of an explanation as I'm going to get, I let it go with a quiet contemplation. I've always looked at magic as a strange, unfamiliar power. But he's right. Magic is all around me.

It's in me.

I might not be able to wield magic in the same manner the fae do, but it doesn't make my life any less remarkable.

Rainer passes me, heading down the staircase to the main floor, and I follow him. I stare after him with a new sense of awe. He's so tormented yet views the world through such a beautiful lens.

"Where are you going?" He looks over his shoulder at me as he descends the stairs.

My fingers trail the intricate iron banner. "I'm… hungry, if that's ok?"

We get to the bottom and he stops abruptly. I crash into his muscular back. Reaching out to steady myself, I accidentally grip his tapered waist. Rainer exhales sharply, turning to face me. I back up a couple steps to give us space, face heating at the close proximity. His delightfully dark, floral scent encompasses me.

My cheeks flush and I drop my gaze to the floor.

"Are you always like this?" he asks.

"Like what?"

He reaches forward, placing a finger under my chin and forcing me to look him in the eyes. "Skittish?"

I start to lift a shoulder in a half-shrug, but then his words about being strong come back to me. I decide to instill a little backbone and give him the fight he's searching for.

"I wouldn't expect you to understand." I swat his hand away.

"And why not?"

I gesture toward him. "Because you're—fae."

"And?"

I wave a hand around. "Look at this space. Look at you. You're a prince. A leader. You want for nothing." My words come out rushed, and I realize it's the opinion of him I've been biting back.

He pauses, cocking his head at me. "And you assume my life came easy simply because I'm a faerie? That I've had no struggles of my own?"

"You have freedom."

"Debatable."

"I'd do anything to have the privileges you have," I mumble.

As soon as the words leave my mouth, I know it was the wrong thing to say. His sympathetic look immediately dissipates, his icy eyes narrowing.

"Be careful what you wish for. You don't know the cost of my life, and I doubt it's a price you'd be willing to pay."

My mouth goes dry. My first instinct is to reign it in, to apologize to him. I'm not normally confrontational, and didn't intend to create conflict. But apologies aren't received well around here. So, instead, I keep up the fight I started.

"You don't know *what* I'd be willing to do for my freedom."

"And you know nothing about my life."

"I might not. But you know nothing of mine either. Yet you insist on poking me, insulting me. And, yes, I might be timid, but I'd rather be that than be an ill-mannered barbarian like you!"

The words tumble out.

I fight the urge to recoil into myself, but when amusement dances in his eyes, it gives me an inkling of satisfaction. I know it's the type of response he was hoping for.

"Barbarian?"

"Savage," I confirm.

"Keep going."

"Brute. Bastard. Arse."

"Careful, little rose, your thorns are showing." He cocks his head at me, a smirk playing on his lips. "Are you going to apologize for such harsh words?"

He's baiting me.

I shake my head, refusing to give in. "I only came to this wretched realm for a chance to survive, to live. I hoped for freedom. Instead, I got stuck with a brooding prince who uses manipulative, magical tactics to keep me against my will." I pause and take a deep inhale.

Whew, it's nice to speak my mind without fear of punishment or retribution. That alone is a liberation I've never had before.

Rainer's brow quirks up. "Is that all?"

"For now." I cross my arms angrily, narrowing my eyes at him.

"If there's more, do come find me. I rather like it when you show a bit of spine, human." He shoots me a wink before sauntering down the hall. Then he pauses. Slowly, he turns to face me. "I see you."

"What?"

My face must betray my confusion, because he clears his throat and clarifies.

"What you said about Fern the other day. 'All you have to do is look'... I see *you*, human."

Without another word, he strides off.

This time, there's nothing cruel in his tone when he calls me human. I'm left standing at the bottom of the stairs, my palms sweating and stomach all twisted up, wondering what just happened. I swear Rainer went through four different moods in the span of one short conversation—concerned, to angered, to amused... to flirtatious?

There's more to the prince than first appears. Perhaps he doesn't hate me as much as I thought he did. And most curiously, I'm left wondering: did the faerie prince just flirt with me?

Eleven

Like the Little Rose She Is

Rainer

I wake in the middle of the night with a violent jolt, my hair slicked back with sweat. My palms shake as I grasp the sheets beneath me. I growl into the dark night.

The same nightmare.

Again.

I can't escape it.

In it, I'm with my mother, my father, and my brother. We're happy. Until we're not. And it all ends in bloodshed.

Refusing to give the nightmare anymore power, I push it from my thoughts. I won't dwell on the details, nor will I replay it in my mind. I need to let it go, in order to survive.

I hop out of bed, smoothing down the black satin sheets. Striding to my balcony, I push the set of double-doors open, taking a deep breath. The air holds a hint of humidity, rife with the sweet, floral scents I hold dear.

The scents reminding me of the best parts of my mother.

Tilting my head up toward the pitch-black canvas overhead, I close my eyes and let the sounds of crickets and night-critters consume me.

With a few minutes of deep breathing, the nightmare is gone. Unfortunately, so is any opportunity for peaceful sleep.

My mind wanders, finding an image of the scrawny girl with too-big eyes, a freckled nose, and white-blonde hair. The human girl with the lightning-shaped tattoo marking her porcelain skin.

The thought of someone holding her down at just five years old, piercing her skin with their ink and needle, marking her like cattle enrages me. My fists shake at my sides, and I have to fight all over again to calm myself down.

The human girl reminds me of the most fragile bits of myself.

I hate it.

I'm not a fan of humans as is. From their egos, to the way they disregard the earth and each other, to how pathetically weak-minded they are. Already, I've taken in Fern, and now, I have another occupying too much time in my mind.

I should hate the new human.

Alessia.

I tried hard not to say her name aloud, not to give it power. Names carry meaning for the fae, and now that I've tasted her name on my lips, it'll be even harder to let her go.

I hate that someone dared put their hands on her, leaving marks on her soft, pale skin. She's like a rose—delicate and sweet, but with thorns that prick if you get too close.

A few times, when I couldn't sleep, I passed her room while I was roaming the halls. On multiple occasions I heard whimpering. It was a sad, broken noise, and she called for Char. Her best friend, as I now know.

Like me, she seems plagued by the inability to sleep. Visited by nightmares and terrors. I hardly sleep these days because of them.

From the little I know of her, she's survived through so much. Yet she doesn't believe in herself. I was right on the first day, she does have a spark in her eye. But it's like she works to tamper it down, to put it out. It's another thing I recognize. Something I'm familiar with.

Where subduing herself looks as if to come easy, though, it's a constant battle for me.

If she stays, at best, she will only be a distraction. At worst, she could unravel everything I've spent my life gaining control over. There's something about her that is utterly bewitching.

Despite her fragility, she owns a quiet, unassuming type of power. For something so frail and timid, she hasn't broken. Her spirit hasn't been diminished. There are moments, sure, where she can no longer look me in the eye, or she recoils or hesitates, but despite all of that, she appears wholly in control of herself.

Maybe I envy her for that.

Or maybe I hate her extra for that.

There was a moment, when she was watching me and Kenisius train, that I didn't see grief or fear in her eyes.

I saw hunger. Not for me, but for the battle itself. That combined with knowing someone in a position of power hurt her? It makes my chest ache. A feat that catches me wholly off guard.

It could be wise to set her up with Kenisius for training. It could bring forth her inner strength. It could protect her from *me*.

Deciding my mind will only continue spinning in circles if I let it, I head back into my room. Crossing past my bed and armoire, I exit into the hallway, striding quietly and quickly in the direction of Alessia's wing. Some desperate part of me hopes she's awake. For what? I don't know.

Maybe I just don't want to be alone anymore.

It takes a few minutes to get there. My quarters are in the castle's turret, five stories high, and on the opposite side of the castle. The distance is useful for quelling any…temptations.

It means I have plenty of time for logic to kick in, to turn away and return to my rooms. Except, I don't. There's an invisible rope tugging me closer and closer to her. Until finally, I'm standing outside her door.

As I'm debating knocking, her sad whimpers reach my ears.

"*Charlotta*," she cries softly. "*Please. No. Please.*"

Resting my head on the door, I press my hand against the wood, fingers splayed out. I listen to her cry. My ribs squeeze.

Should I wake her?

Should I leave her in peace?

Whatever she suffers from in her sleep, I can only hope it isn't as horrible as my nightmares.

My eyes shut, and I stand there—empathizing with her pain—until her whimpers die down a few minutes later. One of the pixies buzzes down the hall, flitting nearby. When they spot me, they freeze, fluttering in place.

"Hi," they squeak out.

"Get out of here," I hiss. "Stay out of this wing entirely."

They buzz off immediately, flying down the hallway and around the corner. I don't need the nosy creature flapping its lips about the girl's night terrors.

Normally, it's not something I'd spare a thought on, but I have an unrelenting drive to protect her. To ease her suffering.

I head back to my room as quickly as possible, not wanting to engage in conversation with any of the night servants.

Exiting onto my balcony again, I glare up at the night sky.

"Why do I care so damn much?" I yell at the hiding moon, as my eyes search the night sky for answers I won't find.

I shouldn't care.

I don't want to care.

I should hate Alessia.

Despise her—simply for what she is. What her humanity constantly reminds me of.

And I need to let her go—force her to go.

But if that's true, why can't I loosen my grip? Why do I harness that inexplicable urge to protect her, to keep her close? Despite the way she angers me...I find a piece of my soul at ease with her around. I've never... felt a tug quite like that before.

Maybe it's because, for the first time, I don't see someone who pities me, judges me, or fears me. Yes, she is fearful of me, but it's not the same. It's on the same level of fear and apprehension she holds for everything and everyone else. I'm not special in that regard.

No.

In those grey eyes of hers, I see a challenge. Potential for an equal. Someone who might understand me because they're not so different deep down.

My lips tilt up at the thought, then I quickly smother it.

Because that can *never* happen. I will never allow a human—especially not a skittish thing like Alessia—be the one who cracks me open and spills my secrets.

I will never allow her to make me weak like her.

And even if I did allow it, she could never survive it.

My fascination with her is dangerous, but I can't help the natural response my body and attention has to her.

If she weren't human, I'd wonder if perhaps she was my—

No.

That thought is not worth entertaining. She *is* entirely human. I can smell her humanity radiating off her. Even if she were somehow glamoured to look human, perhaps, her blood would still carry the distinct scent of faerie.

It's impossible to hide from someone like me.

And her scent is unmistakably human.

She is not *mine*, and she never will be. The best I can do is protect her, help her grow, and send her on her way before she ruins me.

Yes. I *will* have Kenisius train with her.

I will not pluck her or keep her. But I can prune her. Water her. Watch her grow, like the little rose she is.

Twelve

On Rainer's Terms Only

Alessia

The next day flies by, and though I'm tired, when night comes, I toss and turn for what seems like hours. My mind is a whirlwind of panicky thoughts and regrets. It's easier to ignore them during the day, when I'm up and moving. But when I try to rest, they all float to the surface, desperate to drag me down and drown me.

Someone knocks on the door late into the night, right as I'm on the verge of being consumed by my thoughts.

"Who is it?" I call, my voice hoarse with exhaustion.

A grunt greets me. "Just open the door, girl."

I throw the covers off me and jump out of bed, swinging the door open to see Das Celyn with an annoyed look and a tray in their hands. They thrust it at me, and some liquid splashes my thumb.

"Ow!" I quickly set the tray down on the table by the chaise, wiping the hot tea off my finger. "I didn't ask for food or tea."

"And I didn't ask to serve you at this hour, either."

I sniff it. Chamomile.

"Does this have valerian root in it?"

"Yes." They squint. "I was informed you needed help sleeping."

"By the pixies?" My brow scrunches and I look past them into the hallway, wondering if the little creatures are indeed eavesdropping despite what Rainer said.

I have yet to spot one. I'm skeptical of their existence.

Das Celyn snorts. "No."

"Then who—"

"Doesn't matter." They point to the tray, where a couple of pastries sit. "Saw you eyeing those earlier. Had some extras."

"Tha—" I curse myself for almost using my manners again. It's weird not using pleasantries. It's rude, but I guess it's something I have to get used to.

Instead of thanking Das Celyn, I say, "I can make my own meals, you know."

"I'm sure ya can." They begin fluffing my pillows.

"I can make my own bed, too."

"Good for you."

"You don't have to care for me."

They grunt. "I don't have to do anything I don't want."

"So you admit it, you *want* to take care of me?" I ask with a teasing smirk.

"No." They pause, popping a hip and placing a hand on it. "What I *want* is to do my job, without interruptions."

I grab a pastry, biting into it to keep from talking. It's clear Das Celyn wants little to do with me, even when I try to lighten the mood. It's a bad habit I've built over the years—trying to appease others or make them feel better, even when I'm wrecked on the inside. Or, in the lord's case, even when they don't deserve it.

After I finish my muffin, I can't help but break the awkward silence.

"Does it ever get cold here?" I ask, gesturing toward the impeccably clean chimney. It looks like it's never seen a flame.

"No."

"Does the sun ever come out?"

"Do you ever stop talking?" They grunt, and a growling noise comes from their stomach and I can't help but relax slightly at the normalcy of it.

"Are you hungry?" I ask. "Would you like to sit?"

"No."

Their stomach rumbles again.

I take in how rail-thin they are, and the pieces begin clicking into place. Das Celyn might be bad-tempered, but if they're not eating, it's no wonder why they're in a less than pleasant mood.

It reminds me of how Lady Nilda used to withhold my meals when she caught her husband's eyes roaming my body. She thought she could starve me away—as if she could keep me so thin I'd eventually become invisible.

Luckily I had Char looking out for me and sneaking me scraps, so I rarely went hungry for long.

My throat grows thick at the thought, and suddenly I'm not so hungry anymore. A piece of me softens toward Das Celyn. Not in pity, but understanding.

"I insist." I pat the burgundy cushion beside me, beckoning Das Celyn over. "These are incredible. Try some."

They scoff, but reluctantly take the seat beside me and grab a muffin. A smile crosses my lips at the small win.

"I know how incredible they are. I made them."

"*We* made them," I lean in, knocking their arm with my own.

Their eyes flutter shut and they lean back as they eat leisurely. A pang forms in my chest at the sight. How long has it been since they last ate?

"Why doesn't he—Prince Rainer let you eat?" I ask.

Das Celyn jerks their eyes open and glances down at the muffin in their hand before tossing it onto the table and standing. They wipe their hands on their apron, a coldness overtaking their features.

"Who said he doesn't let me eat?"

"I just—you seem so hungry."

"You shouldn't jump to conclusions."

I thought something changed between us during our shared meal, but clearly I hit a sensitive spot. It only makes my heart hurt for them, just as it hurts for Fern.

Why does everyone here—save for Ken—seem so troubled? Faerie prince included.

"I only want to make sure you're okay."

"That I'm okay?" Their anger morphs to disbelief. "Said as if you care."

"I do care," I whisper. Seeing Das Celyn hungry and angry reminds me so much of myself—when I was at the verge of breaking at the lord's hand. Char was the person who continuously checked on me over the years, who broke through the walls I built around my heart at a young age, and taught me how to trust. To love.

I'm not setting out to save anyone, but if I can help Fern and Das Celyn the way Char helped me, I could potentially save a life.

I don't know what Fern, or Das Celyn, or Prince Rainer have gone through, but I see bits of my own suffering in each of them. These strangers are mirrors, each reflecting back a piece of me I've hidden away.

"You don't know me."

"It doesn't matter. If there's something I can do to prevent your suffering, I'll do it."

"Focus on your own self, girl." Their voice is softer, lacking the bite it had before. They pause on the way out, turning to me. "Whatever you think you know about me, or the prince, or anyone else here, you're wrong. And we don't owe you any explanations. We owe you nothing. Remember that."

A tense beat passes.

"Understood," I whisper. It's a harsh reminder I'm wanted here about as much as I want to be here. "Do you know when the prince will let me leave? Or if he will be back to talk to me?"

Celyn narrows their eyes. "He does what he wants. I'm not privy to his thoughts."

Before I can ask anything else or find another way to get them to lower their guard again, they snatch the tray and head for the hallway.

"Drink the tea and sleep," they say without looking back.

Shrugging it off, I let the tea cool and then I chug it to the dregs, figuring I might as well enjoy a deep sleep at the hands of this potent herbal remedy.

Soft light filters in through the trees, bouncing off the golden river. It flows silently, like a satin ribbon kissed by a soft summer breeze.

It's so ethereal, so beautiful that I can't help but smile. Looking up, there is no canopy of trees blocking my view, no clouds suppressing the sun, only bright, open skies in the most beautiful shade of blue.

I walk to the edge of the water and dip a toe in. It feels like silk-sheets. Smooth, luxurious.

Just like the sheets I'm currently wrapped in.

"This is a dream," I say aloud with a laugh.

I'm safe knowing it's just a dream—a lucid one. One that wraps its welcoming arms around me and allows me to shed the heart-crushing emotions that plague my waking life. It's been a while since I've had a lucid dream like this—one where I'm aware I am dreaming, able to manipulate the dreamscape.

I jump into the water feet first.

Water rushes up my nose, as I sink to the bottom, but I can breathe. I propel myself upward, breaking the surface.

I giggle, loving the warmth and love exuding from the dreamscape.

"Hello, human," a familiar voice calls out.

I spin around, the golden water rippling outward around me, as my gaze connects with a pair of hypnotic blue eyes. My giggles grow into a full-blown fit of laughter. Mostly at the fact that I'm dreaming of Rainer.

"I like this," I say with a smile.

He sits at the river's edge, feet dangling in the silky water, in nothing but a pair of black briefs, with a smile of his own. The expression is positively dazzling on his face.

"Dimples," I murmur. "You have the cutest dimples."

I wonder if he has dimples in real life too, or if it's only a dream-conjured image. I haven't seen him wear a true smile yet—only crooked grins, smirks, and sneers. But smiles evade him like my freedom evades me.

I double take the muscles lining his physique, and I spend a moment appreciating the excess of tattoos marking his almost-naked body. My mouth waters.

He's a decadent specimen.

I rather like this dream. It's a nice reprieve from my reality, and I don't want to wake up anytime soon.

Tilting my head up to the sky, I close my eyes and bask in the joy that is sunshine. Until the subtle scent of roses fills my nose, and I'm aware of his presence in my proximity.

I tilt my head up to gaze at dream-Rainer, our mouths inches apart. Everything else falls away and it's only the two of us floating in an abyss.

He leans in, moving so close we share a single breath.

When his eyes roam over my lips, his pupils dilate. "What a treasure you are, little rose."

Instead of closing the distance between us like I'm aching to, I grab his hand, and pull him under the silk-water with me. As much as I crave his physical touch, it's a simple moment of fun and freedom that speaks to me most.

It's intimate in its own way.

When we submerge ourselves beneath the surface. The water takes on a more aquatic form—translucent with specks of glittering gold.

It's magical.

We play like this for what seems like hours, wordlessly laughing with each other, splashing each other with water that turns into confetti midair, manifesting various colorful fish that swim around our legs.

"I needed this," he mutters. "A break from the nightmares."

His words flutter around me. At first I'm confused, but then I realize he's only a manifestation of my mind—my own subconscious. Which means his words are too. And they're right. I did need this break. From the nightmares I face in both the day and the night.

"Alessia!"

I hear my name being called, even from beneath the surface.

"Did you hear that?" I ask Rainer without surfacing.

He smiles at me, shaking his head no before swimming in circles around me.

"My Alessia!"

My heart stops for a moment as I recognize the voice.

I pop my head out of the water.

"Char?" I call, scanning for her familiar face.

"What is it?" Rainer asks, confused, popping up at my side, sparkling gold from the river.

"Shhhh," I reply. "Listen."

Char calls my voice again, and I see her standing further down the river, on the edge, where the dreamscape seems to end and fade into dark.

"Come find me," she says, a look of concern on her withered face.

I try to walk towards her, but all of a sudden my body grows heavy, its as if my feet are glued to the river's floor and I can no longer move.

"Char!"

"Meet me where I rest, Alessia. I have your answers."

"What answers?"

There's a cracking noise—like a burst of thunder—and both Rainer and Char are gone.

The dreamworld dissipates, fading away to nothingness.

"Wakey wakey, eggs and bakey!"

There's a swoosh of curtains opening, and orange light assaults my eyelids.

"Stop, Das Celyn," I mutter. I keep my eyes squeezed shut and throw an arm over my face. "I'm getting up."

The dream from last night comes back to me—vivid as ever. So realistic. And it makes me long for the Rainer I met there, even though it was a simple manifestation of my own subconscious. Clearly the loneliness and unwanted desire are building up—

"Whoa, little human, what's got your heart rate speeding up?"

I crack an eye open, and when I spot Ken standing beside the bed, I shoot upright, clutching the sheets around me. He wears a goofy grin, his brown leathers, and has a sword strapped to his back.

"Where's Das Celyn?" I ask, looking around.

"You're stuck with me today instead." He throws some clothes onto the bed. "Anyone ever tell ya you sleep a lot?"

"Never." I shake my head.

I've never had a chance to sleep this much. It was unexpectedly kind of Rainer to send the chamomile and valerian tea up last night—at least, that's who I'm assuming sent it up considering he's the only one who's asked about how I'm sleeping. Clearly my body needed the rest.

"Well, rise and shine, little human. Get those perky buns up. We have things to do today."

My spirits lift. "I'm getting out of here?"

He cocks his head, pointing at the clothes he's laid out. "You'll find out if you get dressed."

Apprehensively, I drag myself out of bed and head over to the bathroom to change. Ken is rambling, so I keep the door cracked to listen.

"I've missed ya, little human," he says. "Heard you've been getting on with Das Celyn and Fern." There's a hint of surprise in his voice.

"If that's what you can call it," I reply. "I managed to offend both upon meeting them."

"Heard about that."

"From the pixies?"

Ken chortles. "Das Celyn didn't appreciate you nixing their title."

"*Das* is a title?"

"Of high standing—it's a term of respect, a title of honor," he calls over my shoulder as I browse the clothing options.

"Das Celyn implied they weren't High Fae though."

"They're not. Das is a title reserved for Low Fae. It's a renowned title earned through years of unwaveringly loyal support and service to the royal family."

"Are there others with that title?"

"A few…yes."

My brow scrunches as I finish throwing on my clothes and braiding my hair. Exiting the bathroom, I sit on the edge of the bed while Ken pokes around, inspecting things nosily.

"So some actually choose to serve the prince?"

Ken laughs, and it's a hearty noise. "Some are forced to serve as punishment for crimes committed. But for others, like Das Celyn, it's a lucrative position. Not only for them, but for their family."

It's hard for me to comprehend why anyone would want a life of servitude. Perhaps I can't imagine it because Dovenak is utterly opposite. All servants are forced into their roles, purchased from the Trade.

"There's a hierarchy," he says. "We have Royal Fae such as Prince Rainer at the top—also technically High Fae. Below them we have the regular High Fae who don't come from royal lines or hold formal titles. Then we have the Low Fae who've been bestowed with the Das title, followed by the remaining Low Fae."

"That's—" I think of something to say "Are the classes based on how much magic one has?"

He nods. "Low Fae are born with less powerful magic than the High Fae. The Das title offers Low Fae an incentive to rise through the hierarchy through hard work and loyalty. It's not something I expect you to understand. But it would be kind of you to use the title, regardless of your understanding. It's important to fae like Das Celyn."

My cheeks heat. "Of course."

I naturally assumed Rainer was cruel, that he forced his servants into servitude. It never struck me that some of the faeries, like Das Celyn, *choose* to work here.

It makes me wonder what else I was wrong about.

Rainer's words about Fern, about assuming to know the story there, echo in my mind.

I've seen a side of him that is…harsh, yes, but also kind. It's confusing. He appears torn between cruel indifference and unwanted empathy. I can't help but wonder if maybe there's a deeper meaning to my dream last night. Perhaps it's a message to trust the prince.

I break my fast with porridge, courtesy of a tight-lipped Das Celyn, slurping it down in a very unladylike manner. Ken and I sit on the chaise before my room's unused fireplace. The entire time, he watches with humor playing on his lips. He laughs at almost everything I do, but not in a cruel way. It's lighthearted, entertained.

In fact, I find it contagious and much appreciated given the gravity of the last couple weeks.

"You look like a miniature, blonde version of me in that getup, little human." His grin widens, his teeth practically blinding me.

"This is surprisingly comfortable," I say, palming the soft fabric of the tunic. I'm dressed in brown leather pants, a cotton tunic, and boots of my own. My curls are pulled back into a braid to keep them out of my face. I've always been fond of my dresses and skirts, but these pants are much more efficient for moving. It feels... more natural to me.

"Good. Because we're about to get very uncomfortable." I give him a puzzled look and he barks a laugh. "You're working with me and Viv today. Some basic training drills."

"Training? Me?" My heart beats quicker at the prospect of leaving the room and doing something.

"Yup." He leans forward, bopping me on the nose with a beefy finger. "Time to put some meat on those bones, little human. Get that strength up."

"Why do you care about my strength?" I ask skeptically. I find it hard to believe they'd want to train me simply to help me.

"Did you forget how you almost died—*twice*—the day I met you?"

"Of course not!"

"You being so weak is no fun at all." A sheepish expression takes over his face. "Plus, we could use a human to practice with. You move differently than us. Could help us prepare better for attacks from Dovenak."

"So, you want to use me as a mock target."

His face splits into a wide grin. "Can't do it til you toughen up a bit."

Of course it's for their own benefit.

"Does Dovenak attack often?"

His eyes dart to the door then back to me. "Not exactly. But I'm afraid I can't discuss official matters openly, little human. Sorry."

I sigh, plopping the empty porridge bowl down on the table before us. "So you can 'toughen me up,'" I say, with air quotes, "to kick my arse, but you can't tell me *why* exactly you're doing it?"

Ken grips his gut, howling with laughter. "Good gods you don't quit. No one is kicking your arse. Let's just get going—see for yourself."

"Is Rainer going to allow me to leave the room?"

"Well, it was his idea to get you outside."

Before I can overthink it, I bolt down the corridor, taking the stairs two at a time until I reach the ground level. I'm ready to test the boundaries. Behind me, Ken barks a laugh as he keeps up with ease.

"Where the feck are you running off to like that, little human?"

I make it to the foyer, sprinting over the grimly painted floors. Once I reach the massive doors, I grip the cool iron knobs and tug them open. They're heavy, and the groan they make echoes through the foyer.

My lips turn up into a smile. I don't know where I'm going, but as long as I can go, I'll figure it out.

But as soon as I walk forward, I smack face first into an invisible forcefield.

Ken howls, trying and failing to smother his laughter behind his big hand. Shooting a scowl at him, I rub my nose and forehead where they smashed into the magic wall.

"*Not again!*" A tiny, high-pitched voice says.

I turn to catch a little creature no bigger than my fist hovering in the air a few feet in front of me. Its iridescent green wings move so fast that they're a blur of color.

"Pixie?" I ask, dumbfounded.

It giggles, flittering away before I can get a response.

My eyes widen and I stare in the direction it flew, stunned silent. They *do* exist.

"Is my nose bleeding?" I finally ask Ken.

He double-takes, eyes widening. But then he inspects me, and when everything looks okay, he exhales heavily and his shoulders relax.

"You should probably stop charging into the magicked walls like that," he says. "You're giving those big-mouthed pixies plenty of gossip fodder, you know."

I huff under my breath, glancing out the front door at the rose-wrapped iron gates, and to the forest beyond. There, in the distance, a humanoid shadow wafts at the treeline.

A chill walks up my spine, and I suppose it's for the best I can't leave... yet.

I'm not mentally—or physically—equipped to handle whatever happens in those woods.

Slamming the doors with a sigh, I drag my feet after Ken as we head toward the back of the castle.

"You can exit into the back or side yards," he says. "Plenty of fresh air and freedom." He gives me a sidelong glance. "You just can't leave the grounds or go out the front."

"Clearly," I mumble.

I'm still a prisoner, is what he means.

My extended freedoms are fake. Granted on Rainer's terms only.

Thirteen

What Do They Get Out of This?

Alessia

A feminine shriek pierces my ears.

It rings out loud and angry, reminding me of the moment Lady Nilda found her husband bleeding out on her kitchen floor.

I blink, and the image of Char in her last moments fills my vision. Of the lady advancing on me.

My chest tightens, and I lose my breath.

Panicked, I duck down behind a bush of pale pink roses, squeezing my eyes shut. The sharp clang of metal reaches my ears, along with some grunting.

"A little overeager, Viveka," Rainer's voice says from somewhere out of sight. The sound loosens the knot in my chest. "More patience before you strike."

Slowly, I reopen my eyes. Ironically, the prince's voice is like a balm to my fear. Knowing it's him and Viveka, not the lord or lady, offers me a sense of safety.

My breath hitches in my throat. I'm caught off guard by the realization.

That I'm feeling... *safe* here.

Ken squats down in the bushes next to me, and I turn my attention to him, steadying my rapid pulse.

"She's a durable gal, that Viv," he whispers, with a bright smile. "Before you can be rude and ask what kind of fae she is, she's a shifter."

"I wouldn't ask." My cheeks flush. *Yes I would.*

"You're lying, but that's all right."

"Great. You can smell when I'm lying?" I ask, resigned.

"Smell? No." His shoulders shake with silent laughter. "Your breathing and heart rate increased, and unless you're incredibly aroused or frightened right now, I'd say you're lying to me."

"Definitely not aroused," I mutter. And I don't like that he'd be able to tell if I was.

"I didn't think so. *That* I'd be able to smell."

"That's…incredibly uncomfortable to know." I refuse to look him in the eye after that tidbit.

He seems unfazed.

"Ya gonna tell me what we're doing in the bushes, little human?"

"I—" What do I even say? Someone *screamed* and I got so scared that my first reaction was to hide in the rose bush? He already thinks I'm weak, that I need *training* to become even a useful sparring dummy.

So, I improvise. I take a huge inhale of a nearby bright pink rose as if that was my intention all along.

It smells absolutely divine—sweet and soft, with a hint of something citrusy.

"Roses are my favorite," I tell the shifter, and though *that* is not a lie, the next part is. "I simply wanted to smell them. That's all."

His grin grows. "Little, little liar."

"That is unfair!"

"And those"—he points to the flowers—"are Damask roses." He leans closer to me, waggling his brows and whispering conspiratorially. "Aphrodisiacs."

I jerk away from them. The absolute last thing I need is to get turned on by magical faerie roses. Especially after the nugget of information he dropped on me about him sensing my...various states.

"Of course," I mutter.

"One sniff won't hurt, but I wouldn't take another anytime soon if I were you. You might fall in lust with the first thing that walks by." He winks. "I don't need you getting rowdy during training."

My cheeks flame, and I fear my face is as pink as the roses.

I nod. "I'll take your word for it."

"Only the Damask ones, though—the hot pink ones. The others are harmless."

I glance beyond the aphrodisiac roses, to the red, yellow, and purple ones beyond.

My eyes widen in awe. From my window, I thought the gardens were filled with a variety of colorful flowers. Up close, I realize this section—down below my window, near the training yard—are *all* roses.

In almost every color imaginable.

"They're lovely," I whisper breathlessly. "I had no idea roses came in so many colors."

He chuckles, and his shoulders shake. "Hopefully you didn't take too big of an inhale. If you did, try to keep your pants on during training, all right? I know my muscles are big and enticing, but you're not my type, little human."

"You rascal," I hiss as he chuckles. "I am *not* taking my pants off." I straighten my back and cross my arms. "And *you* are not *my* type either!"

"Good to know," a melodic voice says, sending a bolt of lightning through my spine.

My eyes flick up to Rainer, who's standing above us. One brow arches as he peers down at where we crouch behind the bushes.

I shoot to my feet, as Ken straightens out beside me. He laughs heartily.

"This isn't funny," I say to him before turning to Rainer, my body rigid.

Rainer's lips twitch. In his all black leather armor, and matching matte-black sword sheathed at his back, he looks like a deadlier, shadowy version of Ken. Albeit slightly younger and paler. But no less lethal. My pulse increases as I observe the sharp curve of his features… His full lips.

Lips that would feel so—

"Stay away from my roses," Rainer says flatly. "*All* of them."

"But I—"

He spins on his heels before I can get my reply out.

I turn to Ken, frowning. "He's still mad about what I did?"

The flowers are all so beautiful, and the fit I threw was incredibly petty, ruining the flowers to get to the prince. I'm glad they appear unharmed. Shame burns brightly in me.

"Rai is very… particular about his flowers." He sniffs the air, then his coy eyes lock onto mine. "Grumpy, tortured princes are your type, huh?" He gives me a toothy grin. "It seems our little human finds the prince alluring."

"Gross." I frown.

And though it's embarrassing that he can sense certain things about me, Ken himself doesn't discomfit me. I remind myself this is normal for the fae, that it's *me* stepping into their world. So if they don't make it a big deal, I won't either.

Ken howls with laughter and I huff, pushing the big guy's shoulders. He doesn't budge an inch.

"You keep that to yourself, bruin." I stride past him, muttering, "I can't wait to learn how to train so I can kick your arse."

Ken cackles behind me. "That makes two of us, little human."

Viveka's eyes are keen and sharp, and despite her tall height and broad shoulders, her movements are light—like that of a dancer. Rich brown skin contrasts with her cropped, snowy hair, and confidence radiates from her.

I'm immediately in awe.

She doesn't notice me as she unsheathes her sword and nods at Rainer. He mimics the action.

Ken and I grab a seat on the edge of the grassy yard, giving them plenty of space to engage in a nimble dance of clashing steel. Both of their physiques are fit, muscular, but despite this they move with a predatory grace. Quick on their feet, fast to react, and even faster to strike.

The swords strike together in a deadly melody. I watch, mesmerized, flinching every time the blades meet.

Ken leans toward me so I can hear him over the grunts and clangs. "Viv is from Terra Court."

From what I gathered from Fern, it's the closest court to Umbra.

"So, who runs Terra Court?" I ask, unsure of how fae politics work.

"Princess Sennah and her brother run Terra Court."

"There's no queen? Or king?"

"There's a faerie queen, but she doesn't involve herself in the courts. She is very, very old, even by immortal standards. More of a relic than anything. She oversees larger matters between the realms, but the courts are mostly left to the Royal Fae and their families."

Immortal?

Realms?

My head spins with questions. The more I learn about this place, the more incomprehensible it is.

"There are other realms? Besides Avylon and Dovenak?"

"Yup." Ken slaps his thighs, giving me a grin. "Many more, little human." He watches my face morph into shock, then barks a laugh. "You didn't think we were the only ones around, huh?"

"Well…" I've never heard about any other realms. Then again, Tradelings aren't privy to such education and information.

"Any more questions for me while we're at it?" Ken asks.

"*So* many questions," I whisper.

My eyes track Rainer's movements as he engages with Viv. His face is stern, his movements sharp and fierce. I'm captivated by the show.

"Is Rainer… immortal?" I ask.

"Not quite. Fae still age, albeit very slowly. Now that his mind and body have reached peak maturity, his aging process will slow. Many fae only live to be hundreds of years old. The faerie queen is an exception. Her power is enormous." He shrugs. "There's a reason she's queen."

My mouth drops, and I gape at him.

"Rainer is only twenty-six," he says. "Very, very young for fae standards."

He's only a few years older than me? I mean, that's what I would've assumed based on appearances. But with immortality and extended lifespans on the table, it'd be impossible to guess ages here.

"And how old are you?" I ask.

Ken lowers his voice conspiratorially. "Over a hundred years young, little human."

My eyes practically bulge out of my head, and his shoulders shake with laughter. I would've guessed thirties, if we were talking human years.

"And you're fine serving someone only a fraction of your age?"

"Why wouldn't I be? I've served the Umbra Court since I was a cub. We don't place as much importance on age as you humans do."

"You served Rainer's family? Where are they?" Still around, I'd assume, based on their long lives.

Ken shakes his head, his face morphing to worry as he glances in Rainer's direction. "They—they're gone."

I want to press for an answer, but Rainer's eyes swing in my direction briefly. I swallow down the question, wanting to ask the prince himself about his family.

A good chunk of time passes and I'm certain the battle between Rainer and Viv will go on forever, with neither one conceding. Their energy seems endless.

"What of your family?" I ask, picking the conversation back up.

Ken's smile returns. "I have a big ol' family. They live all around Avylon. Much of them live on the other side of the Cursed Wood."

"Cursed Wood—that's what the forest is called?"

Fitting.

Ken gives me a long look. "It's—"

Viveka shrieks. I jerk, my gaze zeroing in on her as her face contorts, shifting between a look of agony and fierce determination. She stares past Rainer, as if seeing something invisible to the rest of us. My head whips to Ken, who appears unconcerned. He leans forward, watching with rapt attention.

"Speaking of," he mutters.

I ignore him, torn between running to Viv's side or staying back.

Rainer continues to stares at Viv with a look of boredom, until she drops her sword and falls to her knees.

Her head thrashes from side to side, as if she's fighting some invisible force. I'm about to jump up and run to her, but Ken puts an arm up to stop me.

"Don't interrupt."

"But she's—"

"She's fine."

Time seems to drag on, as Viv grits her teeth and trembles before Rainer. Finally, her body goes still with relief. Then she punches the ground, an angry roar ripping out of her.

"Better," Rainer says. "But still not good enough."

He sheaths his sword and wipes the sweat off his brows with the hem of his shirt. I blush at the sight of his abs, quickly averting my eyes to his feet—focusing anywhere other than his sweaty muscles and too-pretty features.

Rainer extends a hand to Viveka, helping her up. The two clasp forearms and she smiles at him appreciatively, her previous rage nowhere to be found.

"Good run, Umbra Prince."

"You lasted longer than last time," he says. "You're getting better. Until you can stave it off entirely, you'll keep your shifts short and trade with Ken before nightfall."

"What was that?" I whisper to Ken.

"Don't worry. We'll start you with the infantile lessons."

"I'm serious—what did he just do to her?"

Ken chews his bottom lip, looking past me as he debates his words. "It's a… special lesson." He stops talking, and I gesture for him to continue. He chuckles. "Like I mentioned, Viv and I guard the Cursed Wood. The trees feed on fear. We must practice overcoming our fears, train ourselves not to react. It's the only way we can hope to survive out there."

My forehead wrinkles in confusion. It makes sense what he's saying in terms of overcoming his fear, but I'm still caught up on how the trees feed on fear.

It finally explains what I saw the day I ran and hallucinated the lord, lady, and Char. It was a firsthand account of how the trees can incite terror.

"Is that how I almost died?"

"Yep," Ken says. "But you didn't. *You* survived. Most don't." He cocks his head, giving me a serious look.

His words sink in.

"What does it mean?" I whisper. If the trees feed on fear, killing most humans who encounter it, but I survived, does that mean I am able to overcome my fears?

"That you're stronger than you give yourself credit for, little human." He nods in Rainer's direction. "That you give the prince his own twisted sort of hope."

"Hope for what exactly?"

"That, maybe, he's not as alone as he feels."

"He's *not* alone. He has you, and Fern, and Das Celyn, and the pixies, and—"

Ken cuts me off with a pointed look, pursing his lips at me. "There are different types of loneliness, and I'm not referring to friendship. I'm referring to the type of loneliness that's bone-deep, only cured by finding the one who matches your soul."

We sit silently, as I process his words. I almost laugh at the absurdity of his implication.

"Are you trying to set me, a measly human, up with your prince?" I ask teasingly.

He shrugs, his expression staying serious. "I smell something there. That's all."

"Gross."

I shift around, plucking a few blades of grass. Not knowing how to respond to that. It seems as if there's more Ken isn't saying, but I push it aside for now, focusing on the forest instead.

"So the trees just... scare people to death then eat them?" I ask.

Ken lets his thick, curly hair down, shaking it out before retying it into a bun at the nape of his neck. "Funny story, actually," he says, in a tone telling me it's indeed not a funny story at all. "It was an enchantment gone wrong. The woods were normal some years ago, but magic was used in an attempt to keep the humans at bay." He gives me an apologetic look. "I'm sure you've noticed, not all the fae like humans. It's nothing personal, humans are just… careless about anything other than themselves. They would cross the Gleam, destroying our land for their own enjoyment."

I tilt my head at him, waiting for him to continue.

"Initially, the woods were enchanted to bring one's fears to life in an illusion of sorts. Just enough to scare them back across the border to where they came from. But over time, the trees began to grow sentient, feeding off that fear. It powered the dark magic, multiplying it. The enchantment spread like poison, throughout the entire forest, shifting into the curse it is today. Uncontrollable. Now, the trees manifest fears of fae and humans alike, literally scaring them to death and draining them of life."

"So you and Viv? You two train yourselves to what, ignore your fear? So the trees can't trick you?"

"Something like that. We train ourselves not to react—to not let our fears control our emotions. The woods only win when we react."

A realization strikes me. "And I survived the woods—a mere, *weak* human with no training. That's why you want to train with me? To better understand *how* I overcome my fears and use that strategy for yourselves?"

"It's more than that. Rainer wants you to—"

"Human!" Rainer strides toward us, and his hypnotic gaze sends a shiver through my body.

"Speak of the devil," I mutter, not breaking eye contact.

Ken snickers.

I try to tamper down my nervousness at his approach.

Rainer's gaze narrows, shooting a zing of danger up my spine. I squirm as he draws closer, growing hot and unsettled in his proximity.

"Your chatting is distracting," Rainer says.

He says nothing else as he passes, but I catch a whiff of his scent. It's so deliciously raw. Sweet and masculine, at the same time.

Like sweat and roses.

My stomach tightens with something akin to lust, which subsequently brings burning shame along with it.

I turn, watching him leave over my shoulder. He turns back, too, and a brief flicker of surprise crosses his features. He pauses and we stare at each other for a long, painfully tense moment. My stomach turns inside out with anticipation. I think he might come back, or say something to me, but he doesn't move.

Instead, he scowls at me and saunters away.

"What was that?" Ken smirks.

"Does he bathe in rose petals or something?" I jerk a thumb over my shoulder, in the direction Rainer went.

He probably wears the scent of his aphrodisiac roses as a form of manipulation, tricking others into lusting after him.

Ken's reply is a hearty, good-natured laugh. "If you're trying to blame your speedy little heart rate on something other than your own desire, you're out of luck. Rai's scent is richer, less sweet than the Damasks. More like regular ol' roses." He taps his nose. "Shifter senses, sorry."

My cheeks heat. I shouldn't have said anything. Not only did Ken sense my body's interest in Rainer, but now I've acknowledged it aloud. And worse, I *can't* blame the aphrodisiac roses for it.

"If you say anything to him about this—"

"Our little secret." He puts his hands up, still cracking up at the situation.

Despite my embarrassment, I find myself chuckling in return. "I mean it, Ken."

"I'm a bear of my word."

"Can we start training now? Forget about this?"

"Oh, I will *never* forget this, little human."

"Then at least teach me how to fight so I can kick your arse if you ever repeat this."

"Look at you growing a backbone." He claps slowly. "You'll be something to reckon with if you keep that confidence up."

I bite down the smile forming on my lips, kicking the grass bashfully. He's right. I am growing more confident. It's a combination of things: losing Char, being free of the lord, going toe-to-toe with Rainer, and the buzzy excitement about training.

For a few moments, I forget about escaping.

Viveka makes her way to us, wiping her forehead with a cloth and drinking water from a canteen with her other hand.

She screws the canteen's cap back on and tosses it aside. Inclining her head, she scans me from head to toe. Her eyes crinkle in the corner as she smiles.

"You must be Alessia," she says.

A stupid grin crosses my face at someone finally using my name instead of *human*.

"And you're Viveka?"

"Just Viv." She nods.

Up close, I'm in even more awe of her. She's powerful with muscular arms, thick thighs, and an aura of leadership about her.

Women are not trained in any sort of battle in Dovenak. They're only to be seen, not heard. If they're not in the Trade then they're meant to keep house, tend their husbands, and host social gatherings. Not wear pants, and definitely not wield swords.

I want that.

To be truly strong. Not only mentally, like I am, but physically, too.

"Wanting a go, little human?" Ken asks, eyeing me.

"Absolutely." I stand extra straight, trying to maximize my own height, as if I can somehow convince these warriors I'm one of them.

Even if the fae are using me for their own training, a pawn in their game of fears, I don't care. I'll benefit from whatever they have to show me. It can't break me; it can only make me stronger.

"Can you teach me to do that?" I ask, gesturing toward her blade.

Viv tilts her head to the side. Her pale bangs stick to her forehead. "Sword fight?"

"Yes. I'm a quick learner."

She laughs again and it's a throaty, enveloping sound. I like the energy she exudes. She reminds me so much of Kenisius, and I wonder if it's a shifter thing.

"Really though, can you teach me?" I ask again, trying not to sound desperate.

"Have you ever used a sword before?"

"No."

"Held one?"

I shake my head.

"Are you familiar with hand-to-hand combat at least?"

"Not really."

"Not really?" She quirks a brow at me, smacking her lips with a contemplative pop while Ken looks on with his typical amused expression.

"I can do it," I surmise.

"Only one way to find out," Viv snags the handle of her sword and tosses it into the grass at my feet. She reaches out toward Ken, wiggling her fingers until he hands over his own weapon.

My heart pounds with excitement. I didn't think they'd really let me join in. For once, I feel included rather than excluded. Ken and Viv are not denying me because I'm marked, a Tradeling—the Lord's property.

Or because I'm a woman.

An ember of freedom burns through my veins, and I ache to stoke it. For the first time since losing Char, I'm filled with hope. A new kind. One that foreshadows a new future—one where I am able to defend myself and fight for my freedom.

I lift the sword from the ground, surprised at how heavy the thing is. Even with two hands, it's a workout to simply lift it. My face crumples as I realize this is not going to be as easy as Rainer and Viv made it look.

Ken claps his hands together, hooting his encouragement from near the rose bushes behind me.

Before I can prepare myself, Viv takes a slash at me and whacks the sword out of my hands.

I recoil, stunned at her speed and precision. My arms vibrate from the impact, my palms burn.

I pick the sword back up, and once again, Viv's blade slams into my own, knocking it from my grip.

A grunt of pain and annoyance leaves me. Every time I pick up the sword, she repeats the action.

Again and again and again.

Until finally, I'm so exhausted and frustrated, I leave the sword on the ground.

My arms shake with the exertion, nothing more than limp noodles at my sides. My palms and underarms are doused in sweat, fingers blistered, and the blood pounds in my head.

I want to scream, ask if this is some sort of joke. Ask if I'm a laughing matter for the fae's entertainment. But when I meet Viv's warm brown eyes, my anger quickly dissipates. She looks so kind, so patient, that I can't be angry at her for disarming me so quickly.

Whatever she's doing, it doesn't seem malicious. There's no taunting in her features.

"This isn't… what I…meant," I spit out in between heavy breaths. I plop down onto the grass as Ken accepts his sword back from Viv and sheaths it. He gives me a consolatory pat on the shoulder with his meaty paw.

"You did better than I expected," Viv says.

"I did absolutely nothing!" The frustration is apparent in my voice, and I take a few more breaths to rein it in. "You and Rainer are right," I say to Ken. "I *am* pathetic."

"Hey, there's no self-pity allowed in sword fighting," Ken says sternly. "Viv is only making a point. She's testing your tenacity."

"Sword fighting isn't as easy as it looks," she adds. "It's not just a battle—it's an art. The blade isn't only a weapon either. It's a tool that's meant to be respected. You have to learn to understand and respect your own body—your own tool—before you can add anything into the mix."

I chew on my bottom lip, not responding immediately. She has a point. Even holding the darned thing was hard for me. Just because they make it look easy, doesn't mean it is.

"How do I learn to do that?"

"With these." She holds up her hands, wiggling her fingers. "Listen, if you meet me and Ken down here at dawn daily, we'll teach you how to work with your body and find your own grace."

"Will it help with the sword?"

"Yes. Yes it will. But the goal is not to wield the sword, the goal is to wield your own body with purpose."

"Tha—" I catch myself before I can give her thanks. "I appreciate it, I mean. You doing this for me, Viv."

She nods, her eyes flashing with pride.

I'll never be in another position where I'm taken advantage of. Never again will I surrender to a cruel lord, or an arrogant fae prince—no matter how handsome—or anyone else.

I grin up at the two of them, excited about this renewed sense of purpose. As soon as I learn how to fight, maybe I can go back to Dovenak and seek vengeance for Char.

It seems like a farfetched goal, something I'd never have considered before. But with Viv and Ken training me? Perhaps it'll become a real possibility. At the very least, it gives me a sense of purpose in the present.

I had figured they'd throw me back in the forest. Study me. Learn how I overcame my fears in the trees. I hadn't expected them to dedicate actual time and energy teaching me how to fight like this.

There's no way they're doing this out of the kindness of their hearts. To simply *help* me.

Right?

The fae are malicious. Cruel. Treacherous.

Heartless.

Aren't they?

So what do they get out of this?

Fourteen
Not That Bad After All
Alessia

My next day off, I spend time sitting in the rose garden, enjoying the floral scents—without getting too close to the Damask roses.

Moments like this, when I'm totally alone, with only my mind to keep me company, it's when I miss Char the hardest. A wave of grief makes a sudden appearance. I'm glad no one's around to see the tears fall.

Grief is a funny thing.

I'll go about my day as if I carry no sorrow with me, then a pang will come to my heart, nearly stealing my breath and knocking me to my knees. I'll be kneading dough, laughing at something snarky Das Celyn said, then my brain shouts at me, reminding me that Char is gone, and suddenly, the peace I found is wiped away.

I call it a *wave* of grief, because that's exactly what it is. It washes over me in a rhythmic pattern, lapping at the shores of my mind like a wave. Sometimes, all is calm, and there are no waves at all. Other times, it's a storm, and the waves crash into me relentlessly. As I sniffle through the tears, letting the newest bout subside, I turn my head up to the pale sky.

Movement in one of the windows on the second floor catches my attention.

Rainer.

I can't make out his expression from behind the glass, but I know it's him from the shape of his body. His strong, yet lanky frame takes up most of the window. His shoulders are rounded, as if he's tired from carrying weight on them.

The fire in his gaze stokes the flames inside me.

Ken's words replay in my head. *There's a type of loneliness that's bone-deep, only cured by finding the one who matches your soul.*

I wonder if Rainer ever feels out of control of his life. If he's truly as lonely as I feel.

Before I can contemplate it any further, the prince disappears from view.

When night comes, I toss and turn in my bed, desperate for sleep. Das Celyn didn't bring up tea tonight, like they have been, and I can't help but feel a little let down. They don't owe me anything, and I hate that they wait on me, but I look forward to the deep tea-slumbers.

Instead of suffering through my dark thoughts, and continuing to let sleep evade me, I make my way downstairs to the kitchen to locate chamomile and valerian root myself.

After so many weeks of working with the faeries, the massive kitchen is easy to find. It's almost second nature by now.

It rests on the first floor, in the heart of the castle.

In the kitchen, a collection of pots and pans dangle from a centerpiece hovering over the central island counter space. Matching slate counters line the far wall, offering plenty of space for prep.

My bare feet slap gently against the stone flooring as I move from cupboard to cupboard, searching for the tea. I normally assist with the baking duties, so I often stay near the hearth and counter-space on the far right of the room.

I realize I have no idea where the tea is stored.

It's so quiet, so empty, that I swear I can hear each breath echoing in the wide open space. The eerie silence sends a shudder through me, and I wrap my arms around my body.

Since I can't find the tea, I settle for taking a walk on the grounds, hoping it might make me sleepy. I leave the kitchen and pause. My head swivels both directions down the broad hallway.

I'm tempted to head left to the foyer, to try the front door again, test the barrier, but it's pointless. Even if the barrier is finally gone—which I doubt it is—I'm definitely not heading into the woods at night.

The woods are more of a threat than Rainer is at this point.

Deciding to visit the gardens, I head right, toward the doors at the back of the palace.

Luckily, no invisible force field stops me as I hesitantly poke a foot over the threshold and step through the garden doors. I smile to myself as the still night air welcomes me. Ignoring the stone pathway, I opt to walk through the grass instead. Thick blades tickle my bare feet.

Little freedoms like this are new to me. Something I never had back at the lord's estate. From now on, I promise myself never to take these moments for granted.

The moon and stars hide behind clouds, the entire sky one stretch of endless black, but I know they're up there. It's an innate sense of trust—*knowing* the moon and stars are there even when they're out of sight.

I wish I had someone in my life I trusted as much as the moon. Someone who would show up, night after night, no matter what the day held.

Shaking my head, I focus on the flowers around me and stroll leisurely around the rose bushes.

They carry a delicious floral aroma that's grown familiar. They remind me of Rainer—beautiful, enticing, but prickly. Covered in thorns to keep others at bay. Is that why he likes his roses so much?

Because they're like him?

The breeze picks up a touch, and I swear I hear a whisper in the wind.

"*Alessssssia.*"

My blood turns to ice. I stop, holding my breath as I squint into the dark shadows haunting the edges of my vision.

"Who's there?" I whisper, my voice shaky.

"*Alesssssia.*"

The voice sounds familiar.

It sounds like… like Char.

A voice I'd recognize no matter how much time separated us. I pinch the skin on my arm, wincing when it brings with it a jolt of pain.

Pain means I'm awake, which means Char is truly here. This isn't another one of my vivid dreams.

Dashing across the manicured lawn, I head toward one of the small gates built into the stone. I peer between the bars with unruly vines and roses curving around the iron, squinting into the night. The clouds break, and a sliver of moonlight rains down, illuminating a dark figure among the trees.

"Char?" I call out. "Is that you?"

I open the latch with a soft click, slowly swinging the gate open.

"Char?" I whisper into the darkness.

"My Alessia."

Her voice is soft, kind. There's nothing ominous about it.

But dread forms in the pit of my stomach.

"Char, I'm here."

Gripping the gate door with both hands, I keep my feet firmly planted inside the wall's perimeters, afraid to submit to the forest's night form.

"Come to me," Char calls.

I'm tempted to take a step forward, to leave the safety of the stone wall. But it *can't* be Char. It's impossible. The trees must be playing tricks.

"No," I say. "You need to come to me, Char."

The woods tricked me before. I won't let it happen again.

"Please, my Alessia. It is truly me."

Hesitating, I try to decide if it's worth the risk. What if Char survived the attack somehow and made her way here? I can't just leave her out here alone.

But...then again, I witnessed her die with my own two eyes. There's no way she could've survived the attack. Lady Nilda severed a vital artery in her neck. There was so much blood—

Shifting my weight between my feet, I hesitate. The figure doesn't move either.

Even *if* it's the trees, I survived them once. I can quickly investigate, see if it's truly Char, and if it's not, return before any harm comes.

I release the gate and step forward.

Before the gate has time to swing shut behind me, something crashes into me, sending me flailing backwards.

A sharp exhale steals the air from of my lungs as I land hard.

A solid body weighs me down, preventing my breath from returning. For a second, I lie there stunned with the other body pressing on me. Our chests rise and fall rapidly in sync, both of us clearly on edge.

My eyes lift, and in the moonlight I can make out an icy gaze inches away from my own.

We pant, practically sharing breaths. My eyes flick across his face, trying and failing to read his expression.

When he speaks, his voice is low and his warm breath caresses my lips. "What the feck are you thinking?"

I realize his hand cradles the back of my head, protecting it from the fall. His other hand presses into the ground beside me. It's an intimate hold. I can feel almost every inch of his body pressed against me. I could easily lean forward, close the gap between us—

No.

The lack of oxygen is muddling my thoughts.

"Get off of me!" I push Rainer's solid body off of me, lying there trying to process what happened as the oxygen whooshes back into my lungs and brain.

"Did you recognize who that was?" he asks.

Pushing himself to stand, he reaches down to offer me a hand. I slap it away, pressing myself up instead.

"I don't need your help"

"Clearly you do." He latches the gate, peering beyond it for a second before turning back to me. "What are you thinking—leaving the grounds?!"

"Hypocritical, don't you think." Considering *he* was just out there. How else would he have been able to tackle me like that?

I rub my aching tailbone, wincing. His eyes follow the movement.

"Are you hurt?" The concern in his voice catches me off guard.

"No," I lie. "What were *you* doing out there?"

His jaw tightens. "That doesn't concern you."

"My friend is out there." I glance past him, into the dark woods beyond the iron gate. "We need to find her."

"Whatever you saw, it wasn't what you think it was."

"You saw her too?"

He doesn't reply immediately.

If he saw her, too, it means it wasn't my fear. It wasn't the trees manipulating me.

Striding past him, I head for the gate. His hand flashes out, gripping my wrist.

"Don't," he pleads.

It's his tender tone that causes me to pause.

"Why not?"

"It's not safe." He grits his teeth. "You can't leave the property."

"Thanks for the reminder, captor."

"You could very well be lying in the woods dead if I weren't here right now." He releases me, and my skin tingles where his touch was. "How could you be so—so stupid?"

"*Me,* stupid? You're the imbecile! You didn't have to attack me when you have your infuriating magick boundary popping up anytime I even *try* to leave. Surely it would've—"

"No. If it wasn't for me you—" He smooths his hands over his face with a growl. "Forget it."

Char's words from before she died rush into me. She had specifically said, "Do not linger in the forest, on either side, especially if it calls to you."

She clearly knew *something* about the Cursed Wood and its capabilities.

What else did you know, Char?

My blood boils at the fact that Rainer is right. But I refuse to admit it.

"I didn't realize the trees could call to me from within the wards," I say, prodding him. Wondering if he'll tell me what it really was, if it wasn't Char.

"It wasn't—they can't," he says flatly. "The thing you saw—that was something else. But it doesn't matter what it was. Once you enter the forest, you're at the trees' mercy."

Something else?

I shudder, working to steady my breath. If the woods weren't ominous enough before, they certainly are now. Why would a creepy shadow call to me, pretending to be Char?

It was difficult to resist the call. I was compelled… almost in a trance, trying to seek the voice. As if the voice was luring me out.

"I'm stuck on the part where you thought slamming into me was the solution." I wipe the grass and dirt off my butt. "Was a bit rough."

I might not be able to make out his features in the dark, even from just a few feet away, but it makes our interaction that much more intimate.

He steps forward, until he's crowding my space, and his warmth pulls me in.

"I wish you no harm," he mutters.

He reaches out, tracing my jaw. His fingers trail down to my collarbone, then down my arm.

My face heats, and a pulse builds in my core as I imagine all the ways he might get rough with me if I *ask*.

Hopefully he can't sense my arousal like Ken.

Oh gods, that would be mortifying.

My skin pebbles and I try to suppress a shudder. There's no way he's *not* aware of my reaction. Based on the barely audible chuckle that leaves him, he definitely knows.

As the clouds break again, moonlight illuminates his grin.

"Do I need to lock you in your room again to keep you out of trouble?"

My lips tighten. "You wouldn't dare."

Oh, but he would.

He chuckles again. "Test me, human."

"You wouldn't," I say bravely. He wants me to test him? Fine. I will. "For some reason, which I can't figure out yet, you care about me. If you didn't, you wouldn't have slammed into me like some dramatic savior. You would've let me walk into the forest."

"Don't be delusional. Keeping you from death doesn't mean I'm fond of you. You're a nuisance. More work than you're worth."

"Yet you work awfully hard to protect me."

I squint at him. His words and actions are at odds. He's saved me twice now, kept me comfortable, allowed me freedom and resources to train. I catch him staring when he thinks I'm not looking. Yet when we're face-to-face, he acts as if he's unfazed by me.

"You're a prince, don't you have better things to do instead of entertaining me?"

He tilts his head. "At this hour?"

"Why are you out here?"

"The same reason as you."

"Can't sleep?"

He sighs.

Rainer might not want to admit it aloud for whatever reason, but I hear what he's not saying. My chest squeezes, knowing he has his own troubles that keep him up. Haunted by his own mind, like me.

Ken said his family is gone, and I'm betting it's grief Rainer faces based on the way his eyes gloss over and he gets this hollow look. It's not an expression of terror or pain so much as regret.

"There's a tea that Das Celyn brings for me," I say, trying to lighten the air between us. "It's incredibly helpful."

The air between us is so thick with tension and unspoken words that it's hard to breathe.

"Though they forgot to bring it up tonight," I say.

Rainer cups the back of his neck, offering me a sheepish grin, and my stomach flutters at the sight.

"Don't blame Das Celyn for that," he says quietly. "I was planning to bring your tea up myself—but time slipped away from me. I worried it was too late to disturb you by the time I finished my day's duties."

I dip my chin, hoping the night hides the blush overtaking my cheeks. I had a feeling it was him sending the tea up.

"So it's your fault I almost got eaten by a creepy shadow monster?"

"Is this your way of admitting you needed me to save you?"

"Never." I cross my arms, feigning annoyance, but I rather like bantering with the prince. "I'm not as weak or pathetic as you think I am."

His eyes darken, a smug expression working its way onto his face. "You don't like it when I call you that." It's not a question.

"No."

"And why not?"

"Because it's not true." My fists ball up at my sides. He glances at my hands and chuckles under his breath. I hate that I love the sound.

"It's true for the girl who asks what the *point* of fighting is." He steps even closer, until we're sharing body heat. "But it isn't true for the girl who fights for herself. Now, which one are you? Because I've seen hints of both, but I have yet to figure it out."

Thinking of his previous words—about how giving up is just as hard as fighting—and how empowering training felt today, it's an easy decision. Despite my inability to even hold the sword, I felt renewed. Those failures still felt like successes, because I was trying. I was working toward bettering myself. It was a start.

"The one who fights," I whisper.

Slowly, I tilt my head up to look at him. His eyes are hooded as he stares down at me. His gaze flits to my lips. We're frozen in time as we share this moment, and I wonder which of us will close the distance.

But then Rainer sighs and steps back.

"The one who fights," he repeats. "Then we shall make you strong, Alessia, inside and out."

Hearing him say my name makes me giddy. Hearing him agree to help me toughen up? That's the most beautiful sound of all—the sound of empowerment.

I should worry about his intentions. What does he get out of helping me? But for a moment, I simply exist in the joy of the moment. I'm safe. I'm fed. I have a renewed purpose.

"Join me for tea?" I ask, trying to wedge this door between us open even further.

Rainer hesitates, shifting his weight between his feet before turning and walking away. At first, I think he's going to leave me standing there, but then he turns and calls over his shoulder, "You coming?"

Perhaps it's not the tea that sounds nice, but the extra time spent with the prince in the middle of the night, with the castle quiet and only the moon's attention on us. Perhaps I should be more hesitant, but then again, I've already experienced my worst fears and lived to tell the tale. There's nothing he can take from me that I haven't already lost.

As I follow him toward the castle, my scalp prickles with awareness. I glance over my shoulder, and beyond the iron bars, the shadowy figure stands—watching us. I swear it raises a wispy arm, reaching between the bars. I shudder, stepping closer to the prince as if he'll protect me.

And when he lends me an arm, tugging me to his side, I know he would.

Perhaps the Prince of Fear is not that bad after all.

FIFTEEN

MORE ALONE THAN EVER

ALESSIA

R ainer was actually decent to me last night. There was no more lighthearted teasing as we sipped our tea. No heartfelt conversations. Only peaceful silence. Rainer reverted to his brooding ways, but he also didn't press me about *why* I can't sleep or why I'm searching for safety in Avylon.

It was exactly what I needed—company, without the stipulations of niceties.

It felt safe. Comforting.

It's almost like Rainer understands my struggles. Or at least, maybe he recognizes them. It felt big when he admitted his trouble sleeping to me—even though it was more of a reluctant acknowledgment than a verbal admission—as if we share something important.

I spend the remainder of the afternoon with Das Celyn in the kitchen. But as night comes, and I'm alone in my bed, my chest pangs for Char again.

I never feel as alone as I do at night.

Throwing on a thin nightgown to combat the warm evening, I exit my room for an evening walk. I decide to stay indoors, hesitant to go outside after my encounter with the shadow being.

Plus, I'd be lying if I said I wasn't hoping to run into Rainer.

After roaming the first floor for what seems like hours, I push open double-doors into a wing I haven't yet been in. One that Das Celyn has never showed me, never cleaned when I've accompanied them.

It's a haphazard of blooming life, obviously well cared for despite the disorder.

The air is humid, fragrant. Floral scents and moist earth fill my nose. A couple of watering cans and empty pots litter the floor. Vines crawl up the walls, around the doorways that line the left. The ceiling and entire right wall are made of glass, like a greenhouse. The natural light during the day must be spectacular.

Perfect for the plants to thrive.

It's no wonder this area of the house was chosen for the plants. But, I wonder why they're here, tucked away out of sight in an otherwise abandoned wing of the house.

Following the hallway, I pass the bulk of plant-life. Something moves out of the corner of my eye, but when I turn my head, everything is still. Perhaps it's exhaustion, but I swear some of the plants twitch as I drift by.

I pass a couple of closed doors, and at the end of the hallway sits a pocket door. I slide it open to reveal a small spiral staircase tucked away in a sitting room. White sheets are thrown over the furniture, which piques my curiosity.

I patter up the narrow staircase, which curves up to the second floor. Immediately, I'm greeted by a hallway with much cooler, drier air. As if it's temperature controlled.

Magic, surely.

Creepy portraits of what I assume to be the royal family line the hall. In the most recent portraits—more vibrant in color, less faded—there's one of a woman with raven hair and ethereal blue eyes like Rainer, one of a man with greying hair and stormy dark eyes, and one of Rainer.

None of them smile, and they all glance off into the distance with a glazed over stare. Pointed ears poke through their hair.

Rainer looks lifeless albeit regal. Something in his haunted gaze makes me sad. Whereas the couple—likely his parents—stand proud and confident, Rainer's shoulders are slumped, his lips and brow tight.

The portraits give the royal faerie family a sense of humanity. I wonder what happened to his parents. I wonder why none of them have a portrait *together*—only individually.

I try to shake the chill that's made a home in my bones, but I can't.

Dim light seeps out of an open door at the end of the hallway, as if it's inviting me in. I accept the draw, creeping into the room.

A sharp exhale leaves me as I take in *why* the area needs to be temperature controlled. Inside, books of all sizes, colors, and styles line the large room, floor-to-ceiling, in dozens of rows.

Other than the books I stole, and the letters Char snuck me, I've never been much of a reader. Then again, I never had a true chance to read for pleasure. It was more a mandatory lesson for me, courtesy of Char, than anything fun.

I finger the hardback spines as I walk down a row, and inhale the smell of ink, leather, and paper. It's musty and dank, but somehow relaxing. There's another scent mixed in that reminds me of Rainer, and begrudgingly I revel in that as well.

My bones relax.

When I remove my hand from the books, I'm surprised there isn't a speck of dust on my fingers. As old and worn as these books are, the space is well-cared for, just like the plants in the hall. I like this wing of the house. It's homier, more inviting. Especially with the tattered, ornate rug beneath my feet and the sagging wingback chairs that sit around without rhyme or reason.

These shelves are filled with stories of all sorts, and the thought makes me giddy.

The deeper I get into the aisles, light from the oil lamps at the front of the room recedes, but I can still make out the titles in the dim light. As I turn the last corner, I'm too distracted by the books that I don't see the dark figure ahead of me.

When I finally notice him, I'm so startled that I jump, knocking into the shelves.

Rainer's hand flashes out to steady me before I lose my footing altogether. I gasp, staining the silence with the sharp noise.

"Gods!" I whisper, clutching my chest. "You scared me."

"What are you doing in this wing?" he asks in a cold tone.

He's in tight black slacks with his light-grey collared shirt untucked and unbuttoned. The sight of his skin peeking out does funny things to my body, and I quickly divert my eyes.

"I—" What do I tell him? That I was looking for tea and decided to roam instead, hoping I'd run into him? "Couldn't sleep."

As our eyes meet, his rigidness melts away. The fight leaves his face as his expression softens.

Rainer is a prince. A wealthy, magical prince with everything he needs at his fingertips. A prince surrounded by friends and abundance. Yet he wears his pain like a second skin.

He sighs, not giving me a response as he looks down at the indigo hardback in his hands. He gives it a thump, running his fingers over the broken spine. The letters on the cover are so worn I can't make out the title, other than the word *Gardens*.

"This was my mother's favorite book."

"She's gone?" The question slips out.

"She's dead." His voice is flat as he turns and puts the book back on the shelf.

I wonder if that's what keeps him up at night—her death.

On instinct, I reach out, placing a hand on his shoulder in comfort. He turns to me slowly, and I swear I see a glimmer of unshed tears in his eyes. It's too dark to be certain, but I'm almost positive.

His jaw clenches as he looks away.

This strong, arrogant prince standing before me, with tears glimmering in his beautiful eyes makes my heart ache. He's so vulnerable in this moment that it makes me want to wrap my arms around him and tell him everything will be okay, even if it's a lie. It's what Char used to do for me when I was hurting.

"I never had a mother," I tell him, opening up in return. "At least not one I remember. But I had Char. She was—all I had."

Moisture accumulates in my eyes, and a fat tear breaks free, sliding down my cheek.

Rainer surprises me as he reaches out, swiping it away with his thumb. My heart picks up its pace at the comforting gesture.

We continue to stare at each other, the space between us heating up with the heaviness of the conversation. His thumb gently caresses my cheek, and I lean into his hand.

"She's who you were calling for the other night," he murmurs. Then quickly, he adds, "At the gate, I mean."

I nod. "She was everything to me. If it weren't for her, I'd be illiterate." I point to the shelves, and a smile spreads on my lips at the memory.

"That's what picture books are for."

Did he just make a joke?

When I glimpse Rainer's small smile, I laugh, my shoulders loosening up. His hand slowly lowers from my face. I ache to reach out, to grasp his hand and keep him in my grip.

"That wasn't the only thing she taught me." If it wasn't for her nurturing me, loving me, it's likely I'd have left this world behind long ago. "Not all of my memories are horrible," I continue, opening up to him. "But almost every single one of my good memories is because of her." I glance over my shoulder, in the direction of the hallway where the various plants sit. "Most of my favorite memories are of us baking together. Or gardening in the nicer weather."

"You were allowed to keep a garden?"

I sigh. "*We* weren't. But the lady allowed us to tend *her* garden." I chuckle sarcastically but Rainer's frown deepens. "Forget-me-nots and roses were always my favorite, but the lady didn't have very many...of either. The roses were hard to keep alive. Maybe it was the soil—anyways, I once tried to smuggle a rose, but—" I bite my lip and glance at the floor.

That was one of the few times the lady hit me herself—the back of her hand across my face. And, of course, she implored her husband to punish me when he returned home that same evening.

"Nevermind," I whisper.

"There are thousands of roses," Rainer says, picking up on my obvious mood shift. "Did you know that different colors have different scents? Different meanings?" He doesn't wait for me to respond. Instead, he glances at his nails, twisting a ring around his finger anxiously. "They're not meant to bloom without sunlight. Not native to the Umbra Court, where the days are gloomy, the skies dark. But my mother didn't care. She grew them anyway." His lips tilt up as he meets my eyes. "I learned how to care for them, with the help of pixie magic. I learned how to grow almost anything. Except her favorite rose of all."

That explains a lot. His troubled nature, from missing his mother. His penchant for gardening, to feel closer to her.

My lungs constrict when I realize I'd tried to ruin his late mother's flowers with my fit all those weeks back. I already carry guilt about that outburst, but it grows tenfold.

"What happened to her?" I whisper.

My need to know is selfish. I seek reassurance that I'm not alone in my grief. That despite being as different as they come—fae and human, rich and poor, prince and Tradeling—we are the same deep down. Despite the things that separate us, our lives are truly not that different. The pain we carry in our hearts is the same.

He closes his eyes, as if he's wincing, then so quietly I almost don't hear it, he whispers, "She was murdered."

"I'm s—"

"Don't," he growls.

When he opens his eyes, they're darker than the pale blue I've come to find solace in. They're a stormier color. Almost cobalt. But before I can get a closer look, he turns and walks off, leaving me behind without another acknowledgment.

"Rainer, wait—" I call after him, but he puts a hand up and shakes his head as he stalks off.

"Take whichever books you like, but do *not* touch my plants."

He strides out of sight.

I glance around the cozy library, but the moment of excitement has passed. In its place is sorrow for the prince.

This must have been his mother's wing.

The library, the plants.

Surely they all belonged to her.

It's why the wing is unused, untouched.

As I exit the room, I spot Rainer rapping on one of the doors. I linger at the library's entrance, waiting to see who answers. And when Fern greets him, tugs him inside, and slams the door behind him, my chest grows hollow with jealousy.

Apparently I had it all wrong. I thought she was a victim. Trapped here against her will. But she's important enough to stay here, willingly, in Rainer's late mother's wing.

The chasm in my heart grows, and I'm more alone than ever.

SIXTEEN

WE ARE NOT FRIENDS

ALESSIA

The next morning, after training, I clean up and change into something comfortable—slacks and a tunic swallowing me whole. I tie my hair back into a braid to keep it out of my face. My body is here, but my mind is faraway, swirling with thoughts of Char, the woods, and Rainer. I can't help the nagging feeling that it's all connected.

Maybe it's because I dreamt about Char again last night—or rather, her last words to me. Her apology for lying. At first, I had thought she was apologizing for saying she's not my family. We both know that was a lie. But, what if that's not what she was apologizing for? What if it was something bigger.

She had her secrets—such as the healing salve, her insights on the fae, her warnings about the woods. Granted, so did Felix.

So was I the only one in the dark?

My stomach rumbles, drawing me back to the present. With all the training lately, I'm hungrier than normal.

Glee fills me as I step into the hallway, still able to leave without the barrier stopping me. At least Rainer isn't mad at me for invading his space. I was worried the fickle fae might've reinstated the barrier to keep me locked away after last night.

I hang a left toward the stairs, on a mission to find food, and ask Das Celyn what our duties are today.

The kitchen is mostly empty when I arrive through the swinging double doors, save for two fae.

My shoes squish against the shiny floors as I pass a female with freckles. Her long brown hair is spotted white with flour as she kneads dough. A stout fellow talks animatedly at her side, a rhythmic *whoosh* coming from his whisk as he stirs whatever is in his bowl.

My stomach growls and they eye me curiously. I haven't met these two yet; they're unfamiliar.

"Where's Das Celyn?" I ask.

The female shrugs.

I wonder if that means we're not working today.

Passing the ovens, countertops, and various cupboards and shelves packed with cooking utensils, I make my way to the back wall. The faes' eyes burn into my back, but I ignore them as I pull open one of the few doors I know leads to a pantry.

The dark room is lined with shelves, filled with herbs, berries, flowers, and spices of all sorts. It's bigger than mine and Char's shared bedroom back in Dovenak.

Scanning the baskets and boxes of goodies, I search for something to snack on. When I come across a basket filled with thumbnail-sized berries shaped like crescent moons, curiosity gets the best of me. The berries are pushed off into a corner on a low shelf, but it's the silver-blue iridescent coloring that holds my attention.

I snag the basket and sniff the small fruit cautiously. The berries smell sweet, citrusy. Absolutely divine. My mouth salivates, and I'm tempted to throw all caution to the wind and give them a try.

I've never seen anything like them back in Dovenak. If they weren't safe they wouldn't be in the pantry, so accessible on a low shelf.

Das Celyn has never mentioned anything being off limits for me in here—we often snack as we work.

I plop a berry into my mouth. It explodes in a delicious burst of sweetness, with a hint of sourness.

"Mmm," I hum appreciatively.

I reach for a couple more, closing my eyes and savoring the unique flavor as I munch on them. They're so good, I can't stop. Loud laughter rings through the kitchen as I grab a few more. Startled, I almost drop the basket. I wipe my mouth on the back of my hand and carefully place the fruit basket back where I found it. I poke my head out of the door to see the two servants are still going at it, pulling fresh baked goods from the oversized oven.

The fae prince himself stands before the servants, as they smile up at him with bright eyes.

"Take a tray to Das Celyn," Rainer tells the male fae. "Along with the whole oat porridge."

"They won't accept, Prince," the male says right as the female says, "They haven't been eating much lately."

"Not acceptable. Tell them these were sent from the prince, that he insists they eat. They are prohibited from resuming tasks until they eat something."

"As you wish, Prince." The male bows his head and scurries away with a tray.

"Wait," Rainer calls after him. When the male pauses and looks back, Rainer says, "Das Lulu can manage the kitchens alone today.

Send for Das Celyn's family in the village. Perhaps a visit will do them some good."

Surprise roots me in place.

Rainer is trying to get Das Celyn to eat?

My skin grows clammy. I practically accosted Das Celyn, slinging accusations of Rainer withholding their food. They warned me that I shouldn't jump to conclusions.

How right they were.

It's clear that Rainer isn't the reason for Das Celyn's starving, bony frame, or bad attitude. In fact, it seems like the opposite. Like he cares about the state they're in and wants to help.

The revelation softens my heart toward the prince even further. He's not cruel—he's misunderstood.

After the male faerie scurries out of the room, I wait a few beats before making my presence known.

I clear my throat and step into sight, letting the pantry door swing shut behind me.

"Are those—cinnamon rolls?" I ask as warm vanilla and cinnamon scents assault me.

Rainer's eyes dart between me and the pantry I exited, and his brow cocks, but he doesn't say anything.

"Doughnuts," the female servant—Das Lulu, I presume—says. She stops what she's doing, turning to me with a wide smile. "Prince Rainer's favorite." She winks at him, and he offers her a soft smile back.

On cue, my stomach rumbles in response to the scent.

Rainer's frown deepens and I shrug.

Striding to the counter, Rainer stops next to the female servant. "May I?"

"Of course, Prince." She slides a tray of deserts toward him and nods graciously as he accepts it.

When he returns to my side, he holds out the puffy rings of dough to me. I'm caught off guard.

With holes in the center, they're a strange looking dessert. The lord and lady are partial to pies, even the occasional cinnamon roll.

"I've never had a doughnut before," I murmur.

Rainer's face softens.

"You can fry 'em in grease or oil too, but we like baking 'em. Fluffier that way," Das Lulu says, clapping her hands excitedly.

After a moment's hesitation, I reluctantly accept one of the dough-rings with a chocolate paste on top. I take a large bite. Sugary sweetness overwhelms my tastebuds.

"Wow," I say through a mouthful.

"I prefer the chocolate frosted, too." Rainer grabs an identical dessert off the tray before placing the rest back on the counter by Das Lulu. He taps his doughnut against mine and says, "Sláinte."

Swallowing my mouthful, I watch the prince with confusion.

He's been unpredictable and impossible to read. At times, I think he's being kind to me, but then he grows an attitude out of nowhere, keeping me an arm's length away.

It doesn't matter if he gives me or Das Celyn food, it doesn't make him a *good* guy. I remind myself of that so I don't let my guard down around him.

But when he's not scowling at me, he's quite civil…charming even. His full lips wrap around the edge of his doughnut and his eyes shut as he chews. His throat bobs as he swallows.

When his eyes flutter open and catch me staring, blood rushes to my cheeks. I quickly take a bite of my own doughnut, trying to hide behind it.

Rainer steps closer to me and my body heats up.

"Here," he says. "You have a little—" His thumb reaches up to gently swipe a spot of chocolate from my chin, which he then licks off his finger.

Oh gods.

It's so quiet as we finish the desserts, that I'm afraid he can hear the erratic pounding in my chest. I'm all too aware of Das Lulu watching us with open curiosity. Her eyes are wide, her mouth slack. When she realizes I'm looking at her, she quickly turns away.

What the heck was that?

I want to thank them for the treat, but I remember not to at the last moment. Instead, I nod with appreciation.

"That was delicious," I say, my voice high-pitched.

I'm reeling from Rainer's touch. The kindness in his eyes. The way he ensured Das Celyn is looked after. I need to put space between us before I read too far into his actions or make a fool of myself.

Like I did last night.

The memory of him sneaking into Fern's room hurts my stomach. I'm dumbstruck by the jealous pang in my heart.

Without waiting for a response, I dart toward the door.

Between him setting me up with Ken and Viv for training, bringing me tea, saving me from the shadow in the woods, opening up about his mother, flirting with me, and offering me doughnuts, I'm torn.

The only thing worse than Rainer being awful to me, is him being nice to me. It's confusing and unsettling.

I don't know what his motives are. Gods help me. If I'm going to focus on myself and my resilience, I don't need a Rainer-shaped distraction hovering in my mind.

He might not hate me anymore, but we are *not* friends.

SEVENTEEN

I'VE BEEN FREE

ALESSIA

I head outside, assuming I'm not working today since Das Celyn is not around. I figure I'll get some fresh air by myself.

The gardens have quickly become my new favorite place on the grounds. Rich, vibrant tones of red, white, yellow, and purple roses make up the majority of buds. There are even a few black roses, and the pink ones—Damask roses—that I avoid carefully.

It's such a bright contrast against the cloudy, grey day. A sliver of joy among the castle's dark gothic aura. It's obvious Rainer takes much pride in caring for his mother's old gardens. Floral scents fill the air, mixing into its own beautiful perfume—better than anything in the bottles upstairs.

Following the flat rock path that leads through the gardens, I curve around the side of the castle, crossing the wide open expanse of grass we normally use for training. Without shoes on, the soft blades are like a thick rug. The fresh air warms my skin.

Everything about being outdoors here is comforting—I noticed it from the moment I stepped foot over the Gleam—and it makes me realize just how little time I've spent outside in my life. Lyson's winters are long and bare, and even in the better seasons, I never spent much time beyond the estate's walls. Never had an opportunity to fall in love with the outdoors like this. Chores seldom required me to migrate away from the estate's interior. Unless I was assisting Char in the gardens, or washing windows from the exterior, I stayed indoors.

Here, it reminds me of some of my favorite moments with Char, outside in the fresh air and sunshine as we tended the flowerbeds.

Pausing, I turn my face up to the skies, pretending the sun is shining and washing over me. For a second, rays peek out and bathe my eyelids in an orange hue.

I giggle.

Rainer is right: these little moments are magic.

A smile graces my lips, and suddenly my head is light and airy beyond a normal, natural euphoria.

My skin buzzes with pleasure.

"Is the weather always this delightful?" I ask aloud.

There's a niggling in the back of mind that tells me something is off, but I can't quite figure out what it is.

It feels too good to care, really.

"It's quite temperate, yes."

Whipping around, I spot Rainer a few paces behind me, staring with narrowed eyes. His head cocks to the side, as if he's trying to make sense of me. His gaze is unintentionally seductive.

It's the way he stares at me—like he's trying to strip me naked and see my soul.

Like he truly sees me.

My skin prickles under his attention, but instead of feeling shy or unsettled, I giggle harder.

The colors around me brighten, becoming sharper. The floral scent of the gardens grows stronger.

"Whoa," I say, my voice coming out warbly. "I sound funny."

"You didn't," he says flatly.

"Hullo, princey poo!"

"You did." He runs a palm down his face and heaves a sigh. "Gods save me."

I twirl around, wishing I was in a dress instead of pants, just so I could make the fabric spin around my ankles.

"You are too pretty to be so mean, you know," I say.

He doesn't respond. Instead, he grabs my hand, interlacing our fingers. My skin burns where his soft skin touches my own. But it's not a sweet or romantic gesture—no, he practically drags me along. We pass a few willowy trees, plopping me down in a patch of grass out of sight from the castle.

"Stay here," he orders.

"You are a bossy faerie."

He blinks slowly, clearly unamused. The blades of grass beneath me tickle my skin, and I want nothing more than to lie down and roll around.

So I do.

"Stop that."

"Make me." I giggle and Rainer sighs heavily. Somewhere deep down, beneath the lightness and fuzzy feelings, I recognize something isn't right, but I'm too happy—too free, for once—to care.

"Is this what freedom is?"

"What, exactly?"

"Happy. Light. Safe." I pet the grass beneath me, loving the softness. "Am I safe here, Rai Rai?"

Rainer's body goes rigid. After a beat, he loosens up and grabs a seat on the grass next to me.

He glances up at the sky and mutters, "feckin' hell." Then he turns to me. "Do you feel safe here?"

"Yes," I whisper. "I *want* to be safe here."

He cocks his head, taking me in with interest.

"And I also want—" I stop to think. I've never taken the time to truly consider what I want. What I want has never mattered. "I want a family. I want friends. I want Char." This time when I say her name, my heart flutters with love and peace. There's no grief—no sadness attached. "I want muscles like Viveka. I want beauty like Fern. I—"

"You don't need her beauty," Rainer says, his brows furrowed. "You have plenty of your own."

My stomach clenches at his words, and the way he says them with such vigor.

"You think I'm beautiful?"

"I don't think it. I know it. You *are* beautiful, Alessia." The way he says my name melts my insides. He glances away, muttering under his breath, "too beautiful."

If I was standing, surely my legs would've given out at those words.

Seeing this muscular fae prince, dressed in dark colors, with his gold jewelry and tattoos, sitting so casually in the middle of a flowery lawn would be humorous if he hadn't just called me beautiful. I'm melting in a puddle of lust and yearning. For him.

"I'm onto you mister," I tell him. "You secretly look out for others, but you hide it behind sharp words and cruel scowls. Why?"

His eyes widen in surprise. He turns away, trying to hide his reaction, but I saw it. It makes me wonder how often others point out the good in Rainer. If he even sees it himself.

"I see you," I whisper. "I want you."

Eager to eliminate the distance between us, I launch myself at Rainer. With a knee on either side of his thighs, I straddle him. His hands grip my waist, holding me into place as he watches my lips with a heated gaze.

I don't know what's gotten into me, but I don't care. With one quick tug, I rip his shirt open and buttons go flying everywhere.

"Alessia," he warns.

His eyes darken, flashing to a deep cobalt. I pause, double-taking, but they're back to their normal pale coloring. It was probably a trick of the light.

His shirt falls open a little wider, and I'm able to see the scripture up close. A language I don't recognize with intricate designs mixed in.

My fingers brush the dark ink on his chest, and he shudders beneath my touch. He's all hard muscles and soft skin. An enticing contrast. I want to press my bare skin against his.

"I want to feel all of you."

He grabs my wrists. "No."

Despite whatever trance I'm under—whatever has my head buzzing and my emotions soaring high—I'm able to understand no means no.

I should apologize. Or maybe I shouldn't, because the fae don't seem to respond well to apologies.

"I shouldn't have done that."

"It's not—" He sighs, still gripping my wrists.

He's hard beneath me, I can feel him through our layers. It's clear the attraction between us is mutual, but it doesn't matter if he doesn't want this.

I nod, not fighting him on this. His grip tightens when I try to pull free from his lap. Logically, I should be mortified by his rejection. But, I'm not. Instead, my body buzzes with joy.

"We can't do this," he mutters.

His eyes flicker between shades of ice and navy, as if reflecting his inner battle. I blink a few times, wondering if I'm hallucinating again.

"You're with Fern," I mutter. She said he wasn't her boyfriend, but he snuck into her room. They're clearly together in some manner. "I get it."

"What? I'm not—it has nothing to do with her."

"I saw you go to her room. After the library. It's—"

A large figure appears at our side out of seemingly nowhere, and I squeak, startled.

"Moonberries, aye?" Ken says.

Rainer removes his grip from me, and I tumble off his lap into the grass with a fit of laughter.

"Hi, little human." Ken stands over me, peering down with a wide grin. "I see you're having a good day."

"Why, hello," I say, smiling. "A great day indeed!" Not even Rainer's rejection can get me down.

Ken's toothy smile flashes at me as his eyes jump between me and Rainer. "Why did no one think to invite me?"

"This wasn't planned," Rainer says. He points at me. "I found the human wandering the gardens, high as a bird."

"High?" I snort, rubbing my hands on the ground. The grass is so soft. So soft.

Holy gods.

Am I high?

"I didn't sniff the pink roses, Rai Rai," I say.

"By herself?" Ken asks Rainer, ignoring me.

"Apparently so."

How am I high?

I didn't smell any of the naughty flowers. Or drink anything weird. I only ate the same doughnut as Rainer, and the—

"Berries," I mutter. *Moonberries.* "I knew eating them was a bad idea."

"Yet you ate them anyway."

I snort a laugh. Rainer's scowl returns. His messy hair tumbles around his face alluringly, framing his broad jaw and thick brows, with sharp ears peeking out. I want to trace them, touch them. They're so enchanting.

I reach forward, but Rainer jumps to his feet before I can touch him.

"This is not playtime."

"I think she wants to play with you, *Rai Rai*." Ken teases with a sly look.

"No," Rainer says, his voice frosty. "I am not touching her."

Her.

He not only finally used my name, but he stopped referring to me as an it.

My chest warms. The berries certainly did a swell job of getting me high if the bar for romance is this low. It's like I suddenly don't care that he's holding me hostage or that he's condescending.

Laughter bubbles out of me.

"This is so funny," I say. My head buzzes with excitement. The colors are so bright I can feel them, and the sounds are so loud I can taste them. Everything is comforting, and I'm safe. So safe. So happy.

"Funny, indeed," Kenisius says, his eyes gleaming. "What color are your panties?"

"White!" I blurt, unable to prevent the words from spilling out, and he snorts a laugh.

"Ken," Rainer warns.

"What?" Ken asks with a sly grin. "I'm not asking for me. I'm asking for you."

"I don't need you to—"

"Have you ever taken a lover?"

"Yes! Only one though."

Felix.

Why don't I miss him more? I thought that since we connected on an intimate level, he'd be more important to me. But Char's death, coming here, flirting with Rainer, all overshadowed him. It goes to show that physical intimacy is sometimes just that—physical. Nothing deeper or more meaningful than surface level pleasure.

Rainer closes his eyes and scrubs at his brow aggressively as Ken continues his line of questioning.

"Was he very good?"

"He was… selfish." I lower my voice and scandalously add, "I never had an…orgasm with him."

Rainer's eyes flicker navy again, and he swallows a groan.

The ground is so soft that I want to roll around in it. I want to cover myself in all the grass like a cocoon and never leave. So soft.

"I like these berries," I mumble.

"And what was your pathetic lover called?" Ken looks all too amused with himself, enjoying the fact that I can't stop from answering.

"Felix."

A vague image of his face crosses my mind. I'm sure he doesn't even miss me. And the revelation doesn't hurt, surprisingly. We only kept each other company because we were both lonely and sought affection. Other than the physical aspect, there was never substance between us.

"Have you—"

"Enough, Kenisius!" Rainer gives the shifter a pointed look. He looks entirely distraught, as he strokes his jaw. "This is *not* an appropriate line of questioning."

Kenisus throws his head back in a howling laugh, and his shoulders shake with the force. "When is appropriate ever any fun?"

"Alessia." Rainer turns to me, and I'm so buzzy and disconnected, that I can only smile up at him. "How many berries did you have?"

"A lot, by the looks of it," Ken says.

He's right. I close my eyes and lean back on the ground. I'm floating… floating… floating. The sun warms my skin and it's like a million soft kisses.

Wait—when did the sun come out? Am I imagining it?

"Why didn't you let me kiss you?" I ask Rainer without looking at him.

"You're not thinking clearly," he replies.

"Yes I am. I certainly didn't imagine your erection poking me before Ken interrupted."

Ken howls with laughter and Rainer must give him a look, because the shifter immediately swallows his humor down with a fake cough.

"You asked what I want," I say with my eyes still closed, and my arms behind my head. "I want Char back. I want her to be alive. I want to know why Felix wouldn't choose me over the lord. I want the lord and the lady to pay for what they did to me and Char. I want Dovenak to change, for the Trade to no longer exist so everyone can be safe and free and happy—" I pause. "I want more doughnuts. I want to see you naked. And I want to have an orgasm not by my own hand for once."

A few moments of silence pass, before Rainer says, "I'm taking you to bed."

"Oh goodie." My lips tilt up into a smile, and I try to open my eyes but my eyelids are too heavy. "I'm glad you've agreed to make one of my wishes come true."

"No," he says, clearly exasperated. "I'm putting you to bed—alone. You need to sleep this off."

I don't want to go to sleep. I try to say it, but my lips don't move. They tingle. My whole body tingles. I could stay here forever. Right here.

I'm scooped up into a pair of strong arms, and I sigh, wrapping my arms around the owner's neck. I immediately know it's the prince based on the way he smells floral yet masculine. He grips me tight, and I'm safe with him.

My eyes stay shut and I nuzzle into his neck. "You smell like roses."

"And you smell like bad decisions and regret. My undoing."

I chuckle, and he stills when my parted lips caress his skin.

"She needs to sleep it off," Rainer repeats, his chest rumbling. Ken says something I don't quite hear, to which Rainer replies, "I've got this, Kenisius."

Rainer starts walking, and I cling to his warm frame.

"Will I be okay?" I mumble.

"You'll be fine," he tells me. "Nothing a nap won't fix."

"I don't want a hangover."

"Moonberries don't give you hangovers."

"What do they do?"

His chest shakes with silent laughter, and I can't help the pride that washes over me at making the cold prince laugh. But when he speaks, his voice is rough, "they prevent you from speaking lies" —he sighs— "and influence you to act out your… truest desires."

"Oh." This will be awkward tomorrow. "Why are they in the pantry…just sitting there?"

"For Ostara. It's coming up soon."

"Ostara?" I mutter.

I must doze off in his arms, because next thing I know, he's tucking me into silky sheets. My eyelids are practically glued shut with sleep, my mouth dry.

"Will you stay with me?" I mumble.

There's a pause, as if he's contemplating an answer. "No," Rainer says softly. "Not like this."

"Why not?"

"Because I can't."

"Can't or won't?"

"Both."

"You just said it yourself," I murmur, my eyes finally peeling open. "You're not with Fern. And the berries only bring out true desires. I want this, Rai Rai. I want something good. Something pure and pleasurable."

"I am the antithesis of good or pure, Alessia."

"Then I want bad. Tainted. Wicked. I want *you*."

His jaw tenses and he turns away from me, so I shut my eyes again. "I can't give you that. But I can give you a single truth: I don't want to hurt you" —he sighs— "and I will. It's inevitable."

Hurt me? How could he possibly hurt me?

Sleep begins to pull me back under, and I ask for one more thing before it takes me: "Can you remove the stupid magical barrier?" I mutter. "I'm sick of running into it."

"My silly little rose," he whispers, "I've considered your debt paid for quite some time now."

Soft lips brush my forehead, before his boots thump across the floor. The door creaks open before closing with a click.

I'm hit with a realization then: I've been able to move freely about the castle. I stepped foot outside the walls when the shadow called to me the other night.

There haven't been any barriers to stop me.

I haven't even noticed, but I've been *free*.

Eighteen

Now I Have to See My Nemesis

Rainer

Lying to myself about hating Alessia isn't working anymore. I'm drawn to her inexplicably and dangerously. And she's starting to notice. Worse, she said she wants me.

Me.

And it was the whole, honest truth because it's impossible to lie while high on moonberries. Gods help me, I almost lost control. It's no small miracle that I was able to walk away from her and leave her untouched in that bed.

My veins sizzle beneath my skin, and burning desire propels me through the castle.

I storm to the indoor greenhouse hallway—my mother's old wing—wearing a scowl that keeps everyone at bay. I am angry, but at myself. With Alessia around, my control is waning.

Already, in such a short time, she's threatening the years of self-control I've worked on. Kenisius overestimated my restraint, but the moment he saw my eyes shifting, he finally realized I was serious about my control slipping.

He also knows I'm drawn to Alessia.

He'll want to talk to me. Check on me. But I don't need him right now.

Unfortunately, I need Fern.

I hate that I need her. I hate that I keep her tucked away in my mother's old wing. It's starting to feel like the place I keep all my dirty secrets—my plants, my family history, my human, and much of my trauma.

As much as I love my mother—even in death—I hate her for what she did. For what she made me. I've always had trouble separating hate from love, both emotions intense, devastating in their own way. And now, I'm doing it again.

With Alessia.

I hate her for what she is and what she can do to me. But dare I say, the line between hate and love is getting thinner and thinner. I'm doing a poor job at pushing her away. Or she's doing a better job at pushing her way into my heart.

My blood heats up, and my eyes flicker. I'm on the verge of falling apart, and I don't need a mirror to see the change occurring in my irises. It's the telltale sign. My senses enhance, too, and I can smell her from this distance. Not just Alessia, but Fern too.

Both of them.

Their humanity is impossible to ignore.

One of them I want, crave, in a way that will end in devastation. The other, I don't want at all, but I *need*.

The plants reach for me as I enter the old wing. Bowing almost, as if they know I'm their master.

A few fiddle-leaf figs as tall as me stand strong and healthy. Their leaves a robust green.

Those figs should be dead. They *were* dead. I killed them. Denied them water for weeks. Burned them until they were nothing more than ash. Yet here they are, a day later, as healthy as can be.

I suppose it won't matter if I don't water them, after all.

Cursed things.

I never should've poured my magic into them, desperate to understand the curse coursing through the woods. Desperate to learn how to undo it. I'm only making it worse.

The plants might be alive, but they're tainted.

I ruin everything I touch.

I should embrace my demon, give up on searching for a way to break the curse, but it feels much like giving up in general. It's almost symbolic of my relationship—or lack thereof—with Alessia at this point.

A terrifying growl rips through me.

The last few inches of my resolve shorten. I curse, snagging one of the empty pots from the walkway and chucking it at the library's closed doors. It shatters, ceramic raining down in chunks.

On cue, a door on my left opens and Fern steps into the hallway hesitantly. She's dressed in nothing more than a robe, gazing at me with sleepy eyes.

"Rai?" She calls to me in that grating voice of hers. Her eyes flit to the figs, and when she sees the rage on my face, she stumbles back, desperate to put distance between her and them.

She's wise to fear them. Fear *me*.

It's proof that whatever thread ties me to Alessia isn't just a matter of being drawn to her humanness. Alessia doesn't fear me innately.

"I wasn't expecting you," Fern says, forcing a smile.

"I can't promise I'll be gentle," I say through gritted teeth. "Not this time."

It's my way of giving her an out, letting her know I can find another way to deal with what's plaguing me.

Her eyes dash to the windows, checking that it's still daytime, then back to me. She's too easy to read.

Normally I only call on her in the night. And not every night either. Never in the day when someone might witness. Not even here, in the wing everyone is banned from.

Everyone except Alessia, apparently.

I didn't ward it or scare her off the way I should have the other night. I let her stay in my mother's library. I *told* her about my mother. Part of it, at least.

The thought of Alessia does it. My last thread snaps and I charge at Fern. Her eyes go wide.

"I can handle it," she says.

My hands wrap around her throat as I press her against the wall, too undone to even make it into the room. I can't help but scoff at the irony that the things I hate most lately—the reminders of my curse—are all plants.

Fern is named after a gods-damned plant.

If the gods still exist, they find humor in torturing me.

Because Alessia? She is beauty and pain wrapped into one.

She's my little rose with buds so beautiful and thorns so fatal.

Afterwards, I bathe, washing the guilt and disgust from my skin. I can't change who I am. As much as I'd like to.

I pace my mother's library, wanting to be away from everyone. Fern is recovering, and facing Alessia is something I can't do until

I settle down. Seeing her in this state of self-loathing will do our budding friendship no good.

I wonder if Alessia would accept me if my exterior reflected the true ugliness inside of me. Would she see me for the beast I truly am? Or would she see past that, and still manage to find the beautiful parts of me?

"Sir," a buzzy voice calls.

I spin around, catching sight of one of the pixies. Smaller than my head, it floats about a foot in front of me.

Closing my eyes, I rub my temples.

"Go on," I say.

"The boy is at the border. The messenger. He brings word from Dovenak."

My eyes whip open. The pixie has my full attention. They like to flit around the Gleam, drawn to the abundant magic there. Something about the vibrant colors mesmerizes them. And somehow, they are left unbothered by the woods.

Given their tendency to gossip, and their ability to fly at incomprehensible speeds, I often use them as messengers to communicate with the humans.

"No letter?" I ask.

It's how the human queen and I prefer our correspondences—sealed letters protected from private eyes and gossipy pixies.

"He says he would like to speak to whomever is in charge, sir."

I blink slowly, wondering who he is to demand to speak with me. Then I imagine it's some sort of trick, a way to try and attack me or my land.

"Does this boy have a name?"

"I didn't ask, sir."

Turning away from the pixie, I contemplate the situation.

Given he's the human's messenger, it's very likely he lives close to the Gleam. Just as Alessia did. And if he knows anything about her, or where she came from, well, that is information I want.

"Tell him to remain in place," I say to the pixie. "I'm on my way."

First, I need to find Kenisius and Viveka.

A short while later, the three of us make it through the forest. I instruct Kenisius and Viveka to stay in their animi forms, hidden away in the bushes. With me nearby, the forest won't dare touch them.

I trudge through the clearing toward the Gleam. It's no more than a translucent shimmer in the air. A ripple in space and time where two realms converge.

How unfortunate that it leads to the humans of all beings.

And that it's on *my* property.

"He's over here," the pixie squeaks out. Its wings beat tirelessly behind its tiny body, as it flits in and out of the Gleam, disappearing and reappearing. "Over here!"

"Is he alone?"

"Yes!"

I scan the perimeter, wondering what his angle is. The humans are not to be trusted.

"Have him enter."

The pixie hums in response and flits through the Gleam once more. I don't expect the messenger to agree—normally it's the idiot soldiers and spies crossing through, not a mere errand boy—but a moment later I'm left surprised.

A boy about Alessia's age, only a few years younger than me, steps through.

His skin is a burnished brown, his hair tight and curly to his scalp. With wide eyes and shaky hands, he stares at me.

"You requested a meeting?" I drawl.

"Y—yes."

I can practically smell the terror radiating off of him. A whisper of wind works its way through the trees, as if they, too, can smell it.

Gritting my teeth, I quickly wonder if this is a waste of time.

"Get on with it, then."

He clears his throat, eyes zeroing in on my face. "You're the one who—mutilates them?"

"You're the one who finds them?" I counter.

Neither of us says anything further for a moment. Clearly he knows—or *thinks* he knows—what I'm capable of. And I realize he can stomach much more than he might be letting on.

"I don't suppose that's what you came to ask." I glance at his empty hands, which clench and unclench at his sides. "I haven't received a letter from the queen in weeks. I don't suppose that's why you're here?"

He shakes his head. "Haven't received anything new."

"Well then?" I cross my arms, letting the annoyance settle on my face.

Again, he clears his throat. Standing up a little taller and finding his confidence.

"A girl crossed." He raises a hand up around shoulder-height. "About ye tall. Unruly hair. Lots of curls. So blonde it's almost silver. I—" He swallows and glances away before looking back at me. "Her body was never sent back."

Alessia.

Ah.

Perhaps this little venture wasn't such a waste after all. It would appear our messenger does know my little rose.

"And who might you be?" I ask, with an air of disinterest as I inspect my nails.

"Felix," he says.

For a second, it's impossible to hide my surprise.

Her unskilled lover, she revealed while high on moonberries.

The bushes rustle a short distance to my side, and I know it's Kenisius in his bear form, likely finding humor in this exchange.

A dark smile crosses my face as I take Felix in. He has a pretty face, nice shape to his muscles, and despite his initial fear when he arrived, he still crossed into Avylon—alone.

All to request Alessia's *body*?

"She crossed many weeks ago," I say in a lethal tone. My eyes narrow, and I feel them flickering—darkening into their cobalt warning.

"So you saw her?" he asks, perking up. "Is she—?"

It takes me a second to speak, I'm so stunned at his audacity.

"You spent weeks…waiting around…for me to return her *dead body* to you?"

He chews his bottom lip. "I was hoping she would return."

"And when she didn't? You never thought to—well, I don't know, find her?"

Glancing past me, he eyes the forest nervously. "I value my life."

No matter how *brave* he is to appear before me today, this boy is as spineless as they come.

"You value your *life*." A sarcastic laugh escapes me. "Of course you do."

Images of Alessia on her first day here flit through my mind: tangled in the vines deep in the woods; the slices criss-crossing her feet from her barefoot run; wincing when she woke from her slumber, backside aching with unseen wounds; flinching away from me and Kenisius the first few days; wrapping her arms around herself, trying to make herself smaller.

I don't know exactly what treacherous things she ran from, but I am willing to bet this coward played a hand in it—intentionally or not.

He expected her to die. The thought is enough to send fire through my veins.

It was such a given to him, that he hadn't even bothered searching for her or asking after her sooner.

But she *survived*.

And beyond that, she is thriving.

All plants have a chance to grow when provided a proper environment. And whether she realizes it or not, Alessia's environment is here.

In Umbra Court.

With *me*.

Human or not.

New images replace the painful ones: Alessia angrily challenging me; throwing creams and oils out the window at me—knocking me in the head; making Das Celyn laugh; sticking up for Fern; training with Viveka and Kenisius; trying a doughnut for the first time; listening to me talk about my *mother*.

Something inside of me erupts, and I stalk toward Felix.

I'm before him in the blink of an eye. He doesn't have a chance to respond as I grip him by the neck, cutting off his oxygen.

"How dare you assume Alessia is so weak that you'd given up entirely on the prospect of her survival," I spit.

My words are ironic, considering I once thought the same. But I hadn't known her then. And he supposedly *knows* her. Rage engulfs me. A small part of my anger is likely misplaced. Perhaps it's anger at myself, for also assuming so little of her.

But he deserves the reckoning coming his way.

I drop the boy on the ground.

He coughs and gags, rubbing his throat. Quickly, he pulls himself to a stand, widening his eyes at me.

"I never told you her name," he says hoarsely.

"Oh, but she told me yours." I grin. "She told me all about how selfish you are. How you're unable to bring a woman even the most simplistic forms of pleasure."

It's a gross exaggeration, but based on the way Felix's face contorts with shock, then anger, and finally settles on disgust, it was worth it.

"You're fecking her," he says, shaking his head. "You gods-damned monster!"

He charges at me, but I'm quicker.

Swiftly, I pull a blade from my pocket, flicking it open. I press it against his throat, stopping him in his tracks. My other hand grips the back of his neck, holding him in place.

When he swallows, his skin presses against the blade a bead of blood appears.

"I never denied what I am, but I also never denied what Alessia is capable of."

I let go of his neck, grasping his wrist instead. He doesn't even fight me. Just stands there, petrified. It's laughable, really.

"Your hands might not have put those marks on Alessia," I say, "but they did nothing to protect her, either."

"What marks?" he whispers.

I scoff. "You will never touch a woman again. Not for pleasure. And certainly not for pain."

Before he can react, I bring the knife down on his wrist, slicing through flesh, bone, and tendon as if it's cake—tender and moist. With the blade made of faerie iron, it meets no resistance.

His hand hits the grass with a *thud*.

It's instantaneous.

Blood spurts from the stump of Felix's wrist before he realizes what has happened.

A moment later, the pain hits and he screams in agony.

The metallic, tangy scent of human blood hits the air and my face scrunches. My eyes flicker, holding their cobalt form. I had intended to slice *both* hands off, but leave the boy with his life. In case Alessia truly does care for him.

Or incase she wanted to seek her own revenge.

But as the blood stains the grass beneath us, a long, animalistic growl rips from my throat. My body grows hot, as if I'm burning alive. And I need it to stop.

Need it to—

I lunge at Felix.

No longer myself.

Giving myself over fully to—

Crunch.

Something slams into me, pressing me into the ground. Claws press down on my hands, breaking my bones with their weight.

A black nose and furry face hover inches above me.

When the bear roars, it blasts hot air into my face, momentarily snapping me to reality.

Distantly, I hear Viveka's voice telling the boy to run and not come back—not ever.

I squirm and wiggle, trying to wrestle the bear and break free. But Kenisius doesn't let me go. His weight continues to hold me down, crushing me, breaking bone.

Viveka's face comes into sight, drained of all color. "That's enough, Ken." She rests a hand on the bear's shoulder. "We need to leave. The trees smell the blood. And in that state—" she glances at me, frowning. "He can't protect us."

The bear grunts in agreement.

"We need to get him to Eoin," Viveka responds.

As if this day can't possibly get any worse, now I have to see my nemesis.

Nineteen
Help Me, Please!
Alessia

The last six weeks or so, I've stayed busy with training. The sessions are only a few hours long in the mornings. We've progressed from bodyweight to strength training with boulders, logs, and iron. But still no weaponry work yet. Sometimes the sessions are so brutal I spend the rest of my day eating and sleeping. Recovering.

My clothes are starting to fit differently, hugging my developing curves. There are hints of muscles along my body. Though I'm no stranger to labor and activity, this is the first time in my life I've been able to eat enough to support new muscle growth.

Putting on muscle requires eating in a surplus, Ken informed me, which is quite all right with me. The extra doughnuts I've been indulging in are a delight.

It's crazy what eating *more* can do for one's mind and body.

Though my debt is officially paid to Rainer, on days when I have enough energy to be useful, I tag along with Das Celyn, cooking and baking. It's therapeutic. Best of all, I can sometimes convince Das Celyn to take meals with me. They've been eating more, and their mood reflects it. They have more patience, more color in their cheeks. And when Das Lulu is around, we even smile and make jokes.

It reminds me so much of my time with Char. My heart still aches at the loss, and I'm not sure it'll ever stop aching, but it's becoming more manageable. I'm learning to swim through the waves of grief.

Ever since I made a fool of myself with the berries, I've barely seen Rainer. We almost kissed. *That* I'm sure of. Or rather, I almost kissed him. But I'm not sure if I hallucinated the attraction between us.

Perhaps it was one-sided.

I've continued to dream of him, which is a nice change of pace from the nightmares I had before. But whenever I actually see him in real life, he glares at me. That's if he doesn't swiftly exit the room and dodge me altogether. That's what makes me think I imagined his softer side. I'm a fool for it.

Even with Rainer reining in his hospitality, I can't believe I've been here just shy of two months already. I can't believe how at home I'm starting to become here.

Today, I dress in black tights, a fitted earthy-green tunic, and my training boots. Parting my ashy curls down the middle, I braid each side into its own long tail, tying the ends with a thin strip of cloth. When I'm done, I peek at myself in the mirror.

The girl reflected back at me in the gold-rimmed mirror looks like a stranger. Her forehead is relaxed, no longer marred with worry-lines, her grey eyes softer. There are no longer dark half-circles under her eyes, and her skin radiates a healthy peach coloring, sprinkled with light freckles.

She looks younger, happier, healthier.

I certainly feel it, too.

I'm still exhausted, but in a different way, a better way, and my new lifestyle is reflected in my appearance. Training outside in the fresh air each morning is good for me. Making friends—if that's what I can call them; I've never had friends beside Char and Felix—is a new comfort. The nutritious meals with a plethora of fruits, vegetables, and proteins really benefit my body. The sleep and abuse-free environment benefit my mind.

If this short time has been so good to me, I can't imagine what living here permanently would be like. The more time that passes, the harder I expect it will be to leave. But I shake the thought off. I don't belong here, no matter how comfortable I am at the moment. The point of staying, training, is to grow strong enough to forge my own path forward. Whether I want to return to Dovenak and seek my vengeance on the lord and lady, or continue my search for peace in Avylon, I don't know yet. But either way, that decision belongs to me.

Rainer, despite his rudeness, has truly given me a gift I cannot repay—the gift of my own life back. A place to thrive and grow.

But I know I cannot stay here forever.

When I make my way out to the manicured section of the lawn for training, I spot Viv and Ken waiting for me. Next to them are four different sized boulders ranging from the size of my head, all the way up to the size of a carriage wheel.

I suppress a groan. "Are you really going to make me carry boulders again today?"

"We're working on strength," Viv says.

She does a little shimmy, shaking her chest in joy. The clouds break, and sunshine peeks out, glittering off her feathery white hair. It appears almost translucent.

"Carrying them, kicking them, pushing them," Ken says. "Do what you gotta do, little human." He claps his hands together excitedly.

"Ken's thrilled about this workout, and he's in rare form today," Viv warns. "We have a spot in the grass marked off, see the rope on the ground there?" She points over next to a rose bush at the edge of the garden, where a rope sits stretched out on the ground. "You're going to start with the smallest boulder. Get that boulder all the way down to the rope, bring it back, move to the next largest and repeat, until you've completed the task with all four."

Sounds easy enough in theory. I've done enough labor at the lord's estates—carrying water-filled buckets, rearranging the furniture, carrying the lady's packages to her chambers. I'm fairly confident in my own strength. The first two look small enough to carry without too much trouble, the third and fourth look difficult.

I grin, rubbing my hands together. "Let's do this."

"First run is to get a feel for it. We'll see how fast you get in the following weeks. Think of this as a way to gauge your strength and speed over time."

It was a mistake thinking the task would be easy.

The first boulder is a lot heavier than I expected, and though I can pick it up, I move a lot slower with the extra weight. My arms strain to keep a grip on it, and I'm winded by the time I make it over to the rope. I drop the boulder, letting it fall heavily on the grass. Using the hem of my tunic, I wipe the sweat from my forehead. Luckily the sun is still crawling up from the East, and the house blocks a lot of the direct light, offering me a bit of reprieve.

After I get through the first boulder, I can barely keep a grip on the second. With each run, I'm slower and slower. I have to push the last two—even opting to scoot on my arse and push with my feet for a bit, to give my arms a break.

"Use those legs, little human!" Ken cheers, picking blackberries from a bush in the garden and flicking them up with his thumb, in a high arch, before tilting his head back and catching them in his mouth. He grins at me with purple-stained lips that match his berry juice-covered fingers.

"Keep your core tight! Don't put your back into it." Viveka has her hands cupped around her mouth as she barks instructions from my side.

I grunt a reply, focusing on finishing. I don't know how much time has passed, but the shade is slowly diminishing as the sun makes a surprise appearance.

When I finally finish, soaked with sweat and trembling, Viv and Ken run up to each other, jumping, and bumping their chests together with a celebratory yell.

Letting my legs give out, I flop onto my back, squinting up at the bright sky. I close my eyes for a moment, to relax, but a stream of cold water trickles onto my head.

I yelp, jolting into an upright position. Ken slaps his thigh in laughter.

"Stay hydrated," he says, before handing me a glass of water. He holds an empty pitcher in his other hand.

"I can't drink it if you dump it all on me." I pretend to scowl at him, but I can't deny how refreshing the sensation of cool water on my sweaty scalp is.

"You did well," Viv says, coming to sit next to me. I have no idea how they wear their leathers all the time. It's not that hot, but the physical activity definitely makes it a few degrees warmer. "You have good form. The speed and strength will come with practice. We'll give your body time to rest, and then the day after tomorrow we will start our rope climbing drills."

"Rope climbing?"

"Yup. We hang ropes from both the trees and the perimeter wall. We'll teach you how to rappel and how to free-climb. All in good time. It's all upper body strength, really. As you build more muscle, it'll get easier."

I contemplate that for a moment. That could be a useful skill, especially if I decide to seek my revenge on the lord and lady. Perhaps I can rappel out of a window and disappear into the night without being caught. I like the idea. I'm still holding out for learning weaponry, as that will be my best advantage though.

My fingers ache to wield steel like Viv.

"Aren't you warm?" I ask, gesturing to her outfit.

With the slivers of sunshine, it's much warmer today than usual.

"Enchanted fabric baby, it's cooling," Ken says.

Viv chuckles. "The gear is spelled to reappear when we shift back into fae form, too. Otherwise, we'd be stuck nude."

"I wouldn't complain." Ken purrs at Viv.

"You goon." She pushes his shoulder, rolling her eyes.

"Where were those clothes the day we met?" I ask, feigning shock. "I could've gone without seeing your" —what was it that he called it?— "your *tallywacker*?"

Viv's eyes crinkle with tears as she laughs. "Ken!"

Meanwhile, Ken looks proud. "Hey now. I'm perfectly comfortable in my skin."

"No wonder the poor girl was so shy when she got here."

A sense of pride builds in my chest at Viv's words. She used shy in past tense, as if I'm finally growing past the timid girl that arrived here a short while ago.

"Do you have energy left to work on combat stances?" She asks, taking charge of the conversation before Ken gets too carried away.

I'm exhausted, but there's no way I'm admitting that. I bob my head up and down enthusiastically as I down the last of the water, dribbling some onto my tunic.

We go over footing, proper arm positioning, and how to keep the core engaged—foundations of combat, as Viv says. Ken, despite being a goof, is extremely knowledgeable on the topic and a great coach. His patience and enthusiasm are contagious, and he always roots for me even when I'm a failure.

We take another water break. Viv and Ken take the opportunity to talk through their own drills for their shifts in the woods. I still don't know much about the woods, other than the fact that the trees are cursed and cause people to hallucinate their worst fears. They don't talk much about it in front of me, and I don't bother them about it. Usually, I'm filled with questions related to training. It's extremely kind that these two busy warriors take time out of their morning routine to train me daily. They don't owe me anything, yet they give me their most precious gift—their time. I figure it's best not to impose any further or demand answers that don't belong to me.

I'm sure a day will come when I decide it's not enough, but for now, I'm content with the gifts they give me.

Once we finish up for the day, I lay on my back in the grass, catching my breath. Viv and Ken talk animatedly off to the side of the castle, leaving me to recover.

Finally, when my lungs no longer burn and I have the energy to stand, I wander over to the stone wall guarding the entire property. It's thrice as tall as me. When I first arrived here, I thought the wall was to keep prisoners like me in. I don't think that's the case anymore. At some point, I stopped looking at myself as a prisoner. And now, I realize the wall is designed to protect the Umbra Court—to keep the woods at bay and those in the castle safe.

The wind picks up, rustling the bushes.

"*Alesssssssssia.*"

Pausing, I question if I really heard what I think I heard. I look around the bushes at the base of the wall, but there's no one there.

Maybe I'm hearing things.

I spin, eyeing Ken and Viv who are still talking passionately, both flailing their arms around animatedly. It wasn't them. Maybe I didn't hear anything at all.

But then my name is whispered again, barely audible.

"*Alesssssssssia.*"

I scan the yard, searching for the origin. It's a faint, whisper, drawling out my name, almost like the sound of whistling wind, except, the leaves over head sit still, no sign of a breeze.

Coming from…where exactly, though? The other side of the wall?

"Nope," I mutter to myself.

I learned my lesson the night Rainer saved me. As much as I hate that he had to rescue me, I'm secretly grateful he was there. Who knows what could've happened had the shadows got me.

"Forgive me for lying," the wind whispers.

A chill takes over my body and I freeze.

"Forgive me, my Alessia."

Char's last words.

My resolve snaps and I search for a way over the wall. The iron gate is further down, closer to where Ken and Viv are. I don't want them to see me peeking into the forest. And that's all I plan to do—get a better look.

A sturdy willow tree with low hanging branches stands a few yards to my right. I head over, trying to hoist myself up onto the low branch.

After my training session, my arms are as pliable as cooked noodles. I struggle at first, using the tree's trunk for foot support as I shimmy up. It takes a few tries but I successfully lift myself onto the thick branch.

I make my way up, scooting just a touch higher through the branches, until I'm level with the wall. Carefully, I crawl to where the branch meets the wall, parting the droopy, thick curtain of willow leaves.

I don't see anybody, or anything on the other side of the wall other than a very normal looking forest packed with trees of all sorts. Trees full of leaves and life and greenery.

As I prepare to scoot back to the willow's center, and descend the branches, something catches my eye.

A dark, shadowy figure standing by the tree line.

As if it sees me, it begins to lengthen—forming into a taller shadow, until it takes on the silhouette of a faceless human. Not quite opaque, but definitely a dark shade of grey, almost black. It reaches out, with a wispy, gaseous arm, as if it's beckoning to me.

The face begins to morph into something familiar—something that resembles Char. But I know it isn't her. Terror courses through me as I scoot backwards. The arm continues to extend, reaching out to me. The shadow grows impossibly long as it lengthens and weaves its way toward me.

"Agghhhh!" A scream rips through my throat as I scramble back, losing my footing completely and tipping out of the tree.

I slam into the ground so hard my bones rattle.

The air escapes my lungs and I gasp. Fire shoots up my spine, the pain blinding.

Help me, I try to cry out, but the words won't come. Somebody, *help me, please!*

Twenty
I Hope He's Harmless
Alessia

My lungs plead desperately for oxygen. I choke in raspy breaths, but no matter how much air I suck in, it's not enough. And with each expansion of my lungs, my ribs and spine scream in pain.

Then, the pain goes silent. Fading away.

But I can't move.

My legs and arms won't work.

A tear slides out of the corner of my eye as I gasp.

"Help!" I call out, my voice finally working. It's raw, desperate. "Please!"

I continue to cry, shamelessly screaming for help until there's a soft patter of boots on grass as someone runs toward me.

"Gods!" Ken yells. In a flash, he's standing over me, looking the most serious I've ever seen him. He turns his head, barking out an order to Viv who has appeared at his side. "Get Rainer!" I think he grabs my hand, but I don't know because I can't feel it. "It'll be okay, little human."

Viv runs off, and Ken's head continues to whip around, searching.

He mutters profanities under his breath, his face crumpled. I've never seen the shifter so distraught.

Over and over again he continues to tell me that it'll be okay. That I'll be fine.

But I don't believe him.

"Don't move her!" an unfamiliar voice calls out.

I hear someone bolting across the grass, but I can't turn to look.

"She fell hard," Ken says with concern. "Straight onto her little human back."

I wait for a smart remark from Ken, to distract me, but nothing comes. That's how I know it's bad.

A male I've never seen before leans over me, popping into my sight. With concerned honey-brown eyes, and curly golden-kissed hair, he's less severe in appearance than Rainer. Sweeter, more boyish looking.

His pointy ears peek through his curls, letting me know he's also a faerie.

"That was quite a fall," he murmurs. "Hold on." He looks me over. "Can you feel this?"

"Feel what?" I rasp.

He shares a look with Ken. "How about this?"

"No," I whisper. "I feel nothing.

"It'll be okay," Ken repeats. "Tell her. Tell her she'll be fine. She's talking. That's a good sign, right?"

My eyes squeeze shut as I try to hold back the tears threatening to fall. I realize what nobody wants to say: I'm paralyzed.

I'm alive, but I will never again be okay.

As I'm processing what this means, my body begins to tingle. A warm, prickling sensation takes over as the feeling spreads through my veins. As it builds, the pain comes back. But not for long. The agony turns to discomfort, which slowly diminishes.

Until there's nothing left.

I can breathe fully, no longer hurting.

Carefully, I push myself up to a sitting position.

"Little human!" Ken says.

"Oh my gods. I can feel. I'm—"

The golden-faerie thuds to the ground beside me, face contorting with pain. He gasps for air, like he's choking. His body writhes and shudders, until he goes completely still, blank eyes staring at the sky.

"What's happening?" I ask Ken, alarmed.

Ken ignores me, wrapping me into a sweaty bear hug. "You're okay! You're okay, little human. I knew you'd be—"

I push away from him, dropping to my knees in the grass next to the male.

"We need to do something to help him, Ken!"

Ken nudges him with the toe of his boot. "He's fine."

"Fine?" I cry. "He doesn't look fine."

"He took your wounds."

"What do you mean he took them?"

"Eoin is an empath. He can heal, but only by absorbing the pain of others."

Eoin.

Panic courses through me as Eoin grits his teeth, his movement returning. I reach for him, but then I drop my hand, unsure of what to do.

Meanwhile, Ken seems entirely unconcerned.

"It'll pass." He must sense my uncertainty, because he pats me on the shoulder. "Eoin knows the price of his magic, little human. Give him a minute, and he'll be fine."

Sure enough, a moment later, Eoin gasps for breath, clutching his chest. He sits up and offers me a timid smile, as if he wasn't just dying in the grass.

As if *I* wasn't the reason he was dying in the grass.

"Are you all right?" I ask him warily.

"Yes. Are *you* okay?"

His voice is low and smooth. It warms my skin, like sunlight on a chilly day.

"Yes—yes I am. Tha—" I almost say *thanks to you.*

He cocks his head, his eyes boring into mine.

I clear my throat. "I appreciate you helping me."

Humor dances in his eyes. "My pleasure."

"More like *my* pain," I mutter. When he laughs, my shoulders relax. "I feel awful that you had to experience it."

He shrugs lazily. "I'm used to it."

"What did Ken mean—the price of your magic? Do you always feel others' pain when you heal them?"

"It's a balance." His eyes bounce between mine as he studies me. "Our magic always takes as much from us as we take from it. We give as much as we receive. In my case, I quite literally assume the wounds I heal. Luckily for me, I also happen to mend quite rapidly. It's no thing, really."

I wonder what other abilities fae possess, and what their payments are. It reminds me of what Rainer said a while back about the cost of his life.

What is Rainer's power?

What's *his* cost?

A beat of silence passes between us, and neither of us break eye contact until Ken clears his throat.

"I'm Alessia," I whisper.

"That's a pretty name. A pretty name for a pretty girl."

I'm about to burst from embarrassment and flattery. I bite my lip and glance away, just in time to see Rainer and Viv rushing our way.

"Eoin," Rainer says as he reaches us, without taking his eyes off me.

"Rainer. It's a pleasure to see you again. And so soon after fixing—"

"Much too soon," Rainer says.

"How's that hand?"

Rainer scowls, narrowing his eyes at Eoin.

My gaze flits to Rainer's hand in time to catch him flexing it at his side. I had no idea he was recently wounded. I wonder what happened.

To me, Eoin says, "I suppose my introduction's been stolen out from under me. I'm Eoin."

"Hi," I whisper, flustered by all the attention.

"Hi," he repeats with a kind smile.

"You healed her," Rainer says.

Warring emotions flit across his face, and I can't tell if he's annoyed or relieved.

"He did," I say. "I'm fine."

Eoin gives me a long look. "She's fine now, but she had shattered her spine."

"Her tiny, fragile, little human spine," Ken cries out. "I'm almost tempted to thank Eoin. Debts be damned."

"Me too," I agree.

Everyone chuckles—except for Rainer. My eyes meet his, and something sad crosses his face before he smothers it with disinterest.

My stomach sinks at his demeanor. It's almost like Rainer has two sides, and I can never tell which one I'm going to get.

Eoin stands, holding a hand out for me. I accept it graciously, allowing him to pull me to my feet. He doesn't immediately release me, and I catch Rainer staring at us with an odd expression. He glances down to where Eoin and I connect, and his jaw tightens.

Inexplicably guilty, I drop Eoin's hand and sidestep to put space between us.

"I didn't mean to cause such a ruckus," I say.

Eoin flashes a soft smile at me. "Nonsense. It's a good thing I was here for you." He winks and my stomach knots itself at the unwanted attention.

"Yes," Rainer says with narrowed eyes. "A good thing you were here—doing what exactly, Eoin? Lurking the grounds? I wasn't expecting you again until tomorrow."

Despite the attitude he's receiving, Eoin laughs. He jerks a thumb over his shoulder toward the flowers. "I was simply admiring the gardens, you know how much I appreciate a good garden."

"I'm well aware."

"The pixies are helping keep your roses alive, I see."

"Yes."

"You've yet to grow—"

"Where's your sister?" Rainer asks, crossing his arms.

Eoin grins at Rainer. "She won't be here until tomorrow." He turns to me. "If you enjoy flowers, you should come see the Infinite Gardens at Terra court."

"She'll pass," Rainer says. "My gardens here are plenty fine."

My cheeks heat. What's gotten into him?

Rainer's eyes narrow as he sniffs the air, slowly turning his attention to me. "You're bleeding."

"Well, I did fall out of a tree." I expect him to light up at my sarcasm, the way he does when I stick up for myself, but his jaw tics.

"Clean yourself up," he growls. His eyes darken a shade. "Now."

He darts away, leaving me with Eoin, Ken, and Viv.

"What's his problem now?" I ask, off-put by his demeanor.

My eyes track Rainer as he bolts across the yard and into the castle without looking back. I frown, not liking the coldness he's directing at me lately. Or maybe I'm simply holding out hope that somewhere deep down beneath his ribs, a kind heart beats.

It's my fault for romanticizing the fae prince.

"That's how he always is." Eoin shrugs.

"I don't think he likes you very much."

"It's jealousy. Mostly of the gardens I grow at Terra Court." Eoin's eyes flash with something like pity. "Yet he refuses to accept any help. With the flick of a wrist, our elemental fae could manipulate the earth, air, and water, create a perfect environment for those roses he tries—and fails—to grow. But, alas..." Eoin shakes his head. "Stubborn as a fool."

His bountiful gardens are perfect to me—overflowing with successful beauty—but I suppose it wouldn't matter if he couldn't grow the one he wanted most.

His mother's favorite rose, I surmise.

"Are you sure you're all right?" Viv reaches out a hand to brush my hair out of my face with a worried look of her own.

"I am."

"Good. It's easy for us to forget how fragile humans are sometimes. That was a sobering reminder."

It warms me that she and Ken care enough about my wellbeing. It's starting to feel like we're friends, and I hate that it took getting injured to see that.

Eoin steps toward me, scratching the back of his neck. His eyes crinkle around the edges as he smiles at me. He doesn't appear much older than me, perhaps around his mid-twenties, but that doesn't mean anything here.

"I'm truly grateful you're all right, Alessia," he says. He reaches for my hand again, bringing it up to his lips and planting a tender kiss on the back of it. I can't help the smile that grows on my lips. "I should catch up with Rainer, but I do hope we meet again under more favorable circumstances."

"Me too," I whisper.

He leaves the three of us, and I try to process what just happened. Falling, Rainer's attitude and rude departure, Eoin healing me.

"Rainer really hates me, huh?" I ask Ken, unable to shake it off.

As dramatic as it sounds, his attitude feels like a knife to the gut. It hurts almost as much as falling from the tree.

Ken sighs, rubbing his beard as Viv glances away awkwardly.

"It's not you," he says.

"Could've fooled me," I mumble.

"It's not." There's a pause before he continues, "Rainer is constantly in a battle with himself...with his inner demon."

I frown. "Yeah, well, everyone has demons."

"Do you ever free yours?" He asks. "Let them out? Let them win?"

I give him a puzzled expression, shaking my head. No way. That's where patience and self-control come into play.

"Then you're stronger than Rainer."

Stronger than...yeah right. I scoff.

"Sometimes he loses control," Ken says. "Loses the battle against himself. He keeps a safe distance away to protect others."

"That's not an excuse for being cruel to others."

"You're not expected to understand, little human, but things are different here. Yes, Rainer has his own internal struggles, but he is a well-respected ruler of the Umbra Court. He's in his position for a reason, and his reputation precedes him."

"A reputation of being rude?"

"Something like that." Ken grins. "He might not be all sweet and charming like mister Eoin, and he might not be as handsome and funny as me, but you're lucky you ended up here with him, rather than in the clutches of another. You might think he hates you, but he's quite fond of you."

He has a strange way of showing it. Especially with how he's pulled back ever since the moonberry incident. Then again, it sounds like Rainer's struggles have less to do with me and more to do with his own life. The entire conversation is awfully vague, and once again, doesn't answer any of my pressing questions.

"This is all I'm getting from you, isn't it?" I ask.

"Yup."

Viv speaks up this time, "It really isn't our place to speak about our prince at all. Ken threw you a bone."

I nod in acceptance, grateful for any tidbit of information I get. I also realize she called him *our* prince, despite being from Terra Court herself.

Ken gives me a coy look. "So, how about those climbing skills, eh?"

I crack a soft smile at him, grateful for the normalcy that's taking over.

"I wasn't trying to. There's—there was something over there." I point to the wall, the reason for my fall coming back to me. Now that the pain is gone, and I'm healed, fear seeps back into my heart. "Something dark, like a shadow. It called my name then morphed into a bigger shadow and—"

I realize how insane it all sounds, but Ken's smile melts away, replaced by a serious look. "Like the one you and Rainer saw a couple weeks ago?"

I nod, surprised that Rainer told him about that. But then again, Ken does guard the woods.

The two of them share a glance, and Viv nods in a sort of silent understanding.

Her dark skin begins to glow. In a few short seconds, she shrinks down to a smaller form. The beautiful, strong, warrior no longer stands before me. Instead, she's a snow owl with dark eyes, standing about two feet tall. The owl inclines its head at me—and I swear it winks—before flying up over the wall.

"Whoa."

I remind myself to breathe. This is a normal thing here, I can't freak out. But it is incredible to witness.

"Beautiful, innit?"

"Can shifters just… change into anything?" I ask.

All this time, and for some reason, I naturally assumed that both Ken and Viv were bear shifters. I hadn't realized there were other...forms.

He laughs, scratching his beard. "No. We each have a single animi form."

"She's an owl!" I laugh, covering my mouth with a hand. "I just—I hadn't expected that. It's still unbelievable to me." I pluck a twig out of my braid, trying to smooth back some stray hairs. Eoin had sad something about the cost of using magic. "What's the price of your magic?"

"We can't stay in our animi forms indefinitely. We need to spend equal time out of form as we do in form. If we stay too long, we lose sense of our faemanity—get it? Like humanity?" I smack my forehead playfully at his pun. "And if we don't turn back in time, we risk getting stuck in our animi forms."

It's hard to wrap my brain around. "Has that ever happened?"

"Not to me."

"Would you ever be able to return to your fae form again?"

He chuckles. "I would rather not find out."

A few minutes pass as we wait for Viv to finish scouting.

"Is it normal for the woods to call to us like that?" I ask, thinking of the night Rainer saved me from—whatever it was.

He gives me a contemplative look.

"No. It's not the woods." His honesty catches me off guard, and my brows raise. "This has nothing to do with the wood's curse. The trees make you hallucinate your fears. Things no one else can see. But the shadows? You both saw them that night. It wasn't a hallucination. It was a—well, we're monitoring the situation."

A chill overtakes my body and I brush it off. "Whatever it was, can it get in here?"

Ken shakes his head. "The grounds are warded. You're safe within the walls."

"Do you know what it was?"

He cocks his head. "We have an idea, yes."

"So it wasn't my friend," I whisper.

He rubs his beard, glancing at the wall guarding us from the forest. "Don't worry, little human, it's under control."

"What about the curse? Can you break the wood's curse?"

"We haven't been able to yet, no."

"Who cursed it in the first place?"

Ken glances at the castle, then back to me. "It was never meant to be like this."

Rainer.

Of course it was Rainer. Who else could it possibly be?

Now it all makes sense—why they call him the Prince of Fear.

I want to ask more, but Viv returns, shifting back into her regular form—fully clothed and all. Convenience of enchanted leathers.

She looks at Ken and nods, before offering me a small smile.

"Perimeter is clear. Wards haven't been breached."

Something unspoken passes between them. I know they're trying not to frighten me, but I can tell something is up by the way Viv's brows are drawn down towards her eyes.

"Are you sure everything is fine?"

"Yes." Her lips form a tight smile. She glances at Ken. "We should find Rainer and debrief."

She shoots me an apologetic look, but I don't blame her for not saying more in front of me. It's an understandable security measure, so I don't press her. I accept her answer, for now, and leave them to find the prince.

I'm starting to find the troubled fae prince safer than whatever lies beyond the walls.

He might be unpleasant, but at least he's harmless.

I think.

My stomach churns, unsettled.

Gods, I *hope* he's harmless.

Twenty-One
Up to My Innards In Conflict
Rainer

I lean over the desk in my father's old first-floor office, my back to the room as I face the windows. Out of all the rooms in the castle, this is the one I like the least.

It's the one that reminds me of *him*.

Unlike my mother's old rooms, which offer comfort, my father's old rooms contain fury and condemnation within its walls. Or I'm projecting again.

The leather-bound books and manuscripts decorating the floor-to-ceiling bookshelves are just that—decoration. Everything in here, from the shelves on two of the walls and the fireplace on the far wall, to the oversized desk in the center of the room and unwelcome red-velvet sofa are for show.

But I must meet with Eoin, and I'd rather not share my more precious and private spaces with him. That's what this room has become—a receiving space for the guests I don't much care for.

Fitting that unwanted business take place in an unwanted space.

Seeing Eoin near Alessia, healing her, flashing that disgustingly charming grin at her, it made me sick to my stomach with something I'm not used to.

Envy.

I'm jealous of the Terra Prince. For all the things he has that I don't. For everything he can be that I can't.

And now? For everything he can offer Alessia that I can't.

That earth faerie twit has a penchant for taking anything I'm fond of for himself.

The last thing I need is him cozying up to the woman I'm so drawn to.

I shouldn't lust after a human. I can't. It's…an impossibility that will only hurt us both. She's had enough pain in her life; she doesn't need me adding to it. Arguably, I've done a great job at avoiding her these past two weeks, ever since she straddled me in the gardens, high on moonberries.

Ever since I almost lost control entirely.

When she told me she wanted me, when she revealed all the good she sees in me, it almost tipped me over the edge of no return.

I avoid her in the halls, never getting too close. But at night, I'm the weakest. I'm lonely, and when I can't sleep, I crave her simple conversation. Her attention. Like a fool, I've waited in the kitchen every night over these past couple of weeks, just to watch her make her valerian tea from the shadows.

She's never sought me out. It's for the best. It means she doesn't crave my presence as much as I crave hers.

At least one of us is strong.

It *should* be me. I know better. I know the risk we pose each other, yet still, I watch her from afar every night, hoping she'll make a midnight appearance in the kitchens.

Maybe I refuse to push her away because for the first time in a decade I can sleep without nightmares. Not every night, but some nights. On those nights, it's her face that fills my subconscious. Her laughter and sparkling grey eyes allow me to relax and catch up on sleep.

I see her in my dreams, and by the gods, it's a glorious sight.

She offers me reprieve without even knowing it—an escape from my usual, recurring nightmares. I can't remember the last time I had good dreams, but ever since Alessia showed up, I've had sweet, enticing dreams about her. In them, we're entirely normal. Not plagued by my curses or the differences between us.

If only they were real. If only I could touch her like I do in my dreams.

And maybe that's why I push so much for her to find her strength. Because I knew I would crumble, that really, deep down, it's me that's weak and I need her to be strong when I can't.

There's a knock and the doors open with a creak behind me.

"Prince Eoin to see you, Prince Rainer," a servant says, before shutting the doors with a soft *click*.

I sigh, running a hand through my messy waves before turning around to face the Terra Prince. My jaw aches, the tension radiating into my head.

"I'm almost offended you chose to receive me in such a stale room," Eoin says with a grin that's much too friendly for my liking. He swipes a finger over the doorjamb. "This must be the only room in your entire estate with dust," he says, mockingly appalled.

"It was my father's." The words taste bitter on my tongue. "It's a fine room."

"Fine indeed, but not your preferred receiving room. One might think you're being unwelcome. That you don't want me here. It's no secret how you feel about your late father."

Eoin is wise enough to pick up on it. Good. Let him be offended.

"It's a shame considering how kind I've been toward you." His grin turns smug. "Healing your wounds and all. *That* is a debt unpaid, I'm sure you realize."

Shrugging, I pick up a decanter of wine and offer him a glass. He nods, and I pour us both a generous serving. We'll need it.

"The Iorworths always pay their debts," I mutter. "Now tell me, *why* are you really here a day early?"

Though, I know the answer to that. Cleary it's to scope out my court. It's a common fact he wants Umbra Court. He thinks I'm failing my people. Thinks that he could be a better ruler.

His ego is appalling.

"Why are you so fond of that human girl?" he counters, ignoring my question.

My eyes narrow as I throw back the glass of wine, reaching to pour more. He chuckles into his own glass and sips it without removing his gaze from mine.

I clench my teeth. "I'm not."

"She is a pretty little thing. Those soft, supple lips. Those braids you could just wrap around your fists." He squeezes his fists in the air, mimicking a tugging motion. "I get it."

Without warning, I chuck my glass at Eoin. He ducks, and it crashes into the door, dripping red wine and glass all over the carpet.

Eoin raises a brow at me. "I thought you weren't fond of her?"

"If I wanted to hit you, I would've."

"I don't doubt it. But I also don't doubt that the human is special to you. But the question is, why? And where is your other human? The redhead with the drinking problem?"

"None of your business."

"Oh, but I think it is." He steps toward me, a gleam in his sharp eyes. "It is my business when people from *your* city beg to move to Terra Court, complaining about the unruly forest. A forest we both know you could do something about."

I don't correct him about the forest—that I can't do anything about it. At least not yet. But it's my first time hearing about my citizens wanting to move to Terra Court. I keep the surprise off my face.

As far as fixing the curse, I've tried. I've transformed my mother's entire greenhouse wing into a magic experiment—trying and failing to enchant the plants only to practice calling back my magic. Testing the ways my magic moves through the plants, giving them sentience. But no matter what I do, nothing offers insight on breaking the curse in the woods.

I've even purposefully killed the plants, hoping that in death the curse would rot, too. They simply came back to life, as if nothing had ever happened. Even the ones relegated to ash.

The woods are a problem, yes, but it's my mistake to own. I've kept my court safe. I don't need Eoin sticking his nose in it. Nor do I need him sniffing around Alessia.

"This has nothing to do with either of my humans."

"No, maybe not, but it's another mystery that surrounds you, Prince of Fear. My sister might not demand answers, but the woods reeks of *your* magic. It's no coincidence you both deal in terror."

I simply shrug, as arrogant as can be, as if his words have no effect on me. "You came a day early to talk about trees?"

He gives me a toothy grin and mirrors my shrug. "Perhaps I missed my old friend and wanted to see the happenings at Umbra Court."

"I invited you for Ostara preparation—starting *tomorrow,* mind you—as a courtesy to your sister. I did not invite *you* to linger in my court," I say sternly. "And we are most certainly not friends."

I chuckle at the thought of us being allies.

"You know, my court is fond of humans, unlike yours. You should grant me the honor of taking Alessia back to Terra Court after Ostara. Maybe I'll look the other way when your people ask to move to my court."

He's giving me an out without being aware of it. This is an easy way to wash my hands of Alessia, without him even knowing he's helping me.

But the thought of him being near her, making her laugh, *touching* her—absolutely not. I squeeze my hands into fists.

Worst of all, is the thought of me not being *near* her. The mere thought alone feels like I'm being shredded from the inside out.

I can't part with her.

I'm a selfish bastard to refuse his offer. But I never pretend to be anything other. I told Alessia that I'm not good, nor am I pure, and I meant it.

"The girl stays with me," I say.

"Your intentions are worrisome, Rainer."

"As if yours are any better."

"Mine would truly be to help the girl, not harm her."

"She doesn't need your help."

"It didn't seem that way a little while ago. She would've been paralyzed without my help." He arches an eyebrow. "You think we don't know of the mortals that go missing inside your woods? Or worse, inside your castle walls? You think Viv is loyal to you?"

Anger rises inside of me. We plucked Viveka from Terra Court—she's one of their best warriors. I'm not disillusioned enough to think her loyalties lie with me. It was always a risk bringing her in. But despite that, I think Eoin is bluffing about how much Viveka tells him.

Especially considering how much his own sister keeps from him.

What he seems to be forgetting is that Viveka is an old friend of Kenisius's. Shifters have a loyalty of their own. On top of that, she hates unnecessary conflict, and we've never had any issues that require Terra Court's involvement. So she has nothing to report to Eoin.

"You lie," I say.

He smirks. "Whatever she doesn't tell me, the pixies do."

Gods damned pixies.

"This conversation is pointless. Whatever you think you know, you don't."

I swipe a new glass from my desk, fill it to the brim with wine, and sip it as he scrutinizes me.

A second later, Kenisius and Viveka burst through the door. It's a relief, to say the least. Another second alone with Eoin would've been agony. It's hard to understand why his court loves him so much, he's punchable at best.

Kenisius opens his mouth to speak, but he glances at the burgundy-red stain on the carpet, then Eoin, then back to me. He does a piss job of hiding the smirk budding on his lips.

Luckily, Eoin does us both a favor and dismisses himself. The servant will be waiting in the hallway, ready to show him to his rooms, so I'm not worried about him roaming.

As soon as he leaves, Kenisius speaks. "The shadow called to her again."

"And?"

"I flew over the forest to check," Viveka says.

"And?"

She clears her throat. "It was a shadow-spirit. Affirmed."

I pinch the bridge of my nose. Every day new problems seem to arise, and right now, Eoin is the smallest of them. The only thing worse than a cursed forest, is a cursed forest with a loose shadow-spirit.

"That's twice in a few weeks," Kenisius confirms.

"Yes," I say, huffing. "I realize this. How many did you spot?"

"Only the one," she says. "It dissipated before she could catch up to it."

"It knows Alessia," I mutter. "And she can hear their call."

"Should I send for Tynan?" Kenisius asks. "Have him round it up? We shouldn't wait to investigate the happenings in Shyga. What if there are more?"

Tynan.

My half-brother who guards the resting grounds for faerie spirits.

Another one of my many secrets, and the other bane of my existence—somewhere behind Felix and Eoin.

The last thing I want is Tynan *and* Eoin around, especially with Alessia here. I've already mutilated her dear friend Felix for simply not protecting her, and I'm starting to accept that I have no limitations on what I might do to protect her myself.

But Kenisius is right. This can't wait. My fingers tap against my thigh anxiously as I work to quell the fury at the base of my spine.

Nodding at Viveka, I give her the approval to find him. "Go."

She isn't aware Tynan and I are brothers—only Kenisius is—and it'll stay that way.

Without hesitation, she heads out of the room, likely to shift into her owl form and head to Shyga. It's a dark, ominous bog, leeched of all life, where the spirits of fae who've died linger, their souls tethered to the swamp.

Shadow-spirits are mostly harmless entities, but that's not the issue.

The issue is that they should be contained in Shyga, not roaming my forest. Not calling for my human. And as Shyga's guard, Tynan should've been the first one to inform me of this matter. If he hasn't noticed, that means he's been drinking again, and that's an issue.

I already deal with one alcoholic—Fern.

Two is two too many.

Kenisius gives me a sheepish look. "It's odd that it showed up shortly after little human did. That it calls for her."

"I'm well aware." Another reason I find the situation concerning. Especially considering Kenisius went to Dovenak—to her village in Lyson—and secretly gathered whatever information he could on her. "And we're certain the only people in her life who've died were human?"

She certainly smells human.

Kenisius nods. "Like I told you, her parents died when she was young. In a house fire. And her fellow Tradeling—the older woman, Charlotta Kimmen, according to the death certificate—died in a self-defense accident. In other words, the wife of their owner killed her. Makes sense why the little human ran."

My stomach roils at the thought of the man who dared hurt Alessia. I've been itching to drag him to the woods, hang him alive by his innards and watch the trees terrorize him. The only reason I haven't is because that's Alessia's vengeance, not mine. I refuse to steal her opportunity at revenge. She deserves to be the one to cut him down, to watch the life fade out of his eyes.

If she wants it.

"None of them were fae," Kenisius repeats. "To my knowledge, she didn't encounter any fae before us."

Then whose spirit could possibly be calling for her?

Kenisius interrupts my thoughts before I can dive too deep into the mystery. "One more thing."

I groan. "What now?"

"The human queen finally sent further correspondence. She's not playing nice anymore. She demands you reinstate the treaty."

"Of course she does."

Yet it's *her* people who broke it. *Her* people she's lying to.

He clears his throat. "She found out about—" he holds up a hand and waves it around. "Stumpy."

"I knew I should've cut his tongue out," I mutter.

"If I had known you were going to get so impassioned by the bloodlust, I would've stayed in fae-form and done it for you."

He pats me on the shoulder and I nod. Kenisius's loyalty is commendable.

The human queen's demand is gobshite.

Her little messenger technically stepped into my realm—he was fair game. But of course she wants the treaty reinstated.

I have more important issues than the safeguard she wants implemented to make her people feel safe about living near the Gleam.

Yeah, Kenisius stole letters between Lord Edvin and Queen Wyetta when he paid Alessia's old village a visit. And as always, the exchanged words revealed the exact reason why I hate humans. They're more concerned with money, power, and ego, than they are making an actual effort to mend the ripped edges between our realm.

Perhaps when I'm done solving my issues, I'll pay the human queen a visit, too, and make demands of my own. Ones revolving around her despicable Trade. Or better, perhaps I'll present a reminder of why her people fear mine so much. After all, there's no treaty to protect them. I can use my magic in Dovenak.

If I can keep this quiet enough, the faerie queen won't need to know what's going on between the realms. Considering it's my court that backs up to the Gleam and Dovenak, and my family—the Iorworths—who initially instilled the treaty generations ago, it should be my problem to deal with anyway.

No need to involve our queen. Honestly, she's more of a relic than anything, using her immense power as a last resort when absolutely needed. I've never even seen the woman. Only communicated with her through her wind-whisperer.

I smirk at the thought. Yeah, visiting the human queen myself sounds good. I might not be as powerful as our queen, but I'm more powerful than the humans. I'll do it. Once I'm not up to my innards in conflict.

Twenty-Two
Screaming His Name
Alessia

Little by little, thinking of Char no longer makes my stomach feel like a bag of bricks. The pain of grief is there, and I think it will always live inside me, but now it allows me to breathe.

It's loosened its grip on my heart.

I've allowed this new space to offer me a fresh start, instead of resisting it. It's made all the difference. I'm able to move forward, one foot in front of the other, without being haunted by the ghost of Char's movements and memories.

Or perhaps it was the whole falling out of a tree and basically breaking my back thing that shook me up. It made me realize how fragile human life is, just like Viv had said.

As I relax in bed, a whiff of clove and rose sifts through the air. It's grown comforting. Calming. Relaxing. I like the new familiarity of it. I focus on my breathing, staring at the dark ceiling overhead.

It's so quiet, almost too quiet. My eyes scan the dark ceiling.

Today proved, yet again, that without Rainer's manipulation holding me here, the woods are dangerous. I don't stand a chance of leaving on my own. But if Eoin made it here, visiting from another court somewhere beyond the walls, that means there must be a safe way to travel. He appeared kind enough, caring. Perhaps he would be willing to assist me with an escape—when I'm ready to go.

But maybe…just maybe, I don't want to go. Not anymore. It's the first time I've admitted to myself that it's more than staying for training or healthy meals. I'm starting to understand why Rainer is so rough around the edges. Though I know nothing much of his life or past, it's like Ken said: he battles himself. Battles demons that have nothing to do with me.

And that draws me to him. It's deeper than his appearance. It has called to me since I first met him, but now it screams louder, refusing to let me go, even when he pushes me away. There's no pressure to be something I'm not around him. It's easier to be damaged around others who are just as broken, than it is to pretend to be whole.

And Das Celyn with their "hate the world" attitude and refusal to eat? Rainer with his self-hatred and grief? Fern with her drinking problems and insecurities? We're different on the surface, but we're all the same deep down. We're all existing, trying to survive despite carrying invisible, fatal wounds—hurt hidden deep beneath our rib cages, haunting our hearts.

It doesn't matter *what* happened as much as it matters that we survived it. That we're all *still* surviving it, day in and day out.

When I first arrived, the fae made fun of me for being weak, but they're wrong. Fighting through mental and physical pain for years without reprieve has forged me stronger than anyone expects. They don't see my strength, so they assume it doesn't exist, but it's there. I've been forced to be tough for so long.

It's the same thing I tell myself every night as I rest my head: I am not weak. I am strong.

I'm fine, and it'll be fine.

But what if I don't want to be fine? What if I want to let my shattered pieces show, like Rainer does? Like Das Celyn and Fern do? They're not ashamed of their jagged edges. They don't hide them. Maybe it's time I do the same. Stop behaving like a human—like a Tradeling—and start acting like the fae.

I count backwards from one hundred, closing my eyes and shutting out the too-quiet silence.

Bright sunshine beats against me as I blink, adjusting. I hold up a hand, blocking out the rays so I can get a good look around me.

The castle's gardens spread out endlessly, like a sea of color.

I spot Rainer with a copper watering can, tending to a rosebush. My eyes roam over the blossoms. They're deep orange in the center, with a brighter, pinker tint on the edges of the petals.

"Those are gorgeous," I say on an exhale.

Rainer stops watering and turns to greet me with a smile. "Sunset roses. My favorite."

It's cute that he has a favorite flower.

"I can see why. They're quite lovely."

Rainer smirks, taking a step closer and gently snagging a lock of my curls between his fingers. He gives it a slight tug, and I bite my lip. The way he gazes at me, so full of awe and intrigue, it makes my heart flutter.

His dimples pop out, and I can't help but smile back at him. He's my comfort. My salvation after each day.

Too bad this Rainer doesn't exist.

Because, of course, I'm dreaming. I almost wish I didn't realize it was a dream, so I could lose myself into it that much more.

He releases my curl, letting his fingers trail over my shoulder and down my arm. Goosebumps rise in their wake.

I glance at him in wonder.

"My dreams are always sweeter with you, mo róisín," he says.

"I know," I say with a soft sigh.

If only I could bring him into my waking reality, swap him out for the real Rainer. At first I chuckle at the thought, then my heart pangs. Real-Rainer might not be as soft and sweet as dream-Rainer, but he doesn't need to be. It's his wounds, his tortured soul and conflicted heart that make him what he is. It makes the kindness he does offer that much more special.

"What are you thinking, Alessia?"

I smile at him. "I was wishing that dreams were reality." That I could keep both you and real-Rainer, but instead, I get neither. Bits of each, but wholes of neither.

"So was I," he whispers.

He gives me an indecipherable look. I step closer, reaching up to run a finger over the tip of his ear. His body relaxes under my touch, cold eyes blazing with heat, and I fight the urge to close the small distance between us and wrap my arms around him. My subconscious surely knows how to tease me with him.

I miss touch.

I miss being touched.

If it's only a dream. Why fight it at all?

I give in at precisely the same moment Rainer does. We move toward each other, and when we connect, it's with something more powerful than simple attraction.

He cups my cheeks in his hands, forcing me to look up at him, and I run my fingers through the back of his hair.

"I wish this were real, mo róisín," he whispers, leaning toward me. I think he might kiss me, but instead, he rests his forehead against mine.

His lips hover above mine tentatively, as if testing the territory. My stomach twists with a beautiful mix of nervousness and desire. His warm breath caresses my mouth.

Leaning into him, I press our mouths together. He groans, gripping the back of my head with a strong hand to keep me in place. His plump lips are so soft, so sweet, as we kiss desperately.

A fire builds inside me, unlike everything I'd ever experienced. I want more of him.

But the world around us goes dark. It shakes and shatters, everything around us crumbling as it disappears.

I wake with a start. My body is hot with desire and confusion, and my core aches for release.

Without giving it too much thought, I give in to what the dream started. My fingers travel down my body, lifting up my nightgown and slipping beneath. My back arches slightly when I find my tender spot.

Pressure builds—a mixture of blind need and pending release—as I imagine Rainer's head between my legs.

Moments later, as I tip over the edge, moaning softly to myself, the door flies open. Light from the hallway floods me, and I yelp.

"Human," Rainer calls. "We—" He freezes, his eyes wide as he catches me in the compromising position.

Frazzled, I yank my dress down and pull the sheets up around me, scrambling to cover up my naked lower half. But I know it's too late.

Glancing up at him, even in the dim light, I can see a flush coloring his cheeks. I'm sure it matches my own.

"I was just—" I say, at the same time he says, "I should have knocked."

He clears his throat, refusing to look at me. His eyes stay glued to the ceiling.

"What do you need?" I ask, anger rising in place of the mortification. He has no right to barge in during the night.

"I—nevermind. It can wait." His voice is thicker than usual.

Before I have a chance to press him, or scold him for his poor manners, he says in a strained tone, "stay in your rooms for the night. It's—not safe to leave the castle right now," and swiftly exits the way he came, slamming the door behind him.

"Unreal." I flop over, shove my face into a pillow, and groan.

Well, it could have been worse. I could have been screaming his name.

TWENTY-THREE

He's a True Nightmare

Alessia

The next morning, a beam of light bursts from behind my eyelids.

Cracking my eyes open, I inwardly curse at the sight of Das Celyn standing before the window. Tracking their movements with sleepy eyes, I wipe away a bit of crust with my sleeve. They move with purpose to the armoire, yanking out a dress and tossing it onto the bed where I sit.

Great.

As if last night wasn't terrible enough with Rainer walking in on me pleasuring myself—to thoughts of him no less—now I have to contend with Das Celyn instead of Ken this morning. I've grown rather fond of my training routine with the shifter.

"Get dressed," they say.

I take in the dress they chose—a frilly purple thing. "I can't wear that to training." A bit of humor bubbles up at the absurdity of the dress. "And what's with the attitude? I thought you were finally warming up to me."

"You're not training today." They cast me a stern face, ignoring my question.

"What? Why not?"

"We have guests and I need your help tending them."

"And I must wear a dress? *This* dress?" It's a straightforward question. I'm not pouting or throwing a fit about it, but Das Celyn, who is now rummaging through a leather bag, rolls their eyes all the same.

"You must be presentable."

"I'm presentable in pants."

They pull out a few various cosmetics, entering and exiting my bathing room swiftly and returning with a hairbrush and scented oils.

"No you're not. And honestly, I don't think the dress will be enough to help you either. At this point, only magic could help you."

"Ouch," I say, mockingly rubbing at my heart.

"Oh please. You know it's true." They gesture toward me. "Look at your curls! They're a knotted nest. Better suited for the birds than anything."

"That's… kind of mean." If I cared more about my appearance, their words might hurt. But I really could not care less about how I look. After living with the lord's wandering eyes and drunken touches, the last thing I ever cared about was being pretty.

Except… maybe deep down I do care.

A small wave of jealousy washes over me as I remember seeing Fern the first night I met her and Rainer. She looked absolutely stunning, confident. Maybe a small part of me wishes that, for once, I could care about my appearance, make myself pretty, and attract the attention of someone I like.

Like the prince.

Perhaps I could be the one pulling him into *my* room instead, living out my fantasies in reality instead of in dreams.

A blush paints my cheek and I chew my lip.

"Fine. Yes. I see where you're coming from."

"Then get over here." They pat the settee, clearly ready to clean me up and make me over. "I've been hoping to do this since I met you."

"What, insult me? You *have* been doing that since you met me." I hop out of bed and join them where they've set up their tools for making me over. I perch on the settee as they use their fingers to unknot my curls.

A rare smile crosses their lips. "No, fix your damn hair. I've been aching to tame those curls for you."

"That sounds an awful lot like you want to help me. Out of kindness."

"Don't get it twisted."

"Does Das Celyn have a heart?" I tease.

"This is a purely selfish act. It's only because I can't look at your raggedy appearance a second longer. It pains me."

"Whatever you say, but I think I'm starting to grow on you."

"Like fungus on an unwashed buttock."

A burst of laughter escapes me.

"You're growing on me, too," I say. "Everyone here is." I think about the kindness Ken and Viv have showed me. The care in Eoin's eyes yesterday when he healed me—despite being strangers to one another. "Except Rainer," I lie.

"Good thing he doesn't care about a measly human's opinion of him."

Thinking back to Das Celyn's rumbling stomach, and taking in their small frame, a surge of pity overcomes me.

But Rainer sent up food that day in the kitchen, the day we shared doughnuts. I suppose I'm desperate to know if the soft sides I've seen of him are real.

I *need* to know.

"Das Celyn, does the prince treat you poorly?" I whisper.

Their eyes narrow and they plant a hand on their practically nonexistent hip. "You think he treats me poorly?"

"I hope not." My hands twist in my lap. "It's just—I don't know. Nevermind."

They finish running their fingers through my curls. Then they put a bit of cream on their hands, rubbing them together, before returning to my hair. They yank a little too hard and I let out a yelp.

"Whoops," they say. "That was an accident."

"It's fine."

Another silence drags on.

"You didn't answer me," I say quietly.

"Mind your business, gal."

"If you need help, I can—"

"You can, what?" Das Celyn steps in front of me and leans down. We're so close that we're eye-to-eye with just a few inches separating our faces. I can smell the berries on their breath. "You think that you—a *human*—knows best? You think you know everything? That you can help everyone?" They shake their head, backing away while they mutter something to themselves.

"I didn't—" I don't know how to react to their outburst. I was only trying to help them. Steeling myself with a heavy breath, I say, "I don't know why everyone takes offense when I offer to help them, but where I come from, it's a kind offer. It's not meant to offend."

"Fern said you offered to help her, too."

"I did."

That was so many weeks ago, and though I've given up on thinking she needs the help, the offer still stands.

"Neither of us need your help, nor do we want it. Like I said, you know nothing. Just because you dislike the prince, it doesn't mean we all do. And he doesn't starve me, so stop flapping your lips about that."

Swallowing the knot in my throat, I shake my head. "I don't dislike him."

"Then stop digging. Let it go."

"It seems like I'll be here for a while." I wouldn't go as far to say this place is my home, but it's starting to become a lot better than where I come from. "I just wish he'd stop treating me like a—a—"

"Like what? Like a human?" Das Celyn smiles smugly at me, their annoyance from a moment ago washed away. They reach for a tin of cosmetics on the table beside me, rubbing a pale peach coloring on their finger before softly smearing it across my forehead and cheeks. "This is the tin you chucked at his head, by the way."

I scrunch my face, still embarrassed about that.

"Relax your face. Stop moving like that." I oblige, and they continue blending the color in. "Good aim, by the way."

"It was an accident," I mutter.

"So you didn't mean to hit him?"

"No—I meant to. I just didn't think I actually would."

Das Celyn covers their laugh with a cough and I chuckle. After a second, we both lose it, snorting with laughter.

They set the tin down, squatting down so we're eye to eye.

"Not all humans get laid up in such luxurious accommodations," they say. "Not all humans get the privilege of training with Viv and Ken—two of the most prolific warriors from the courts. Stop pouting and be grateful for what he's given you."

The words sink in, and I slowly nod. I see where they're coming from. The situation is a lot better than I initially had thought, when it's put like that.

"I am extremely grateful for that. But it's hard to call this place home when I'm so unwanted here."

Das Celyn snorts. "You *are* unwanted here. Yet here you are."

"Gee, great."

"At least you're learning." They pull back, tilting their head to the side as they eye their handiwork.

After a few beats of silence as they smudge kohl on my eyes, I can't help but saying, "Rainer likes Fern."

Das Celyn snorts so hard that I flinch. "Is that jealousy I hear?"

"What? No!" *Yes.* My cheeks heat as I think of my dream last night... and even worse, of Rainer walking in on me afterward.

"Well, *I* don't like Fern. Neither does Ken. Consider yourself at an advantage there."

My lips twitch at the admission from Das Celyn. Whether they realize it or not, they just admitted to liking me. At least in their own way. For some reason, it does little to soften the sharp pang in my heart at the idea of Rainer not liking me, though.

"Rainer doesn't much care for her either," they say, eyeing me curiously. "I've told you before: stop assuming things."

"Fair enough. But can I ask something else?" They grunt, and I take it as a reluctant affirmative. "Is Fern really okay? She seems..."

"It's nothing personal," Das Celyn says.

"No. It's not that." I chew my lip, glancing away. "I saw her take a pill."

Das Celyn surprises me when they step back and level a serious stare at me. "Fern struggles with her reality. She depends on substances to survive." They reach for a small tapered brush, leaning forward to dust a translucent powder across my skin.

"An addict?" My brows pinch with confusion.

"Stop wrinkling your face." Das Celyn grips my chin as they continue to work. "Something like that."

"She doesn't look like an addict."

Das Celyn purses her lips as she scrutinizes me. "And what do you suppose an addict looks like, huh?"

"I don't know. But she's so pretty—"

"You can't assume to know one's internal struggles based on their outward appearance." They grunt. "And you can't place someone's value solely on their beauty."

I wince, embarrassed. "Well, why does Rainer just let her live here and have access to the pills and wine? Isn't that feeding her addiction?"

"I don't see how that's your business." Das Celyn glances toward the door then lowers their voice. "But I'll do you the favor of explaining, so long as you let it go."

I nod.

"Fern would likely be dead without Rainer's help," they say. "She's addicted to the *magic* infused in many of our products—the wine, the moonberries, as I'm sure you recall." They give me a pointed look, and I know they're referring to the time I ate a few berries and tried to take Rainer's clothes off. I wish they didn't know about that. "She's consumed so much over the years that her body adapted. It now requires a certain dosage of magic every so often, in order to survive. If she quit entirely, her organs would shut down. At least here the prince can give Fern a safe space with periodic doses of magic to keep her heart beating."

My heart skips a beat as it dawns on me.

I thought Rainer was starving Das Celyn, but he was trying to feed them. I thought he was keeping Fern intoxicated, but he's keeping her alive.

I thought he was keeping me against my will, but this whole time, he's been giving me a will to live.

My lungs constrict and I ache to see him, ask if it's all true.

"How did Fern get here in the first place?" I ask.

"Again, not your business, and it would be wise not to traipse around running your mouth, but Fern's a changeling."

"Changeling?" I've never heard of that term before.

Das Celyn sighs and scrubs at their face with a hand. "Yes, Alessia. A set of fae parents swapped out their own babe with a human infant—Fern—and intended to raise her as their own instead."

My heart drops at the admission. The fae *do* steal human babies.

"And before you ask," Das Celyn says, "I don't know why they did it, or how they did it. Changelings aren't common, and it isn't my business. But typically," they lean in and whisper conspiratorially, "faerie parents swap out their sick babies for a healthy human. It's rare, but from the stories I've heard, it has happened before."

"So Fern was raised as fae?"

Das Celyn scoffs. "The fae aren't dense. They knew she was human, and humans aren't exactly welcomed around Umbra. She was targeted by her peers and neighbors as she grew up. As she got older, she turned to substances for comfort. An escape, if you will."

"Why didn't she go back to Dovenak?"

They look at me with narrowed eyes. "Why don't *you* go back to Dovenak?"

Point taken.

"I'm surprised Rainer wanted to help her."

"Oh don't be mistaken, he made a bargain with her." Das Celyn busies themselves with cleaning their powder brush and wiping their hands on their apron. "He receives plenty in return."

Once again, a blush takes over my cheeks. I don't care to ask what it is Rainer gets in return from Fern. It's clear as day.

She doesn't have to be his girlfriend for him to have sex with her. He doesn't even have to like her to enjoy her body.

The more I think about it, the more I realize that's all it was between me and Felix. Strictly physical. A distraction. A carnal need satisfied.

Despite the niggling jealousy at the thought of Rainer's hands on Fern, I can't blame her for accepting the bargain. They both get something out of the deal. It sounds mutually beneficial.

But I also can't help but pity Fern. I almost wish she'd open up to me. It's not like I've had many friends in my life, so I'm not sure I could offer her a true friendship, but everyone deserves someone who understands them. And I understand what it's like to never feel quite at home and to question if life is worth living.

I'll need to make a better effort to be her friend.

"Rainer might have a good heart, but he also has a thing for manipulation," I mutter. "With all those stupid bargains and deals and—"

They *tsk* at me. "We do things differently around here. Trust me when I say, that is the prince's way of showing kindness." They wipe some stray powder off my sleeve. "You keep trying to compare our world to yours, but the fae will *never* be human, as similar as we may be. Stop using your own experiences and culture as the baseline for normalcy."

I open my mouth to reply, but they cut me off.

"Don't bother asking more, either. It's personal, and not my place to share."

They help me into the frilly dress, straightening out the material and ensuring the sleeves sit right on my shoulders. They work in silence for a bit longer, until I can no longer bear the awkwardness. "How did you end up here?"

"Gods have mercy, you humans love to chat. I thought we were done with the questions? You'd make great company for the pixies." Das Celyn stares off into the distance for a minute before speaking again. "Rainer took me in. Saved me."

I nod softly, itching to ask for more, but not wanting to get on Das Celyn's bad side now that they're finally opening up to me.

Luckily, they continue with their story. "I was born weak. With very little magic. My parents were High Fae, but I was born with such little magic that I was not worthy of the same title. My parents could not bear the prospect of rearing a Low Fae. They thought a dead child would be better than no child, so they poisoned my plate one evening."

I gasp, my hand flying up to my mouth. "Das Celyn… I'm so—"

"Oh stop with the pity, human." They shoot daggers at me. "I'm fine now, aren't I?"

It makes so much sense now, why they refuse to eat. Food trauma. Their own parents attempted to murder them. My lungs constrict at the realization.

"Rainer hired me on for a hefty salary at a very young age, after I recovered. I worked hard, stayed loyal, and loved my job. I still do. After a few years, Rainer bestowed me with the coveted title of Das. It wasn't enough to outrank my parents, but it is as high as a Low Fae like me will ever rise."

"Did your parents accept you once you earned the title?"

"No. They were dead by then."

"Oh. What happened?"

"Rainer killed them." I choke on the air and end up in a coughing fit. "Drained them of their blood and left their meat for the trees."

My jaw goes slack. "That's—"

"The best thing that little bastard ever did for me." They smile, reminiscing. "Even better than gifting me the title of house steward and Das."

A tremble creeps through me. I had *not* expected the story to take that turn. And I suppose I hadn't realized how ruthlessly terrifying Rainer was. Nor did I anticipate Das Celyn's lax attitude about gruesome murder.

It's a reminder of how malicious the fae can be. How normal it is for them.

"Do you have any remaining family?" I know they do—I overheard Rainer send for them.

They grunt. "A partner and two young of my own."

Das Celyn is a parent, and after all our time together the past couple of weeks, I hadn't known. Guilt weighs on my shoulders. I should've asked. Gotten to know them. Instead, I've only worried about my own problems.

"How long ago did Rainer bring you on?"

"That was twelve years ago. When I was only eight."

"Rainer's only twenty-six though," I say, trying to put the timeline together in my head.

"Yup."

It doesn't make sense to me. How could someone so young make those sorts of decisions? How could someone... murder at that age? Where was his family?

"He was fourteen when he hired you? When he... killed your parents?"

"I told you, things are different here. Age doesn't matter like it does for you." Das Celyn looks me dead in the eyes and says, "And Rainer is no stranger to being a leader, nor a killer. He is better than you could possibly imagine, yes, but he is also worse than you could ever expect."

Despite the warm air, Das Celyn's words chill me to the bone.

They finish with, "If you ever cross him, well, he's a true nightmare."

TWENTY-FOUR

I Am the Girl Who Fights

ALESSIA

I am reeling after all the revelations Das Celyn gifted me with. About them. About Fern. About Rainer.

Maybe I fit in here better than I could've ever expected. And I wasn't wrong about everyone carrying their own trauma.

Das Celyn leads me downstairs. The purple ruffled skirts swish around my ankles, and the bell sleeves billow around my arms obnoxiously. With its sweetheart neckline, the dress is much more revealing than I'm used to, showing my collarbones and upper chest area. But with the excess of tulle and layered skirts, its smothering me.

My hair wraps tightly around my head in a sort-of braided crown, and already it's giving me a headache.

"I look ridiculous," I whisper to Das Celyn.

"You look clean for once," they hiss back.

We pass by the kitchen, and Das Celyn spots a few servants struggling to balance trays with a plethora of foods.

"For fae's sake," they mutter.

"What is it?"

"I step away for an hour to help you get ready and they fall behind."

The kitchen is much busier today, with every surface covered with food. Smoky scents fill the air, dancing with the lighter, sweeter scents of desserts. About a dozen fae run around, manning the various ovens and stacking fancy trays high with artful designs of fruits, baked goods, cheese, and meats.

"We got hands, Benjo," Das Celyn calls out to a flustered male who's barking orders around the room. There's no animosity in their voice, just acknowledgement. Turning to me, they say, "Grab a tray."

I try to ignore it, swallowing the lump in my throat. "What exactly is going on today?"

"The prince is hosting an important brunch between courts today." Das Celyn sighs. "I have much work to do, so if you're done with the irrelevant questions, let's move before Benjo puts us on slop duty. Grab a tray, bring it to the formal dining room, and get your scrawny buns back here and do it all again."

Slop duty doesn't sound like something I want to familiarize myself with, so I follow their lead.

Das Celyn grabs a tray right before one of the servants almost drops it. "Take this."

They thrust the silver tray hosting a pyramid of chocolate-glazed doughnuts at me, and I quickly accept it, careful not to let the pastries lose their balance.

"You want me to… serve this?"

They narrow their eyes at me. "What? You've been upgraded to training with the shifters and now kitchen work is beneath you?"

"No it's not that. I just—" I glance down at my fancy dress, confused. Lowering my voice, I whisper, "Why am I dressed like this?"

"It's customary to dress up when serving royalty."

My nose scrunches. I've never seen anyone dress up to serve Rainer. "I didn't get the impression—"

"Stop gabbing and let's go. We need to drop these off and get back here. Clearly the kitchen is struggling without me."

I don't miss the flicker of pride crossing their face at the thought of being needed.

We carry our trays down the hallway. I take it slow, careful not to let the doughnuts topple over. A few faeries pass, carrying a variety of trays and plates and pitchers, but none are dressed as elaborately as me.

My stomach pitches.

We enter the formal dining room. Flames flicker overhead from the ivory chandeliers, casting an orange glow around the windowless room. Paneled walls display a variety of tapestries and portraits, and an ornamental rug leads us from the door to the dining table.

Rows of cushioned, high-back chairs line either side of a grand table, with enough space for a few dozen. Only four chairs are taken though, at the far end of the table.

Rainer and Ken sit on one side, across from Eoin and Viveka. Annoyance builds in my stomach at seeing Rainer. Leaning back casually in his chair, his black long-sleeve shirt is unbuttoned a few inches down, allowing me to preview his chest like always. His pants are pressed today, though, shoes shiny, but his hair still has the same mussed-up look, like he just rolled out of bed. Gold jewelry peeks out from his ears, matching the rings on the slender fingers tapping an inaudible rhythm on the armrest.

As arrogant as ever.

But what truly angers me is the way Fern sits perched on Rainer's lap as she runs one arm around his neck, her fingers dancing through his raven hair.

Eoin gives me a soft smile in greeting. I return it, ignoring the dark faerie prince who's currently ignoring me in favor of the girl on his lap.

"Oh my gods," Fern yells, and all remaining eyes swing toward me. "What are you wearing?" She giggles, and I squeeze the tray so tight that the steel edges bite into my skin, threatening to break the skin.

"I thought—" What exactly did I think?

I think I trusted Das Celyn, despite feeling like something was off about the situation.

Mortification flushes my cheeks as I glance down at the frilly dress. Fern wears a silky dress that hugs her frame delicately. Viv looks like a badass in her leathers. And here I am in a joke of a dress.

I turn, catching Das Celyn with a smirk on their face. It grows into a full-on smile as they wink and scurry away. Facing the table, I slowly carry my serving tray over.

"Ah, the Low Fae do enjoy their jokes." Rainer tilts a glass to his lips.

Mischievous tricksters, indeed.

My hands clam up and my breathing grows shallow.

I mentally beg myself to let Fern's taunting go—she has issues of her own—but it doesn't prevent the tears from pricking at my eyes.

I could copy the servants before me. Set down the tray politely, bow, and hustle out of sight. But so many times before, I had wished I stood up to the lord and lady. I had dreamed of fighting back for so many nights, of sticking up for myself, but I never did. Char finally did it for me—and look at the price she paid. I refuse to be a puppet, a prisoner in my own skin again. Fae prince or not, I won't let myself cower before Rainer. I won't let myself cower in front of Fern and her judgements.

Fueled by petty jealousy and embarrassment, I nudge my way between Rainer and Ken, plopping the platter in front of Rainer with a loud clang. A doughnut from the top of the pyramid topples onto the floor.

I force a smile at the prince. "Your favorite."

My hands ball into fists, trying to hide the trembling.

Silence sits heavy in the air. The other fae servants carefully place their trays down, and scurry out of the room, leaving me to fend for myself.

Fern snickers, muttering something under her breath. The whites of her eyes are red, her lids heavy.

Viv looks at me with her mouth open agape while Fern snickers. I refuse to meet Eoin's eyes. We just met yesterday, but twice now he's seeing me at a low point.

And I don't care.

Fern has been through a lot, and whatever she and Rainer have doesn't involve me, but her taunting sets me on edge.

"Someone's hungry," Ken murmurs as he licks jam off his fingers.

Rainer stares up at me from his seat, no emotion on his face.

"Sit," he says, pointing to the open chair beside him.

"No."

There's a collection of sharp inhales as the others observe our exchange.

I was a fool for thinking I could belong here. Clearly, Rainer and his pals are playing with me for their own humor.

Ignoring the room's tension, Rainer deposits Fern into the chair beside him. She pouts, but he ignores her, leaning forward to grab a chocolate-covered doughnut. He chews methodically while everyone stares at him waiting to see what he'll do. As I turn to leave, he swallows and catches my eyes. Waves of heat flutter through my stomach.

A flashback to last night's dream passes through my mind, and I break eye contact before he can see the desire building in me, or worse, before Ken can scent it. I pray Rainer forgot what he saw me doing last night.

My blush deepens at the thought. Sure, the prince has the most kissable lips, hair I want to run my fingers through, and penetrating, icy eyes that twist my stomach into knots, but he's a right bastard.

Ken clears his throat, giving me a humored look. My face burns so hot that I fear I might pass out. I hate all the eyes on me.

"Sit. Have a doughnut." Rainer's lips twitch as he beckons to the chair on his left—the one Fern now sits in with her arms crossed and a glare on her face. "I insist."

"That seat is taken," I say stupidly. "And I'm not sitting on your lap."

Rainer says, "She was just leaving."

Fern narrows her eyes at me. It's one thing for the fae to be cruel, but I refuse to take the attitude from another human woman—someone who should understand how difficult it is to fit in here.

"Sit," Rainer commands.

"No," I say.

Someone inhales sharply, and there's a murmur from the table. I snag a doughnut before retreating and striding toward the archway.

"Run away now." Fern laughs. Her words are slurred, and I can tell she's high on something. It brings out her mean side. "You don't belong here."

"Shut it," Rainer growls.

"Showing favorites now, Rainer?" Eoin asks.

It takes a few deep breaths to ignore Fern's taunting. Slowly, I turn back to the table.

"You know what? You're right, Fern. I don't belong here." I look to Rainer next. "And I am pathetic. I am weak. Just like you all constantly remind me. Is that what you want to hear? Does that make you happy?"

"Oh, no, little human," Ken mutters with a shake of his head.

I grip my purple skirts, shaking them out aggressively. "This is just one big joke to you all. Playing with me like some sort of living, breathing toy." A *dolly*. "Sure, feck with the human for a few faerie laughs."

"She said *feck*," Ken whispers, leaning forward with wide eyes. "I think she's mad."

Rainer frowns, but when his eyes dart back to Eoin—who's scrutinizing him—he carefully schools his expression and turns back to me.

I wait for anyone to say something, anything, to tell me that I'm more than a joke to them.

I wait for Rainer to stick up for me, to show me the kind side of him.

"Is it true?" I whisper, my voice cracking. "I'm just here for your entertainment?"

Another beat stretches by. Eoin gives Rainer a smug grin, waiting for his response.

"Tell us, Prince of Fear," Eoin says, taking a quick sip of his wine, "does this human mean something to you?"

"No." Rainer's tone is devoid of emotion. He locks eyes with me, and I feel like I'm drowning, stuck beneath the surface with no air. "Like she said, she's here for entertainment and nothing else."

My heart shatters in my chest.

Eoin points at Fern. "And what of that one?"

"She's good for one purpose, and one purpose only," Rainer says, without sparring her a glance.

Fern's cheeks burn bright red, but she says nothing. When she reaches for a glass of wine, Rainer puts up a hand, blocking her.

"Leave."

Fern stands with a huff, storming from the room.

Eoin raises a brow at Rainer, a weird tension lining the room. The two males stare at each other, as if caught in some sort of silent battle. Rainer's fingers tap out a rhythm on his knee, the only indication that he's unsettled.

"So, one entertains you in the bedroom—good choice, by the way," Eoin says. He throws me a boyish grin. "No offense, of course, darling. I find your innocence wholly alluring." The grin melts off his face as he turns back to Rainer. "But how exactly *does* the innocent one entertain you?"

I twist my hands around my skirts, frozen there like an idiot. I'm brought back to all those times the lord made me feel small, lesser-than, useless.

Entertainment.

Eoin leans back in the chair, crossing his legs cockily. Ken and Viv busy themselves eating, ignoring the unraveling scene. Rainer studies me, his jaw tense. I swear his eyes flicker from pale-blue to cobalt, then back to their normal pale coloring.

"Are you sure she's merely your entertainment, Rainer?" Eoin taunts. "It appears you've caught a liking to the—"

"No," Rainer growls.

"I've had enough," I say, finding my voice. "I'm leaving."

"Leaving where exactly?" Rainer asks.

His fingers pick up their pace, dancing erratically on his thigh. If I wasn't mistaken, I'd say he's nervous. On edge.

"None of your business," I say.

"Surely not back to Dovenak?"

"Let her go," Eoin says with shrug. "If she means so little to you, Rainer, let her leave."

Rainer's jaw tics, but other than that he remains perfectly still.

"What in fae's sake is going on?" Viv whispers.

Eoin's gaze bounces between me and Rainer. Ken keeps stuffing food in his mouth, as if he's fighting the urge to talk.

"You should get your humans under control, Rainer. Unless you view them as equals?" Eoin asks, raising a brow. "Again, no offense, of course, Alessia." He shakes his head with a tut. "Though you're accepted in *my* court, you'll never be equal to the fae in Umbra's eyes."

Tears threaten to fall, so I turn away quickly. A fire burns inside of me as I trudge toward the exit with all eyes on me. Halfway across the room, a sparking warmth crawls up my spine and slides through my veins. Similar to the sensation of the Gleam, or when I accidentally thanked Rainer and bound myself to him.

Magic.

I've no time to analyze the feeling, because two familiar figures enter the doorway, pausing me dead in my tracks.

"There you are, my little Dolly," Lord Edvin says.

My heart stops momentarily and the doughnut I'm still holding slips from my fingers, crashing onto the shiny wood floors beneath me in a heap of crumbs and chocolate.

Impossible.

Rainer brought the lord here.

Has he been training me all this time just to summon the lord and have me fight to the death as a sick form of brunch entertainment?

Grubby fingers extend toward me, and I jump back out of reach. Lord Edvin's face resembles a tomato—all red and swollen, his eyes swimming with intoxication.

"Such a disobedient creature," Lady Nilda spits out, patting her husband on the shoulder. "Punish her good for that, husband."

Turning back to the table, four pairs of eyes lock onto me. Eoin is halfway out of his seat, his eyes wide, but Viv has an arm out, holding him back. Ken watches curiously with raised brows. Rainer's leg bounces as his fingers drum on his knee, but other than that, his face doesn't give anything away.

He *knows* where I came from—what I escaped. Yet he sought out my owners, bringing them here to retrieve me.

He betrayed me. Set me up.

Made me believe he cared about my safety—in his own, twisted way.

Made me think I could be something more than a weak, pathetic Tradeling.

But it was a lie. They're sending me to my death.

"How could you?" My voice cracks.

A flash of concern crosses his face before he snags a goblet from the table and sips it carefully, hiding his expression from me.

The lord steps up beside me. "Time to go."

He grabs me, binding my wrists together beneath his impossible grip in a move that causes me to yelp. His fingers squeeze so tight that I worry he'll break my wrists. Breath bitter with whiskey fills my nostrils and I gag at the memories it brings.

"Please! Please, no!" Tears stream down my face as the lord pushes me toward the door, forcing me to take steps by nudging the back of my calves with his boots. The lady laughs beside me. I scream at her too, before spitting in her face in a bold move.

"You imbecile!" Her hand whips out, cracking against my cheek. The lord releases me. I fall to the floor in a heap of purple fabric.

"That's enough!" Eoin's voice booms through the room in a sharp command, sounding nothing like the kind man I spoke to yesterday. A chair screeches, and suddenly Eoin is at my side, helping me to my feet. I tremble, barely able to stand.

"Release her, now!"

At first, I think he's talking to the lord until I hear Rainer sigh exasperatedly.

"So dramatic, Eoin," Rainer says in a bored tone. "Satisfied?"

"You've made your point." Eoin seethes. "Heartless as always."

"There. Done. She's released."

Eoin holds me against his chest as I collapse with a sob. I clutch him desperately as his lemongrass scent washes over me, reminding me of the soap Char and I used to clean with at the estate. It only makes me cry harder.

Despite him being as big an arse as Rainer, I cling to him like he's a safety line.

"It's okay," he whispers into my hair. "Whatever it is, it's gone. You're safe now."

No one says anything as I pull back, wiping my tears on my dress's hideous sleeve and glancing around the room. Only... the lord and lady are nowhere to be found.

Spinning around desperately, I try to pinpoint where the two of them have gone so quickly. There's only one open door—the archway—which was in my line of sight the entire time. I hadn't heard them cross the room. Hadn't heard any of the other doors opening. Not that they would've had time to cross the room that fast.

My face stings with the impact of the lady's hand, my wrists ache from the lord's grip—phantom pains now, and the only indicator they were even here.

"Where are they?" I rasp. "Where—"

"Shh. No one's here," Eoin says reassuringly. "You're safe, Alessia."

"How could you—" I gasp out between breaths, my words aimed at Rainer. "How could you—?"

"Come. Sit," he says. "Eat."

His fingers, glinting with rings, twirling a glass of ruby-red liquid, as he brings it up to his lips and drinking deeply, keeping his eyes on mine the entire time.

Ken and Viv look between one another, and Ken chews his bottom lip like he's still fighting to hold his tongue. Viv shakes her head at him and gives him a look.

"It's okay, Alessia," Eoin whispers so only I can hear him. "I've got you."

My fear of Rainer calling the lord and lady back spurs me into action. Eoin gently takes my hand, leading me to his side of the table. Every few feet, my head swings around, vigilant in case they return.

I'd much rather sit here in a hideous dress, for the fae prince's entertainment, than be back in the lord's grip.

It's choosing between a demon and a devil. How can one pick when they're both equally horrible in their own way? In fact, there's a saying I once heard: "better the devil you know, than the one you don't."

I disagree with that sentiment.

Sometimes the devil you know is the worst one of all.

Seeing my former owners reminds me of what I escaped from. *Anything* is better than going back with the lord, especially without Char there to comfort and protect me.

I slink down into the seat next to Eoin, across from Rainer. Mortification gnaws on me. I'm embarrassed they all saw me at my weakest, *again*.

With a sniffle, I wipe the last of the moisture from my cheeks with the heel of my hand before sitting up tall.

"You're safe, Alessia," Eoin says. He keeps our fingers interlaced on my lap, caressing the back of my hand with his thumb.

I avoid looking at Rainer, even though his intense gaze burns a hole into me. I want to beg, plead with him not to give me back to the lord.

"Whatever you saw wasn't real," Rainer mutters.

Gripping Eoin's hand tightly, as if I can draw courage from him, I finally glance at Rainer. His jaw tics as he looks from me to Eoin, back to me again, but he doesn't say anything further. His usual coldness slides back into place.

"That was amazing, little human! Most humans, hells, most fae can't handle—"

"Ken," Viv interrupts.

She mimics a shut it motion with her hand, and Ken puts his meaty paws up in a submissive gesture. "My bad."

His eyes glow with excitement when he looks at me.

"What do you mean he wasn't real? What about the lady? She slapped me." My hand flies up to my right cheek, still smarting from the smack.

But it starts coming together as my adrenaline wears off and my heart rate finds its baseline.

Magic.

The prickling sensation I experienced right before I saw the lord and lady.

Prince of *Fear.*

Like the magic in the Cursed Wood—magic, Ken said, belonging to Rainer.

It was—

"An illusion," Rainer says. "Whatever you saw was one of your fears manifested. Minds are a fickle thing. Sometimes we believe something so fully that it presents itself in physical form, such as an injury, but it's merely a parlor trick."

I grit my teeth, steadying my breath before speaking.

"How could you? How could you?" My voice is borderline hysterical, and I work hard to tamper down my emotions.

When Rainer doesn't reply, Ken speaks up. "Rainer is a fearcaller."

"She was asking a rhetorical question, Ken," Viv admonishes under her breath.

I'm outraged. It's incredulous that this haughty brute would use his powers against me, to trick me like that.

"Is this another one of your manipulative games? Scaring me into obedience?"

"I had no way of knowing what would appear for you," he says, as if that makes it better.

"But you knew it would be something I dread."

"Rai's only trying to—" Ken starts, but I don't let him finish.

"How dare you!" Scooting the chair back with a loud screech, I jump to my feet, ready to put distance between us.

"Wait—Alessia," Eoin calls to me.

"Now who needs to let her go?" Rainer hisses at Eoin. I have no idea what he's talking about and I couldn't care less. "Let her cool down."

Cool down…

The mild annoyance and embarrassment I felt earlier has been wholly replaced. Rainer made a fool of me. It's clear that whatever his intentions are, they're not in my favor. He truly is playing games.

I'm filled with burgeoning fury. My hands clench into fists at my side.

"You might be the Prince of Fear, Rainer, but *you* are a manipulative coward. I don't need to know anything else about you to know that is all you will ever be." I stand, curving around the table to where he sits. Leaning towards him, I meet him eye-to-eye with a hand on his armrest. "If that's all you have—silly parlor tricks" —I chuckle sarcastically— "then that's lackluster."

My hands shake as I grip his chair and a few stray tears stream down my cheeks. But I don't waver. I keep my eyes trained on Rainer. He can put me through my worst nightmares all he wants. I refuse to let his illusions break me after surviving the real thing.

I lower my voice to a whisper, fighting to keep it steady.

"You will get what's coming to you," I grit out. "And so will the lord and lady."

He tampers down a small smile as his eyes flit to my lips and back up.

He leans forward until there's practically no air between us.

"And there she is," he whispers against my lips for only me to hear. "The girl who fights."

My belly flutters, but I push off his chair, shaking my head.

Without looking back, I stomp out of the room with my head held high and tears staining my cheeks. But Rainer's words ring in my head: I *am* the girl who fights.

Twenty-Five
She Will Always Be Mine
Rainer

I tune out the bottomless brunch chatter as I sit back in my chair. I focus on the doughnut on my plate, tapping my fingers against my leg.

Most beings cower in the face of their fears.

But some blossom.

Alessia?

She blossoms like the little rose she is. Slowly but surely, as her vines snake their way around my heart.

As proud of her as I am, my self-loathing has hit an all time high. If I didn't already hate myself, I surely would now. Watching Alessia suffer like that took my breath away. It crushed me. After it was over, I wanted nothing more than to taste those tears on her lips.

To wipe them away, telling her how strong she's become.

She's not weak. Not at all. I was wrong when I first thought that about her, but I was correct in my assessment that a fire lives behind those beautiful grey eyes of hers—eyes that were so sad, and so tired when she first arrived.

Slowly, gracefully, she's discovered her strength and reclaimed her life. The irony is she hasn't even noticed. She wanted safety? She got it. Freedom? She has it.

They both belong to her, yet she still acts as if I have her leashed. But I hold neither her nor her leash in my fist.

Using my power on her was manipulative, but in a different way than she assumes. It wasn't meant to control her or prove she's weak. No, the fearcalling was intended to get Eoin's eyes off her—off us. To convince him that she means nothing to me.

Convince *her* that she means nothing to me.

Again, I'm protecting someone I shouldn't care about, at the expense of my true emotions. She was softening up around me, and I've shut it all down.

It was a fight to use my powers on her in the first place. It was even more of a challenge to allow Fern to perch on my lap, to pretend as if I don't loathe her touch.

All a show for Eoin. So he knows that both my humans are equally as important, and equally as unimportant to me. They're both tools to be used, and nothing more.

Eoin is already intrigued by Alessia because he thinks I am fond of her. If he sees her as something I care for, he sees a weakness. I doubt he will stop at anything to acquire her for himself. He's wanted to gain control of Umbra Court for as long as we've been old enough to disagree. Eoin would do anything to gain a foothold over me, even if it means using Alessia as a pawn.

The irony of it all is that she might truly be safer in the Terra Court. Eoin would never harm her—he's a healer for fae's sake—and there are a handful of humans that reside there. He doesn't pose a risk to her like I do.

But she certainly wouldn't get the opportunity to grow and thrive.

He would never train her. He would keep her like a prize, put her on a pedestal. Use her against me. He'd pluck her, where I would water her.

She would wither instead of flourish.

The truth is selfish: I don't want him to steal Alessia away.

Watching her grow comfortable in my castle has been a thing of beauty, but it's dangerous. Not just for me, but for her. With Eoin here, and Tynan coming, I can't let either of them see that she means something to me. I can't let them see I am protecting her.

And though I worry about hurting her, I would never hurt her the way they did in Dovenak.

It's necessary for her to hate me in hopes that she'll avoid me. I had never wanted to use my fearcaller power on her. But I needed to remind her that I am not her friend, not her savior.

I am cruel.

I am evil.

I am a walking nightmare—The Prince of Fear.

And if Eoin thinks I don't care for her, he'll lose interest.

But watching him comfort her, hold her hand so casually, it made my chest ache. It was eerie. It took everything in me to keep the emotions from splaying on my face. It made me realize that as much as I lie to everyone around me, I can't lie to myself.

Alessia means something to me.

I don't hate her. Not at all. I tried, but I can't.

It's more than the juxtaposition of her sweet innocence mixed with a fiery spirit. It's the way she watches Kenisius and Viveka with unabashed respect during their morning training sessions, hanging onto every word with eagerness. The way she'll work herself to the verge of passing out, never wanting to disappoint her teachers. Striving to be the best she can.

It's the way she doesn't give up on Das Celyn. Instead, she patiently coaxes them into eating in a way that's neither pushy nor too forward, helping them overcome their cibophobia—their fear of eating.

It's the way she stands up for herself against Fern's taunting, and my cruelty. How she fights for herself despite her earlier notion of it being pointless.

Most of all, it's the way she watches me when she thinks I'm not looking. It's never with pity or disgust—always understanding and curiosity. She's asked about my flowers, my mother. Things most people overlook or ignore. But she sees it all—my good, my bad. But if I can have it my way, I'll protect her from my ugly.

There's a third reason for using my power on Alessia. I needed to see for myself that she can survive her fear. That she reacts…differently to my power.

Unlike most, she did not become petrified.

She fought through it.

Just like she did the trees.

Such a feat should not be possible by a mere human with a sorrowful upbringing. It only deepens the mystery between us. The mystery of her.

I can only hope that one day I'll get a chance to explain, that I can make it right. But if not, as long as I can keep her safe, it's worth it.

And as long as she stays far away from me, I can control myself while protecting her.

I might not be able to have her, but no one else can have her either.

Even if it's from afar, she will always be *mine*.

Twenty-Six
I Don't Owe Him Anything
Alessia

With my mind spinning as I process Rainer's powers, I storm to my room. My gaudy dress is drenched with sweat, sticking to my body in an unsightly fashion. I rip and tug, desperate to free myself from the material.

Once the dress is off, I give the seams a yank, growling as I tear it to pieces, the purple scraps fluttering down around me.

What a load of shite.

I can't believe Das Celyn would set me up, and for what? For a gods-damned laugh?

As I put on a pair of leggings and a tunic, I turn the new bits of information over in my mind. Some of the mysteries surrounding Rainer and the Umbra Court are finally coming together for me.

If Rainer is a fearcaller, it explains how the forest feeds on fear—the trees' sentient power must be connected to Rainer's somehow. It also explains what happened during that training session with Viv. Rainer used his power on her, like he did me, to mimic what she might see out there in the forest.

To prepare her.

Most of all, it explains why he's so off-putting at times—he's a literal nightmare. Everyone's worst fear, personified. I have no intention of getting close to him again.

I blame the moonberries and my dreams about him for the false romanticization. But no more. Finally, I see the truth.

He's *not* nice. He does not care about my best interests.

He's a feckin' faerie, after all.

If I were going to leave, now would be the perfect time. No one is around. I don't have any belongings to retrieve. I could easily slip away unnoticed, risk braving the woods.

But…despite my revelations about Rainer, being here has been good for me. Training with Viv and Ken has been good for me. It's ignited something I didn't think I'd find—hope.

Hope that I can learn something for myself.

Hope that I can protect myself.

Hope that I can create a better life.

A few more weeks, or even months, here could be the difference I need to grow from a weak girl to a strong woman.

It could be the difference between life or death for me.

I can't let Rainer's cruelty hold me back from being my best self. I refuse to let him ruin my life now that I'm finally getting it back.

Getting it for the first time, actually.

If I can stick out the lord for almost eighteen years, I can stick out an arrogant faerie prince for a few more months. I can subdue my stubbornness in the name of survival.

And for Char—for the life she wanted for me.

I'll endure their taunts and teasing. Brave their mischievous manipulations. Let them train me, let them teach me their ways of cunningness and confidence, *then* I can return to Dovenak and seek revenge on Lord Edvin and Lady Nilda.

I'll also be strong enough to forge my own path forward.

I refuse to let Rainer break me.

My stomach growls, reminding me that I haven't yet eaten. Leaving my room, I trudge down to the kitchen.

"The girl who fights," I mutter to myself as I make my way through the hallways.

If he was trying to break me… why would he look so satisfied when I threatened him. There was a wicked gleam in his eye, and for a second it almost seemed like he was going to kiss me.

Another faerie game, I bet.

More fuel for my desire to grow strong and stand up for myself.

Not wanting to pass the main dining room, I take the long way to the kitchen. After a bit of walking around the first floor, and passing some weird art—mostly nonsensical paintings—and more doors than I can count, the hallway dumps me into the main foyer.

Somehow I got turned around.

The ridiculous bone chandelier hangs precariously above the center of the room, and I remember how terrified I was the first time I saw it. Now, it irritates me.

Light leaks in from the stained glass windows above the massive front doors. It sprays color around the room. For a moment, I stand there, watching in awe, mystified by the colors.

Suddenly, the front doors slam open with dramatic force. I jump, and so does my heart.

"Ryyyyyye-nerrrrrrr," a high-pitched voice calls out. "I'm late, I know. Spare me. It's been a day."

A curvy female fae with a warm-golden coloring similar to Eoin's and flowing honey-brown hair enters the room. Jewelry decorates the sharp points of her ears. Matching gold bands wrap around each of her biceps, and layers of dainty chains rest on her sternum.

The dress she wears is as gilded as her hair, with thin straps and a plunging neckline.

The more I stare at her, the deeper my frown grows. She looks just like Eoin... except fancier. Royal. Yesterday, when I fell from the tree, Rainer had mentioned something about Eoin's sister coming today. This must be her.

She steps closer, towering over me with her dancer-like grace.

"And who do we have here?" she asks, her amber eyes soaking me up. She pops a generous hip, placing her hand on it as she smiles brightly at me. "What a doll!"

Hearing the Lord's old nickname for me instantly causes me to recoil. My arms itch to reach around my midsection on their own accord, but I force myself to keep my hands at my side.

I'm done being a toy.

I am no one's dolly.

"Oh, this is delightful," she says, clapping her hands together. "You must be the new human Rai's acquired. Did he finally drain that wretched Fern?"

"He did not acquire me," I mutter, causing her to laugh.

"Sennah, stop making my human uncomfortable," Rainer says.

I feel his energy before I even see him. And I fight the urge to flee.

I am not weak.

I am strong.

"Hello little Prince of Fear," Sennah says.

The little hairs on my neck stand up, and I know without looking that he's behind me—maybe only a few feet away. His mere presence seems to heat the space up a few degrees, and a quick flashback to last night's dream makes me even warmer.

Sennah ignores Rainer completely, stepping closer to me and lowering her voice. "Does it hurt?"

"Does what hurt?" I ask, puzzled.

"You know." She wiggles her brows at me. "When he—"

"Sennah!" Rainer's voice booms. "I will rescind your invitation to my court."

"So dramatic, Rai." Sennah rolls her eyes. To me she says, "I didn't mean to make you uncomfortable."

"I'm fine," I mutter, wanting to put distance between all the unwelcome chaos this morning.

"I should've known better," she says to Rainer this time. "You do enjoy caring for the broken ones."

My brows raise at that. It's not a coincidence that a hodgepodge of suffering folk hide away in Rainer's gothic castle. Is it because he gives us freedom to exist as we are? Or is it because he beats us down and keeps us broken?

Rainer moves forward to stand at my side. When I shrink away, I swear I see a flicker of hurt on his face. He steps aside, too, as if he agrees with putting space between us.

"You're late, Sennah," he says.

"Have you already discussed the Ostara plans without me?" She smiles, twirling a lock of hair around her index finger.

"No."

"Then I'm on time."

"I'm not arguing about this."

"Sounds like you are though."

"You are an incredible pain in my arse," Rainer mutters.

"Insult me again, Rainer. Let's see what Eoin thinks of that."

"I care little about your brother's opinions."

Sennah flicks a wrist at Rainer, and at first I think it's just a sign of dismissal, but then his eyes widen almost humorously. He opens his mouth to speak, but no hint of sound escapes. His hands fly up to his throat as he drops to his knees, staring up at Sennah in disbelief.

I have no idea what's happening, but I think she's magicking him somehow. If that's even what it's called. My stomach contorts with fear.

Is she really going to kill Rainer in front of me like this? I don't care for him right now, but I don't want him dead.

My eyes dart between the two of them, and before I can think it through, I jump between the pair.

"Sennah, please! Don't!"

She double-takes at me with a frown. A single brow slowly raises in question, but she obliges and drops her hand.

Rainer gasps for breath, still on his knees, and I bolt to his side. "Are you all right?"

He ignores me, standing and straightening his shirt and running a hand through his hair.

"Feckin' elemental faerie," he mumbles.

Sennah laughs, and I see red—fueled by anger—until Rainer chuckles softly too.

"Bastard faerie," she shoots back. I glance between the two wondering what the hell just happened. "It would be more fun if you'd fight back."

"Which is exactly why I refuse to."

She steps forward and gives him a hug. He awkwardly pats her shoulder in return before pushing her away.

"Alessia, this is Princess Sennah of Terra Court," Rainer says, as if the entire morning never happened. As if we are casual acquaintances and he didn't slice our budding friendship in half.

I wipe my sweaty palms on my slacks, aware of the nervous disaster I am.

"Unless you're staff, Sennah is just fine," she corrects.

"Apparently I'm the entertainment," I mutter.

Rainer rubs his jaw, staring at me intensely. As if he's trying to relay a message. I turn my attention to the princess, instead. She simply cocks her head, watching us with interest.

Faerie courts and politics are baffling. In Dovenak, I only know of one royal—Queen Wyetta, the one who reigns over the entire Wessex Peninsula. She has no heirs, no princes or princesses in line for the throne. There are other royals in other parts of the continent, beyond the Barrens, and sometimes they marry their heirs off to one another to ensure political neutrality or combine resources, but we don't often hear about them.

"Where's Eoin?" Sennah gazes up at the chandelier in awe, as it spins beacons of light throughout the room. Without waiting for Rainer's response, she says, "Always did love your space, Rai. Spooky and stunning, just like you."

Rainer strokes his temples, as if he's annoyed at the princess.

"Peppy Princess, what an unpleasant surprise!" Ken's booming voice fills the space as he enters with Viv and Eoin at his side. I notice he's swapped his armor for dress slacks and tunics, similar to Rainer's, but Viv stands regal as ever in her leather vest with matching scabbard.

"My favorite cub!" Sennah screeches. "Give me a bear hug."

Ken groans, but he wraps his arms around her, embracing like old friends.

When they release, Ken ruffles my hair and asks, "Glad to see you're okay, little human."

"I'm fine," I mutter lamely, watching everyone cautiously.

"Finally, you made it, sister," Eoin says as he steps beside me. We're so close that our pinkies brush. After his sister greets him, he leans in so only I can hear, "I went searching for you."

Turning to face him, I blush when I see his forehead marred with concern. When I offer a reassuring smile, his eyes crinkle adorably around the corners.

"Just not used to… faeries I suppose."

He chuckles, and the sound makes my stomach turn over. "Not all the fae are like Rainer. Some of us have morals, you know."

It hits me then, if his sister is the princess— "You're a prince, too."

He scratches the back of his neck, looking bashful. "Technically, yes, though my sister oversees much of the court. It's not really my thing."

"Of course you are," I mutter. His face drops at that. "Oh—I didn't mean it like that."

"It's all right. I get it."

"No, seriously. That was rude of me. Especially after how kind you've been. I'd say I owe you… but you faeries and your bargains."

He offers me a shy smile. "I know a way you can make it up to me. Without an official bargain."

Sennah and Ken burst into laughter at their separate conversation, startling me, and reminding me that we're not alone. I glance over at the group to see Rainer's penetrating gaze focused on me, his lips pulled down in a frown. I squirm, not understanding what the intense stare-down is for. No one else seems to notice as they chat amongst themselves, catching up lightheartedly.

"How about it?" Eoin asks, elbowing me playfully.

"Huh? I—what did you say?"

"How do you feel about making it up to me?"

Oh. He's serious about that. "I—"

"Enough time wasting," Rainer's sharp voice cuts in, his eyes still locked onto mine. A muscle tics in his cheek. "We're all busy, so let's get on with it."

"What is this meeting for?" I ask Eoin.

"Ostara preparation," Rainer replies, narrowing his eyes at Eoin. "And it doesn't involve humans."

Of course it doesn't. Any time I start to feel remotely normal here, Rainer reminds me of what a lowly human I am. How could I possibly forget?

"Are you coming?" Eoin whispers to me.

"No. I'd rather..." go find anything else to do. "Rainer just said it doesn't involve humans."

"Ignore him. Ostara is fun," Eoin says, whispering in my ear. "Come back to brunch with us. For me? You need to eat."

I shudder at the way his hot breath tickles the shell of my ear. And when he reaches out to touch my shoulder, I relax beneath his touch. A tingle courses through me—warm, comforting, magical. But I don't think much of it.

Rainer's nostrils flare and he storms off.

My stomach clenches with regret, but I have nothing to be sorry for. I don't owe him anything.

TWENTY-SEVEN

AN EQUALLY TROUBLED BROTHER

ALESSIA

Never have I eaten as many fruits as I have here in Avylon. I eat just enough to keep my stomach from grumbling, then I use my fork to push a blueberry around my plate as I listen to the fae's conversation about Ostara.

To be honest, it isn't nearly as exciting as I had hoped it would be. Ostara, apparently, is a fae holiday celebrated during the spring equinox. Folk from both courts along with some courts further away, get together to eat, dance, and drink. It's a cultural way to honor Mother Nature for her magic and bounties.

"I'm appalled your gracious host hasn't properly informed you of what Ostara is!" Sennah says. "Actually, I rescind that. It's entirely in his character."

"Oh, cut the prince some slack." Viv angles her glass at the princess and purses her lips. I'm surprised when she speaks up on Rainer's behalf. He dips his chin at her in a show of solidarity. She looks at me next. "Don't you celebrate the Mother in Dovenak?"

I shake my head. "We have some similar celebrations—or rather, the wealthy do—but no one worships Mother Nature. They never did. Our celebrations originated from the gods. But no one even worships them anymore. Now, it's more of a show for the rich to celebrate their own power and money. I guess you can say they worship themselves, in a sense."

I hated holidays at the estate. Char and I would rush around, tending to the lord's drunken acquaintances while simultaneously trying to remain invisible. The only thing worse than an intoxicated Lord Edvin, was an intoxicated Lord Edvin with a dozen of his closest and equally grotesque companions.

"Shame. Likely why humans possess no magic at all."

"Because we don't worship the Mother?"

"Among other things."

"Like your blatant disregard for nature," Rainer says.

Viv picks apart a muffin hungrily and Ken looks down his shirt, searching for fallen crumbs distractedly. Eoin chuckles softly. Rainer cocks a brow.

Sennah smiles, and it's so genuine that I feel my own lips mirroring the motion. "The Mother is the one who gave us our magic."

It hits me how easily I've fallen back in with the fae, and I mentally remind myself that they are not my allies. This isn't a conversation between friends. Simply a way of gathering information as a matter of survival.

"Is she a goddess?" I ask.

"Sort of. She's *the* goddess. Our balance. The original source of power. Fae have a much deeper respect for her—and the lesser gods she created—than the humans ever did."

I lean forward, intrigued by the conversation. "So the gods are real?"

"The gods *were* real," she confirms. "They were created by the Mother, tasked with watching over the unruly humans. They wielded an unimaginable level of power. Humans co-existed with them, honoring and worshiping them. But, of course, they began finding themselves jealous of the gods and desperate for their power. They stopped acknowledging the gods at all, stopped worshiping them and believing in them. Over time, the less the humans worshiped them, the weaker they grew until they became mortal altogether."

"Jealous, power-crazed, feckin'—" Ken catches my eye and cuts his rant short. "No offense, little human."

"Not all humans fall into that category." Viv purses her lips at Ken. "You can't stereotype them all because of a select few."

"As the gods began to weaken, humans began to slaughter them and perform obscene rituals in attempts to harness their magic—which, of course, failed. The Mother, in a last effort to preserve their magic, created a new species—our ancestors, fae—to protect the magic," Sennah continues, ignoring the side remarks. "We were designed to be keepers of magic, protectors of elements, preservers of balance and harmony. The gods even designed us specifically to look similar enough to humans, in hopes that we could merge back into humanity incongruously. Some fae have heightened senses and extreme beauty" —she points to herself with a smug grin— "and we watch over the courts. But some have wings and take to the skies, and some have fins and guard the waters."

"And some are born of two forms, a link between animi and humanoid forms," Ken adds. "There are many different fae beyond shifters and faeries."

"Anyway," Sennah continues, "Of course, it didn't work out. The human race was more outraged than ever. They felt tricked by the gods, disgusted that instead of recruiting them as keepers of magic, an entire new species was born and gifted with magic."

"Resulting in the War of Chaos," I mumble, thinking back to the story Char had told me.

"Yes, actually."

"So what happened?"

"Well, instilled with an inherent desire to protect the magic at all costs, fae combined their magic to open a portal to another realm beside the human realm. Though, humans tried to spoil that by entering the realm with malicious intent."

"That's why the treaty is in place," I whisper.

Eoin's face twists with discomfort. He shares a look with Sennah. But it's Rainer that speaks up, "There is no treaty."

"But, I thought—"

"Not anymore." Rainer runs a slender finger around the lip of his wine goblet. "It was broken."

"Do the humans know?" I ask, worry swirling in my gut. I shouldn't care—I don't know why I do. But the humans still think the treaty is in place, protecting them. At least from what I've heard and read back at the estate.

"They're the ones who broke it," he says flatly.

"And now they want it reinstated," Ken mutters.

I frown. That means there are no current protections in place, yet the fae have not started conflict. It's been the humans who challenge things. More interestingly, it means the fae could very well use their magic in Dovenak if they choose to.

"How did they break it?" I ask.

Rainer leans forward, lowering his voice. "They began mating with the gods, birthing humans with magic. Not quite human, but not quite fae, either."

"And definitely not gods," Ken chimes in.

"They sent those kin into our realm as spies, as destroyers of our land. It was a way around our treaty."

"Because the treaty banned humans from entering right?" I ask. "But these half-human, half-gods weren't technically human, right? At least not fully." That explains how I was able to cross the Gleam—there was no treaty keeping humans out of Avylon. Not anymore. In all the chaos, I never even realized that. I figured I had simply heard wrong about what the treaty entails.

"Precisely." The look he levels at me is ice cold, and I wrap my arms around myself nervously. The pieces are starting to fit together now. "You think we are mischievous and manipulative, but it's the humans who strive to wipe out anything they don't like."

"That's why you cursed the forest," I whisper. The treaty ended. He was trying to protect his court—his people by scaring the humans back to Dovenak.

"I didn't curse it," he hisses.

"Enchanted it," I amend.

"You did curse it though, Rainer." Eoin's tone is accusatory. "Your dark magic—your court—is Avylon's stain."

I gasp at his words, my eyes widening at him. He gives me a pitying look and slowly sips his drink. Sennah bites her lip, whispering something to Viv.

"It's the truth," Eoin continues. "You could've reinstated the treaty, but instead, you put your entire court at risk."

"Watch yourself, Eoin Glenn Orion."

"Why so sensitive Rainer Rohan Iorworth?" Eoin taunts, mimicking Rainer's tone. "You chose to tell the story. Why not tell the whole story?"

Iorworth.

The Treaty of Wessex-Iorworth.

The treaty struck with the most terrifying family in Avylon—Rainer's ancestors. His family.

My eyes practically bulge out of my head, yet it makes perfect sense, considering what I've seen of him. Not to mention his court is the closest to the Gleam.

"You think you are so much better than me because you can heal," Rainer spits.

"It's better than scaring people to death." Eoin's lips tighten. His words aren't said with cruelty as much as they are matter-of-factly. "At least one of us has useful magic."

Rainer steeples his hands, trying to appear unaffected, but I see the way his jaw tics. There's a fury in his eyes, directed at Eoin.

Ken reaches for a glass of wine and chugs it to the dregs, before planting it back on the table. "You know I don't like all the quarreling when I'm sober!" He beckons for a servant who's been lingering along the side wall, and requests more wine.

"Enough." Rainer slams his fist on the table, rattling the glasses. I jump, gripping the edge of my chair nervously.

"Welcome to your first Ostara preparation, Alessia," Sennah says cheerfully, as if these arguments are totally normal. "Hoorah!" Raising her glass, she clinks it with Ken's freshly poured one.

"Oh, don't be so sensitive, fearcaller," Eoin says, his tone light again. "Come to Terra Court, and we'll teach you how to grow those pretty little roses you love so much."

"What roses?" I whisper.

"Haven't you seen the gardens?" Eoin asks me. I nod, my brows drawn tight in confusion as I think of the endless bushes of roses—hues of red, violet, pink. "Rainer has a thing for flowers—"

"Eoin," Sennah hisses.

"What? He does a fabulous job, but he just can't get his mother's favorite roses right, and he's too stubborn to let any elemental faeries help him. It's the kind of male he is. He'd rather suffer alone in his pain than let anyone lend him a hand. He hates me for no reason other than the fact I can grow the one flower he can't."

Everyone's quiet for a second, and when I meet the prince of fear's eyes, I see an unexpected expression there—something akin to an apology. He bites his bottom lip, fiddling with his fork.

"What flower can't you grow?" I ask.

"Sunset Roses," Eoin says. "They're a crossbreed. Actually quite easy to grow, especially if you know what you're doing, but alas—" He gives Rainer a pointed look.

He keeps speaking, but my ears ring and my head spins.

The words sink inside of me like a boulder in a lake.

Sunset roses.

I dream of Rainer and his sunset roses. Often. How could I possibly have known about his desire to grow them? That they were his mother's favorite?

"I dreamt it," I whisper. Rainer rubs the back of his neck and a blush stains his cheek. "I dreamt of *you.*"

Magic.

Again.

It has to be.

I don't believe in coincidences—not like this.

Rainer tenses, his jaw tightening. Ken must have heard me, too, because he goes stock still, leaning forward in his chair.

"What does *mo róisín* mean, Rainer?" I demand.

I've never heard that phrase anywhere other than my dream. How could I hear it in my subconscious without hearing it in my waking life? Unless my dreams were somehow real all along. Perhaps he somehow used magic to enter my dreams or bring my dreams to life. I'm not sure exactly what my theory is, but I hold my breath as I wait for his response.

I realize Eoin, Sennah, Ken, and Viv are silently watching the two of us as they eat slowly, as if they're afraid to make a move or speak up.

"What's going on?" Eoin finally asks as he reaches for my hand, giving me a reassuring squeeze.

Rainer tracks the movement, narrowing his eyes. "Nothing that concerns you."

"What does it mean, Rainer?" I repeat, my voice stern this time.

"Not here. Not now, Alessia."

"Tell me. *Now*."

He sighs. "It means… *my little rose*."

"You—you—!" I can't even speak.

Rainer… was in my dreams.

Real-Rainer is dream-Rainer.

I release Eoin's hand and push my chair back, standing to leave.

I had wondered how I heard the new, unfamiliar phrase in my dreams. I dusted it off, figuring I heard it somewhere and it lingered in my subconscious. But no. It was Rainer all along.

I'm violated by the revelation that my dreams weren't innocent at all. They were—I don't know—but they weren't private. They didn't belong to me. My cheeks flush as I realize I kissed him. We kissed. I almost—oh gods. It's somehow worse than him walking in on me pleasuring myself to the memory of his kiss.

A kiss that was real.

"Alessia—"

"How could you?"

Rainer's icy eyes soften. "Alessia, *please*. It's not what you think."

My knees go weak. The desperation in his voice heats my blood. I've never heard him use the word *please*. Somehow, it feels monumental. My head tells me I'm being stupid, but my body responds to his effortlessly, falling for the kind act by becoming lax.

How have I become such a silly, stupid girl—the one who lusts after a cruel faerie prince, simply because he says her name and uses the word please?

Char would be disappointed in me.

After a moment of hesitation, I sit.

I'm not fleeing.

I'll wait out the brunch so I can catch Rainer alone afterward. This isn't a conversation I want to have in front of nosey ears. If I can wait out the lord's violent punishments, I can wait out an awkward brunch. Both are painful in their own way, but I'd still rather be here than facedown on the lord's table getting whipped. So, this? This is nothing. I'll sit here quietly and bide my time, as I simmer in my newfound rage.

As much of a disappointment as I've become, at least my self-control would make Char proud.

After brunch finishes up, Eoin plants a kiss on my hand. Rainer watches us from across the room, even though he's engaged in conversation with Sennah, Viv, and Ken, and his eyes flash dark blue again.

I wonder if it's related to his emotions, or his magic, or both.

"You could come with me," Eoin says. My attention snaps back to him. "To Terra Court. If you feel unsafe here." He glances at Rainer to make his point.

"I—"

The answer should be an easy yes, especially after how Rainer used his power on me, and how unwelcoming most of the Umbra Court has been, but a tug deep inside me anchors me to the ground. Something in the way Rainer said "please," earlier haunts my mind. Though I'm irrefutably bothered by his actions and misuse of magic to influence both my fears and dreams, I need to know why.

Mostly, I need to know if the Rainer in my dreams is truly the fae I know. If so, it changes everything. It certainly complicates things, but it changes it all.

"I can't go with you, Eoin."

"If you change your mind, Viv can bring you to us. You'll be safe at my court."

"It's beyond the Cursed Wood?"

"Yes—the opposite direction of the Gleam."

"How do you get through the forest?"

"We don't. We fly."

"You—what?" I peek over his shoulder, checking for wings.

"Not me." He laughs. "Our court has fae warriors with wings. They transport us."

"That's—" A lot to take in. But Sennah did mention there were tons of different types of fae. "Wow."

Eoin smiles at me, his eyes sweet like melted chocolate. "If you'd prefer not to fly, Ostara is the only time of year the curse on the woods is broken. The veil is thin between the Mother and our power, and it temporarily neutralizes the curse."

"That's why the Ostara celebration is held here," I murmur.

"Yes. We used to hold the celebration in our court, but since it's the only night to safely travel the forest, we've gifted Rainer the honor of hosting."

"He doesn't seem like a celebration type."

"Oh—he isn't. It's less for him and more for his people."

Sometimes it's hard to remember that Rainer is a prince, that he oversees an entire court.

Eoin's expression turns serious. "Alessia, be careful here."

"I will."

"I mean it. There are things about the prince that are...off. Between his forest and his dislike for humans, I worry for you."

"Don't."

"If you truly knew, I think you'd take my offer up and leave with me."

My gut squeezes. "What aren't you telling me, Eoin?"

He steps forward, placing a hand on my shoulder.

"Get your hands off of her." Rainer strides up to us, his gaze lethal as he pins Eoin with his stare.

Eoin ignores him, but he doesn't try to finish whatever thought he had a moment ago. Instead, he sighs and says, "Be safe." He turns and walks out with his sister, Viv, and Ken, giving me one last worried glance over his shoulder.

What secrets are Rainer keeping, and why does the Terra Prince care so much?

"I don't like him," Rainer says.

"I can tell."

"He'll try to take you away, simply to get at me."

That infuriates me. "I'm not a pawn for you spoiled princes to play with."

"*I* know you're not." Rainer offers a lopsided smile, and it catches me entirely off guard. The air whooshes out of my lungs at the sight of his dimples.

Dimples.

Like my dream.

He's been there since the beginning. Since the very first dream I've had about him.

"Do you really know that though?" I whisper-yell. "Because how dare you."

A blue-haired servant with jerky movements, scurries around the table collecting our dirty dishes. At my tone towards Rainer, they bug their eyes at me. Rainer tilts his head to the side, dismissing them with a flick of his hand.

Once we're alone, he props himself up on the edge of the table, swinging his legs and staring at me with an oddly expectant expression. He flicks a blueberry upward, catching it effortlessly in his mouth.

"How dare I what exactly?"

"You know what! You—you—bastard."

A warm, inviting laugh leaves him, totally at odds with the cold demeanor I normally see from him. It almost reminds me of the Rainer from my dream. The lighthearted, fun, easy-going Rainer. I shrug the thought away, reminding myself it doesn't matter if he seems happier or nicer now, he explicitly violated my privacy when he entered my dream.

"Enlighten me, please."

"You invaded my privacy. Somehow you—your magic—you practically assaulted me in my own dream!"

"Your—what?" His expression grows serious. "I told you I would never touch someone against their will."

"Yeah, well…It doesn't matter because you were still technically taking advantage of me while I dreamed."

He hops down off the table, rolling up his sleeves to show-case tattoos on his muscular left forearm, as he strolls toward me with arrogance. He stops a few inches away, and leans forward to whisper into my ear. His eyes darken to navy then fade back to pale-blue.

"No, Alessia, taking advantage would have been having my way with you when you consumed those berries. When you straddled me in the grass. When you begged me to join you in bed."

His tone makes my stomach tumble, and I'm immediately too hot and cold at the same time. I step back to put some distance between us, wiping my hands on my thighs.

"Stay out of my dreams you dirty, manipulative—"

"Feckin' hell." He grips my chin firmly yet gently, forcing me to look at him. "Damn it, Alessia! I've *never* been in your dreams. That's not how my power works."

"But the sunset roses and—"

"Bloody hell."

"Stop cursing!"

"I had a feeling... but you're..." he mutters. "Gods."

"*What?!*"

"I didn't know." He runs his hands over his face with a groan. "I—" Shaking his head, he gives me a sad look. "I should've known something was up the moment I had a good dream."

"What does that mean?"

"I've had nothing but nightmares for years. Part of being a fearcaller. I deal in fears, nightmares if you will, and that's the price I pay. But with you—anytime I dream of you, it's a good dream. My nightmares have mostly subsided since you showed up."

"Because it's not your dream you're having." I cross my arms. "I don't know how you're entering my dreams, but stop it."

"That's the thing." He gives me a perplexed look. "It's not—I'm not—"

"You are infuriating." My list of questions seems to be growing the longer I stay here. "Feckin' faerie," I mutter.

He steps so close our chests almost touch, and he reaches out to push a curl out of my face. "Did you just swear at me?" His lips twitch. "I'm a bad influence on you, it would appear."

I almost laugh, but I catch myself. "This isn't funny."

"Alessia—"

"Brother!" A booming voice calls out, heavy boots thundering through the hall.

The moment between us shatters as Rainer steps back.

A figure marches towards us. He looks eerily similar to Rainer, but with slightly darker skin, and his sheared hair shows off soft, rounded ears. He's shorter and more muscular than Rainer, and dressed in simple, all black leathers—similar to the regalia of Viv and Ken. There's a scar that cuts through his left eyebrow, and as he gets closer, I see similar scars on his neck and hands.

He must be a warrior—no doubt.

But brother?

"Tynan, keep it down or I'll put you down." Rainer presses a finger into his temple. "What an honor to see you in these halls," he says sarcastically.

"You know I never pass on festivities."

"Oh, but you always do."

"And who is this lovely creature?" His eyes turn to me, a darker, stormier blue than Rainer's. He takes my hand in his, placing a lingering kiss on the back of it as a way of greeting. My skin crawls as he licks his lips.

Rainer moves between the two of us and his brother drops my hand immediately.

"Oh, do tell, is she yours?" His brother asks.

"His?" I balk. I step away, putting space between me and Rainer. "I'm not—" Rainer glances over his shoulder at me, his nostrils flaring in warning before returning his attention to his brother.

Something in his gaze inspires me to keep my mouth shut.

"She is *mine*," he hisses with lethal possession.

The words send butterflies through my stomach. The words should terrify me—especially coming from him. But for some reason they give me a feeling of empowerment.

There's an invisible pull between me and Rainer, and in that moment, I can't help the possessiveness that overcomes me in response.

He is mine, echoes in my skull. *Mine. Mine. Mine.*

I squeeze my eyes shut, shaking away the strange feeling.

"Too bad," Tynan says. "As much as I cherish these delightful reunions, Rainer, I'm informed we have things to discuss."

Rainer goes rigid. "We do," he says. "Yet you waited until I sought you out instead of coming to me the moment something was amiss."

"I'm here now, aren't I?" Tynan yawns dramatically. "I could use a nap and a meal. How bout it, *Prince*?" His lips pull up into a smug smile. "Then we can talk Shyga and restless spirits."

"Spirits?" My eyes bulge.

"You're drunk." Rainer sighs. He turns to me and says, "We're not done with our conversation." Then he walks past his brother with controlled confidence and a snap of his fingers.

After another pointed look tossed in my direction, Tynan says, "And you, sweet thing, shouldn't get too comfortable."

He winks, and I shift uncomfortably.

Tynan follows Rainer. The two of them disappear down the hallway, the click-clack of their boots fading out.

My heart thumps wildly in my chest, and I exhale a long breath. Why haven't I heard about Rainer's brother? They don't seem to get along. Not that Rainer seems to get along with anyone, really.

And what the hell is Shyga? Spirits?

Curiosity burns brightly inside me.

More importantly than all of that, Rainer and I need to finish this conversation about our shared dreams—about whatever magic he's using to invade them and why. I refuse to sleep until he gives me answers.

Temptation to follow the brothers arises, but Tynan is unsettling. I'd rather not spend another moment in his presence.

The only thing worse than a cruel fae prince is a cruel fae prince with an equally troubled brother.

Twenty-Eight
Instinct Ends Up Being Right
Rainer

Everything changes with the dream-sharing revelation. I still haven't fully wrapped my head around the implication. It *should* be impossible. A human cannot dreamwalk…yet, Alessia was definitely in my dreams.

She can fight my magic.

She can dreamwalk with me.

Until I confirm that it means what I think it means, and find out *how* it's even possible, I need to keep this little nugget of information quiet. It will attract unwanted attention. And *if* it somehow is what I think—

No!

It just can't be.

I refuse to accept it…even though it explains my inexplicable draw to her—*why* I can't let her go. Why I'm driven to protect her.

Sighing, I run a hand over my face. This is a mess.

Tynan and Alessia's paths were not supposed to cross. But sure enough, Tynan just couldn't wait for me in my father's old office. I had asked the servants to bring him there when he arrived, but I can't blame them for their inability to hold him there against his will.

He's a very… persuasive male.

Which is part of the reason I stationed him away from my court.

Now, I'll work overtime to keep him away from Alessia. I can't trust Tynan not to glamour her, to influence her, but I had new wards instated this morning. He's the brother with the power of persuasion. That skill didn't come in my repertoire.

Alessia is going to want answers. Not only about the dreamwalking situation—which I don't even know where to begin with—but also about my brother and Shyga. I avoided gauging her reaction at those new bits of information, because I know Tynan is trying to stir up drama already.

I lean against my father's glossy-oak desk, crossing my arms. Staring down my brother, I push all other thoughts aside for the moment. He runs his grubby finger over the leather spines on the bookshelf, acting interested.

As if he's ever read a book in his life.

"You need to watch your mouth under my roof, Tynan."

He knows the rules and expectations I've set between us. No one is to know we're brothers. A feat he's already disrespected by announcing it to Alessia.

Thank the gods the others were gone.

Kenisius knows the truth—he's the only one who knows all of my secrets—and I'd prefer to keep it that way.

"What are you so scared of, brother? Afraid your beloved court will learn the truth?"

I grit my teeth. Without responding, I call forth my power, focusing on Tynan's stocky, swaggering frame. When his steps falter, and he sucks in a sharp breath, I smirk to myself.

I've learned how to block out his glamour, yet he can't block my fearcaller power out. It gives me a smug sense of satisfaction.

"Rai—" Tynan grips his head, his eyes wide.

Cocking my head, I focus on him for a few more seconds, letting him simmer in whatever invisible nightmare I've conjured up for him. I'm curious to know what his fears are, but I suppose it doesn't matter. It never really matters what they are, just that they exist.

I clear my throat, rolling up my sleeves, before dropping the mental connection between us and releasing him from my power.

"You're a prick, you know?" Tynan tries to laugh off the moment, but it's forced.

Good.

I've unsettled him.

Having Tynan here, it reminds me of how much I hate this room and why. It belonged to Seamus Iorworth, the faerie who I thought was my blood. The male who should've been my father—who everyone thinks was my father.

He was also the man who smacked my mother around so badly before I was born, that she sought secret solace in another man's arms. And after I was born, Seamus smacked us both around.

Anyone who hits a defenseless child is disturbed.

And having Tynan here reminds me that most of my life, as perceived from the outside, is a lie. We share a father, who in many ways, is worse than Seamus could ever be.

My heart breaks all over again for my mother, for her poor choice in males, and the way they used and abused us both.

Perching on the edge of the desk, I gesture for Tynan to grab a seat on the red-velvet sofa. He obliges.

"Speak," I say.

"The spirits are unsettled."

I cross my arms, unamused. "Clearly."

"They've been unsettled for a few weeks—"

"And you've waited this long to inform me?"

He rubs the back of his neck and grins. "I had it under control."

"Wrong answer."

"Instead of crossing over, or resting in Shyga as they should, there are a few shadow-spirits trying to escape."

"They shouldn't be able to escape," I mutter.

"No shite, brother," he says sarcastically. He leans back, resting his ankle on his opposite knee.

The arrogance sickens me.

"I've been able to round them up and draw them back to the bog, and they don't appear to be causing any damage."

"For now." I shake my head. "Considering they shouldn't be free-roaming in the first place, we shouldn't allow ourselves to get complacent when it comes to their capabilities."

"They're just spirits, brother, relax."

"I say this with zero respect, *brother*, feck yourself."

He barks a laugh. "Your knickers must be on too tight again."

Running a hand through my hair, I close my eyes and will my patience to stay with me a little longer.

"If ruling is getting to be too much for you, I'll be glad to switch posts. You can look after the spirits yourself."

"You will never rule my court."

"Does the court truly even belong to you? What do you think your people would say if they knew your mother was a whore and your bloodline is impure?"

I growl, launching myself toward Tynan. Fisting his shirt in both hands, I pull him up so he's level with me. "Talk about my mother again, and I will string you up by your innards. Do not test me."

"Awfully protective, coming from the boy who killed her."

Black and red spots fill my vision, and I crash my fist into his face. His head snaps back, and blood immediately spurts out of his nostrils. He squeezes the bridge of his nose to staunch it.

"Nice punch, little brother." He smiles, and blood drips down into his mouth, staining his teeth crimson.

The sight of his blood is another stab in the heart. It's a reminder that deep down, Tynan and I are the same. It's *his* blood, our father's blood, that cursed me.

Poisoned my veins.

Tynan is a reminder of all the things wrong in my life.

"You need to head back to Shyga," I demand.

Tynan slips his shirt off, using it to wipe the blood from his face. "Can't."

"What do you mean you can't," I grumble.

"There is one more shadow-spirit missing. I haven't located it yet. Though I did track it to your little forest."

Bloody hell.

I stride to the desk, placing my palms on the surface and leaning forward with a heavy sigh.

Tynan and Eoin are both a threat to my court. Eoin wants my throne, and Tynan has the information that could potentially help him earn it. Worse, they're both a threat to Alessia. And the surprising nugget of our dreamwalking changes things.

"You're banned from using your glamour while you're here, Tynan."

I'd ban him from speaking to members of the court, and attending the Ostara celebration next week, but unfortunately, that would only tempt him further. At least with wards on the grounds,

I can physically ban him from accessing his magic. It's the best I can do for now. That, and hope he's gone before Ostara.

I need my brother to find the spirit and take it back to Shyga—to get away from me, my court, and the human girl who's weaseled her way under my skin. The one I feel an innate obligation to protect with every fiber of my being, despite her warranted hatred for me.

A hatred I provoked—for good reason—but now regret.

Especially if my instinct ends up being right.

Twenty-Nine
Like A Sunset Rose
Alessia

The next few days are a blur. I train each morning with the shifter duo. They make it easier to remind myself to be patient—that once I'm comfortable and confident with my newly developing self-defense skills, I can leave.

I can leave whenever I want.

That's what I'm holding onto. No one is forcing me to stay here, and the simple fact that it's my choice to stay gives me the sense of freedom I've sought for so long. Freedom isn't always about having a perfect, pleasant life, sometimes it's merely about having the ability to *choose* which hard route you want to take.

Other than that, if I'm not in my room, I mostly stick to the kitchens, helping Das Celyn and Das Lulu with Ostara festivity preparations.

The autonomy is nice.

In fact, I've been toying with taking Eoin up on his offer. Though it seems as if I'm safe here, I can't help the new feeling of my safety being an illusion. I don't trust Rainer and his power.

As grateful as I am for Viv and Ken, I can't fully trust them either. We've known each other less than two months, but they've been with Rainer for who knows how long.

They're fae.

They're loyal to each other.

I'm simply a human in passing.

Over the week, I don't see Rainer in person or in my dreams, much to both my pleasure and dismay. We have unfinished business, and I've been aching to speak with him—even if I have to seek him in my dreams. But he's heeded my warnings and stayed away. Too little, too late.

I hope he's sleeping. That he's not having nightmares. Not that he deserves the peaceful rest, but I still hurt for him and whatever life he's lived before me.

The castle bustles with more servants than ever. Everyone is working double-time to prepare for this Ostara festivity.

The Terra princess uses her magic to help the gardens blossom and bloom into an even more beautiful sight—something I hadn't thought possible. It's ethereal how lovely it looks. The entire castle is crawling with rose vines—inside and out. The Terra prince, Eoin, shapes the hedges with Ken and Viv, taming the overgrowth.

I'm pleasantly surprised the royals are comfortable getting their hands dirty.

Inside, the deep dark hues are swapped out for swaths of color. Everything shimmers and shines.

After seeing the weird shadow things in the trees twice now, and meeting Rainer's brother, I'm almost grateful everyone is too busy to pay me mind. And with all the ominous warnings—especially the most recent ones from Eoin and Tynan—I need the valerian root tea to sleep again.

Sometimes I swear I hear my name whispered in the wind, the shadow-spirit beckoning for me, but I ignore it. And whenever I glimpse a shadow moving in the trees, I avert my eyes.

Tonight, I chug the valerian tea like I have nights past. As soon as I lay my head on the pillow, I fall fast asleep.

It smells like cinnamon and something woodsy—pine, perhaps? Laughter carries down the hallway. I pass a handful of doors until I approach an open doorway. Chatter trickles out. I poke my head in to see what appears to be a family sitting near a giant pine wreath, eating sweets.

The room is decorated elaborately, with sparkling ornaments and tinsel.

"Snickahdoodles are my favorite," a little boy with black curls says as he fists a cookie into his mouth. He's probably no more than eight, sitting on the worn-in sofa with what I presume to be his parents nearby.

"Snickerdoodles, Rainer," the father says, casting him a disgusted glance. "You sound like a child."

"He is *a child, Seamus," the mother says, her voice small and timid. "Let him be."*

They're a beautiful couple, with pointed ears and layers of expensive clothing and gold jewelry. But they're rigid. I recognize them from the portraits in Rainer's mother's wing.

Looking around, it's clear this is Rainer's current estate, but it's filled with much more—just, more. There are portraits lining the walls, decorations and knick-knacks in crystal displays, furniture that's clearly worn and used.

Yet it's somehow colder than the castle I know in waking.

It's missing something.

I pop back out into the hallway, a strange feeling in my stomach from witnessing such an intimate moment between Rainer's family.

From seeing a young Rainer. It feels less like a dream and more like a memory.

"Why the hell am I dreaming about Rainer's childhood?" I groan aloud.

"You're not."

I gasp. Leaning lazily against the hallway's wall, arms crossed across his chest, Rainer stares at me with a hollow expression.

"Stop sneaking up on me you dirty dreamstalker," I hiss.

"Dreamwalker," he mutters. "And you're *the dreamwalker. It's my dream you're in." He sighs, peering over at a decorative grandfather clock, just as the bell tolls out in a midnight call. "Nightmare, actually."*

Even in the dream, his forehead is marred with lines. His lips tug down. He's tired. Worn out. Defeated.

"What do you mean?"

The little boy in the room screams, and I wince.

"Keep your hands off him, Seamus!" The woman cries.

There's a loud thump, and she yelps.

Rainer flinches at the sound.

"You're awfully convinced that I would violate your privacy and lie about it." His eyes meet mine, unwavering. "Which is curious considering I've been nothing but kind to you."

"Kind? You think you've been kind *to me?"*

His brows scrunch. "In more ways than you'll know."

The family's voices fade, and the otherwise bright space begins to dim. My body grows heavy, weighed down. Trying to take a step feels like I'm moving in slow motion.

"You admitted you were in my dreams," I say, but my voice is warbled. "You never denied it."

"You misunderstood. I never said I was in your dream." His icy blue eyes peer into mine, with a hint of challenge. "But you, mo róisín, are in mine. Again."

"Wait, what?"

"I recommend staying close."

Screams burst free of the room where the family sits. I move in slow-motion—trying to get a view of what's happening.

I beg my feet to move quicker, but Rainer's hand snakes out, reaching for my own. He shakes his head.

"Don't." His eyes plead with mine, his mouth in a tight line.

Whatever is happening in that room, he doesn't want me to see it. Disobeying his wishes would be entirely hypocritical, considering I thought he was violating me by being in my *dreams initially.*

Hesitantly, I reach out and accept his hand. We interlace fingers and run down the hall, away from the room filled with desperate screams.

"We have to move," he says, tugging me along.

I swallow the lump in my throat.

The screams get louder and a metallic scent reaches my nose.

"What's happening?" I whisper.

Rainer's color drains from his face, he looks as if he might be sick.

After a few more yards, he slows until he stops moving entirely, frozen in the hall with a pained expression.

"Come on, you said we have to keep moving." I tug his hand, but he stays still as stone.

I'm not sure why *we have to keep moving, if it's just a dream nothing can harm us, right? Just the fact that I'm questioning the possibility is enough to make me lose confidence, and either way, based on Rainer's reaction, I don't think staying here is a good idea.*

But it feels like my feet have turned to stone. I try to walk but I can't.

The hallway gets darker and darker, then the screaming stops, leaving us in silence.

A thumping noise comes from the room we left behind.

The scrape of something heavy dragging across the hardwood floors reaches my ears, sending a chill across my skin.

"Hold your breath, Alessia," Rainer whispers.

A tidal wave of bright crimson blood rushes out of the open door- ways, surging down the hall toward us.

A scream escapes me, and I shut my eyes just as the warm liquid rushes over us.

It's just a dream.

Just a dream.

Just a dream.

Please get me out of here.

Please.

Please.

I chant the words in my head, as my lungs burst—desperate for air. I'm clinging to Rainer's hand for dear life, desperate to get us both out of here.

I picture the golden river Rainer and I played in before. I imagine the sun on our skin and laughter in our lungs. I focus so hard I feel like I'm going to drive myself insane.

After a moment, a tingling sensation surrounds my body. And all of a sudden, we burst through to the surface, gasping for breaths.

The soft ripple of water traverses through the river. The air even smells fresher—no longer thick with warm cinnamon spice.

Rainer releases my hand.

I open my eyes and see that we are truly at the river. We're no longer in the house where something terrible is happening. Instead, we stand in front of the golden dream-river once again. The entire tone has altered. The air is lighter, clearer. My body grows lighter again.

Rainer stares at me with awe, a longing he doesn't attempt to hide.

"It's real," he mutters, more to himself than me. "You—"

I sit silently, waiting for him to go on.

"That nightmare. Even I can't—" His tone sounds almost accusing, and he eyes me warily as if he doesn't trust me. "But you're a bloody human."

"What was happening back there?" I ask, looking away and sitting at the edge of the water.

"I don't—I can't talk about it." His voice cracks with emotion on the last part.

Witnessing such a vulnerable moment of his makes me feel like an intruder.

With a heavy sigh, he plops down next to me, keeping a few paces between us. Hurt and brokenness mar his expression.

Despite being irked, I can't help but ache for him. Rainer is so different in the dreamscape. I've seen him laugh and play, and now, I've seen him trembling with fear. He's so alive in his dreams. So filled with emotion and vulnerability, and it's so unlike the Rainer I've met in person. He appears almost human himself, nothing more than a broken man.

That, combined with the realization that I'm the one invading his dreams—not the other way around—tugs at my heartstrings.

I make a deal with myself. For tonight, in this dream, I will forget about Rainer's transgressions. Here, he cannot harm me. I've proved to be in control. I have nothing to fear.

Slowly scooting over, I wrap my arms around him as we continue to face the river. I'm shocked when he responds by pulling me into his chest.

Rainer suffered something unfathomable.

The clues are all there in front of me. It shouldn't be my concern at all, except that I've been dragged, quite literally, into his nightmares. I can't shake the ominous feeling that I'm here for a reason, as crazy as it seems. This strong, arrogant prince hides a broken little boy deep inside. His trauma shaped him. And I'll be damned if I don't understand that in my soul.

I toss and turn for the rest of the night after I wake from Rainer's nightmare. I can't stop thinking about what he said before about his mother: she was murdered.

If his dream is anything to go off, he was only a child. Was his father the one who murdered his mother? How did Rainer survive? Where was his brother?

It takes everything in me to stay firmly planted in bed. I want to run to him, to hold him and reassure him everything will be all right, just as I did in my dream.

But why?

I don't owe him anything. He's been wishy-washy with me since I've arrived. Then, at brunch, he made a fool of me and subjected me to my own fears. He never apologized, not that I expect a fae to. I can't shake the draw I have toward him despite it all. And seeing tears—I swear he had tears last night—really got to me.

In the morning, I go through the motions of training with Ken and Viv, though I'm distracted the entire time. Much to my benefit, they're equally as distracted with it being the Ostara celebration tonight.

The one night a year the curse is lifted—a curse I still don't fully comprehend.

When I return to my room, I find a single pink rose sitting at my door. Not the bright, hot pink like the Damask roses, but a lighter, softer color.

Rainer once said different colored roses have different meanings. This flower is a peace offering, and I wonder what it means, exactly.

I eat and nap, spending the day with my thoughts, until Das Celyn breezes into the room in a cloud of perfume.

I dash from the settee to greet them, desperate for answers. Though I'm still wary of them after the stunt they pulled, I'm relieved to see a familiar face.

"Das Celyn—where have you been?"

"Preparations for festivities aren't completed with idle hands, ya know."

Dressed in shiny black shoes, loose dark slacks and matching tucked-in vest, with a white bowtie at their neck and a matching hair bow at the back of their head, they look sophisticated.

"Well, you look fabulous."

They've gained some color and density to their cheeks, slowly opening themselves up to eating more over the weeks. An ounce of pride flickers in my chest.

Their lips tug up in a smile as they finger their vest.

"I happen to like Ostara. Now, let's get you dolled up."

A tremble runs through me at the choice of words.

Dolly.

Even when things seem lighter, easier, my life is forever tainted by his shadow. I choke it down, forcing a smile.

I am not weak.

I am strong.

I refuse to give the lord, and my memories of him, power over me any longer.

Das Celyn, oblivious to my inner struggle, trudges to the armoire, flinging it open and searching for something.

"Aha. Perfect for the celebration." They pull out a frilly, white dress with awful shoulder caps that distracts me from my inner turmoil.

"No! Absolutely not." I bolt to Das Celyn, ripping the dress from their hands. "I am still downright furious with you about the first dress you put me in."

Instead of scolding me like I expect, they only laugh. I'm stunned silent as I watch their face light up in humor. Their entire body vibrates with laughter.

"I was wondering when you'd finally start fighting back."

"You dressed me in that treacherous purple ensemble for your own amusement." I grumble to myself as I toss the white dress aside. "You are *not* doing it again."

"It was quite funny."

"Not for me!"

"I had only hoped to help you snag the prince's attention."

I don't have to ask which one—I know she's talking about Rainer. I blush.

"Don't act like you were doing me a favor," I say.

"Humans," they mutter. "Believe it or not, playing tricks and pranks is our way of showing our fondness."

I yank a bunch of dresses aside in the armoire, searching for something better than they picked out for me. They can entertain themselves another way, not by making me their joke.

"Yes, I tricked you into that purple thing," they admit. "Partly for amusement—it can get dull around here—but mostly because I've been waiting for the day you stand up for yourself. I figured throwing you to the wolves might be the quickest way to sharpen you up."

Their words remind me of something similar Rainer said once, about fighting for myself. "What do you mean?"

"You came to us so weak, so broken, Alessia. You would never stand a chance here—anywhere for that matter—with how namby-by-pamby you were."

"Namby-pamby?"

"Weak-kneed. Spineless—"

"Pathetic," I finish. I plop to the ground, resting my head against the armoire.

"We weren't making fun of you, Alessia. We were pushing you to stand up for yourself."

"By bullying me?"

"Bullying is not the term we'd use. Fae don't take as much offense to insolence and sass as humans do. If a fae cares enough to help you grow—to push you to be stronger—well, they care about you. It's as simple and as complicated as it sounds." They shrug.

"Ah, so you *do* care about me." I smile smugly at Das Celyn. "What was that you said about me? I'm growing like a wart on your arse?"

Das Celyn laughs even harder, wiping a small bit of moisture that gathered beneath their left eye. "Like a fungus on an unwashed buttock."

"Yeah that's a very heartening term of endearment."

They grunt, continuing to rummage through the armoire without sparing me a glance.

Their words bring Rainer to the forefront of my mind. He let me stay here, despite clearly not wanting to. He pushed me to train.

But he also pushed me away.

After experiencing his vulnerability in that nightmare last night, I'm starting to think his unsympathetic act is just that—an act. There has to be a reason he's pushing me away, and maybe I can convince him to open up to me, or at the very least, stop pushing me away.

Is he afraid to get close to others because he lost his parents? Or is there more to it? Is he truly afraid of hurting me?

I'm choosing to overlook the use of his fearcaller power on me. At least temporarily. We've made too much progress over the past month for everything between us to be phony. And now that I know our dreams together are real, that dream-Rainer himself is the real Rainer, it's easier to forgive him.

He's not human, after all. He's fae. They have different rules and standards than I'm used to.

After letting my anger and shock subside, his words finally sunk in: he's not the one invading my dreams, I've been invading his. I'm not sure how it's possible, or what it means except that he hasn't been violating me like I initially assumed.

If I'm not mistaken, it's as if he hadn't noticed it was truly me in his dreams until I mentioned it at brunch. Even with his indifferent mask on, he couldn't hide the flash of shock that coursed through him at the revelation, which confuses me further.

"Das Celyn?"

"Hmm?" They grunt as they pull a few dresses out, but I'm not partial to any of them.

"What do pink roses mean?"

"Pale pink, coral, or fuchsia?"

I glance at the rose sitting atop my nightstand, and their eyes follow as they pull back from the armoire.

"Ah. Peach." A smirk tugs at their lips. "Gratitude. Appreciation. Sincerity. *Friendship*."

They wink with the last word.

Heat blossoms beneath my rib cage. That is absolutely a peace offering. He's making an effort. In his own way, he's trying to draw me in instead of pushing me away.

Das Celyn steps aside and I move forward, rummaging through the armoire myself. Finally, I spot a beautiful gossamer gown—it's bell-shaped and shimmery, gorgeous for how simple it is. I pull it free, and I realize it's not only a pink tone like it first appears. When the light hits it, it shimmers, as if it's changing colors, morphing into deeper pink with orange tones.

"Perfect," I whisper.

They stare at me, scrutinizing my face and then nod. "Good choice."

Before I can change into the dress, I let Das Celyn help me with my hair.

"You're really good at this, you know." That's as close as I can get to thanking them.

"I used to do hair and makeup for the courtesans in the city," Das Celyn says so quietly I almost didn't hear them. "When I was young."

"Do you ever miss it?"

"Yes," they whisper.

And their talent shows, because they've outdone themselves.

When I glance into the mirror, my lungs tighten with disbelief. I look… stunning.

The dress has a fitted bodice, with small beads decorating my bust and emphasizing the curves there, before flaring out with a fun, gossamer skirt that reaches just above my knees. Most of my ashy curls are loose and down my back, but each side has a section braided back from my face, tying together loosely in the back.

My fingers ghost over the spot where my mark usually is—now covered by Das Celyn's cosmetics. It's the first time I've seen myself without the Tradeling tattoo, and it brings a swarm of feelings. Relief, gratitude, pride—at what I've overcome. I don't miss the mark by any means, and will gladly keep it covered for the night, but suddenly I realize that that marking no longer owns me.

I own it.

It's my badge of strength.

"That's a swell color with your complexion," Das Celyn says, pulling me from my thoughts.

I nod, still choking up at my reflection. I've never looked—or felt—so lovely in all my life.

They add a bit of kohl to my lash lines.

"Don't cry now, you'll smudge it," Das Celyn says, brushing a bit of powder onto my cheeks to finish off the look.

I feel like a princess. Not that I ever desired being one—if anything, I'd rather be a warrior like Viv—but there's nothing wrong with appreciating a beautiful dress as much as a deadly sword. I like that here I can have both.

I don't have to be just one thing or the other. I can be a sweaty, bruised mess in the morning, and a clean, pretty lady in the evening.

I also appreciate that nothing is forced upon me; if I hadn't liked this dress so deeply, no one would force me to wear it. I could've refused the purple dress. I could've stuck up for myself.

The fae push me, but not to break me. To build me.

Quickly slipping into a pair of matching pale pink flats, I follow Das Celyn out to the gardens, eager to experience Ostara firsthand with the fae.

As I glance down at my dress again, I realize why I'm so fond of it: I look like a sunset rose.

THIRTY

THE MERCY HE NEEDS

ALESSIA

The night sky is void of starlight, but twinkles with mischief instead. Fireflies sparkle in harmony with the stars and a bonfire roars with a cozy warmth beyond the gardens.

A few yards away from me, flower-covered tables—sporting vases of those alluring, aphrodisiac Damask roses—sit in a ring around a makeshift dance floor, where fae of all sorts work their feet skillfully to keep up with the rhythmic strings filling the air.

Though almost everyone is decked out in stunning, wispy dresses and silkiest fabrics, their feet are bare. Many wear flowers in their hair as they dance upon the grass.

Laughter and joy wash over me, and I relax as I realize this is the first time I'll be at an event for something other than servitude. Granted, the lord's events were typically balls, auction, or charity events—black-tie, stifling, uptight—whereas this event seems carefree and harmonious.

A curvy brunette female runs past us with no top—her nipples puckered and exposed. I balk and look away bashfully.

"Fae don't find bodies as revolting as humans do—it's part of nature," Das Celyn whispers to me.

"I'm not used to this," I say, my face hot with secondhand embarrassment.

"Bodies are nothing more than flesh and bones."

I ponder their words for a moment. "That is true I suppose."

"Enjoy the eve. Stay away from the faerie wine. I'll see you around." With a stern look, Das Celyn falls into a crowd.

"Wait, don't leave me!" I call after them, but they're already lost in the crowd.

My hands grip my skirts, as I nervously scan the yard. Other than the curious stares—no one pays me much mind.

A beautiful female with a headful of curls passes me, offering me a rose. I take it with a smile. When she's not looking, I hand it off to someone else nearby. Based on the amount of roses, moonberries, and wine overflowing on tables and in hands in every direction, it's clear this party is meant to incite pleasure.

Since I've already made a fool of myself with the moonberries, I'll stay away from those and the roses tonight. I want a clear head when I speak with Rainer. And I will speak with him. I'll demand it.

Besides, I'll let Fern's story be a lesson. A warning. About what can happen when a human loses themselves to faerie magic.

Making my way to the food tables, I find myself mindlessly swaying to the music. The itch to dance builds in me. Rainer isn't anywhere to be found, but I continue searching for him.

Right away, I spot another familiar face—the beloved bear shifter.

"Little human!" Ken roars at me, blocking me from the table I was approaching. A few eyes swing our way, crinkled with humor.

"Human," a passing fae scoffs, glaring at me.

"Gee, announce to everyone that I'm human, why don't you."

"Oh, we all know when there's one in our midst." He winks. "Why are you empty-handed? Want some wine?" He offers me his chalice.

"Das Celyn warned me not to indulge."

"Das Celyn doesn't know how to enjoy a night off work."

He tugs me to him in a friendly side hug, then I pull away to admire his bright slacks and tied back hair. He looks tidier than I've ever seen.

A burly male with a glass eye sidles up and wraps a hairy arm around Ken's neck affectionately. "There ya are, big fella."

Wanting to find Rainer anyway, I sidestep their large forms and move towards the food table.

Someone steps up beside me, the warmth of their body giving me goosebumps.

"Has anyone yet told you—" a soft, sensual accent caresses my ear as they whisper.

"—to stay away from the wine?" I interrupt. "Yes they have."

Turning to face Eoin, I offer him as true a smile as I can muster, but there's an inkling of disappointment that it's him and not Rainer.

Eoin chuckles. "The wine is quite fun, actually."

He smiles, full on, with a chiseled jaw, twinkling honey-brown eyes, and golden-kissed curls—a few shades darker than my own ashy curls, and bordering on light brown. He has the sort of tanned skin that outdoor servants get in the summer—bronzed—but he looks nothing like a servant in his white button up and tight fitting brown pants and brown lace-up boots. His pointy ears sport golden jewels, and he's much fancier in appearance than he was the last time I saw him.

"I was only asking if anyone has yet told you how stunning you are."

"Oh that's—that's sweet," I stammer, blushing.

"It's the honest truth."

He reaches up and brushes a lock of hair back from my face, and I bite my lip to keep a goofy smile from gracing my lips. I'm not at all used to the strange, ethereal beauty the fae possess. Felix wasn't ugly by any means, but my stomach never felt like it was being flipped inside out when I looked at him.

"You look wonderful yourself," I tell Eoin.

"We do make a darling pair tonight, if I might say so myself." He leans in, lowering his voice. "And I've thought of a way you can pay me back."

"Pay you back?" I jerk. "Pay you back for what?"

"I'm surprised you forgot so quickly." He chuckles. "You agreed to pay me back for being kind to you."

"Oh." My face falls. "You were serious about that?" Of course a faerie expects to be repaid for being kind. Everything is manipulation or a bargain here.

"I did say I knew of a way you could make it up to me."

When I go rigid, he seems to notice my change in demeanor and playfully bumps my shoulder.

"Hey now, I had only intended to ask you to dance. Nothing nefarious, I swear."

"That's it?"

"Dance with me." He puts a hand out. "We'll call it even." The crinkle at the corners of his eyes and upturned lips are inviting. "I'm not the Prince of Fear, I will not use and abuse you. Unlike Court Umbra, *we* like humans just fine."

He's right... he's *not* Rainer. That fact has the opposite effect of what he intended. I really want to go find him.

"Will you excuse me?"

Without waiting for an answer, I turn on my heels and try to look composed as I maneuver through the bubbling crowd, looking for the familiar set of icy eyes I crave.

As I push through the crowd of dancing, twirling fae, I run into both Ken and Das Celyn again, but no Rainer. I even spot Viv—still dressed in her warrior leathers—engaging in a dance with Princess Sennah, who's dressed dashingly in a floor-length, sky-blue strapless dress with flushed cheeks.

They stare at each other with stars in their eyes and swollen lips.

Viv has been nothing but kind to me the past few weeks during training, and I'm glad to see her so happy. I like seeing her loosen up like this—even if she refuses to lose the warrior garb.

My skin prickles with the sensation of someone watching me. When I glance up, I see just who I am looking for. Rainer lounges at a lazy angle with his ankles crossed and his back pressed against an oak tree, facing the partygoers. His black button-up sits open to reveal his ink as he sips slowly from a goblet. A few males and females bob around him desperate for his attention, but he continues to stare directly at me, ignoring their fuss.

He raises his glass in a salute, one side of his mouth tipping up in a grin that gives me a preview of those dimples.

My chest flutters with excitement. Just as I get my feet moving again, someone steps in front of me, cutting off my path.

Eoin.

"You ran away from me." He puts a hand over his heart and gives me a flirtatious grin. "Have I offended you?"

I muster a polite smile, biting back the human apology sitting on my tongue. My eyes dart past Eoin's shoulder, towards where Rainer stood under the magnolia tree. But now the tree stands alone. I scan the nearby folk, and only see the giggling fae but no Rainer.

"Looking for someone?" Eoin asks, following my line of sight.

"Yes I—I am, actually."

"Maybe I can help?"

I shake my head and dart off again, leaving him behind a second time.

I have to relieve my bladder anyways, so I head inside to my chambers. I figure it'll be a good starting place to search for Rainer. I'm borderline obsessed with finding him. I tell myself that it's because of our unfinished conversation last week, but part of me knows that's just an excuse.

There's the tense moments when we're alone, the desire I have for him, the connections in the dreamscape—which, now that I've had time to sit on it, I'm no longer angry about. I'd wished for Rainer from my dreams to be real...and he is.

I can't be mad at how it happened. It happened, and for that, I'm grateful.

Everyone sees the Prince of Fear—a cruel, angry male. And for a minute, when he used his fearcaller power on me, I saw that too. But now I see a broken little boy who grew into a heartbroken male. A male who shoulders too much trauma on his own.

Char once told me "all broken things heal, and broken girls heal into indestructible women," but what do broken little princes heal into?

After I do my business and clean up, I leave my chambers. Sconces in the hallway light my path as I head back toward the stairs. Just as I make it to the top of the stairwell, a figure steps out in front of me and I plow into them.

I grunt, stumbling backward. A hand flashes out to steady me, and I find myself staring up at Rainer's scowling face.

"There you are," I say awkwardly. "I've been looking for you."

"Yes. Looking very hard indeed…though I don't think you'll find me in a set of Terra eyes."

My brows shoot up. "Are you jealous of Eoin?"

His jaw clenches but he says nothing.

"I'm not interested in him."

"Well, he's taken an interest in you."

"Is that really so bad?" I ask. I'm pushing his buttons now, just a little, but I can't help it. He really has no clue that it's *him* I'm drawn to. Him I've been seeking out tonight. Him I'm dressed for.

His little display of jealousy makes me feel like he might even feel the same way. It at least shows me that he feels something.

"No," he answers. "I can't blame him."

Rainer runs a hand through his shaggy hair, avoiding eye contact. I try not to stare at his beautiful face, or his broad chest. His eyes roam over my dress. He sucks in a sharp inhale and his eyes soften. It's as if he's seeing me for the first time tonight. Truly seeing me. He rubs a hand over his jaw, his mouth agape.

"You look—wow. You look radiant, mo róisín."

My skin warms under his gaze and I duck my chin.

"I got your rose," I whisper. "Is that your way of showing appreciation?"

He licks his lips, removing his gaze from mine. "It's—I'm not the best with words. Or…feelings."

"Understandable."

"There are much more important things we need to discuss, though," he says.

"I agree."

I need answers about the dreamwalking and the shadows that call to me. And I'd appreciate answers about his attitude toward me. Something tells me they're not as disconnected as they might first seem.

Voices float up the stairs.

"Not here."

Rainer sighs, and beckons me into a door at the top of the stairs, leading me into what appears to be yet another small sitting room. With one window facing out into the yard, the only light comes from the bonfire down below, casting just enough of an orange glow to peek around the space. A few shelves filled with dark, dull spines line the space. There's a worn sofa and a couple of wingback chairs in a semicircle in the middle of the room, and a writing desk pressed up against the wall beside the door.

I step towards one of the shelves, eager to see the titles, when my foot catches on the area rug and I trip.

My hand flashes out, and I try to grab the desk and steady myself, but I miss. I go all the way down, slicing my palm on the sharp edge of the desk instead, and landing heavily on my knees.

"Gods!" I hiss, cursing under my breath. It stings, but it's definitely not the worst wound I've endured.

Rainer runs to my side. "Did you hurt yourself?"

"No," I lie.

My knees burn where they hit the carpet, and my hand stings where I sliced it, but I won't admit that. Tears well in my eyes, but I blink rapidly to hold them back. Balling my wounded hand up, I hope that it isn't bleeding enough to drip on my dress. I'd hate to ruin it.

I'm hyperaware of Rainer kneeling down beside me. He sits on his knees, leaning over me. We're close. We're alone. And he's staring at me with a heated gaze, inches from my face. I bite my bottom lip to silence myself from saying something stupid.

"Let me see," he says sternly.

I'm attuned to his body heat, and the way both of our chests rise and fall at a quicker pace than normal. His scent of rose and clove encompasses me, drowning me in the best way.

Muffled voices and the music of the party fade away as I tune everything out. Everything but Rainer and his beautiful blue eyes. His usually expressionless face is now filled with the same emotion I feel.

"Be careful or I might think you actually care," I whisper.

"I *do* care." His voice comes out in a low rumble, but he doesn't freeze up or look away this time.

"Why do you wear such an apathetic mask, Rainer? I know that's not you." *Not after spending time with you in our dreams.*

"That's where you're wrong."

I shake my head, wishing he could see himself through my eyes right now—how vulnerable, kind, and warm he is. If only it was as easy as that.

"But it's not," I whisper. "In my dreams you're—"

"Dreams aren't reality, Alessia." His tone is cold as he slams his eyes shut. "*This* is reality. And I am what I am—a monster. A demon."

My heart pangs for him. For whatever he's going through. He doesn't deserve to brave it alone. "Your demons don't define you."

"I don't *have* demons." His voice gets loud with frustration. "I *am* the demon, Alessia." I shake my head, opening my mouth to disagree, but he continues, "You don't know what I've done. What I've gone through."

My features twist. "Then tell me."

He shakes his head. "It's my burden to carry, not yours. You don't deserve to be stuck with me." Stuck with him? What is he talking about? He broke the oath binding us, didn't he? "I'm a demon cursed with malice. And you, sweet Alessia, are a human cursed with mercy."

"Mercy isn't a curse," I whisper.

My forehead wrinkles in confusion. He's speaking in riddles.

"It is a curse when you're as unforgivable as I am," he whispers.

The air between us grows thicker.

"We're all a little unforgivable at times. Me included."

We sit there in silence, his face contorting in pain.

Before I can second guess myself, I let my attraction to him rule and allow myself to take action. I lean up, without hesitation, and press my lips to his. Even though I'm trembling with need, the kiss I gift him is soft and controlled.

It's to seal my words and show him I care. I don't know why, and maybe I shouldn't, but I do.

He groans into my mouth as he kisses me back. My hands travel into his thick, dark hair. His lips are so warm and soft, so right. Our tongues meet as I deepen the kiss. There's no awkwardness or self-consciousness as we explore each other's mouths. It's as if we were designed for this—this incredible, perfect kiss. For each other. If I thought one kiss would satisfy my want, I was sorely mistaken. It only lights the fire between us.

His hurting heart and his honesty only deepen my attraction to him. Ignoring my fresh wound, I grab his face with both hands, pulling him closer.

His mouth stops moving, pausing our kisses.

"Alessia—" his voice is hoarse when he speaks.

His eyes darken into a stormy blue. He pushes me away and turns his back to me, climbing to his feet hastily and facing out the window.

"Rainer? Your eyes—" It's not the first time they've changed color, either. It wasn't my imagination after all. "Are you—"

A strangled noise leaves his throat. "Leave."

I sit there on the floor stunned, with the desk between us and his back to me.

"I'm not going anywhere. You can't close me out anymore. I know you're struggling, but you're not alone. I'm sorry for kissing you, but I don't regret it. You told me to be strong, Rainer. So here I am. Standing up for myself and what I want."

"Leave."

"We still have things to discuss. The dreams. The shadows that call to—"

"Go!"

"Rainer—"

"I said leave. Now." His voice cuts me like shards of glass.

I'm so jarred by the change in demeanor—it's like someone dumped ice down my shirt. I sit there confused, feeling the memory of his lips on my own just a second prior.

"Don't make me call upon your fears." Any sign of the warmth and emotion he just revealed to me is gone.

He threatened me.

My hands shake with anger.

I can understand if he's hurting, in pain. But I can't understand how he can lead me on, open up, just to tear me down and push me away. Again.

"You're bleeding," he croaks. "I need you to go. Now!"

A tear slides down my cheek as I back away and out the door. I look back one last time at Rainer's broad back, just in time to see him slamming his fist into the wall. The door latches shut and I'm left staring at the barrier between us, more confused than ever.

Without the distraction of Rainer's lips on mine, the pain in my hand and knees come rushing back. I glance down at the cut on my palm. It's not that deep, but it's smeared with blood, and I realize I forgot about Rainer's aversion to blood...the trauma he faced as a young boy.

Blood triggers him, as the word dolly triggers me.

Shame floods me, guilt for not being more cognizant of the issue.

I rest my forehead against the door, wishing for Rainer to be all right.

Him being alone in his pain stings worse than my hand.

I'm reluctant to leave, not wanting to abandon him in this state. But after a few moments of silence, when it's clear he isn't exiting, I retreat, giving him the space he needs. Hopefully, the broken prince will let me be the mercy he deserves—the mercy he needs.

Thirty-One
Annihilate the People I Love
Rainer

M y breath comes in short, quick pants as I try to regain control.

We kissed—she kissed me—and it snapped my resolve. It was too much. Too sweet. Too pure. Too *everything*. In one fleeting moment, she built me up and demolished me all at once.

Kenisius is wrong, I *can't* control myself around her. Even without the scent of blood—which pushed me over the edge—it was too much.

She has become a part of me. And she wants me, too. But we cannot have each other the way we desire.

I fist my hair with both hands, battling the darkness inside of me. What a fool I was to think I could have Alessia to myself. We're destined to ruin each other. The only way I can have her is in my dreams, and that's not fair to her.

She deserves more.

How could fate be so cruel to us?

How could I be given the most precious gift, only to doom her?

The floorboards creak beneath me as I pace. The revelers celebrate in the yard below. They're filled with carefree joy, lust, pleasure. They have no cares in the world. Part of me wishes I could join them, find the freedom Alessia thinks I have, but the other part of me knows I never can.

She needs to leave—get as far away from me as she can. Thank the gods she left when she did.

I could've hurt her.

I could've killed her.

"Bloody hell!"

It's too hot in here.

My veins crawl beneath my skin, like hundreds of live worms trying to dig their way out. and I'm hungry... so hungry.

The scent of her lingers. I move to the window, cracking it to let the air in, hoping it'll wash her delicious smell away. It drives me insane. Sucking in big inhales of air does nothing to quell the burn in my lungs.

Music from the festivities below filter in through the open window, carrying with it laughter and whoops of joy. Alessia deserves to be down there. She deserves to enjoy everything Avylon has to offer. And here in the Umbra Court isn't the place for her.

Maybe she would be better off with the Terra Prince. She'd be safe there. As much as I dislike Eoin, he isn't plagued by the curses I am.

And fate has reassured me that even though I can't be with her, he can never fully be with her either. Alessia and I are no good for one another, but we belong to each other.

Whether she knows it or not.

I am hers.

A guttural noise rips from my lungs and I grip the doorframe, refusing to leave until she's long gone.

After another minute passes, I sniff the air, grateful to discover Alessia is no longer lingering in the hall.

Thank gods.

I'm on the verge of combusting.

Yanking open the door, I fly from the room to locate Fern. As much as I hate it, she can curb my needs.

Without her, I would succumb to the violence inside of me. I would devastate.

Like I've done before.

Annihilate the people I love.

Thirty-Two

A Thousand Little Pieces
Alessia

I return to the celebration in poor spirits, hurt that Rainer rejected me so adamantly, but hurting more for him and whatever he's gone through to make him jaded. The things that haunt him: his family issues; losing his mother; cursing the forest.

"Little human graces us with her presence once again!" Ken's voice booms over the steady melody of music. His heavy arm goes around my shoulder. A bunch of nearby writhing and bobbing fae hoot, cheering and clinking glasses of maroon liquid together.

Everyone is having a grand time. More importantly, other than a few glassy second glances, no one seems to care about my presence—my humanity—the same way Rainer does.

I duck out from under Ken's arm. "Why do all the fae really hate humans, Ken?"

He does some kind of gyrating dance move, sloshing wine down his arm carelessly. "Ostara is for dancing, not for negativity." When he glimpses my concern, he grows serious. "If any fae bother you, let me know and I'll deal with them. Did anyone say something to you?"

I'm tickled by his protectiveness. "No, but Rainer has made it clear I'm not welcome here."

"He doesn't speak for everyone, and even if he did, it's *Ostara*." He tilts his head toward the night sky with a goofy grin. "Fae of all sorts have traveled far and wide to party tonight. No one cares what you are. Not tonight at least. Unless you're a demon." He grins, stroking his chin.

"A what?"

"A demon," he whispers conspiratorially.

"What?" I balk at him. "Demons are real?"

He grabs my hands, tugging me toward a dancing group with impossibly beautiful features, and white feathered wings spread out behind them.

"Wine loosens my lips," he mumbles with a head shake. "Ignore me and drop it. We're bringing negativity to the party and that is a no-no. Come join us in some good ol' rump-shaking instead."

All I can do is stare, while actively trying not to stare. Not all the fae around us look human-esque—though the ones with pointed ears and wings almost do, save for a few features and their ethereal beauty. Some, like Ken and Viv, are virtually indistinguishable from humankind. But others have glistening, scaly skin in vibrant colors, translucent wings and shrunken limbs, or other uncommon features. I wonder what demons look like. If they're as awful as Ken implied, surely they're horrible creatures.

The gibbous moon sits high overhead, indicating there are still many hours of partying left before sunrise. Everyone seems to be having a grand time.

Everyone except me…and Rainer.

The angry, blue-eyed faerie with a secretly sweet side he doesn't know how to accept.

"Something's going on with Rainer," I yell over the music to Ken.

"He being a bastard again?"

"Yeah. He—"

"Nothing unusual there." Ken throws his hands over his head and moves his hips in an obscene way. It makes me laugh despite my worries.

"Yes. But he also—he opened up. Told me about his—his curse?" *Cursed with malice,* he said. *Unforgivable.*

Ken stops moving, the smile melting off his face. "He told you?"

"Yes but then we kissed and he pushed me away."

"What truth did he tell you, exactly?" Ken fingers his beard nervously. That question isn't exactly comforting.

How many different truths can Rainer have?

"About his demons."

"What exactly did he say, little human?"

Something clicks in that moment as I replay Rainer's words. "I don't have demons. I am a demon—"

My heart drops into my stomach.

What if he had meant the kind of demon Ken referred to. Is it possible that Rainer isn't a faerie, but a demon?

My body stills, and my arm hair stands up on its end.

I grip Ken's arms, pleadingly. "What don't I know, Ken?"

"Many, many things, little human." He pats my head reassuringly, a genuine smile rising back to his face.

"Why does he hate Tynan?"

"Shhhh." Ken shoves his finger to my lips. He leans forward and lowers his voice. "Don't speak of him so openly."

"But Rainer introduced me—"

"We can't talk with so many shifters around." Ken's eyes widen. "Relax. Have fun."

"But what about Rainer?"

Ken flashes a toothy grin and shakes his head, his sweaty hair flying around his face. "You are as obsessed with him as he is you."

Obsessed? With me?

"He hates me." The lie is bitter on my tongue.

"Give him some space."

That, I can do.

I think we both need space.

Excusing myself, I push through a pulsing group of glistening, half-naked bodies that grind against each other sensually. Away from the dance floor, I pass the snack tables and abandoned chairs—not a single person sits idle tonight. Each body is up and moving to the beat, hollering into the night sky, or joking good-naturedly with another.

A couple of fae play by the fire, tossing a flaming ball between each other. Another comes up beside them, waving a hand and sending a gust of wind toward the ball, sending it sailing up into the skies.

A panther prowls by, following what looks like a normal girl, save for the giant white wings sprouting from her back.

I wonder if they're all High Fae, since they're using magic so casually. Or perhaps it's an Ostara custom. A way to celebrate.

Or maybe they're just drunk and careless.

It's all awe-inducing, and I don't think I'll ever get used to witnessing fae magic.

Under a willow tree off to the side, away from all the action, I spot Viv and Sennah devouring each others' faces.

My lips curve up, happy for them, until I remember how Rainer pushed me away like a diseased rodent after I kissed him.

The sickening acceptance of rejection hits like a punch to the stomach.

After a good thirty minutes or so of moping, I force myself to snap out of it.

For once in my life, I need to stop caring about everyone else, stop catering to their needs. Das Celyn had said, "I've been waiting for the day you stand up for yourself—we all have been." I'm not sure this is exactly what they meant, but they'll all get their wish tonight.

It's time I have some fun and stop worrying about everyone else.

Char would hate to see me squandering an opportunity to be free and have fun. Especially over some boy, as she'd say. She always wanted a better life for me. And though this isn't what I had envisioned, it's better than anything I've ever known. It's Char's smiling, weathered face I see reminding me to seize the moment and live for me.

For her.

For us.

A wall of muscle whips by me—a hairy, shirtless Ken—swinging his untethered, shoulder-length black curls around. Free of all constraints.

"Ken!" I cup my hands around my mouth, shouting so he can hear me. "Hey, Ken!"

"How d'ya do, milady?" He shouts back over the noise. He grins, dark eyes glazed over as beads of sweat drip down his brown chest.

That is exactly what I want.

Not Ken himself. But his attitude. That carefreeness. The all-consuming pleasure without boundaries or self-consciousness. The freedom. Freedom is not a thing nor a place, I'm discovering, but a mindset. I want to be as free as him.

The fruity aroma wafting off his breath hints at how he's achieved such a state.

Wine.

"What exactly happens if I drink the wine?"

"You haven't tried it." He says it matter-of-factly rather than as a question.

"No."

He laughs, a row of white teeth taking over his face. "Faerie wine is a stimulant. It'll keep you up and energized, heightening your emotions. It's probably too much fun for you, little human."

That's it?

The ominous warnings were because it's too much *fun*?

I grin. "Thanks."

"Whoa there, slow it down." Ken wipes the sweat off his forehead with a large green leaf before discarding it onto the ground. He leans in over my shoulder, his hair tickling my collarbone as he whispers. "It also severely lowers your inhibitions and decision making abilities. Rainer has many...enemies. The wine could make you a vulnerable target for anyone wanting to hurt Rai."

"I don't follow, Ken." He bobs to the music and I try to snag his attention again. "No riddles, not tonight, please."

He must sense the seriousness in my tone because he stops moving and frowns at me.

"It's not a secret that you, little human, *you* " —he bops my nose— "are a special guest of Rainer's. One might take advantage of you with the wine coursing through your veins, in attempts to gain information about Rainer."

"I don't know any of his secrets." The lie tastes like ash on my tongue.

Ken gives me a funny look, waggles his eyebrows, then dances off, clapping his hands over head to the rhythm. He can definitely tell I'm lying. And he's definitely intoxicated.

His implication does nothing to deter me. They don't want me to drink the wine because I could put Rainer at risk? It's not enough to hold me back. I'm putting me first tonight.

I make my way over to a table housing a large, crystalline bowl full of the ever-so ominous faerie wine.

A female with midnight skin and bouncy curls pops up out of nowhere and wraps her arms around my neck in a tight hug. I stand like a statue, unsure of a proper response.

"Huuuuuuuman!" She screeches. "So cuuuute!" Then she trounces away, grabbing the hand of a tall red-haired male before disappearing into the gardens, dragging him behind.

Scooping a generous ladle of wine into a gaudy chalice, I inhale the delightfully sweet scent. Here's to not letting that dark-haired arse ruin my night of fun. One sip tells me exactly what I've been missing out on. It's delicious, as expected, with strong notes of raspberries and a slightly smoky aftertaste.

No wonder Fern is addicted to this stuff. I glance around the crowd, wondering where she is this evening. Perhaps Rainer keeps her away, for fear of her spilling his secrets. Does *she* know his secrets?

I shrug, sipping the wine.

Cheers to me and myself.

"I thought you'd been warned off the wine, no?" Eoin sidles up beside me a short while later, as I'm on my second glass.

I turn, eyeing the boyish, golden-haired male. Unlike the rowdy fae trouncing about, shedding clothes and dancing their night away, he stands prim and proper. Even his shirt buttoned all the way up to the collar.

"You don't look sweaty enough to be having a good time," I say.

"Would you like to change that?" He teases, arching a brow.

"You miscreant." I snort a laugh into my wine.

He winks at me, offering a hand. "I only meant by dancing with me." He bats his long eyelashes at me innocently. "How many times must a male ask for you to accept?" He pauses, then quickly adds, "Though if you do say no, truly, I shall leave you be."

Hesitating before accepting his hand, my mind flashes to Rainer. He still hasn't come to seek me out. I was hoping he might. Especially after he gifted me a rose...especially after I dressed like *his* rose.

I can practically hear Char's voice in my head. She'd tell me something like, "You cannot fix him. You cannot find his happiness for him, my Alessia. You can only create your own."

My head buzzes with fuzzy pleasure as I push Rainer out of my thoughts.

Fine.

I'll create my own joy.

"Let's dance." I tilt back my head, downing the entire glass of wine in one gulp.

Eoin chuckles at me before grabbing a glass and doing the same.

I smile up at him, hesitantly placing my hand in his. He interlocks our fingers and leads me over to the dance floor. We push through the throng of fae as my blood starts to warm and a buzzing sensation races through my body. I'm lighter, happier, freer.

Despite the music being fast-paced and upbeat, he draws me close to his chest, his sweet scent putting me at ease. Or maybe it's the wine.

My head spins in the most delightful way.

Unlike when I was high on the moonberries, I'm energized.

We dance for hours, me and Eoin. Even Viv, Sennah, and Ken join us for a few dances. At one point in the night, I spot Tynan, lurking in the shadows, watching me.

"What's the deal with Rainer's brother?" I ask Eoin.

His face scrunches with confusion. "Brother?" He follows my line of sight over his shoulder, to where the broad, brooding man stood a moment ago. But now it's empty. "He doesn't have a brother."

Do people not know who Tynan is? I suppose I know more of Rainer's secrets than I thought.

I trip, missing a step, and Eoin chuckles as he steadies me.

"Nevermind. I was confused." I laugh it off and grab Eoin's hands, tugging him to the wine table.

I try not to let thoughts of Rainer invade me. Grabbing another glass, I chug it to the dregs and return to dancing. I let the music course through my body and take control.

"I've never had this much fun in my life."

Eoin continues to glance past me, searching. I grip his chin and direct his focus back to me.

He flashes me a dazzling smile that makes my heart flutter. "Come with me, Alessia, to my court. I'll ensure you have this much fun everyday for the rest of your life."

"That sounds a little tiring."

"Better get used to it. The fae will dance until sunrise and beyond."

All around us, everyone continues to engage in festivities, none
of them showing signs of slowing down.

"Don't they get tired?"

He chuckles. "Of course they do. But they look forward to Ostara
all year, it's the one time they can make it to the Umbra Court
without harm."

"What about their journey back? Isn't Ostara technically over in
the morning?"

"Yes, but they'll leave before the trees regain their power mid-
day."

Hours pass, wine flows, and we continue to dance together

"This is nice, Golden," I say with a giggle.

"Golden, eh?" His perfect white smile gleams at me, his eyes
crinkling slightly in the corners. He seems genuinely amused, and
that makes me buzzy. He places my arms around his neck, and his
own around my waist as we sway too-slowly to the frantic tunes
around us.

It's like we are floating. Lightweight and untethered.

The emotion courses through me like liquid adrenaline.

"You are golden like sunshine!" A high-pitched giggle reaches
my ears, and when I realize it's coming from me, I laugh even
harder. "I am...aroused!"

"It's the music," he whispers in my ear. "Perhaps the wine as well, but dancing to faerie music heightens one's... intoxication."

"The berries, the roses, the wine, the music..." I trail off, nuzzling Eoin's neck. His shoulders shake as he chuckles. "This place is fun."

"If you think *this* little shindy is fun, you should see the parties we throw at Terra Court." His voice is seductive, and it sends tingles down my spine. "How exactly did one so lovely come to be in such a nefarious place, any way?" He tilts his head, eyeing me with interest.

"Shhh." I whisper, placing a finger to his lips. "It isn't quite bad here, really."

"I'm going to make the assumption you mean here in my arms, and not in this gods-foresaken court."

"Not partial to the Prince of Fear?" A giggle bubbles out of my mouth.

"Is it obvious?" He wraps his arms around me, his fingers dancing along my spine. "I don't want to talk about him right now," he whispers.

Me neither. I give Eoin a sly look, emboldened from all the wine I've drank tonight. "And what do you want to do instead?"

"This."

Before I can prepare for it, he's pressing his mouth against mine. I giggle against his lips, but it quickly subsides as his tongue presses inside and we find a rhythm.

"*Alessia!*"

My name is hissed with venom, snapping me from my moment of fun.

I pull away from Eoin, and lo and behold, the prince I'm trying to ignore stands a few paces away. His arms are crossed across his broad chest. His lips are pursed, his teeth clenched so tight I'm surprised he hasn't cracked them yet.

"You two have matching ears," I say, fingering the shiny studs on Eoin's ears. I lean in and nibble his bottom lobe for good measure.

Rainer's nostrils flare as he seethes.

"Get away from her, Eoin," he growls.

I've never seen him so angry—so possessive.

Chuckling, Eoin turns to face Rainer.

"It's rude to interrupt a lady's good time." He winks at me before flicking his gaze back to Rainer.

Rainer steps forward, features tight and his sharp eyes trained on me.

"Alessia and I need to talk."

"Alessia—" Eoin repeats Rainer, saying my name in a sensual way, as if he's tasting it. He offers me a soft smile before returning a hardened gaze to Rainer. "—is capable of making her own decisions."

"Talk, talk talk," I giggle. "He always wants to talk, but he never says anything worth listening to."

Rainer grits his teeth and looks for my confirmation. "May I have a word?"

"I thought you didn't care for her?" Eoin accuses.

I snort a laugh. "And tonight he suddenly has manners!"

"You drank the wine." Rainer rubs his brow and sighs. He looks at Eoin accusingly. "You let her drink it."

"Eoin didn't *let* me do anything. Perhaps that's why I like him so much. He doesn't cage me and stifle me like you do."

I reach forward, booping Rainer on the nose. His cheeks blaze red, and his eyes flicker.

"Why don't humans have music like this?" I ask. "We miss out on so much."

So many naked bodies, though. I laugh, thinking how funny it is, until I catch Rainer's eye.

He jolts forward, ripping Eoin away from me. "Get out of here."

Eoin steps back, raising his hands with a smirk. "I'll be around if you need me, Alessia."

With that, he winks at me again and strides away.

"Thanks for that," I mutter.

Rainer's mouth twitches. "Why, you are so welcome, little rose."

"No. I didn't mean—"

My head swims.

Light and fuzzy with intoxication.

Stupid faeries and their stupid games.

"What can I assist you with, Princey Poo?" I curtsy with a dramatic flair.

A flash of annoyance appears before he packs it away, reverting to his stoic neutral.

"You're drunk."

"You're drunk," I mimic back in a nasally tone.

I want to pinch his cheeks and tell him to lighten up, have some fun. Be free like me!

The wine is glorious after all!

"For the love of…" He runs a hand through his hair. "We can't talk like this."

"Like what?" I smile sweetly, fluttering my eyelids for good measure.

He pauses, standing more rigid. "Come to bed, Alessia. Sleep it off."

"Nope!" I sing-song it out while twirling my glittering skirt around me. The bonfire and moonlight washes over me, causing my dress to glow in fiery hues of pale peach, pink, and orange. "You always want to ruin my fun."

Except, in this state I can't stay mad. My body wants to lean towards him, even closer. I fight it, willing myself to stay strong.

"You look like a sunset rose," he murmurs.

"I do."

"You dressed for me?" Rainer flexes his hand at his side.

"Maybe."

When he speaks, it's careful, controlled. "But you kissed him."

I twirl, shooting him a toothy grin. "I kissed *you* first." My grin morphs into a frown. "And you pushed me away."

"So you sought solace in the first warm body you could find?"

I scoff. "I'm tired of your games, Rainer. You treat me like I'm nothing to you—even though we both know it's a lie—and instead of letting me in, you push me away. Then you expect me to wait for you? To not take care of myself? I deserve to have a happy moment, Rainer. And you don't get to ruin that for me."

He runs a hand through his onyx waves. "I know."

"For someone with such a pretty face, you have an ugly heart." I don't mean to say it, but it slips out on its own. I wish I could stuff it back in my mouth.

His spine goes ramrod straight, and he pauses, his mouth twisting into a frown. His eyes sparkle with a sadness I recognize, and I'll be damned if it doesn't steal my breath.

"Have fun tonight, mo róisín," he murmurs. "You do deserve it." He pauses, cocking his head at me. His eyes flicker a deep cobalt then back to icy blue. "You deserve everything you want and beyond. But if you kiss Eoin again, I will kill him."

My brows fly up and I blink, trying to understand where that came from.

With his hands stuffed into his pockets, he leaves the revelry behind, heading toward the castle.

I gape after him, wondering why he resorts to pushing me away and threatening me, when it's clear he harbors feelings for me. It's there for both of us, whatever is between us, no matter what he says.

The pang in my chest tells me to go after him, but he's not my responsibility. I already tried to be there for him, and he sent me away. Until he's willing to make an effort and stop with the nonsense, he's not my problem.

So, instead of following him, I mosey on over to the table of faerie wine and pour myself another glass.

"This is for us, Char." I tilt the glass up toward the starless sky and down it whole. "We *do* deserve all the fun."

Let the faerie wine flow.

Somehow, in between seeing Rainer and getting more wine, I get lost in a throng of fae. Or rather, I get sucked into a whirlwind of dancing fae who pull me into their orbit. Time twirls by, and I don't know how much I've lost before I finally manage to pull free.

Stepping away from the mayhem, I move toward the dark gardens to catch my breath and rest my aching feet. I'm searching for the stone benches amidst a sea of overgrown flowers and oak trees when I hear it.

"*Alessssssiaaaa.*"

"What?" I yell, snorting a drunken laugh.

Over the music and chatter, I hear it again—the call of the creepy shadow.

Glancing around, I wonder if anyone else heard it. But no one appears to notice.

The curse in the forest is supposedly muted tonight. If there was ever a time to leave the wards, confront the spooky shadow thing and figure out what it wants, it's now.

Plus, there are so many magical beings around. If anything happens, they can protect me. Right?

The faerie wine swims through my veins, giving me the extra boost of courage I need. My mind screams not to go, but my legs move on their own accord. I let them carry me toward the voice.

Trailing around the castle, out of sight of the revelers once again, I search for a gate further down the wall—one out of immediate sight of the party.

"I'm coming, shadowy friend," I singsong. "Just please, please don't eat me." I snicker, tripping over my feet.

I trail further away from the music and liveliness, desperate for a moment away from everyone.

Turning a corner around the overflowing side gardens, I'm completely alone on this side of the castle. The bonfire's glow no longer reaches me over here. Only the silver-tinted glow of the moon peeking out from the abundance of clouds allows me to see at all.

The perimeter wall is barely visible in the distance, a thick, dark line melting into the shadows beyond.

Turning my head up to the sky, I admire the expanse of darkness.

A soft moan reaches my ears, and my head snaps down, silently scanning for the source of the sound.

"Again? Haven't you had enough tonight," a throaty, feminine voice says. I squint in the direction it came from.

Propped up against the house's stony exterior are two figures—clearly having an intimate moment.

I cover my mouth with a hand, stifling a laugh.

The female has her back pressed into the wall, with her curtain of dark hair pulled over one shoulder, exposing her neck to the male that pins her against the wall.

He leans toward her, and her eyes shutter.

I can't see the guy at all except for his back. His dark clothes blend into the night, concealing them conveniently among the shadows.

Even in the darkness, there's something familiar about the figure.

I step closer, squinting to make out why he looks so familiar, ignoring the fact that I'm spying on such an intimate moment.

The clouds part, gifting me a stream of silver moonlight. Just enough to see as the woman tangles her hands in unruly, dark hair...hair I just had my fingers tangled in earlier tonight while pouring my heart out through my lips.

It's Fern I'm looking at.

And—

"Hurry up, Rainer," she pants.

A terrifying growl leaves him and slams her into the wall, planting his mouth on her neck.

There are many things I'm willing to overlook and forgive. But *this* isn't one of them.

Not wanting to face him, I flee back to the celebration.

Behind me, I hear her gasp in pleasure—or perhaps it's pain?

Or maybe it's the echo of my own pain. The sound of my heart shattering into a thousand little pieces.

THIRTY-THREE
Not Fae At All
ALESSIA

D esperate to put space between me and what I saw, I run back
through the gardens, following the sound of carefree chatter
and music until I find the party.

Seeing Rainer with Fern sobered me up, stole my buzz.

I shouldn't care.

We're only strangers after all.

Our kiss was surely a mistake after all—one I initiated—and one
I won't make again. I'm mistaking my own sympathy, and Rainer's
occasional kindness, for something it isn't.

Damn him for unraveling me like this. It wouldn't hurt as much
if he hadn't been so tender with me, too.

I wish I could find an explanation for *why* Rainer and Fern were
together, alone, in the shadows. But there isn't one. He was kissing
her neck, and she was enjoying it.

Simple as that. I know what I saw.

He didn't push me away tonight because he wanted to be
alone…he just didn't want *me*.

I scoff, plopping down on a boulder beside the wine table, letting my dress flair out around me.

A dress I picked out for Rainer.

"Stupid. Stupid. Stupid."

I hang my head, burrowing my face in my hands and groaning.

"Let me guess?" Eoin asks. "He was displeased that I kissed you."

I chuckle sarcastically. "He doesn't get to care what I do."

"I don't know what's going on between—"

"Nothing. There's nothing between us." *Not anymore.*

"May I keep you company?"

"Only if you don't kiss me again."

"Ouch." He rubs his chest mockingly.

It's not because Rainer threatened him, but because it's not fair that I kiss Eoin while thinking about someone else. Even if there's nothing between me and Rainer, Ken's right, I *am* obsessing over him.

He's consuming my thoughts.

I've gone from drowning in grief to drowning in Rainer.

"I don't want to give you false hope," I tell Eoin. "But I am not interested in anything...*more.*"

"Fair enough." He holds out a hand to me. "Friends?"

A friend sounds nice right about now. I nod.

"I'm done with all of this tonight." I gesture toward the party.

I had fun—until I didn't. And I could continue to drink faerie wine to stave off the emotions sitting on my chest, to ignore the sharp sting in my heart, but part of me wants the hurt. To remember this so I don't make the same mistake. So I don't forgive Rainer as easily as he expects me to.

I am cursed with mercy, after all. I scoff at the thought.

It's ironic: we can break hearts that don't even belong to us.

"May I walk you back?" Eoin asks.

"Yes, actually. I'd like that."

Eoin reaches for my hand, interlacing our fingers as he walks me back toward the castle. The buzz of faerie magic has almost fully worn off. I don't want to be alone. I'd rather wallow in company, like I would do with Char.

Eoin isn't Char, not even close, but he's a friend. He's the only one who has stuck up for me, showed an interest in *me*. That's more than I can say for anyone else around here.

"Come up with me?" I ask Eoin, my cheeks flushing.

He hesitates, glancing up at the castle then back to me. "On one condition."

"Faeries and their conditions," I mumble, garnering another laugh from him.

"I only ask that you allow me to clean up first. I'm afraid I smell rather ripe from all the dancing."

"Deal." I'm sure I smell the same, and a bath does sound enticing.

My eyes travel up the castle's stone exterior as we head inside, and on the third floor, in the soft flicker of candlelight, I make out Rainer's drawn features as he watches me and Eoin.

His shoulder slump in exhaustion. Defeat. I'll be damned if my heart doesn't split down the middle at the sight. But instead of focusing on him, I squeeze Eoin's hand and lead him to my chambers.

"You're sure you're okay sharing a bed with me?" Eoin teases once we clean up, change, and make our way to the only bed in my room.

My eyes roam the bare, tanned muscles of his chest and, and when I get to the thin trail of hair leading below his waistband, my cheeks flush and I look away.

"Yes," I say. It's just *sleep*. "As long as you promise to keep your hands to yourself."

His smile falters, and I fiddle with my nightgown, trying to avoid his eye contact. Did he think I invited him up here for...something else? I mean, I understand how he might assume that, but still.

"Hey, hey, hey." He plops onto my bed, beckoning for me to join him. "I have no intentions of touching you." His grin comes back. "Even if you wanted to do something beyond sleep tonight, I wouldn't allow for it."

That causes me to snort a laugh. "Even if I wanted it?"

"I would never take advantage of you, Alessia," he murmurs, "and you're still riding the high from tonight—the music, the wine, the flowers. Your... whatever is going on between you and Rainer. It wouldn't be right to take advantage of you with those sorts of influences on your emotions."

The sincerity in his voice wins me over, and I crawl under the covers with him. "The same could be said for you."

He chuckles. "Oh trust me, it's you that makes me feel how I do about you. Not any external influences."

My heart flutters. "How do you feel about me?" We just met. What could the Terra prince possibly feel about me?

"Intrigued by. Interested in. Attracted to."

"But I'm only human," I say dumbly.

He brushes the curls out of my face, tucking them behind an ear. "And so what? The conflict between fae and humans comes from our predecessors and their wars and vendettas, not mine nor my courts. Unlike Umbra Court, Terra doesn't hold a grudge. I view us as equals."

It contradicts what he said before at the brunch. "You said I'd never be equal to the fae."

"Not in the eyes of *Umbra*."

"But you're also a prince, and I'm… I'm—"

"Amazing? Incredible?" He smirks. "*Prince* is a job title. Not a definition of who I am inside."

I flush. "I—I didn't think about it like that."

"So how could I possibly be interested in you?" he asks with a teasing lilt to his voice. He taps his chin in feigned contemplation. "Hmm. Let's see. Well, the first time I saw you, you had barely finished an intense training session with Viv and Ken—two of the best warriors around. Trust me, Viv's from Terra Court, I know how tough she is—"

"You were watching that?"

Even in the dark, I can make out the bashful blush to his cheeks. "I was. And I also witnessed how you relentlessly tried to climb that tree and hop the wall triple your height, despite being tired from training—and probably knowing that imminent death lay on the other side."

I nod, agreeing. "Yeah that was stupid."

He pulls me to him, wrapping his arms around me. "Then you fell—hard. And you barely made a peep. No screaming, no crying, no tantrums. You fractured your spine—I know because I felt it—and the pain was unbearable. The numb silence? Even worse. It made me wonder 'who is this girl and what has she gone through in order to be as strong as she is?'"

Strong.

Not pathetic. Not weak. But strong.

"And at brunch, with Rainer's awful magic influencing you, you fought back. You withstood his challenge and didn't give in or break down."

A challenge? Is that what it was to Rainer.

It certainly felt like I broke down.

Eoin's words strike something deep inside of me.

"So, yes, Alessia. We've only just met, but I want to get to know you. I'm attracted to the woman I've seen in the few fleeting moments we've been together, and I want to see more of her."

Eoin sees the good in me and wants more of that. But would he still want me if he saw the darkness I carry, too?

My throat is thick, and I'm unable to reply for a moment.

Finally, I say, "I didn't want to be alone tonight."

"I can understand that." He holds his breath for a second before saying, "I'm glad you asked me to join you."

"Me too."

Eoin *hmms* to himself. A few minutes later he says, "For someone who proclaims to hate humanity, Rainer seems awfully fond of collecting humans."

My stomach sinks at the reminder of Rainer's lips on Fern's neck. "I don't want to talk about him."

"Deal." Eoin shifts beneath me. We lay there in silence until finally he plants a finger under my chin and angles my head up to look at him. "I'm not here to pester you or make you uncomfortable. If at any time you're not comfortable, tell me and I'll leave, okay? I'm here as a friend, because that's what you need tonight, Alessia."

His words settle the doubts gnawing at my stomach, and I offer him a soft smile. When I reach up to cup his cheek, he gently grabs my wrist, eyeing my hand.

"What happened here?" He frowns at the fresh wound from earlier this evening. "I hadn't noticed this earlier."

Eoin can't smell my blood, too? I figured heightened senses were universal for all faeries. I suppose their abilities differ beyond their base powers of fearcalling and healing.

I almost laugh at how opposite the two males are.

"Here," Eoin says as he gently grips my hand.

A warm tingle crawls through my palm, and I know without looking that he's healing. He winces for a second as he absorbs the pain, but then he's done and I'm admiring the soft, unbroken skin on my palm.

"That's amazing," I whisper.

"You're amazing, Alessia."

The conversation lulls, and I realize that, despite being fae, Eoin has been nothing but a perfect gentleman since I've met him. He says all the right things.

He's also open and honest about his feelings and intentions.

But it doesn't warm me from the inside out like Rainer does. I'm not drawn to Eoin in the same way I am Rainer. I hate it. Why can't it be the golden faerie I'm fond of instead?

The silence between us isn't awkward or unsure. It's confident and comfortable. Being here with him, like this, is exactly what I needed. Without Char's friendship and Felix's affections, I've been quite lonely here in Umbra Court. So lonely, that I think I was searching for something in Rainer that he isn't willing to give.

Barely no time passes at all before Eoin dozes off with his arm wrapped tight around my midsection.

It's incredibly intimate, and I'm grateful for his company, but I can't keep my mind from wandering back to Rainer.

It's Rainer's stoic features and icy-blue eyes I see as I begin to doze off, despite the golden-haired male wrapped around me.

The door slams open and I jerk upright, clutching the sheets.

Eoin swears under his breath as light from the hallway washes over us, and he's immediately on his feet ready to fight. "Rainer?"

"*Rainer*?" I repeat.

"I can't do this, mo róisín," he growls. "We need to talk."

My traitorous heart rate picks up at his term of endearment for me. "Now?" I ask. "What time is it?"

"Late," he says at the same time Eoin says, "Early."

They glare at one another.

"Get the feck out, Eoin."

"Yeah, she means nothing to you," Eoin mutters.

Rainer narrows his eyes at Eoin. "I said get *out!*"

Suddenly, Eoin's eyes widen and his face contorts. He scrambles to put space between us.

"Eoin, what—" I whirl on Rainer. "Release him! You can't just do that to people whenever you want."

"I can and I will." Rainer growls before releasing Eoin from his fearcaller hold. I'm simultaneously appalled and awed by the power the Prince of Fear holds. "Keep. Your. Hands. And. Lips. To yourself."

I've never seen Rainer so angry. The energy in the room is tense, and I fear that Eoin might fight back. Instead, he backs away with his hands up.

"She needed a friend." He looks at me as he makes his way out the door. "And when he" —he jerks a thumb at Rainer— "ruins whatever strange thing you two have going on, I'll still be there for you, Alessia." He gives Rainer a stern look. "As a friend. As whatever you need."

Rainer's eyes flicker shades as he slams the door shut in Eoin's face and prowls toward me like a lethal predator, I recoil, flinching back until my calves hit the bed.

His face contorts as if he's pained. His eyes lighten back to pale, icy blue before darkening into cobalt, then black. "I told you to stay away from him."

"You told me not to *kiss* him," I correct.

"I hate the secrets between us. I hate the thought of Eoin's hands on your body—of anyone's hands on you except mine. There's something I need to—"

"I hate the thought of your lips on Fern's neck!" I hop out of bed. My nightgown falls around my thighs as I stomp my way to Rainer. His eyes roam my body, and he visibly relaxes when he sees I'm covered. "You made me feel something for you—you bastard."

"Bloody hell! I feel it too!" Rainer snarls, his eyes darkening to an almost-black. I shudder, my palms growling clammy.

He grips me gently by the throat, holding me in place. Leaning forward, he runs his nose along my jaw, inhaling deeply.

"My little rose," he mutters against my neck. "I tried to stay away, but I can't."

Goosebumps rise on my arms, loving the way his breath tickles my skin. My stomach flutters with excitement. This is so messed up. There's something seriously wrong with Rainer—worse than I initially thought. Yet I can't help the way my body responds to him.

His fingers flex on my throat. Not tight enough to hurt or cut off my air, but just enough to show me who's in charge of this moment.

Heat builds between my legs.

I'm mortified his aggression is turning me on, but I'm also too aroused to stop him. I'm paralyzed with lust and need. Frozen with confusion and shock.

I should hate this.

I should push him away and put distance between us.

But I *love* his hands on me. Love his unhinged possession.

I am *his.*

Slowly, he removes his hand from my throat. His fingers work their way into my hair while his other hand flashes out and grips my waist.

He rests his forehead against mine.

"Rainer, what are—"

"I warned you, Alessia." His tone is deep and low. Dangerous. His breath fans across my lips and I melt with desire. "I am not good. I am not pure."

His hands tremble against my skin, as if he's fighting himself. And there's something so utterly raw about the way he seems to need me, but refuses to admit it.

"I don't need protecting from you," I whisper reassuringly. "Stop fighting it."

"You don't know what you're asking for." He squeezes his eyes shut and curses under his breath. "I am not your hero. I'm a monster."

"Be *my* monster, Rainer."

My whispered words appear to snap him out of whatever fog he's in. He blinks a few times, his eyes returning to their normal pale color.

Then he slams his lips against mine, kissing me so passionately that my sanity dissipates, lost to the heat of his touch.

A moan rises in my throat, and I grip his shirt collar, pulling him flush to me. We topple backwards onto the bed, and he plants a hand on the mattress next to my head to hold himself up.

Rainer pushes himself to a stand, pacing in front of me as he runs his fingers through his hair.

"I—I'm... *sorry,*" Rainer whispers, his eyes bouncing between mine.

My brows quirk and I sit up, perching at the edge of the bed.

He just *apologized*.

I study him with open confusion.

"I tried to stay away, and bloody hell, I hate you so much for making me want you so desperately." His eyes deepen beyond blue again—lingering in black territory.

My brow wrinkles with concern.

"What are you talking about?" I whisper, wrapping my arms around me. "You kissed Fern! To, what, push me away? I have feelings for you, Rainer, but I will not be toyed with. I know you fae enjoy games, but I do not. Not when it comes to—"

"I'm *not* toying with you. Not intentionally. I—" He groans, running his hands over his face.

"What are you doing here?" I'm proud of myself for how steady my voice comes out. "How dare you come in here all aggressive, kicking Eoin out and trying to claim me."

At the sound of Eoin's name, Rainer freezes. His jaw tenses and he levels a serious stare at me.

"Please. *Please*, Alessia. Don't tell me you slept with him."

His voice is so desperate that it sends a pang through my chest.

I hug my midsection tighter. "Who I sleep with is none of your business."

"I'll gut him."

My mouth drops open. "Stop threatening to kill him! You can't just kill someone for pissing you off—especially not another prince!"

"I can and I will."

"Oh my gods, Rainer, do you hear yourself right now?" His words should terrify me, but they only cause my heart to beat faster. I can't deny the thrill that courses through me, and I barely recognize myself right now. I'm almost ashamed.

"You are a hypocrite!" I yell.

He kneels before me, placing his hands on my knees. He grows quiet, leveling me with a serious look.

"I have *never* slept with Fern."

"Maybe not in the sleeping sense," I mutter.

"I have never even *kissed* her. She and I are friends, and barely even that. Nothing more."

I rub my forehead with a sigh. "I saw you two!"

"Whatever you think you saw, you're wrong." His eyes darken.

"No more faerie games. No manipulation. No twisted words, Rainer. I saw what I saw."

"You saw wrong."

"Then wha—"

"I was *feeding*!" He throws his hands up with a growl.

The room grows so silent that I can hear my blood pounding in my head. I don't know what to say.

"*Feeding*?"

His fingers tap a rhythm on his thigh, and he takes a few deep breaths with his eyes shut.

When they reopen, they're back to their normal color.

"I tried to stay away from you, Alessia. To spare you my truths—my curses. But I can't do it anymore."

"I'm not following this conversation." My head spins all sorts of stories as I wait for Rainer to speak.

"My mum was a wonderful woman. A great woman."

"What does she have to do with anything, Rainer?"

"Everything," he murmurs.

I'm still stuck on the feeding part. My body trembles as I wonder if sending Eoin away was smart. Rainer is becoming unhinged. He warned me from the beginning that he would hurt me.

I just didn't understand it then.

I barely understand it now.

He pauses, as if carefully contemplating his words.

"My mother was wonderful," he repeats. "But my father? He was not."

My lungs constrict as I remember his nightmare. He was just a boy. His father seemed cruel—to both him and his mother.

I angle my body at him, watching him as he speaks. He hangs his head, his shoulders slumped in defeat.

Even with my confusion and anger, my hand reflexively reaches for his. I interlace our fingers, giving him a squeeze to let him know I'm here. I needed a friend tonight, and Eoin was there for me. Now Rainer needs a friend, and it's my turn to be there for him. As hurt as I am by his actions, he doesn't owe me anything. The least I can do is hear him out. And based on what I've seen from him, I know this moment is a big deal.

"I'm telling you this, Alessia, because it's important to me that you know *why* I am the way I am. *Why* being together is danger-ous." He clears his throat, glancing away. "This is not information I give freely."

"Then why tell me?" I whisper.

His gaze bores into me. "Because you and I—like it or not, we're connected."

He feels it too.

"My mother had an affair, and she got pregnant with me. In Avylon, there are many polyamorous relationships, open relation-ships, and the likes. However, when a couple declares monogamy, it's taken seriously. Adultery is enough for one to be exiled by their fellow fae. My parents had gone through the monogamy ritual long before I was born. So when my mother had an affair, it's no surprise she kept it secret. Especially as a Royal Fae.

"When I was born, I looked just like her—there were never any questions about her fidelity. We might never have known at all, except—"

I wait with bated breath for him to continue. "What happened, Rainer?" Based on the nightmare I witnessed, I think I know where it's going. "Did your father find out?" I whisper. "Did he kill her?"

Did Rainer witness it all?

He was only a child.

Rainer glances up at me, his eyes brimming with unshed tears.

"Worse," he says hoarsely. "When I turned eight, the magic from my real father's bloodline was triggered. A bloodline my mother *knew* about. But she thought because I looked like her—like a faerie—that I would be unaffected by his bloodline. She chose to keep her secrets and protect herself instead of facing the truth and protecting me. She chose wrong."

His aversion to blood.

Pushing me away—especially when I was bleeding.

Feeding on Fern.

Demons.

"Who was your father, Rainer?" I ask gently. My head grows light. "*What* was he? Fae?"

"No." He shakes his head. "Not fae at all."

THIRTY-FOUR
Who Was Killed?
Alessia

"He was a demon. A vampyr specifically," Rainer says. "I'm half-faerie from my mother's side and half-vampyr from my biological father's side.

I try not to hyperventilate as my breath comes quick and shallow. It takes a few minutes of focusing on my breathing to calm my body. My skin is sweaty, flushed. I shouldn't be surprised. I should've seen this coming.

Ken had mentioned demons tonight—how they're hated.

Even Rainer straight up told me he was a demon.

How did it take me so long to see the truth?

Perhaps it's because I never imagined such a thing to exist.

He *needs* blood.

He's a vampyr.

My mind spirals in circles.

"But you eat doughnuts," I say lamely. "You *like* them."

He chuckles. "I do. I need food to survive, just like other faeries. But I also require blood to replenish my energy and restore my magic."

I blink a few times, trying to comprehend the idea of drinking blood.

"When the bloodlust set in, I hadn't expected it—no one had," Rainer continues. "I wasn't taught to deal with it properly. I was young, confused, and hungry, so hungry. It hit me and I had no idea what was happening. Nothing satisfied my hunger." He fists his hair again, shaking his head. I reach up to pull his hands away and grip them in my own. Finally, he turns to face me. The emotion on his face practically shatters me. "*I* killed them, Alessia. My mother and father—the man I thought was my father. I drained them of their blood. I fed on them. I was so overrun with hunger that there was no shred of morality left in me."

His words turn my veins to ice. I knew there was a darkness inside of him, but never did I guess he murdered his only family. Dropping his hands, I scramble to put space between us.

Something deep in my gut shouts at me to comfort him, to stay close. But the logic tells me to *run*.

It's the shattered expression on his face that keeps me rooted in place—my gut, and heart, beating logic.

I swallow through the thickness, watching him warily.

He was only a child, I remind myself. Only eight years old.

It doesn't make it right, but it makes it less malicious. It wasn't intentional.

"It was an accident?" I whisper. "Right?"

He nods slowly, guilt and shame clouding his features.

Comfort him, something inside me calls. *He needs you.*

There's nothing in this moment I can say that will change the past. Nothing that can possibly ease the pain Rainer harbors. So instead, I let the invisible tug between us win, accepting the inexplicable energy that draws us together. I ignore my own misgivings and pull him to my chest and comfort him as his body silently shakes with sobs.

It's an impossible situation. If his mother would've been honest, he could've been prepared for his true bloodline as a boy. Their deaths and his trauma could have been spared.

Her secrets tore the Iorworth family apart, leaving Rainer an orphan so young. Yet Rainer still loves her, honors her, respects her.

Only someone with an abundance of love and forgiveness in their heart is capable of doing that.

But what hurts most is that he doesn't blame her—he blames himself.

I swallow the thickness in my throat, working to quell my trembling limbs.

After a few minutes, he swipes his palms over his face. He clears his throat. "Ken found me. He covered for me. He let me feed from him, to stave off the bloodlust. And later, when we found Fern—a lone human in Umbra, on the verge of self-induced death—we were able to help each other. I protect her from the ruthless fae. I shelter her, give her everything she needs to live in harmony, and she lets me feed."

That explains his strange relationship with Fern. Why he houses a human. Why his mouth was on her neck. He wasn't *kissing* her. He was drinking her blood.

The thought sends a shudder through me and I squirm.

"But… it's not only human blood you crave? It's all blood?"

Rainer sighs. "Fae blood works well enough to stave off the bloodlust, but human blood is more potent. There's less magic diluting it."

"So when you feed on Fern, you can, what, feed less often?"

"Yes. I've also trained myself to fight it over the years. But having you here—"

I hear the words he isn't saying: having me, a human, is temptation. The worst kind.

"It's not only the temptation of your blood that tests me. It's—attraction. Arousal. Strong feelings of any sort that provoke the bloodlust."

My cheeks heat at the implication.

He kneels before me, his hands on my thighs as he looks up into my face. "That's why I pushed you away, mo róisín. To protect you. To protect myself. It dredged up so many bad memories, and I refuse to lose myself to bloodlust again."

He killed his own mother.

His father.

He feared he would kill me too.

The Prince of Fear is not without his own terrors.

And I want nothing more than to kiss away his pain.

"Is that why Tynan is a secret?" His brows pinch together. "I—I accidentally mentioned your brother in front of Eoin, but he didn't know who I was talking about."

"Yes," Rainer says quietly, running a hand through his hair. "Tynan isn't the secret, but our relationship is. We share the same father—my biological father."

A demon.

"Tynan's a vampyr," I whisper. A chill crawls up my spine. "A full-blooded one?"

Rainer gives a sharp nod. "Fae are not fond of demons. For good reason. They've been banned from Avylon. If word got out about my mother's transgressions, my rule would be challenged on the grounds of an impure bloodline. "

"Ken said something similar tonight," I murmur. "But your magic—being a fearcaller—Eoin called it dark magic. A stain on Avylon. Yet no one has figured out… what you are?"

"My abilities as a fearcaller stem from my mother's side—the royal line. Little does he know the irony of his words."

"That's—convenient." As a half-blooded vampyr, he's able to hide his demon side beneath his faerie appearance and magic.

"Dark magic is rare among faeries, but not unheard of—especially not in the Umbra Court. It's the bloodlust that's my true curse."

Not a literal curse, but a hereditary one. "Speaking of curses, it *was* you that cursed the forest, right?"

"That enchantment was meant to keep the humans away." He scowls.

"Because of your… temptation? The bloodlust?"

"Yes," he whispers.

"You don't hate humans for being human, you fear for them. You've only tried to protect them."

"Don't make me out to be a hero, Alessia. I meant it when I said that isn't me. My intentions were to protect myself, and my court from knowing the truth, moreso than protecting the humans."

I reach up to tenderly cup his cheek. "Not everyone wants a hero, Rainer. Some of us want a monster of their very own."

He brushes a stray curl behind my ear. "Can you forgive me?"

The revelations overwhelm me. It connects so many of the pieces floating around—answers many of my pressing questions. I understand why he pushed me away, why he didn't open up to me. And I'm extremely relieved to know he and Fern are not intimate.

I can forgive him for that, but it still doesn't explain why he found it necessary to be so cruel.

"You used your fearcaller power on me," I accuse. "Why?"

He sighs. "I was trying to protect you—from Eoin, from Tynan, from myself. And I wanted you to see that you *are* strong, Alessia. I wanted you to believe in yourself."

"And did that work out for you?" I ask, sarcastically.

"You've come a long way, so I'll say yes in that regard. But considering you had Eoin in your bed, and now here I am begging for forgiveness, I'd say it backfired."

I arch a brow at him. "Begging? I don't see any begging."

He tightens his grip on my hand, bowing his head.

"Can you forgive me, mo róisín? For hurting you. For keeping secrets. For pushing you away."

I pull my hand out of his grip, crossing my arms and scrutinizing him. We both know I'll forgive him. I don't have it in me to hate him for trying to do the right thing. Especially after losing Char and understanding how valuable friendship and love are.

"I don't know—"

"I never said I was a nice guy, Alessia. Never pretended to be anything other than what I am—but I promise I've only tried to protect you since I met you. I..."

"Yes?"

"I care about you. And I beg you to forgive me." His expression is genuine.

That causes me to crack a smile. "You can't just use manners and expect me to forgive you, Rainer."

He clears his throat, rubbing the back of his neck sheepishly. "*Please?*"

Okay, maybe he can use manners and earn my forgiveness, because his authenticity floods me with emotion. I know the fae don't easily use manners.

"I forgive you," I say. He freezes, a surprised look overtaking his features. "What?" I ask with a laugh.

"I had hoped you'd forgive me, but I hadn't expected it so easily."

"Rainer, I've met many bad people in my life, and you aren't like them."

"I wish I were better for you," he mutters.

My heart lifts at his teasing, his vulnerability. "Let me be the mercy you deserve, Rainer."

"But I hurt you."

A soft laugh flows from my lips. What he's done to me is nothing compared to what I've gone through. I flash back to the lord's whippings, his hands tainting my skin with unwelcome touches. I think of the lady and her taunts and cruelty. Finally, a flash of Felix's face pops into mind—he never once tried to protect me or encourage my dreams.

"I truly despised you at first," he says with a soft chuckle. "For only a brief moment. Because of what you are—what you represent to me. I tried to push you away, but your beauty enraptured me."

"Rainer…"

"I'm not talking about your external beauty—though that comes in abundance—I'm talking about your inner beauty, your strength, your perseverance. I only wanted to stoke your fire, to bring out your fight."

"You did hurt me, Rainer," I repeat, "I know you were only trying to protect me, but you still hurt me."

"And I—I wish I never had. Truly, Alessia."

I know what he is—a fearcaller, a vampyr, a bastard prince with a trauma-filled past and uncontrollable bloodlust—and it doesn't scare me. Because he's also selfless, considerate, and flawed in the most beautiful ways.

And he never kissed Fern.

He wants me.

My body begs to touch him—to finish what we started. Especially now that we've cleared up the biggest secrets between us. I know his truths.

I bite my lip. "Are you going to stop talking and kiss me now?"

"Alessia." His eyes spark with warning, his voice raspy. "My self-control only goes so far."

"Maybe I want you to lose control. Maybe I want you to make *me* lose control."

"I don't want to hurt you."

"Then don't. You *are* in control, Rainer. I trust you."

"Your trust means everything to me, but I can't trust myself." His eyes roam my body, and his eyes flash a stormy blue, and this time, when they darken, they stay black. He groans. "Touching you will ruin us both." Before I can reply, he stands. "Go to sleep, Alessia. Find me in your dreams. I can touch you there."

He backs away, a torn expression on his face. When he turns and bolts away, rejection fills me once again, but then I shake it off. He admitted that he wants me.

He let me in.

He's done avoiding whatever it is between us.

And his eyes.

They change color when he's facing his bloodlust. Brought on by hunger, attraction, arousal, or any strong feelings he had said.

I realize now that he constantly battles his vicious nature when he's around me. And after what he told me about his parents, I can't blame him for taking precautions. It'd be unfair of me to pressure him into something he's not ready for, especially when he believes he could lose control and hurt me.

It's not about me trusting him.

He needs to trust himself, and that's not something I can force. It's not my gift to give.

Instead of mincing his words, I chug a half-mug of cold, leftover valerian tea from my nightstand. Then I wait anxiously to see him in my dreams.

Rose petals scatter all over the room in red, orange, and sunset hues.

His sunset roses.

"Mo róisín," he whispers, reaching for me. "You came."

"I'm still not sure exactly how this works."

"We have much to talk about—"

"Not now."

Giving him a coy look, I decide not to waste any time. We've done the talking tonight, and I don't know how much time we'll have in our dream together. I don't want to waste another second. I slip out of my dress, leaving me in just my undergarments. Shy, and self-conscious, I quickly step forward and press my lips to his. It's gentle at first. We kiss, lost in each other's lips for eternity, yet not nearly long enough at the same time. When he pulls back, I mourn the loss of his firm body.

He drops to his knees before me.

"What are you doing?" I whisper.

He chuckles, his fingers teasing the waistband of my underwear. Slowly, he slips them down over my legs.

I step out of them, standing before him fully nude. My cheeks heat and I fight the urge to wrap my arms around myself. His eyes hood with lust and he runs his hands through his hair, as if he's hanging on by a thread.

"Such a pretty rose," he murmurs. "I bet you taste as sweet as one, too."

My heart rate increases, and even though it's a dream, I swear I'm on the verge of passing out from desire.

"I want you," I whisper.

"Tell me what you want me to do to you."

"I want you to show me how you feel about me." Biting my lip, I grow bold and speak more confidently as I say, "I want you to make me come. I want you to be the first person to make me come, Rainer."

"Those are awfully dirty words for such a good girl."

"Who said I was a good girl?" My cheeks burn at my own bold words.

"Alessia." My name comes out like a warning.

This isn't my first time by any means—Felix and I have had plenty of turns in the sheets—but this is my first time being so forward, driven by the nagging need in my core.

Reaching out to lift the hem of Rainer's shirt, he helps me tug it off over his head. I work the button of his trousers next, slowly working his pants and underwear down his hips. His erection springs out, staring me in the face, and my body heats with anticipation. My hands grow clammy with nervousness.

This is happening.

This is a dream, but it doesn't make it any less real.

Once I get his pants down around his ankles, he steps out of them. Taking a moment to look up at him from where I'm kneeling on the ground, I admire his chiseled, tattooed body, illuminated by the soft glow of my night lamp.

"Gods," I whisper. "You are beautiful."

I want to trace his ink, study it, but he reaches for my hand, interlacing our fingers and pulling me to a stand as his eyes roam my naked body—filled out with new curves from training and eating.

"I am nothing compared to you, mo róisín. The word beauty never had meaning until I laid eyes on you."

Cruel Rainer is dangerously captivating, but it's Sweet Rainer that's my annihilation.

My hands trail around the back of his neck, tangling in his charcoal hair as I pull him flush to me. Our chests rise and fall rapidly in sync. It drives me wild to know I affect him the same way he affects me.

"I don't want to hurt you," he says.

"Then don't."

His gaze flicks around my face, and I see the conflict simmering in his icy blue eyes. "We need a safe word."

"A safe word?" My brow scrunches. "Even here?" I doubt he can hurt me, but if that's what will make him feel better, I'll pick one.

"Even here. If at any time you want me to stop, just say—"

"Mercy," I finish. It's a fitting safe word in more ways than one.

The grin he gives me is so utterly boyish and charming, that I can't help but pull his smiling lips to mine.

It's a gentle kiss, one that stokes the attraction between us. Our lips move lazily, our naked skin pressed together. His hard length jerks between us, pressing against me. Slickness leaks from his tip as he grinds it against me, and the feeling turns me on more than anything. I want nothing more than for him to enter me, fill me up.

He walks us backward until my calves hit the bed, and we tumble onto the mattress together.

It's so familiar with him, yet so different—so invigorating.

Rainer lifts me up, tossing me to the center of the bed. He prowls toward me and I giggle. But he's not laughing with me.

His eyes darken as he grips my thighs. "Spread your legs for me, Alessia." Gently, he tries to pry my legs apart, but I fight him, keeping them shut. I'm suddenly nervous to bare my most intimate parts to him. "You're safe with me, mo róisín, now be a good girl and let me see you."

A flood of wet heat fills my center, and I relax into his touch as he slowly spreads me apart. He releases a deep growl as he takes me in.

"That's a good girl," he whispers. Leaning forward, he runs his nose up my center, inhaling deeply. "You're so wet. So sweet. Better than I've imagined."

I'm squirming now beneath his touch. Seeing him naked with his head between my legs is a sight to behold. But it's not enough. My hips rise, craving his kisses, something to release the impending pressure building deep inside of me.

"Can I taste you?" He asks, licking his lips.

"Please." My voice comes out strained.

He leans forward, hovering over my most sensitive part. When he chuckles, his warm breathe tickles me and I moan. "Tell me this belongs to me."

"It's yours. Please. Please." If I weren't so consumed by desire, I'd be embarrassed by my begging.

"Tell me I'm the only one who gets to taste you."

"Yes. Please touch me now. I'm dying."

"Tell me again," he commands, his voice dangerously low. "Tell me you're mine."

"I'm yours," I whisper breathlessly.

He grunts his approval as he closes the small space between us, planting his hot tongue on my center. I chase the friction, but Rainer grips my hips, holding me down with his strong hands. I'm so small, so delicate beneath him. He's a predator, and I'll be damned if the danger doesn't bring its own wave of excitement with it.

The first few licks of his tongue are teasing, as if he's searching for the spots that make me respond.

He moves confidently, yet unhurriedly. My hands weave their way into his hair, and when he sucks on my most sensitive spot, I moan, holding him in place.

"Right there," I say breathlessly. "Gods this is so much better than my own fingers."

He chuckles, and the vibration of his mouth sends a jolt through me. When he teases my opening with a finger, slowly pressing it inside of me as he works me with his tongue, I cry out.

"It's—I'm so close." My fingers grip his hair so tightly as I hold him in place. "Wait, wait," I say.

He stops, and my wet core throbs, desperate for his return. He peers up at me, his eyes widening with concern. "What's wrong?"

"I don't want to come like this." His brows furrow with confusion. "I want you—inside of me. I want us to come apart, together."

He groans, running a hand over his face. "You're killing me."

"Please?"

"When I'm finally inside of you, Alessia, I promise it will not be here in a dream." His lips tilt up in a wicked grin. Without warning, he plants his lips back on me. After a few minutes of him working in that same, deliciously sensitive spot with relentless consistency, I'm writhing beneath him.

"Rainer!" A storm of pleasure courses through me, and my whole body quivers. Once the waves pass, and I'm too sensitive for his touches, he sits back on his heels and wipes his glistening mouth with the back of his hand.

"Oh my gods," I whisper. "That was—"

I trail off, distracted by the image of him tugging himself. His eyes are half-mast, and his muscles bulge as he works his hand up and down his shaft, twisting in a corkscrew motion. Driven by a new wave of passion, I shift onto my knees and crawl over to him.

Before he can say anything, I lick the head of him tentatively. It's unexpectedly salty, but I like it.

"I've never done this before," I whisper.

He groans. "Bloody hell."

I grip him, my hand looking so small around him. "Will you tell me what to do?"

Before he can reply, there's a loud bang on the door.

"Ignore it," Rainer mutters. "Stay asleep a little longer."

"Rainer," Ken calls. His voice sounds distorted, far away. "It's important."

Rainer tenses, but instead of disengaging me or answering Ken, he grips the back of my head.

"Open your mouth, my little rose." His term of endearment sends a tickle through my belly.

I open wide, and he slides into my mouth. I try not to let my teeth scrape him, pressing his flesh against my tongue as I suck him down.

"Just like that," he whispers. "Take me like a good girl." I moan my agreement, and he fists my hair, picking up his pace as he thrusts into my mouth. "You take my cock so good."

The banging on the door picks up, and it only spurs him on. I can't deny there's a small thrill at being caught.

My eyes water as Rainer hits the back of my throat, and my face is wet—covered in tears and spit. I gag, and he hisses.

"Take it all," he says. With two final thrusts, he grunts and shoots a salty stream into the back of my throat. "Swallow me down."

I obey, swallowing his pleasure and trying not to choke. Finally, he pulls out and I gasp for breath. Gods if that wasn't the most decadent experience of my life.

"You, mo róisín, are a good dream in a world of nightmares." He presses his lips to mine, merging both of our tastes together.

The door bangs open, and I squeal, jolting. My face is flushed, my body still trembling from Rainer's touch.

Eoin stands there, and my cheeks heat with embarrassment. He's unfazed, as if he has no idea what he intruded on. I heard him banging on my door in my dream, just as I apparently heard Ken banging on Rainer's door.

"Thank gods you're all right." He swipes a hand over his mouth and shakes his head. But he won't meet my eyes.

"What is it?"

He takes a deep breath. "I heard they found a body in the woods." He hesitates. "A human body."

"Oh gods." A hand flies up to my mouth, and my thoughts flit to Fern.

"I had to ensure that it wasn't you."

"It's Ostara," I say weakly. No one should be harmed by the trees. "I thought the curse wasn't active tonight."

"Exactly," he says.

Suddenly, I understand the concern. If someone—a *human*—ended up dead in the woods tonight of all nights, it wasn't the curse.

It was murder.

I slide out from under the sheets, my panties still wet from my nighttime escape with Rainer, and the best orgasm I've ever had. As much as I want to revel in the aftershocks, and replay the intimate moments over and over, I don't have time for that now.

I motion for Eoin to turn around and quickly slide on a pair of tights, switching my nightgown out for a tunic.

When I'm finished, Eoin gives me an apologetic glance and we exit into the hallway. Fern's face flashes in my mind. She's the only other human here. Was she killed? And if not her, then who was killed?

Thirty-Five
I Do Recognize Him
Alessia

When I make my way downstairs, Rainer, Ken, Sennah, and Viv stand around a white sheet on the floor. As I get closer, I make out a body laid out on the sheet.

They're talking amongst themselves in a serious tone.

Rainer glances at me with a frown. He subtly shakes his head, warning me from coming closer. After the moment we just shared together—dream or not—I want to run to him. I want to feel his arms around me.

But our moment was stolen away. It no longer belongs to us.

"Don't you normally kill their spies anyway?" Sennah asks. "What's the big deal with this one?"

"This one wasn't a spy," Ken replies.

"How can you tell?" she asks.

Rainer gives me an apologetic look. Clearing his throat, he says, "He's the human queen's messenger."

"And how exactly was he killed?" The princess asks. "Looks to me like he was terrified to death—that expression is filled with fear. Typical of the woods, no?"

"Well, he still has color and his limbs are pliable," Ken says. "Rigor mortis hasn't set in, so it was recent. A fresh kill from tonight. With Ostara, it couldn't have been the trees."

"Couldn't have been far from the property line, either," Viv adds. "Most worrisome… he was drained of blood," she whispers. Her eyes flick to Rainer. "And he's missing a hand. That is" —she coughs into her fist— "odd."

Ken and Rainer share a stern look.

"Drained?" Eoin asks as he strides up to them. "Vampyrs? Can't be. The demons were exiled."

Exiled?

Would Rainer be exiled, too, if they knew the truth about him?

Rainer glances up at me, his features drawn tight.

The fae hate demons. They don't know their Umbra Prince is half-vampyr himself. As he meets my eyes, there's a new emotion there I haven't seen before, not even when he was worried about losing control. It's fear. True terror flits across his expression.

What has the Prince of Fear so distraught?

"Alessia," he warns, shaking his head and striding toward me as if he's trying to block the body from sight.

Before he can stop me, I peer at the body.

It's a man, and he's covered in rust-colored streaks and wounds. It's a gruesome sight, and bile rises in my throat. His limbs are bent at odd angles, and he's missing a hand, but when I observe the man's face—brown eyes wide, lips split open in terror—my heart stops.

Whatever he saw before his death frightened him.

His skin is pallid, and there's a dark spot around the groin of his beige trousers, as if he peed himself out of fear.

My hands fly to my mouth, covering the guttural cry that leaves me.

Everything around me fades away, and I'm stuck staring at the lifeless man.

A man I once knew intimately.

His eyes are open, glossed over and seeing nothing. There's a wound on his neck. Two little puncture marks, tiny black holes.

It reminds me of how I saw Rainer and Fern, with his mouth on her neck. I've never seen wounds on her, but she likely uses the healing salve so others don't notice.

This is careless. Messy.

It wasn't Rainer.

Please.

It couldn't be him.

Seeing this brings back the memory of Char's death—of seeing my only other friend's life fade from her body. Right when I finally made it to the outskirts of grief, it washes back over me like a tsunami, flooding my insides.

"No," I croak out. All eyes flick to me. "No!"

The scream that rips from my lungs is guttural.

Rainer strides to me, catching me right as my legs give out.

"I've got you, mo róisín. I'm here."

He pushes my hair out of my face, planting an uncharacteristically tender kiss on my forehead. But I can't appreciate it right now. Not in this moment.

"What happened to him?" My voice sounds foreign, disconnected. Rainer gives me a look of pity and I fist his shirt. "Tell me what happened to him, Rainer."

But I already know the answer to that. We both do.

"Do you recognize him?" Eoin asks softly, frowning at me.

I can't answer him.

Because yes, I do recognize him.

THIRTY-SIX

I'll See You In My Dreams

ALESSIA

I stare at Felix's lifeless body, frozen in shock. I'm sure I mirror his expression right now, save for the fact I'm filled with life.

The others flit around me, buzzing like bees as they converse. I don't register it for a few minutes, until the shock subsides.

"She's not safe here," Eoin hisses. He's at mine and Rainer's side in a flash.

Rainer ignores him, cupping my face. He brings his forehead to mine. "I didn't do this, Alessia. This wasn't me."

The tears stream down my face as I regain my grip on reality.

Felix is here.

And he's dead.

Drained.

Because of a vampyr.

Because of something like Rainer.

I pull away from him.

"Mo róisín—"

Raising a hand, I cut him off. "I know this wasn't you," I whisper. "I know you wouldn't do this."

"Never. Never like this."

"Why would she think this was you?" Eoin asks in a low tone.

I'm aware of all the eyes on us, but I can't find it in me to care right now. I might've been okay with parting ways with Felix, with never having a full resolution, but I didn't want him dead. He might not have been the best lover, but he was still my friend. He didn't deserve such a brutal death.

And worse, I'm filled with guilt at the realization that he probably came looking for me.

It's my fault he's dead.

"Your brother—" I croak out. "Where is he?"

I saw him at the party when I was dancing with Eoin. He was lingering on the outskirts, watching me. My skin crawls and I shudder. What if I had been alone? Would that be me laying on the sheet instead of Felix?

I was wrong to think my place in the Umbra Court is safer than the lord's estate.

"Brother?" Eoin asks.

Rainer's expressionless mask slips into place as he runs his fingers through his hair. "Kenisius—find Tynan. Now."

Wordlessly, Ken obeys, darting out of the room with Viv on his heels. Sennah is quiet in the background, but I'm all too aware of her attention on us. Eoin looks between Rainer and me, and I know I've revealed too much. The Terra Prince silently places the pieces together.

Not just about me and Rainer... but about what Rainer is.

"You fool." Eoin steps between Rainer and me, planting his hands on Rainer's chest and shoving him—hard. Rainer barely stumbles, but his jaw tics and his fingers flex at his side. "*You* are supposed to be the one who protects the court. Instead, *you* are the curse."

In the short time I've known him, I've never seen Eoin's face so red, so angered.

"What the hell were you thinking? You could've hurt her." Eoin paces, shaking his head rapidly. "Did you do this?" He turns to face Rainer, pointing at Felix's body. "Was this you?"

My palms grow clammy as I wrap my arms around myself, suddenly wishing I could shrink away altogether.

"Of course not!" Rainer roars.

"You could've killed her!" Eoin shoves Rainer harder this time. "You selfish bastard."

Rainer doesn't fight back as Eoin cocks his fist, ready to land a blow. Then suddenly, before his punch can land, Eoin makes a choking sound and grabs his throat. He drops to his knees, gaze flashing to his sister behind Rainer.

I've seen her do this before—elemental magic.

Eoin's eyes bulge. It doesn't last long before Sennah releases her hold on him and he gasps for breath, desperately sucking lungfuls of air down.

"Eoin," she hisses in warning. "Compose yourself. We cannot attack the Umbra Prince in his own court." A stern look crosses her face, and she raises her brows at her brother, as if willing him to challenge her.

He gives her a sharp nod, and takes a few deep inhales. "We'll see how long this bastard rules his court once the truth comes out."

"Eoin—" Sennah says his name carefully. "Let it go. You have your own court to focus on."

"He truly is a bastard." Eoin shakes his head. "A demon bastard." He levels a hard stare at Rainer. "I always knew there was something wrong with you—with your magic. Your soul. I feckin' knew it." He looks at me. "You deserve better, Alessia. Whatever he promised you, it's a lie. You're not safe here. You never will be."

Sennah sighs and throws her flowing blonde hair up into a messy bun. "I'm going to assist Viv and Ken."

"Why are you so nonchalant about this, sister?" Eoin asks, rubbing his temples. Sennah bites her lip, and glances away. His gaze grows deadly. "You knew? This whole time?"

"It's not that big of a deal," she whispers. "You're the one who has a problem with him. Not me. Get your head out of your arse."

"Unbelievable." Eoin's face reddens. "You knowingly let a demon run our neighboring court. I could've taken over long ago had you confided in me, but you chose a bastard over your own blood."

Rainer scowls at Eoin, watching the interaction carefully.

"Eoin—" Sennah's normally kind face morphs into something sharp. Her voice takes on an authoritative tone. The ruler in her comes out. "Maybe you should learn from the *bastard* and take care of your own court. Your own people. Stop focusing on him and focus on yourself. Whether you admit it or not, Rainer runs Umbra Court damn well."

"That's complete shite and we both know it."

"No. It's not." She gives her brother a pointed look. "As your sister, I'm asking you not to repeat anything you've learned tonight. Let it go."

"I can't do that."

"Then as your princess, I am commanding you to keep this information to yourself and to not act on it. The Umbra Court is our ally. It will stay that way."

"This is a mistake, Sennah."

She shrugs at him before exiting the room, mumbling to herself about her brother being an idiot.

Eoin's body twitches with anger, as if he can't stay still. "I'm taking her with me."

His eyes lock onto Rainer, who appears almost bored. "No."

"I am taking Alessia back to Terra Court," Eoin repeats. "She will be safe there."

"Wait a second—" I start, only to get cut off.

"You're a disgrace to Avylon, Rainer, and I don't care what my sister says, we will never be allies. If Alessia stays here, she'll be the next one lying on your floor, staining it with whatever drops of her blood remain—if any remains at all." Eoin cocks a brow. "I'm assuming that's what really happened to your parents? Right? Weren't they found drained of blood, while you were untouched?" Rainer flinches as the words strike home. "*You* murdered your own mother. Your own father."

Rainer gives him a cold look. His fingers dance nervously against his thigh.

"Come with me, Alessia," Eoin pleads. "I can keep you safe."

"I'm not going anywhere." I cross my arms defiantly.

"You have no choice."

Rainer steps forward, his fist balling at his side. "The hells she doesn't—"

"'The Iorworths always pay their debts,'" Eoin says mockingly. "Isn't that what you said to me? Well, consider this your debt paid. I am taking the girl."

Fury burns bright in Rainer's face. He squeezes his eyes shut for a moment.

"Rainer, you can't let him—"

"I don't have a choice." His lips flatten, his voice monotone.

"What?" My heart drops. Did he just use me as a pawn to pay some stupid debt? "You can't be serious, Rainer."

"You need to go anyways, Alessia. You aren't safe here."

He's doing the same thing he did the night I kissed him—pushing me away because he thinks it'll protect me. It's only a facade.

The heartless Prince of Fear does have a heart, even if he hides it.

I grit my teeth. "No."

Rainer sighs, his eyes penetrating me to the core when they finally swing my way. "It's only a matter of time before you end up like Felix." His words are cold, callous, his jaw tight.

Cruel Rainer is back.

And I'll be damned if it doesn't take my breath away in the worst way.

"You're wrong, Rainer. I'm perfectly safe here." But I need him to admit it. Need to hear him say it. Maybe then I can lie to myself.

Because seeing Felix's body laid out on Rainer's floor is all too sobering. It's a reminder of how dangerous it is here.

How deadly Rainer and his kind are.

That I'm only human.

A fresh wave of tears threaten to fall, and I bite my lip.

"Tell me he's wrong, Rainer," I whisper. "Stop pushing me away."

He narrows his eyes. "You think you're an exception? That I won't want a taste of your blood eventually?" His tongue darts out and wets his lip as he looks me over, head to toe predatorily.

"Stop, Rainer," I whisper. "This isn't you."

He gives me a sad smile. "Isn't it, though? If you stay here, this is your fate." He gestures to Felix's body. "It's in my nature."

"No! You are not a bloodthirsty savage, Rai. You are in control. You know your triggers. You're aware of your limits. I trust you. Why can't you trust yourself?"

"I've done it before. I'll do it again." His eyes flicker dark before settling on their normal pale blue.

I shake my head. "You're not the same little boy as you were then. You've grown. You're stronger. You would never do this." I gesture toward Felix's body.

"You're wrong."

I step forward, pounding my fists into his solid chest. He grabs my wrists as tears stream down my cheeks. For a fraction of a second, he softens, but I see the moment his mask slips back into place.

"Use me instead of Fern," I say. "Take what you need from me instead. I can handle it."

"*I* can't."

"But you don't hurt her."

"Because I don't face the same temptations with her as I do you, Alessia! You are a danger to me, and I am a danger to you." His eyes stop shifting, and this time they stay dark and stormy as he exhales a heavy breath.

He whispers so only I can hear, "I'm sorry." Apologies sound sweeter on a fae prince's tongue. But they sting that much sharper. "This is not what I wanted. But we have no choice. Stop fighting me on this."

"We always have a choice!"

After all that talk about learning to be strong, to fight, now he wants me to stop fighting?

"There is something else you should know." Rainer wears a pained expression. Briefly, he closes his eyes and takes a deep breath. When he reopens them, his features are carefully schooled, as if he's fighting any emotion that might appear. He gestures at Felix's body "I am the one responsible for his missing hand."

My eyes widen. "You're...*what?*" My legs give out and a loud sob bursts from my lungs.

Rainer runs a hand through his hair, his shoulders slumping.

"Did you do this?" I ask, my voice cracking. The heaviness in my chest spreads through my body. "Was this *you*, Rainer?"

His face contorts with regret. "No, Alessia, I swear it." He swallows thickly and looks away. "Just the hand."

"*Why?*" I cry. "When?"

Before I can succumb fully to the agony, Eoin's hands are on my shoulders.

"You're okay," Eoin whispers in my ear. Rainer tracks Eoin's movement, his whole body going rigid. His jaw flexes, but he doesn't tell Eoin to get away from me this time.

"Get off me!" I try to push Eoin away. "Don't touch me."

He keeps his grip on me. "Just a second, Alessia."

"No. You bloody bastard!" I claw at Eoin, desperate to get away from him. "You are a rotten apple! Sweet on the outside, poisonous on the inside."

"And you, my dear Alessia, are a worm wiggling your way to my core."

A deadly growl rips from Rainer as he charges toward us.

But then a tingling—like static—spreads from Eoin's touch over the rest of my body.

"Wait," I mutter, holding up a hand.

Rainer stops in his tracks, glaring at Eoin. His body vibrates with anger, as if he's fighting with himself. Battling to adhere to my wishes and not come any closer.

The anger, the grief, the terror…it all melts away, leaving peace in its wake.

I stop fighting and relax into him and he wraps an arm around my shoulder. My feelings are still there somewhere, but they are deep in the background instead of a prominent feature.

"How are you doing?" Eoin asks softly.

"I'm—I'm okay, actually." I gaze up at him. "How am I okay with this?"

He offers me a half-smile, but it looks out of place against his sad eyes. "Empath, remember?"

"I thought you were a healer."

"Yes—but that isn't only physical."

Any other time, I'd be upset that he took away my feelings without my consent. But right now, I'm grateful for his touch of empathy. And I realize, if it's anything like when he healed me before, he's now the one burdening my heavy load. He's the new owner of my worst emotions.

Rainer continues to look at the spot where Eoin touches me, and his entire body is so tight that I'm afraid he'll snap. Those icy eyes conceal so much pain. They begin to flicker between azure blue and cobalt, a warning sign that he's close to snapping.

But I don't care. I feel—*nothing.* Thanks to Eoin's magic touch.

"Don't use your fecking magic on her again or—"

"Or what?" Eoin taunts. "She belongs to me now. You have no say here."

A dark, mean laugh comes from Rainer. "She will never belong to you, Terra Prince."

Rainer glances at me, regret marrs his features. "You belong to yourself. And your heart belongs to *me*."

With a clearer mind, thanks to Eoin's empath magic, I ignore his profession. I stare past him, at the body laid out before us.

Gods, Char and Felix are both dead because of me. It's my fault he came here to find me. Once this magic wears off, the guilt will crush me.

My eyes roam over Felix's crooked limbs. In his intact hand, something white peeks out. It calls to me, and I step forward, prying open his now-cool, stiffening fingers as I pull the crumpled paper out.

Alessia,

I know I will not survive the forest. Most men don't. This is a risk I accept. But I hope this letter meets your eyes. I hope it will make up for my transgressions. I should have stuck up for you sooner.

I meant it when I said there are worse things out there—things you don't know. It seems you have met them for yourself and have somehow been spared. I do not have time and space to elaborate, and if by chance I make it to you alive, I will explain everything. But you need to know—

The last few lines of the letter are drenched with sweat and blood, smeared and entirely illegible.

My heart pounds, blood thumps in my ears.

Oh, Felix. What did you get yourself into?

The irony that he survived the woods, only to die so brutally, is an extra blow to my stomach.

My eyes race over the letter, rereading it, trying to make sense of what he's trying to tell me.

What exactly do I need to know?

Rainer steps closer, wanting to read the note. I swallow the lump in my throat, stuffing the note in my pocket before he can read it. It doesn't concern him.

Eoin waves a hand around the air. "You need to clean up your mess, Rainer. My sister might like you, but I don't, and I will come for your court."

"You will never have my court."

"Oh, but I will. And I'm starting with your human." He pets my cheek and I recoil.

Fury burgeons in Rainer's face. His nostrils flare.

"Come," Eoin tells me.

I refuse, rooted in place. He offers me one of his boyish grins that I now see right through.

"I'm cashing in on a debt owed." He beckons me forth. "You can't resist."

A warming sensation encompasses me. The tingle of magic crawls through my veins. My feet move on their own accord, as I follow Eoin.

"No," I whisper, shaking my head. But I can't stop walking. "Stop this."

Just like the magic of the barriers keeping me against my will, the magic of this new debt propels me toward Eoin.

And I can't fight it.

"I have nothing to do with this!" I yell. "This isn't fair. Release me! *Please!*"

He blabbers something about how I should be grateful he's protecting me. That he's giving me space and safety away from the vampyrs and tainted court.

Except with each step further and further away, my heart aches more for Rainer. It's like the distance between us rips open a chasm in my heart, and even Eoin's empath magic isn't enough to numb the hurt there.

I've never felt a pull like it before.

It's incomprehensible, and every cell in my body screams to turn around and run back to Rainer—despite what he's done.

Glancing over my shoulder, I catch Rainer watching me with longing.

He mouths to me, so no one else will hear, "I'll see you in my dreams."

THIRTY-SEVEN

I Will Do Much Worse to Him

RAINER

A lessia leaving is like ripping my beating heart from my ribcage.

Each step she takes through the foyer steals my breath, and as she steps through the front doors and out of sight, I almost fall to my knees.

All the lessons I've tried to teach her: to fight, to stand up for herself, to protect herself, to believe in her strength. They seem like nothing when I'm the one standing here tearing her down.

For now, Eoin has won. Our debts are paid, we are even.

When I'm certain I can keep Alessia safe, I am coming for her.

As it stands, I can barely protect her from myself, how can I protect her from Tynan?

The spirits?

The woods?

If Tynan is willing to flout our moral code, drain a human and leave them behind so carelessly, what's stopping him from going after Alessia next?

There's no love lost between us brothers, and between him and Eoin, the Terra Prince is the lesser evil. He's a weasel, a threat to my court at worst, an annoyance at best.

As much as I loathe Eoin, he's a decent male when it comes to humans. He has the means to keep Alessia safe and out of harm's way.

He thinks he won this battle, but he hasn't. By agreeing to send Alessia with him as a way to call our debts even, I've won. I protect Alessia, and I protect my court.

Placating Eoin means buying myself time to figure out this mess.

I'm already heavily disliked, and I couldn't care less if I'm ostracized, but I'm in charge of too many people here to let my title slip through my fingers. If I'm replaced, it's likely the entire court would be, too. And I can't let them down.

Kenisius's family has worked in my family's employ for generations. His stipend supports his expansive family. They rely on his job.

Das Celyn's status could be stripped, and they would be left with less than they had before. Their family would reject them, and they'd likely end up on the streets with no home, no title, and no money.

Even Fern, as much as I despise that girl, doesn't deserve to be left for dead. Sure, I need her blood to keep my bloodlust at bay, but she relies on me for safety—from the fae who hate her, and from the faerie magic she's dangerously addicted to.

And those are only a few members of my court. There are hundreds—thousands more—who rely on my leadership. Beyond that, it's *my* magic coursing through the woods. My magic that I *will* one day regain control over.

I've been experimenting with my plants in my mother's old wing, trying to find a way to reign in the magic and keep the trees under control.

I'm close. So close.

Kenisius strides up beside me. "He's gone, Rai. Viv's flying over the woods, searching for any sign of him or…"

More bodies.

He doesn't have to say it, but we both hear it.

I was a fool for thinking I could put Tynan in charge of Shyga. First the issue with the shadow-spirits, and now this mess. It never feckin' ends. This needs to be dealt with—all of this—as soon as possible.

So I can get Alessia back.

I run my hands through my hair, groaning. My fingers twitch anxiously and I begin pacing to quell the burgeoning energy inside me.

"We need to send someone to Shyga."

"I'll go."

I shake my head. "I need you here. We have other issues to deal with. Send Viveka."

"You got it." Kenisius scratches his head as he eyes the body curiously.

"Who found him?" I ask.

"A group of fae headed back to Umbra City. Found him right outside the gates before sun up."

I'm pissed at Tynan—or whoever it was that killed the boy—because now we've lost our chance for intel. We'll never know what his message was, or why he chose to come now.

"Poor boy perished before learning how to properly please a lady." Kenisius toes the body with his boot. He chuckles. "Shame. Well, guess he won't be missed."

I ignore Kenisius's humor, focusing on all the people who failed Alessia. Too many people.

The queen and her Trade.

The lord and his ownership.

The dead boy and his reluctance to be a man and protect the woman in his life.

None of them are innocent. They're all guilty.

And I'll deal with them—one at a time, or altogether in war. Their choice. Once we send the boy's body across the Gleam, the decision will be on their hands. Even if they don't retaliate, I'm coming for them.

"What should I do with the body?" Kenisius asks.

"Send the body across the Gleam." My voice lacks emotion, despite the turmoil in my heart.

"Are you sure?" Kenisius asks. "This isn't a spy or an escaped Tradeling. This is the *messenger*—it will stir the humans up."

Ah, yes. When we had the treaty instated, the messengers were protected. Neutral, if you will. Though there is no longer a treaty in place, surely the death of the messenger will rile up the queen.

"Precisely."

"Are you prepared if they decide to retaliate?"

"We'll be ready." That's if they even make it past the Cursed Wood in the first place.

"Is she worth the risk of another war between the realms?" he asks, observing me carefully.

I smile darkly at him, but it doesn't reach my eyes. "You saw those marks on Alessia when she arrived, Kenisius, the tattoo on her face. Tell me, what do you think?"

He cocks his head, stroking his beard. "I think this is highly unusual. Even for you."

My jaw tenses and I glance away.

"What aren't you telling me, Rai?" he asks. "Why did you really send her with Eoin? Why are you desperate to protect her—no matter the cost?"

Glancing upward, I suck in a huge breath of air. "Because, Kenisius—" my heart thumps faster in my chest as I finally say the words aloud, "—she visited me in my dreams. We can dreamwalk together."

Kenisius stops breathing a moment, and the room goes utterly still and silent.

"Well, I'll be damned," he says. "I *knew* it! I smelled—"

"Keep this to yourself. Nobody is to know."

His face pinches. "Does she—"

"No." I shake my head. "She has no idea."

"Rai, you should probably tell her—"

"I *can't*. She's human. I need to figure out what it means first."

Kenisius whistles long and low, shaking his head. Then he starts laughing. "No wonder you felt confident enough to send her with Eoin. Bastard doesn't stand a chance."

"Still. We can't let him know." I incline my chin. "Send the pixies to keep an eye on things."

He grunts his agreement, and we stand there in silence, staring at the boy's mutilated body before us. I eye the place where I cut off his hand without an ounce of regret. I'd do it all over again if given the chance. And if Eoin tries anything with *my* little rose, I will do much worse to him.

To be continued in book 2, A Dream of Fate and Flesh, coming soon.

Acknowledgments

Here we are, at the end of another book. Except it feels like the start of something brand new. Each book is its own journey and has its own heart. This heart wouldn't beat nearly as strong if it weren't for the amazing team of people who have supported me along the way. This list is in no way exhaustive. Just like this book, it's only a start.

Thank you, as always, to my wonderful husband who encourages and nourishes my weirdness. Thank you for loving me and giving me a safe space to express my creativity. For that, I will always be grateful.

Thank you to my amazing editors RaeAnne and Brit who helped bring this vision to life as cleanly and cohesively as possible. You've both given me great insight on this project. (And Brit, extra thanks for being such a cherished friend. You're a bright spot in my life.)

Thank you to my earliest alpha readers, Charity and Abigail. You two are more than alphas. You're critique buddies. Friends. Family. And you're both stuck with me forever. Thanks for being the best support system and hype team a girl could ever ask for.

Thanks to my awesome critique partner, Alex, for being a chaos pixie like me. You have a talent for story! And Alessia would probably be riding horses incorrectly if it weren't for you.

Thanks to my beta readers: Becky, Brit, Danielle, Laura, and Jess. You each have given me helpful feedback that made ACO-MAM what it is today.

Thanks to my cover designer, Maria, for making an amazing cover. Not just for this book, but the whole series! I can't wait to share the others with you all.

Thank you to all my friends and followers on Bookstagram. Our community is incredible and I am thankful to be a part of something so beautiful.

Big thank you to my early readers, and special shoutout to Ali, who helped me find some big last minute changes that needed to be made. Another big shoutout goes to Ashley—stay chaotically you, always.

And finally, thank YOU! Thank you for reading and giving this lil' indie author a chance. You're supporting my dream and it means everything to me. I appreciate you more than words can describe.

AFTERWORD

If you enjoyed this book, I ask you to please consider leaving a review or sharing it with your friends and followers.

Reviews and word-of-mouth recommendations help indie authors like me so much! I thank you from the bottom of my heart.

About

Miranda Joy believes everyone deserves to fall in love, especially characters with dark pasts who overcome unpleasant situations. She holds a BA in creative writing & English with a fiction concentration from SNHU. She's finishing her MFA and intends to teach collegiate-level writing.

When she's not scratching out notes for her next story or devouring a book on Kindle Unlimited, it's likely she's petting her dogs or doing yoga. She's a long-time fitness coach, sports nutritionist, and RYT-200 yoga instructor. Send her an email or a DM on Instagram to chat!

Also By Miranda Joy

These Wicked Lies

These Wicked Truths (These Wicked Lies Book 2)
These Wicked Gods (These Wicked Lies Book 3 — coming Soon)
A Dream of Fate and Flesh (Courts of Malice 2 — coming soon)

Printed in Great Britain
by Amazon

26219182R10252